R.J. Ellory is the author of eighteen novels published by Orion UK, and his work has been translated into twenty-six languages. He has won the Quebec Booksellers' Prize, the Livre De Poche Award, the Strand Magazine Novel of the Year, the Mystery Booksellers of America Award, the Inaugural Nouvel Observateur Prize, the Quebec Laureat, the Prix du Roman Noir, the Plume d'Or for Thriller Internationale 2016, the Theakston's Crime Novel of the Year, both the St Maur and Villeneuve Readers' Prizes, the Balai d'Or 2016, and has twice won the Grand Prix des Lecteurs. He has been shortlisted for two Barrys, the 813 Trophy, the Europeen Du Point, and two Crime Writers' Association UK awards.

Among other projects, he is the guitarist and vocalist of The Whiskey Poets, and has recently completed the band's third album. His musical compositions have been featured in films and television programs in more than forty countries. He has two television series and two films in pre-production, and has recently premiered his first short film, 'The Road to Gehenna'.

Also by R.J. Ellory

Candlemoth
Ghostheart
A Quiet Vendetta
City of Lies
A Quiet Belief in Angels
A Simple Act of Violence
The Anniversary Man
Saints of New York
Bad Signs
A Dark and Broken Heart
The Devil and the River
Carnival of Shadows
Mockingbird Songs
Kings of America
Three Bullets
Proof of Life
The Darkest Season

NOVELLAS
Three Days in Chicagoland:
1. The Sister
2. The Cop
3. The Killer

THE LAST HIGHWAY

R.J. ELLORY

ORION

First published in Great Britain in 2023 by Orion Fiction,
an imprint of The Orion Publishing Group Ltd.,
Carmelite House, 50 Victoria Embankment
London EC4Y 0DZ

An Hachette UK company

3 5 7 9 10 8 6 4

A CIP catalogue record for this book is
available from the British Library.

ISBN (Hardback) 978 1 3987 1034 4
ISBN (Trade Paperback) 978 1 3987 1245 4
ISBN (eBook) 978 1 3987 1036 8

Typeset at The Spartan Press Ltd,
Lymington, Hants

Printed and bound in Great Britain by Clays Ltd,
Elcograf S.p.A.

www.orionbooks.co.uk

Acknowledgements

This work is dedicated to all those who stood by me through the best of times and the worst of times.

To Victoria, my wife of more than three decades; to my son, now a father himself; to my brother, first reader and judicious critic; to Tim Willocks, a great writer and a very dear friend; to all my French family at Sonatine Editions; to Celia Killen, my astute and understanding editor; to all those at Orion who have now worked with me through eighteen novels.

I owe you all a debt of gratitude that can never be repaid.

I

News of his brother's death came soon after breakfast.

Victor Landis went onto the porch with his coffee and his cigarette and sat on the swing seat. The morning was bright and clear. He looked towards the highway and tried to remember the last time he and his brother had spoken. He could not. It had been a number of years, for sure – eleven, likely closer to twelve now – and the words they'd shared had come to blows. Whatever fraternal bond they'd once shared had been broken beyond repair. There was a history between them, its telling all kinds of different depending on who was asked.

Little more than a year between them, Victor and Frank Landis now shared nothing but blood. That they'd both wound up in law enforcement was attributable to coincidence alone. Neither one had evidenced a hankering for such a thing in their early years. Victor had in fact shown a leaning towards music. Fancied himself a guitar player, much like their father. How the law came about – how it connected and then further separated them – was yet another twisted strand in the barbed-wire fence of their past. For both of them, that past was as good as quicksand – the harder they'd fought to escape, the harder it had dragged them back.

The news that Frank was dead seemed proof enough that persistence invariably paid off. He had finally escaped, though not as he'd intended.

'Thought maybe a hit-and-run,' Dade County Deputy Sheriff explained on the telephone. 'That's what I figured until the coroner got himself out there. Seems whoever run him down backed up and run over him again for good measure. He done moved a good deal too in between, suggesting he weren't gonna quit until they got him flattened three, maybe four more times.'

'Tough as cat meat, my brother,' Victor said, thinking that some people were born to die hard.

'Best get yourself over here soonest,' the deputy said. 'You bein' next-of-kin an' all.'

'I didn't get your name, son,' Landis said.

'Abrams. Paul Abrams. Been your brother's deputy more 'an five years now.'

'Well, I guess you're gonna be the new sheriff soon enough.'

Landis took his time. He had a second cup of coffee, smoked a second cigarette, then telephoned Barbara Wedlock at the office.

'My brother's got himself killed over there in Dade County,' he said. He knew he was saying the words, but it sounded like someone else's voice.

'Oh my, Sheriff,' Barbara said. 'Oh my, oh my.'

Barbara had been at the Sheriff's Office dispatch desk for more years than Landis had been sheriff. She knew everyone's business. Anything she didn't know wasn't worth spit.

'Gonna head over there and identify him and whatnot. Anything comes up, tell Marshall to take care of it.'

'Will do, Sheriff Landis,' she said. 'And condolences to you.'

Landis thanked her and hung up.

The distance from Blairsville to Trenton was all of seventy miles by crow, closer to a hundred by road. Landis took 76 on past Mineral Bluff, turned northwest and joined the highway that followed the Conasauga River. He headed north again until he was nothing but a loud holler from the Tennessee state line, and then he turned back down again across Whitfield County. The Appalachians were bold on the horizon, beneath them the sprawling wonder of the Cherokee National Forest.

En route Victor listened to the radio. There was a station out of Bunker Hill that aired the kind of music he wished he could play. He was working on it, but his hands were more suited to skinning rabbits than plucking strings.

Coming up on the county line, he eased up on the gas. The news had not yet sunk in. Whether it would ever sink was another matter. All he knew was that the cold, broken body of his brother would be laying up on a steel table at the coroner's office and he'd have to say something about a man who was more a stranger than kin. Preparing something was as much use as laundering skunks. Anything planned would be meaningless when the moment came.

Outside of Wildwood he joined Interstate 24 and headed on to Trenton.

The city itself was everything northern Georgia had to offer, nestled there in a fertile valley of the Appalachian foothills, Lookout Mountain to the east, Sand Mountain to the west. Dade County was half the size of Union, maybe a hundred and eighty square miles. Named after Major Francis Langhorne Dade, the man himself killed in the Dade Massacre of the Seminole Indians way back in the mid-1830s. The Cherokee were the next to be routed, the land then raffled off in the Georgia Lotteries. For the first century, there was no road into Dade from Georgia. Anyone venturing there had to take a scenic route by way of Alabama or Tennessee.

Dade was as far north as you could get without actually leaving the state.

*

It was somewhere after 11.00 am when Landis gained the city limits. He pulled over at the first diner he saw. *Mountainview Grill,* a busted neon sign half-heartedly announced. He wanted a cup of coffee, a cigarette or two, a handful of moments to gather his thoughts.

The waitress attending his table was all sunshine and pleasantry. It took a moment, but Landis saw the light go on in her head.

'Well, this must be the strangest thing ever,' she said. 'You look more like the sheriff than the sheriff himself. If you're not his brother then your pa musta been takin' his business elsewhere.'

Landis glanced at her badge. 'I am, Shirley,' he said. 'Frank Landis's brother.'

'Well, my oh my, isn't that a thing. And you're a sheriff, too?'

'Over in Union County, yes.'

Evidently news of Frank's death had yet to reach the folks of Trenton.

Shirley poured coffee, still smiling like the sun had lost its way west in her throat.

'Is that all you'll be wantin', Sheriff?' she asked. 'We have a fine selection of pies up there at the counter.'

'Coffee is good,' Landis said.

'Well, you go on and let me know if you'll be needin' anythin' else, okay?'

'Thank you kindly, Shirley.'

Landis wished he'd changed out of his uniform. He wasn't there in any official capacity, and he didn't much care for the constant glances from those in adjacent seats.

The coffee was good. He took a second cup. He would smoke a cigarette outside and make his way over to the Coroner's Office.

At the counter his money was point-blank refused.

'You go on and visit with your brother,' she said. 'Your money's no good here, Sheriff.'

Landis left. He drove up a block or so and pulled over once more. Being gawked at through the diner windows was something for which he didn't much care.

Landis knew that every true story had a handful of lies woven through it. For most people, the truth was just the most acceptable interpretation of events. Whatever circumstances had resulted in the death of his brother, it would have to be investigated by Trenton officers. Even though he and Frank were estranged, they were close according to the law. Had Frank died in Blairsville, there'd be no way he could have pursued the case. Besides, Trenton not only had a Sheriff's Office but its own Police Department. What little information Landis possessed regarding his brother's affairs he would willingly give them, even though he knew it would be of no real assistance.

Landis smoked two cigarettes, lit a third but let it burn down to the filter while he wrestled with the fact that he was feeling nothing at all. He hadn't missed Frank for all these years, and now he was dead there was no reason to start. A couple of hours' drive between them, it may as well have been the other side of the world.

With his mind as empty as a fairground balloon, Landis got back in the car and headed up to see the coroner.

It was time for a reunion, and – just the same as ever – he and Frank would have nothing to say to one another.

2

Frank and Victor Landis came from a line of hard, laconic people. Their forebears were cautious of words exceeding three syllables, distrusting of banks, insurance men, automatic machinery, vegetarians, things done quickly that demanded patience and time. Their grandparents, great-grandparents before them, hailed from the Mid-West where monolithic barns – angled awkwardly between parched landscape and empty sky – were often the only evidence that man had touched the earth. Their father – Walter Landis – had been a man of deluded hope, forever certain that the future would eclipse the past. He was narrow-shouldered and angular, had never danced and never would. He wore a pawnshop wristwatch, the second hand rattling loose and untethered behind the scratched crystal. *No need for seconds*, he'd say. *Even minutes. Have use for hours, sometimes the days for anniversaries and suchlike, but here we're dealing with the seasons.* He was no stranger to work. Labored all hours. And when he wasn't laboring, he stood quiet and awkward as if awaiting instructions. Either that or he was out on the porch, eyes skyward as if gauging distance between Earth and some other world where he would more easily belong.

Better times and fortunes were always on the horizon, and there they stayed, waiting for the Landis family to arrive. People like Walter Landis died in mechanical accidents or drowned in flooded run-offs while driving steer to safer pastures. Sometimes they died of drink, the liver ridged and perforated, as heavy as stone. Walter was different in that the cancer got him in the fall of '67. No one thought he'd see Christmas, but he did. Saw it twice more, in fact. He finally gave up on December 23, 1970, as bitter in death as he had been in life.

Victor, the eldest of the two sons, had not been fooled. He went east, then north, gravitating back to Georgia when his plans went unrealized. He wound up in the Sheriff's Department, encouraged by words from his younger brother. Frank had joined up in November of '72, just twenty-five years old. Victor followed suit in the fall of '74. The job offered clothes that required no choice, a good salary, a house, a car, a sense of purpose. Everyone needed to feel they were walking on stable ground, and the work gave him that stability. Traffic violations, disturbances of the peace, drunks, jackrollers, conmen and petty thieves. And then there were the dead. Natural causes, a drowning or two, farming accidents, a fall, a murder, a suicide. The dead didn't lie. Except when someone used the dead to hide the truth.

Victor Landis had never tried to guess the future, nor had he worried for the unknown. History was meant to be a lesson, but was ordinarily not. Most times he believed he favored the back of life rather than the front, but found himself drawn to the uncertain, the mystery of things unexplained. He would often say *There's never a light at the mouth of a tunnel*, and he meant it. This was what he looked for, and it seemed that the looking kept him alive.

Before the Sheriff's Office, before Blairsville, Landis had chosen a woman. Married in June of '76, they'd done the best they knew how for a handful of years. He saw her infrequently, their time together stilted and edgy. She read snippets from magazines and newspapers aloud to him, as if these words were part of some earlier incomplete conversation. Mary Landis, née

Symanski (Polish lineage he believed; immigrant farmers who'd settled in Wisconsin and then drifted for a century), never seemed anything other than pleased at her husband's silence. She'd died in December of '80, a disease in the blood, after close to a year of sickness. Landis and his wife never knew the magic of children, perhaps did not feel loneliness as others did. Landis believed that even a man alone could have a place in the history of things. One did not need descendants to be defined.

After Mary's death, Victor drowned himself in work. Four years later he was Sheriff of Union County. He believed he got the job because no one else was willing to take it.

Now Victor's company was books; he read them quietly, methodically, emptying the town library as he went. He liked Hemingway. Hemingway said *One must, above all, endure*, and this was a sentiment he could appreciate.

Forty-six years old – without wife or children, his parents long-dead – he knew there would be nothing left behind of him but that which people chose to remember. He would take his own memories as well, and one of them – perhaps the most vivid – would be the way he found his brother's body on the morning of Saturday August 15, 1992.

3

For a good while Landis just stood and stared at his brother's face.

Frank's eyes had sunk back into the skull. His features were gaunt and stripped clean of all color. Even his hair seemed lifeless, like that of a store mannequin.

Without a word, Landis indicated that the coroner should draw back the sheet that covered Frank's body.

The coroner hesitated, and then did as he was asked.

In his time, Landis had seen no shortage of dead folk. His mother, his father, his grandparents, his wife, beyond that the victims of vehicular accidents, those that died in their sleep, those that fell from trees, from buildings, those that ran out in front of trains believing they were swifter than they turned out to be.

This was different. This was different beyond all measure.

Frank was broken in a dozen or more places. From his arms and legs, the flesh already blue-white and stiff, the snapped bones protruded like rotted teeth.

The coroner was silent, standing back and allowing Landis some time and space to absorb and register what he was seeing. Eventually, when Landis asked for details, he came forward.

'Just as it looks,' the coroner replied. 'Struck at waist level by a vehicle. That first impact fractured his pelvis, shattered the right femur and tibia. From what we can discern, it seems that he was face-down, but turned over and dragged himself forward somehow. When he was struck a second time, the impact broke ribs seven to twelve on the left, also the clavicle, scapula and humerus. The third and final impact crushed the fourth and fifth lumbar vertebra and snapped both his ankles.'

'At what point did he die?' Landis asked.

'Difficult to say how long he lived after that.'

Landis looked up. 'He was still alive when the driver left?'

The coroner nodded. 'Seems he dragged himself a good six feet before he finally gave up. How he did that is anyone's guess.'

'Tough,' Landis said. 'He may have been many things, but he was never a quitter.'

'And then he lay out there a good number of hours before it was reported.'

'Is that so?'

The coroner cleared his throat. 'If I might ask a personal question, Sheriff.'

'Ask away.'

'Your brother's been sheriff here for over ten years. I've known him all that time...'

'And you didn't know he had a brother.'

'No, I didn't.'

Landis gave a wry smile. 'I wouldn't feel left out. Frank spent more years than that convincing himself he didn't have a brother either.'

After a few moments of awkward silence, the coroner said, 'So, you can confirm that this is your brother, Frank Landis?'

'I can and it is,' Landis replied.

'I'll get the paperwork,' the coroner said.

'One question for you. Was he in uniform?'

'No,' the coroner replied. 'He was not in uniform.'

*

It was a short walk to the Sheriff's Office. Landis found Deputy Abrams packing up Frank's personal effects.

After introductions, Abrams said, 'I figured you'd be wantin' to take his things on back with you.'

Landis looked in the box. It was a jumble of worthless knick-knacks, more than likely kept for sentimental reasons known only to Frank. A small, framed photograph caught Landis's eye. It showed a woman and a young girl of six or seven.

'Who would this be?' Landis asked.

'That there is Frank's ex-wife, Eleanor, and his daughter, Jennifer. That was taken a while ago, though.'

'They're here in Trenton?'

'Yes,' Abrams replied.

Landis held Abrams' gaze. 'You're not from here, are you?'

'Not originally, no. Came here for school, wound up stayin'.'

'So where was home?'

'North. Place outside of Columbus, Ohio.'

'Outlander.'

Abrams smiled. 'Yep. That's what I'll always be.'

'How long did it take for them to give you the time of day here?'

'Still workin' on it, you know?'

Landis looked back at the picture.

'How old is the daughter now?'

'I'm guessing ten, maybe eleven.'

'The wife still go by Landis?'

'No, she went back to her maiden name, Boyd.'

Landis stared at the faces. There were lives here that should have been part of his own, and yet of which he knew nothing.

'You didn't know you had family?' Abrams asked.

Landis shook his head. He opened the frame, took out the photograph, put the empty frame back in the box.

'The rest of this stuff you can get rid of,' he said.

Abrams set the box down on the floor.

Landis walked to the window and looked out into the street. His feelings were a confusion of the unfamiliar. The sense that he was somehow connected to what had happened here was unknown territory to him. He was walking blind, unaided, and he didn't know where he was headed.

'Is there anything you want to know?' Abrams asked.

'Where did it happen?' Landis said without turning around.

'Up off of Interstate 24 outside of Wildwood.'

'And what would he have been doing up there?'

'To be straight, I don't honestly know. He was out of county.'

'Meaning?'

'24 heads out of Dade, crosses the edge of Walker County, and then you're in Tennessee.'

'And he was in Tennessee?'

'No, still in Georgia, but he was headin' north.'

'In his own vehicle?'

'Yes.'

'Any leads?' Landis asked.

'Nothing.'

'Who called it in?'

'Anonymous,' Abrams said. 'Some fella just dialed emergency and said there was a dead feller on the road.'

'The coroner said he was layin' up there a while before it was reported. That means he was out there late at night.'

'Seems so, Sheriff Landis.'

'Any notions of your own?'

Abrams paused before answering. 'Nope,' he said. 'Nothin' that ties anythin' up.'

'He a straight shooter?'

'Beg your pardon?'

'My brother. Was he a straight shooter? Law-abiding?'

'Your brother *was* the law, Sheriff.'

'That don't mean a great deal now, does it?'

'Well, all I can tell you is that I've been deputy for all of five years and he seemed like a good man to me.'

'Five years. How's that then? Elections run on the presidential cycle. Last election was back in '89. You take someone else's job, son?'

'I did, yes,' Abrams replied.

'How old are you?'

'Thirty-one.'

'You don't look it.'

'Folks often say that.'

'I got myself a deputy a little younger. Smart boy.'

Again there was an empty silence, unasked questions hanging in the air between them.

'And so here we are,' Landis finally said. 'You gonna head this thing up, or you giving it to the police?'

'The police,' Abrams replied. 'They got trained-up detectives, forensics and whatnot. I figured they're better equipped and experienced for this kind of business.'

'As you said on the telephone, this wasn't no hit-and-run. This was a killing, plain and simple.'

'You plannin' on seein' the assigned detective?'

'Would be bad manners not to,' Landis replied. 'He's gonna come lookin' for me anyhow. Might as well save him the journey.'

'His name is Fredericksen. Mike Fredericksen. You want me to take you up there?'

'That won't be necessary, Deputy. I got my own car. You just point me in the right direction.'

4

The story of Mike Fredericksen's life was etched on his face in sharp betrayals and dull failures. His soul was bruised and drowning. He'd often wondered if he should sink one more time and forget to come up for air.

He had been a good cop, a good detective, but life had battered him with hard choices.

Landis saw these things in the first few minutes of their meeting. The tell-tale signs were in his eyes, his body language, his mannerisms, his speech. Just like Landis's own father, here was a man who'd reached a point in his life where he knew he'd never be anything more or less than what he was. To live with a profound disappointment in yourself was not living at all.

'You're the likeness of your brother, I'll say that much,' Fredericksen said as they took seats in his office.

Landis didn't reply. Nature was set to play this hand until he returned home.

'Bad business. He was a good man, a good sheriff.'

'Any notion of who he could've crossed?' Landis asked. 'Someone sure wanted him good and dead.'

'As of this moment, we have nothing. We don't know why he was out there, we don't have a make on the vehicle, and we have no witnesses. At least no one with a mind to talk.'

'His deputy said he was right up near the Tennessee state line.'

'That he was.'

'And headed north.'

'Seems so, yes.'

Landis waited for Fredericksen to say more, but he kept his tongue in his pocket.

'So how are you starting in on this?' Landis asked.

Fredericksen leaned back in his chair. He looked at the ceiling for moment, and then he sighed. 'You came on over to ID the body, right?'

'I did.'

'And I'm guessing you'll be stayin' for his funeral and whatnot.'

'I don't know about stayin'. I'm just over there in Union. I got my own business to attend to.'

'But you'll be makin' the arrangements, right? After all, he's kin. You ain't got no folks to see to it, have you?'

'Sheriff's Office and the City will take care of that. He was a public servant. If he's the man you said he was, then they'll do a better job than me on that front.'

'You weren't close.'

Landis shook his head.

'Because?'

'Because that's the way it sometimes is with brothers,' Landis said. 'Not that it matters anymore.'

'Not that it's any of my business, either.'

''Cept if it had something to do with why he got himself killed. Which it don't.'

Fredericksen lit a cigarette. He did not offer one to Landis.

'Save going 'round the houses, I'm asking you direct now. You over here intendin' on making this your business?'

Landis looked at Fredericksen for a handful of seconds. There was something about the man's demeanor he didn't much care for. His tone implied superiority, and yet there was nothing about him that warranted it.

'I'm not here for any other reason than to identify my brother's body,' Landis said. 'Unless you're tellin' me that you don't want me here. If that's the case then I'd be interested to know why.'

Fredericksen smiled. 'You're reading tracks where there ain't none,' he said. 'I got no issue with you bein' here as family. I just don't much care for a Union County Sheriff gettin' all up in this matter.'

'I don't plan to get up in anything, Detective.'

'Good to know,' Fredericksen said.

'So are we done?'

'Unless you can tell me anything that might send us in the right direction on this thing, then I don't believe there's much for us to converse about.'

'You have a problem if I take a drive up there, see where it happened?'

'Long as you don't go messin' up a crime scene, I see no reason to dissuade you.'

Landis chose not to take offense at the slight Fredericksen was making. He stood up. He didn't want to shake the man's hand, but he made the effort nevertheless.

People stared at him as he left, perhaps fearful that Frank Landis had risen from the dead and come back to shame them for their sins.

5

I-24 ran ten miles northeast to Wildwood. Beyond that a finger-print of smaller roads led this way and that. The one he needed was clear from the crime-scene tape strung between sawhorses at the turning. He parked up and started walking.

Abrams was there in his patrol car. He got out when he saw Landis and walked down to meet him.

'They got you up here mindin' things, then,' Landis said.

'Just until forensics can come get your brother's car.'

'Show me where they found him.'

Abrams did so, the scattering of dried blood still visible here and there in the sandy dirt.

Landis took care to keep his distance. Irrespective of Fredericksen's comment, he knew precisely what it meant to disturb a crime scene.

'Did you see Mike?' Abrams asked.

'I did.'

'He as brittle as ever?'

'Like he got a hornets' nest in his ass.'

Abrams laughed. 'Don't take it personal.'

'I didn't, and I won't.'

Landis walked a full circle around the spot where his brother had breathed his last. He had sure made an effort to escape whatever was coming back to run him over a second and third time.

Turning north towards Tennessee, Landis knew well enough what was out there. The Appalachians crossed more than four hundred counties in thirteen states, spanning everywhere from Alabama and Kentucky to North Carolina and New York. Almost a separate culture, the mountains created a natural barrier that was nevertheless replete with mineral wealth. Exploited by outlanders, the Appalachian peoples – amongst them Native Americans, Scots, English, Irish, German and Polish – were denied the bounty of their own land and survived as some of the poorest in the nation. Communities were strong and self-sufficient; strangers were viewed with suspicion, though those in need of help were often aided beyond their expectations. If you did not come from here, you would never be accepted. If you left and returned, you would forever be known as a halfback. In his own county, Landis was just ten miles from the North Carolina state line. Up past Ivy Log you drove right into the Nantahala National Forest. There were stories of drunk, joyriding teenagers heading into that, never to be seen again. True or not, it didn't stretch the imagination to appreciate how such a thing could happen.

'You reckon he had some business up there?' Landis asked.

'Up in Tennessee? If he did, I didn't know about it.'

'Would he o' told you if he did?'

'Guess we'll never know.'

'Unless someone starts asking,' Landis replied.

'Yeah, I guess.'

'You have much to do with these folks?'

'In the mountains?' Abrams shook his head. 'Met some. Seem good folks to me. As far as anything official, never had a need to. They mind their own business.'

'Strong community,' Landis said. 'They take care of their own, and if you're in trouble they'll take care of you.'

'I never bought the stereotypes,' Abrams said.

'Good, 'cause there ain't none.'

'You plannin' on gettin' involved?'

'I'm just here as family, son.'

'Did Mike Fredericksen tell you to keep your snout out of the trough?'

'Not as straight as that, but I got the message.'

'And?'

Landis turned back and looked at Abrams. 'If it was your brother, what would you do?'

'I don't got a brother.'

'It's a hypothetical question.'

'I'd wanna know, for sure, but I guess I'd trust the police to figure it out.'

'You think they're gonna do that?' Landis asked.

'Any reason they wouldn't?'

'None that I know of.'

'So I guess the best thing to do is let them get on with it, see how it turns out.'

'Yes, indeed,' Landis said. 'And that's exactly what I'm intending to do.'

Abrams was quiet for a moment, but there was a question in his eyes.

'Go ahead and ask whatever you're thinking of asking,' Landis said.

'Not that it's my business, Sheriff, but I have been wondering what would keep you two apart for so many years, 'specially as how you're both sheriffs and you both seem so alike an' all. Livin' so close to one another, too.'

'What seems obvious and what is are rarely the same thing. Talkin' about it ain't gonna put the skin back on the cat now, is it? Any explanation I could give you wouldn't be worth a damn, and I ain't got a mind to figure out a better one.'

'I'm sorry I asked,' Abrams said. 'I know it ain't my business.'

'No offense taken, son,' Landis replied. 'I guess as long as I stay here, there's gonna be folks who're asking themselves the same thing.'

'I got a flask of coffee in the car,' Abrams said. 'You wanna stay and share a cup?'

'Sure,' Landis replied. 'I ain't in no hurry to be someplace.'

6

As Landis headed back to Union, his thoughts were louder than usual. His head was a mess of things he figured no one would understand, least of all himself.

Hindsight was the only way to fashion something that once was into something that could have been. It was common knowledge, so much so that no one troubled themselves to say it out loud.

Landis had convinced himself that he bore no regrets for what had happened between himself and Frank. Things had a habit of turning out the way they turned out, and often there was nothing you could do to change them. The whys and where-fores seemed so much conjecture. Perhaps Fate played a part. Perhaps not.

He saw Frank's face – as a child, a young man, as an enemy and then a corpse. Whatever had fueled his dislike now seemed to waver and flicker. The force of his animosity – something he'd carried for so many years – was now a redundant burden. Carrying it further served no purpose, but its weight was so familiar he doubted his resolve to set it down.

Arriving back at the Blairsville office, Barbara asked after news.
'He's dead,' Landis said. 'No doubt about it.'
'Accident?'
'Nope. Murder plain and simple.'

'Lordy, lordy, what a business. And they got someone in their sights?'

'They ain't done much thus far but move his body. His car's still out there. Got the Trenton police on it. We'll see what kind of show they make.'

'You want me to get Marshall to cover you for the rest of the day, Sheriff?'

'Now why would he need to do that?'

'Thinkin' maybe you want some reflectin' time an' all. Your brother's dead, ain't he? Usual for folks to want some time alone to ponder things.'

'I ain't got nothin' to ponder, Barbara. He's dead and gone and that's the end of it.'

'Well, if you're stayin' on, them new folks on Garland said they got an abandoned car outside their place for three days now. Think maybe it's been stolen.'

'I'll get over there and check it out,' Landis said. He glanced at his watch. It was close to four.

'If that's all that's happenin', you may as well get yourself on home.'

'I will, but I got a little paperwork to finish up here,' Barbara said.

Landis put on his hat and went to the door.

'See you Monday, Barbara.'

'Sure as there'll be weather, Sheriff.'

The car wasn't stolen. Took no more than a minute to call it up and see who owned it. Landis used the phone in the complainants' house.

'Derry Buck, that you?'

'Depends who's askin'.'

'Sheriff Landis is who's askin'. Got your vehicle out here on Garland. Mr Prentiss say it's been here a while now.'

'Well, I'd say Mr Prentiss'd be right.'

'You gonna come get it or what?'

'It's busted.'

'That may well be, Derry, but you can't leave it out here for ever.'

'Soon as I got me the tow money, I'll get it fetched. You got a problem with that?'

'Not just now, Derry, but there will be if I have to ask you a second time.'

Derry Buck hung up without another word.

'You go on and call Barbara if it's still here tomorrow evening,' he told Prentiss.

Mrs Prentiss thanked Landis for coming out, asked if he wanted a cup of coffee for his trouble.

'Kind of you, ma'am, but I'd best be away.'

Back in the office, Barbara having left, Landis turned out the lights and sat alone as the dark came down. From the file cabinet he fetched a bottle of rye, poured an inch or so into his coffee cup and sipped it slow while he smoked.

When he'd been just a handful of years old, his mother told him he was destined to make a special mark on the world. It was just the kind of thing every doting mother impressed upon a child. No doubt she'd said the very same thing to Frank. The issue was not that it was a lie, nor whether a child believed it. The issue arose when people went on believing it despite all indications to the contrary.

As far as what had happened between his folks, he hadn't appreciated the gravity of things. His father was a drunk, a violent one, on one hand seeing himself as the authoritarian patriarch, on the other wrestling with a profound and debilitating sense of worthlessness. He was all kinds of mad at most everything, and didn't have the stamina to outrun his own fury.

Most people chased something they didn't really need, or ran from something already inside of them. Walter Landis was no different. Later, folks would wonder how he wound up so crazy. In truth, it hadn't been so hard. In truth, he should've been dead a hundred times over, but he was just too dumb to realize it. As dumb as a box of sand, and with half the personality.

Everyone did wrong. It was part and parcel of being human. But what a man did wasn't near as important as what he did next. Their father had a habit of making that next thing even worse. Walter had been his own worst enemy, yet blamed everyone but himself for his inevitable downfall. The sad thing was that his wife – bearing the brunt of all that bitterness – quit first. A suicide. Victor had been fifteen, Frank a year younger. It was only later that her death took on the color of murder. A slow-motion murder, but murder all the same.

Making sense of all that happened back then was a road, plain and simple. Whatever Landis imagined was at the end of the road, he had yet to find it. He was still trying. And if a man stopped trying, he may as well be dead.

When all was said and done, the thing he missed most about the past was not his mother, nor the fact that he and Frank had once lived out of each other's pockets.

The thing he missed most was hope. Hope that it would all make sense when he was older.

7

It was Friday morning before Landis heard word of the funeral. Deputy Abrams called him at the office, surprised to discover that no one else had kept him informed.

'It's tomorrow,' he said. 'Noon. Trenton Community Baptist Church.'

Landis didn't respond. He was considering how little he'd thought about Frank in the previous week.

'You're comin', right,' Abrams said with no hint of a question.

'Guess it would be wrong not to.'

'You want me to get a wreath made up or something?'

'Why do you care so much, Deputy Abrams?'

'I see that you and Frank had your differences, Sheriff. That ain't none of my business. However, I'm guessin' a fight between two people has gotta be over when one of them is dead.'

'You go ahead and get a wreath made up,' Landis said. 'Let me know the cost when I get there.'

'And there'll be a gatherin' at the church hall afterward,' Abrams said. 'Sheriff's Office, Police Department, even the Mayor. Figured maybe you'd wanna meet your sister-in-law and your niece.'

'You mean the ones I never knew I had?'

Landis could sense Abrams' patience wearing thin at the other end of the line.

'Look here,' he said. 'I ain't never had nothin' bad to say about your brother, and I sure as hell don't wanna get mixed up in whatever went on between the two of you. I'm just tryin' to be decent here. If you want me to butt out then you just need to say it straight, Sheriff Landis.'

'I apologize,' Landis said. 'You're gettin' the sharp end of a long stick, son. You done right for lettin' me know, and I appreciate your thoughtfulness. You go on ahead and get them flowers made up, and I'll see you tomorrow.'

That night the cold fell hard. Clothes on the drying line were as stiff as dried meat.

Landis saw them through his bedroom window, swaying back and forth like store shingles. Where the chill snap had come from he did not know, but it was unseasonal.

He had never been a troubled sleeper, but that night – thinking of Frank's funeral, wondering whether he would find any words to share with Frank's ex-wife – he wrestled with awkward emotions. They were sufficiently vague for him to get a grasp on nothing specific. All he felt was a deep sense of unease and disquiet. He wondered for a time if Frank was trying to tell him something. Landis had never been one for religion, had rarely attended church after the death of his mother. He afforded no time to the greater questions that plagued the minds of other men. Who are we? Where did we come from? What happened once we were dead? No one knew because no one ever came back to file a report.

Frank was dead. He was gone. There was nothing left but a uniformed corpse in a wooden box. Frank was not out there emanating messages to anyone through the ether.

Finally, between three and four in the morning, Landis found sleep. He did not dream, but when he woke he felt as if he had. It was as if there was something he was supposed to remember, but when he looked there was nothing at all.

Donning a suit he hadn't worn for a decade, Landis looked at himself in the mirror. He appeared older than his years. He'd heard it said that everyone wore the face they deserved. He didn't know what he'd done to deserve this one.

Nevertheless, he was going there just to be seen, and he was willing to make a degree of effort for the occasion.

As he drove out to Dade for the second time in a week, he hoped this would not become a habit. For him, the funeral would be the end of the matter. He would pay as much respect as he could muster, and then he would come home. Who had killed Frank and why they'd done it was a matter for Fredericksen and his colleagues. If they figured it out, all well and good. If not, then Frank's business would go with him to the hereafter. After all, Landis figured, if the roles in this little drama had been reversed then Frank would've felt no obligation to get involved.

Landis made good time. He was early enough to take some coffee at the Mountainview.

Though Shirley did not bus his table, she saw him from the other side of the room and came on over.

'I just want to say how sorry I am for your brother,' she said. 'I had no idea at all … well, you know, about what had happened when you were here the last time. I found out later and I felt so darn awful about what I said. You know, how you should go on an' enjoy your visit with your brother.'

'It really don't matter none, Shirley,' Landis said. 'You weren't to know, and to tell you the truth, you were nothing but friendly and that was appreciated.'

'Well, I am sorry again. Such a terrible business. He was a good man and a fine sheriff, and I'm sure that however all o' that came about, he's in a better place now.'

Landis doubted this was the case, but he said nothing.

'You need anythin' else?' Shirley asked.

'I'm fine, but thank you for askin'.'

Shirley seemed momentarily awkward, as if there was something else she felt she should say but couldn't get a hold on it.

Landis just smiled until she relaxed, and then she went about her business.

The Trenton Community Baptist Church was filled to capacity. Though narrow and tall, it still accommodated a congregation of two hundred or more. Seemed to Landis that every seat was filled.

Try as he did to stay inconspicuous, Abrams saw him and came over to greet him.

'You should come on up and meet the mayor, the police captain and whoever,' he said. 'Everyone has come. It's a fine turnout.'

'If it's all the same to you, Deputy, I'd rather just stay on back here and—'

'Well, at least come and meet my wife,' Abrams said.

Before he knew it, Landis was being allowed passage along the right-hand side of the room and Abrams' wife – a pretty brunette holding a child of no more than two or three – was getting up from her seat and extending her hand.

'This is my wife, Carole,' Abrams said.

'Pleasure to meet you, Sheriff Landis,' Carole said, 'though a shame it's on such a sad occasion. We had your brother over many a time for supper and football games on the TV and whatnot and I did like him so. I'm real sorry for your loss.'

Landis was courteously monosyllabic.

Abrams insisted Landis take a seat beside Carole. Before he could be discouraged, Abrams was then bringing over the Mayor of Trenton, the Captain of Police, some other official whose name and title went unregistered. One by one they expressed their condolences, said as how Frank was a good man, a fine sheriff, that he would be sorely missed by anyone who'd had the good fortune to know him.

Landis accepted their words but gave none in return. There was a time for speaking and a time for silence. Most folks rarely knew the difference. Whatever he might venture to say would come out twisted in a fashion that gave it some unintended meaning. Ironically, the clearest memory of saying what he meant was in a letter he wrote to Frank, though that letter was never mailed. Just getting it down on paper had given him sufficient respite from the thoughts that troubled him. That letter was still somewhere, buried in a box alongside photos and postcards and the like.

It was then, as people made their way back to their seats, that he saw the girl.

In her features he saw his own mother, his grandmother before, even something of himself. She sat wordless and wide-eyed. She looked at Landis as if transfixed. He had the sense of being clothed in someone else's skin. The girl kept staring. Landis mustered a faint smile, but the girl's fixed expression did not change a whisker. Her mother nudged her. The girl looked ahead, but after a moment she glanced once more over her shoulder. After that she sat still as stone.

This was his niece, Jennifer, and beside her was Frank's ex-wife, Eleanor.

The service began. Landis paid little mind to the words. His attention was drawn back time and again to the woman and her child.

People got up and said what they wanted to say. Some of them were emotional, pausing and breathing and repeating themselves. Others were unused to facing a crowd, their words formal and stiff and seemingly devoid of feeling.

They spoke of a man who should've been closer to Landis

than anyone else in the room. Even the child, Frank's own flesh and blood, should have been relegated to second position in light of the fact that she'd been around for only a quarter of Frank's life. Landis had been there right from the start, and yet he was the most distant of all.

Whatever world Frank had created here – the things he did, the people he knew, the memories he left behind – were utterly foreign to Landis. He did not feel anything so specific as grief or loss; what he felt was far less definable. It was tantamount to being told that something you didn't know you had was now gone.

Abrams and his wife insisted that Landis stay on after the service.

Landis did his best, but his refusal was no match for Abrams' insistence.

Those who'd known Frank were set to acknowledge and celebrate his life. The novelty of not only discovering he had a brother, but that the brother had actually shown up, was something they couldn't ignore.

Faces and voices came and went in a wave. It seemed endless. After a while, the novelty having worn thin, Landis headed out back of the church hall with a glass of rye than was now more ice water than liquor.

Ten yards or so from the rear of the building was a low fence. He set his glass on the post, took out his cigarettes and his lighter. Even before he'd lit one, he was aware of someone behind him.

'I know who you are,' Eleanor Boyd said.

Landis turned.

'He may'nt have told that horde of peckerwoods 'bout you, but he told me.'

Landis smiled. He held out his hand. 'Ms Boyd,' he said.

'Pleasure to meet you, and I'm sorry about Frank, you know? He an' I had our differences and we hadn't spoken for a long time, and so I'm sure your loss is far greater than mine. Your daughter, too.'

'Jenna, sure. She doted on him. Thought he was all kinds of special. And, to be fair, we never went without. Even though he and I were all busted up, he still took care of us. Money came every month, got things fixed up right, forever seemed to have someone owin' him a favor who could sort something out with the house. You know, plumbin', electric fuses, whatever.'

'Yes,' Landis said, all the while wondering how he could extricate himself from this situation and head back to his car.

'Anyways, I'm not here to talk about Frank. I'm here to invite you to our home.'

'Your home?'

'Like it or not, you're my daughter's uncle. She has a will somethin' fierce like her daddy. She'll keep hammerin' at things until they're bent the way she wants.'

'I'm sorry, Ms Boyd, but you know I have my own—'

Eleanor Boyd cut him dead with a look. 'You are so full o' shit,' she said. 'I don't give a rat's-ass what happened between you and Frank, but you got a girl over there goin' on eleven years old who's kin whether you care for it or not. She said to come over here and ask you polite if you'd visit with us a while before you head on back. The day of her daddy's funeral, that's what this is. You gonna tell her no? Is that what you're fixin' on doin', Uncle Sheriff Landis?'

'I guess I ain't now,' Landis replied.

Eleanor Boyd smiled. 'We'll be leavin' in a while. I'll give you the heads-up. You follow us in your own car. It ain't so far, and it's the same direction as where you're headin' anyway.'

With that, she turned and walked away.

31

Landis watched her go, and then he took out his cigarettes once more.

As he lit one, he noticed his hands were shaking. Just a little, but shaking all the same.

8

When his mother died, Victor Landis felt a sense of aloneness unlike anything he'd experienced before. He was fifteen years old, but he felt like a child.

No matter who you were, things changed when you no longer had a place that was home. His mother was the one who'd created that, and in her absence it all fell apart at the seams.

It was this sense of awkward separation and disconnection that he tried to recall as he followed Eleanor Boyd's car out to her home. He was trying to imagine how Frank's daughter would be feeling in that moment, perhaps trying to empathize with her. Landis knew he'd have to find some way to be something more than lost and wordless when they arrived.

He could see them talking in the car ahead. Landis guessed it was about him. Eleanor had not said whether the girl had ever been informed of his existence. He figured he would find out soon enough.

The car ahead slowed and turned left into the driveway of a modest but well-kept house. There was a lawn, flowerbeds patrolling the borders, and up on the porch was a couple of chairs and a wrought-iron table.

Landis drew to a stop against the curb. He didn't want to park in the drive. Making as fast and clean a getaway as possible was foremost in his mind.

Getting out, he stood beside the open door of his car for a moment. Jenna stepped out of her mother's car and looked back at him. She smiled, and it was a smile of such artless simplicity that he could not help but smile back.

Landis closed the door. Jenna walked down towards him. He met her halfway.

Holding out her hand she said, 'I'm Jenna Landis, your niece.'

Landis reciprocated her very businesslike handshake. 'I guess that makes me your Uncle Victor,' he said.

'From a distance you look like my dad,' Jenna said. 'Close up less so.'

'If we're talking looky-likes, then you have a good helping of your grandmother.'

'Was she pretty?'

'Pretty enough for some fellas to wish their own wives was dead an' six feet down.'

Jenna laughed. 'You're funny.'

She turned towards the house. 'Come on, let's go inside,' she said.

Landis followed her without another word.

The three of them sat in a bright yellow kitchen. Had Frank ever lived there, there was no evidence of it. It was very much the home of a woman and her daughter. Perhaps there was now another man in Eleanor Boyd's life, but if so, he was a visitor not a stayer.

'So you're sheriff over there in Union?' Eleanor asked.

'I am, yes.'

'How long for?'

'Oh, seven and a half years or so. Been in the department since back in 1974. Sheriff since '85.'

'So you're the older one, but got into policing after Frank, then.'

'That's right, yes. I went roaming, you know. Up north and thereabouts. Came back to Georgia, and Frank was already enroled. I could see it was doing him good, the predictability, the discipline of it. Seemed to make sense for both of us after what happened when we were younger.'

'What happened when you were younger?' Jenna asked.

'Well, we lost our ma pretty early on, you see?'

'Like me losin' my daddy.'

'Yes,' Landis said. 'We were a bit older, but not much.'

'Did your pa die too?'

'He did, yes, but not for a good few years after.'

'What was he like?' Jenna asked.

'Jenna, sweetheart,' Eleanor interjected, 'I'm quite sure he doesn't want to be hounded with questions just at the moment.'

Jenna looked at him, her eyes like searchlights. 'Do you feel like you're being hounded, Uncle Victor?'

Landis laughed. 'I got to say this is all very unfamiliar to me, but I got no issue with your questions.'

'So what was he like?'

'Your grandfather? Well, he was a tough son-of-a … a real tough character. Yeah, he was a tough character. Someone nailed him together out of timber and saddle hide. He didn't say a great deal. Not a talkative man, you know?'

Jenna smiled. 'You talk funny.'

'Jenna, really,' Eleanor said.

'Well, he does.'

Landis looked at Eleanor. Eleanor shrugged. Landis smiled, started to laugh.

'Guess so,' Landis said. 'Only way I know how, though.'

'So did you always want to be a sheriff?'

'I actually wanted to be a guitar player. Like my daddy.'

'Your daddy was a guitar player?'

'No, but he wanted to be.'

Jenna looked at her mother. 'See?' she said. 'He does talk funny.' She turned back to Landis. 'And you sound just like my father.'

'Okay,' Eleanor said, 'I think that's enough of the third degree, young lady. Let's all have a drink together, and then perhaps Sheriff Landis here will be wantin' to get himself on home.'

'Yes,' Landis said. 'Maybe a cup of coffee, Ms Boyd. If it's no trouble.'

'You'll be wantin' somethin' in that to fire it up some?' she asked.

'Thank you, no,' Landis said. 'I got a drive ahead of me.'

Jenna got up. 'Mom, Uncle Victor and I are gonna sit out front for a while. Can you bring me some lemonade?'

'Sure I can, sweetheart.'

She grabbed Landis's hand.

'Come with me,' she said.

Landis went with her. She didn't release his hand until he was sat out on the porch.

'So,' she said. 'I know that what my ma told me ain't true.'

Landis frowned.

'She said my daddy was killed in a car accident. I know that's a lie.'

'That's no lie. He was killed by someone in a car.'

'But it weren't no accident.'

Landis looked at his niece. He felt as if he'd been cornered by a bear.

'It weren't no accident, was it?'

'I don't know the details of what happened, Jenna,' Landis replied. 'And the police here, maybe Deputy Abrams too, well

36

they're gonna look into it and find out what happened to your daddy, okay?'

'But you're gonna help them right?'

Landis shifted uncomfortably in his chair. 'Well no, as a matter of fact I'm not. I actually can't.'

'You can't, or you don't want to?'

'Him bein' kin an' all means I can't get involved in the investigation itself. When you're family you have to stay out of it.'

'Don't you care what happened to him?'

'Of course I care what happened to him.'

'It doesn't seem like you care.'

'Well, different folks have different ways of showing their feelings.'

'And you show yours by showing nothing at all.'

'Look here, Jenna, I understand you're upset an' all, but I really have no part in this—'

'You do. You're his brother. He was my daddy and you're my uncle, and I want you to find out what happened to him.'

'The police will find out. There's a detective called Mike Fredericksen, and he's taking care of all of that.'

'Well, I ain't stupid. I know two things right now. Mike Fredericksen ain't my daddy's brother, and Mike Fredericksen ain't been over here askin' questions of anyone.'

'I'm sure he'll get to it.'

Jenna didn't say anything immediately. She just fixed Landis with those searchlight eyes. He found himself inadvertently looking away. The girl had a manner about her that was invasive and direct. Like Eleanor had said, she was set to hammering on something until it was bent the way she wanted it.

'If it was my brother,' she finally said, her eyes brimming with tears, 'and no matter what had happened between us, I'd wanna know why someone run him down with a car and broke him all to pieces.'

Her lower lip quivered. Her whole body was wound up tight like a clock spring.

'And if I didn't wanna know, I'd be askin' myself some pretty tough questions about why.'

9

After lunch on Monday, Landis called Mike Fredericksen at Trenton PD.

'Detective Fredericksen, Sheriff Landis down in Union. Just wanted to know how things were progressing on the investigation.'

'Well, I have to say, Sheriff, that *progressing* isn't the word I'd use. We're doing everything we can, but it seems no one saw a thing. Nothing to speak of in the way of forensics evidence either.'

'Someone been on up in the direction he was headed and talked to the families there?'

'Like I said, Sheriff, we're doing everything we can, but we got ourselves a bunch of twos and threes without no picture cards, if you know what I mean.'

'Sure I do,' Landis said. 'I know exactly what you mean.'

There was silence for a moment.

'So?' Landis asked. 'That's your sheriff you got murdered—'

'We're utilizing every resource at our disposal. We've got a reward out for information, and we have as many officers as we can muster canvassin' every which way. We're sure to come up with somethin' sooner or later.'

'Was over with Eleanor Boyd after the funeral on Saturday,' Landis said. 'From what I understand, no one has interviewed her.'

'Why would we interview her, Sheriff Landis? You think she run him over?'

'Why do I think you would interview her? Because they used to be married, Detective Fredericksen. Because she possibly knew him better than anyone else. Because he might've said somethin' to her about some trouble with a case or a suspect maybe, or someone that figured he had it coming to him for a bust he did—'

'Of course, yes,' Fredericksen said. 'Of course we'll get to that. We're following the standard protocol, as we do with any homicide. We know exactly what we're doing.'

Landis wanted to ask Fredericksen why he had the definite impression they'd got no idea what they were doing. Either that, or they were unwilling. He kept his tongue to himself.

'I'm guessing he had a place over there in Trenton.'

'For sure he did. House out on Cooper Road.'

'And you got that place turned inside out?'

'All of that, yes. Like I said before, we're doing everything we can. Seems the best thing you could do is let us get on with it and I'll keep you up to speed with any new information as it comes in.'

'That'd be much appreciated, Detective Fredericksen.'

'Okay then,' Fredericksen replied, and hung up.

Landis leaned back in his chair and looked at the ceiling. The thing stuck in his craw. From the girl's emotionally charged interrogation to the seeming nonchalance of Fredericksen, something didn't sit right. One thing he hadn't done was ask Eleanor Boyd what she thought. Did he actually not want to know what had happened to his own brother? That was now the question foremost in his mind.

In that moment – memory perhaps revived by the funeral – Landis remembered the last time he'd seen Frank. It was back at the start of 1981. They'd talked, argued, near came to blows again. Frank's last words to him were bitter, hard to swallow.

'You were never gonna be anyone other than who I thought you were,' he'd told his brother. 'Well, tomorrow you get a whole new day to break my heart. You've broke it enough for today.'

But there hadn't been a tomorrow, and there now never would be.

Landis got up from his desk and walked through to dispatch.

'You know where Marshall's at?' he asked Barbara.

'On up at Wilbur's. 'Nother fight last night. Some out-o'-towner got his nose busted.'

'And do you know if Derry Buck got his car moved off of Garland like I told him?'

'I'll check, Sheriff.'

'I'm gonna go over Wilbur's then. Got something I want Marshall to do for me.'

'Okey dokey.'

Wilbur Cobb had the least fingers of any man Landis had ever known. How he'd lost them was a different story for everyone who asked, and none of those stories were true. Men were regaled with tales of lightning-fast five-finger fillet, the women with bear-wrestling or babes-in-arms rescued from burning buildings. The truth was that Cobb had driven halfway across the mid-west to see a girl who never showed. On the way back he got caught in a Minnesota blizzard, survived four days in his car before they dug him out of a drift. Frostbite took a thumb and two fingers on the right, the last three digits on the left. His bar was called The Old Tavern. He'd inherited it from his uncle on his mother's side back in the early eighties. It had its fair share of rowdies and drunks. Fights broke out like a rash, especially in the summer, and usually over nothing more calamitous than a lost pool game or a spilled drink.

Marshall's car was parked down the side of the building. Landis parked out front and went on in.

Marshall was up at the bar and halfway through a sandwich.

'Sheriff,' Cobb said. 'You come on over to check on your boy?'

'He ain't a boy and he ain't mine,' Landis said.

Marshall greeted Landis, asked if he'd had lunch.

'Cup of coffee wouldn't go amiss,' Landis said.

'Wilbur. Get the sheriff a cup of coffee, would you? Fresh, mind. None of this over-boiled coal tar you been servin' up.'

Wilbur muttered his way out back.

'This matter get fixed?' Landis asked.

'As good as. Usual story. Some guy runnin' his mouth off. Took a swing at Trent Kelsey. Kelsey busted the kid's nose, got a good kick in when he was down. Half a dozen say it was self-defense.'

'The busted nose?'

'Got it set this morning. Hightailed it out of here. Said he wasn't pressin' charges.'

Wilbur arrived with coffee, refilled Marshall's cup too.

'So, you know the deal with my brother,' Landis said.

'Yeah, I do. Sorry to hear that. I ain't been around for the last coupla days. Got things sendin' me here and there all over the county.'

'No mind,' Landis said. 'Wasn't nothin' for you to concern yourself with. However, I did want to ask you about somethin'.'

'Shoot.'

'You got folks over east, right?'

'Got my daddy's brother and his kin out near Snowbird Mountains if that's what you mean. He settled up there in Murphy.'

'Right, right. I'm thinkin' maybe they know some folks up above Dade County.'

'He's a social feller, no doubt. And all them people out there are good an' close. Why d'you ask?'

'My brother was out that way when he got himself killed. He was near the Tennessee state line, car headed north. It was late on Friday night, and I am itchin' to know what the hell he was doin'.'

'Heard it weren't no accident.'

'You heard right. He got run down three, maybe four times.'

'He was a sheriff, for Chrissake. Surely they got half the National Guard and three units of Feds up there tearin' the place apart.'

'Well, that's the rub right there. Seems they got one detective who's showin' as much interest as a sleepin' dog.'

Marshall looked at Landis. He frowned. 'You think he was into some bad business?'

'I'm not thinkin' anything right now.'

'I can ask around and about, sure.'

'Discreet like.'

'Sure thing.'

Landis took a sip of coffee and grimaced. 'Hell, it really is coal tar, ain't it?'

IO

It was late on Wednesday before there was news.

Barbara had left for the day. Landis was finishing up some long-overdue paperwork when his deputy appeared in the doorway.

'Marshall, how goes it?'

Marshall came into the room and took a seat without a word.

'What's up, son?'

'This business with your brother,' he said. 'I made some calls, spoke to my uncle. Said he didn't know anything directly, but mentioned someone called Jim Tom Moody. You heard o' him?'

'Can't say I have.'

'I looked him up. He got a bunch of stuff goin' on, and way back a while too. Did a stretch for manslaughter when he was barely out of his teens. A whole grocery list of other stuff on file, but it ain't never stuck 'cause no one's ever corroborated or testified or been a witness. Anyways, that's all as may be. What my uncle said is that this Moody feller's runnin' drugs, guns, a whole mess o' things through Carolina, Tennessee, down here too.'

'And he said that this Moody might know something about Frank?'

'He said that if your brother was into anythin' he should'na been then Moody would be the man to ask.'

'Jim Tom Moody.'

'That's the feller.'

'Murphy, North Carolina.'

Marshall nodded. 'Said that's where you'd find him.'

'Appreciated.'

'You want me to follow up on anythin' else?'

'No, that's fine,' Landis replied. 'Just let it lie for the time being. I wanna see how the Trenton investigation plays out.'

'You heard anything else on it?'

'Dead quiet,' Landis said.

'Ain't right, is it?'

'Well, let's just say I ain't never been one for jumpin' to conclusions, but I sure am tempted right now.'

Two days went by. Landis was busy with regular matters. Derry Buck still hadn't moved his vehicle off of Garland so Landis instructed it be towed. He called Buck and told him he was set to pay fifty dollars for the trouble.

'Now, where in Christ almighty's name d'you expect me to get fifty dollars from, Sheriff? If I'd o' had the money I woulda dragged that car off myself.'

'Not my concern, Derry. The car's in the pound. You want it back, you pay the money. Six weeks and then they'll sell it or scrap it.'

'Well, maybe I'll just do us both a favor, eh? Climb that fence and set the thing on fire. Be done with it then.'

Landis tried to hold his tongue but he couldn't. 'You know Derry Buck, you are about three helpin's of useless with a mess of stupid on top. I known you a good while now, and you always got some reason why your trouble is someone else's doin'. You ever gonna be a man, or you gonna spend the rest of your days actin' like a child?'

'I ain't decided on it yet.'

'Well, I think it's high time you growed up, son. Ain't no one gonna make your mark for you.'

'Maybe I don't wanna make a mark.'

'You take care now, Derry,' Landis said, and hung up the phone.

The phone rang almost immediately. Landis picked it up.

'Got some lady on the phone for you,' Barbara said. 'Eleanor Boyd.'

'Put her through, Barb.'

'Ms Boyd?'

'Sheriff Landis, hi. I'm sorry to call you but I figured you were the only person I could talk to.'

'What's up?'

'Well, I got an issue with money.'

'With money?' Landis asked.

'Whatever anyone might've thought about Frank, he was devoted to Jenna. He took care of everything for her, you know? We've been divorced seven years or more now, but he still sent money over every month. I figured it was comin' direct from his wages, but now I find out that it was comin' from someplace else.'

'How d'you mean?'

'Last week of each month he'd put a thousand bucks in my account.'

'A thousand bucks?'

'Seems like a lot, but I got a growin' kid. Dental, school stuff, clothes, whatever. It soon adds up.'

'Surely it's just an administrative thing, Ms Boyd. I mean, he's been gone two weeks. They're gonna be straightenin' out his pension now, and I can only guess that the bulk of that is gonna come to you.'

'Well, that's the thing right there,' she said. 'I called 'em up. They said Frank never sent any money direct from his wages. So I called the bank, asked 'em where the money was comin' from. You know, the money he put in my account. They said they ain't got no record of him.'

'Well, maybe he had another account.'

'Maybe so, but I wouldn't know how to even go about diggin' that up. All I know is that the money ain't here and I need it bad.'

'Okay, okay. So what do you want me to do?'

'Like I said, I'm sorry for bringin' this to your door, but I don't know anyone official. Sheriff's Office over here don't seem to have no interest in helpin' out, so I thought ... well, you know, seein' as how it's really for your niece ...'

Eleanor Boyd let the last statement hang in the air between them.

'I can make some enquiries, Ms Boyd, but you're talkin' about a different county, about banks and whatever. I don't know that I'm gonna be a great deal of help to you.'

'Anything you can do would be mightily appreciated,' she said. 'I got bills comin' out my ears and rent to pay and things, you know?'

'Of course, yes. Leave it with me. I'll see what I can do. Give me your number.'

She did so. Landis wrote it down.

'Thank you, Victor.'

Landis hesitated. The fact that she'd used his first name threw a spanner in the machinery of his thoughts.

'You're welcome, Ms Boyd.'

'You can call me Eleanor, you know?' she said. 'After all, we're as good as family, aren't we?'

'Er... yes, I guess we are.'

The line went dead.

Landis hung up, leaned back, and wondered what the hell he was getting dragged into.

II

From Deputy Abrams' first words, Landis knew that he was on a hide into nowhere.

'Not a clue, Sheriff,' Abrams said. 'I mean, I knew your brother an' all, but only workwise. His personal life was his own business.'

'Of course, yes,' Landis replied, 'but it's a matter that needs to get resolved, if only for the sake of his daughter.'

'Well, Ms Boyd's gonna have to take it up with the administration, isn't she?'

'She has done, but they aren't givin' her any answers to amount to anythin'. They don't seem to know any more than you an' me about this.'

'Hell, I wouldn't go readin' anythin' awkward into it. More than likely he had a different bank account and he paid her from that.'

'Which raises the question of where that money was comin' from.'

'From his wages, I guess.'

'If Dade people are paid the same as Union, then that's about a third of his salary, son. From what she says, his bank ain't got no record of any money goin' out to her or another bank.'

Abrams didn't reply.

'And another thing strikes me while I'm sayin' this. If that money wasn't legal, then why the hell would he be payin' it into a bank account. Seems to me if he had some other source of income he didn't want known, then why wouldn't he pay her from his bank and keep the other money to himself?'

'Like I told you,' Abrams said. 'His personal business wasn't any o' mine.'

'I assume his pension is gettin' sorted.'

'I assume so, too.'

'And Eleanor Boyd would be receivin' a good portion o' that, seein' as how she's got Frank's kid to look after.'

'You're talkin' to the wrong man, Sheriff. You'd need to take that up with the pension folks.'

'Right. Sure. So, what's the deal over there? You sheriff now?'

'Well, I guess I am. In name only, mind. Good while 'fore there's an election. We'll have to see if the higher-ups wanna bring someone else in meantime.'

'Well, if I had a vote you'd get it,' Landis said, wishing to end the call on a friendly note.

'Mighty kind of you, Sheriff Landis. Sorry I couldn't be any help to you on this.'

'No matter, Deputy. You take care now.'

Landis hung up, then buzzed Barbara.

'Barb, can you get me the Georgia Sheriff's Department Pensions Office. I'm guessin' that'll be in Atlanta.'

'Sure thing, Sheriff.'

The call came back within a minute.

'Marjorie Whitmer here,' a young woman said. 'How can I help you?'

'This is Victor Landis. I'm sheriff up in Union. Had a brother, sheriff over in Dade, got hisself killed a couple o' weeks back—'

'Oh, I'm very sorry to hear that, Sheriff,' Marjorie replied.

'I'm chasin' up some information about his service pension. I'm guessin' it's gettin' itself sorted out right now.'

'Well, I would have thought so,' Marjorie replied, 'but I'm not gonna be able to give you any information about that over the phone, you see? That's confidential. You'd have to get us something in writing, and it's gonna have to come through whoever might be dealin' with your brother's estate.'

'You can't even tell me if it's goin' through the necessary channels?'

'I'm sorry, Sheriff. I would if I could but I just can't.'

'Well, okay. I appreciate your time, Marjorie.'

'You're most welcome. And you go on and have a nice day now.'

The call ended, Landis paced back and forth. With no further news from Fredericksen, now two weeks after the fact, he guessed the investigation – or whatever was happening over there in Dade – was going as slow as molasses. Now there was a thousand dollars a month for seven years that seemed to have no identifiable source. That was all of eighty-four thousand dollars. With a sheriff's salary running somewhere around thirty-five and change, that was a good deal of money to come from nowhere.

Landis thought to chase up Trenton PD again, even go over Fredericksen's head, but something in his gut told him that it would be an unwise course of action. If he was going to look into this, then the fewer people who knew the better.

He buzzed Barbara again.

'Want you to find an address for me, Barb. Jim Tom Moody up in Murphy, North Carolina.'

'Just got a call to make,' Barbara said, 'and then I'll get on it.'

'No hurry. Today sometime'd be fine. I'm gonna go out and get me some lunch. Can I bring you somethin' back?'

'No, that's fine, Sheriff. I'm back on my diet, you know.'

Landis drove across town to a ribs place he liked. What they did with them, he hadn't figured out yet, but they turned out good.

While he ate, he wrestled with the conflict he was facing.

In order to resolve the circumstances of Frank's death he had to understand a good deal of his life. That was something he'd never wished to do, and he wasn't of a mind to change. It would be simpler to let it go, but the emotive plea for assistance that had been rendered by Frank's daughter had left him unsettled. She deserved to know what had happened. Had it just been Eleanor, he might have been in a position to pursue it no further. He was not without heart, even though he might have denied it under oath. Every once in a while, he wondered what would have happened if he and his wife had had children. Say they had, maybe a year or so after getting hitched. Kids wouldn't have stopped her dying, and he'd have been left a widower with little ones. Would he have stayed in the sheriff's department or would he have followed some other road? It was all so much hypothesis, and it shouldn't have warranted any thought at all. But there it was, right in the shadows behind him, and every which way it turned it seemed to turn with him.

For all that had happened between them, whatever animosity and aggravation they had caused one another, he and Frank were still brothers. That they'd survived their mother's suicide, the death of their father, they had nevertheless come from the same place and would more than likely end up in the same place too.

It was more a matter of unanswered questions than anything else, and it galled him to think that someone somewhere knew the truth and was all set to withhold it. Fredericksen seemed about as much use as a bucket of holes, and Deputy Abrams – even though he seemed a smart enough young man – was holding down his brother's job.

Wiping rib sauce from his hands with a napkin before he lit a cigarette, Landis came to the inevitable conclusion that he'd have to go talk with Jim Tom Moody. Being the law, he wouldn't be welcome, but he wasn't out to railroad the man. Landis's sole interest was whether Frank had gotten into something that had warranted his killing.

12

The drive from Blairsville to Murphy was all of twenty miles.

Once over the North Carolina state line, Landis skirted the southeast edge of Lake Hiwassee and followed Highway 74. Surrounding him was some of the most beautiful landscape the US had to offer. Running fifteen hundred miles all the way from Newfoundland to central Alabama, the Appalachians never ceased to take his breath away. There were large tracts where industry had torn up the land looking for anthracite, gas, iron and zinc. The non-arable acres they'd left behind were called 'scalds', but surrounding them, seemingly intent on covering up those wretched scars, were forests of hickory, black northern, chestnut and scarlet oak, beneath them great swathes of mountain laurel and huckleberry. The Apalachee Indians were the first to find their home here, but – as was the case right across the country – they had been tracked and cornered, finally routed. They'd come all the way from the Florida Panhandle, only to discover that human greed would be a far greater adversary than anything Nature could offer.

Murphy itself had its own tale to tell. Site of the first trading post in the early 1800s, it later became the site of Fort Butler. Butler was the government collection point for the Cherokee who lived east of the mountains. From there, they went over to the Fort Cass internment camp, and then west beyond the Mississippi into Oklahoma. Murphy was the seat of Cherokee

County, and – just the same as Blairsville and Trenton – it had its own police department. Its sheriff's office was run directly by the Cherokee County Sheriff's Department.

The address Barbara nailed down for Jim Tom Moody was a ways beyond the town limits. Having said that, Landis would have missed Murphy if he'd blinked. Limit to limit, it was barely a mile and a half, and then a slip road took him north and then east until he was driving in the shadow of the Nantahala Forest.

Landis had grown up around these people. Irrespective of the TV stereotypes, they were really no different from anyone else. Mountain talk, so often mimicked and parodied, was far closer to the English of Chaucer and Shakespeare than anyplace else in the States. Hard-working, strong ties to their own community, devoted to the maintenance of family and tradition, these people were as good as you were ever likely to know.

Having eschewed both uniform and department vehicle in favour of civilian clothes and his own beat-to-hell Buick Skyhawk, Landis pulled over to the side of the road close to a mailbox that read Moody. From the back seat he collected a bottle of rye and a box of smoked meats. It would have been discourteous to arrive empty-handed.

Landis walked on up a pathway cut between high oaks, and came out into a wide expanse of land that was bordered by numerous sections of different fencing. Out beyond the fences was a wide run of sideling ground. It looked like someone was putting in beans. Pens holding three dogs were up on the right, and out to his left were a truck, two cars, a flatbed wagon and an old trailer with worn-out tires and rusted hubcaps.

The house itself was substantial. It was wider than it was tall, rooms added one after the other until it spread like the middle of an unfinished jigsaw puzzle.

Before he made it ten yards, a young woman came out onto the porch, her hand over her brow to shield the sun from her

55

eyes. Her hair was a deep auburn, falling around her shoulders in bold waves.

'Be helpin' you now?'

Landis took off his hat. 'Howdy, ma'am,' he said. 'I'm just lookin' to make a visit with Jim Tom Moody.'

'And who might you be?'

'No one special, ma'am. Just had word that he might be able to help me with a matter.'

'He didn't make no invite then?'

'No, he didn't.'

'And who told you he'd have anythin' to say to you?'

'Uncle of a friend of mine pointed me here.'

'What's your name?'

'Landis,' he replied. 'My name is Victor Landis.'

'You carryin'?'

'No, ma'am. Nothin' 'cept some this here whiskey and some smoked meat.'

'You brung that here for Jim Tom?'

'Yes, ma'am, I did.'

'Wait on here a while. I'll see if he's fit for talkin'.'

Landis waited a good fifteen minutes. Curtains twitched in the house. There was the sound of children out back, and then two little ones came haring out of a doorway and ran off into the trees without acknowledging his presence.

The young woman returned.

'Come on up,' she said.

Jim Tom Moody greeted Landis affably. He took the rye and the meat. The young woman went ahead into the house, Landis and Moody following on behind.

The room they wound up in was curtained and dim. Once seated, Landis surveyed the man facing him. He was somewhere in his late fifties, maybe older, his skin the beaten leather of someone accustomed to weather and work. Though slight in stature, there was a tough wiriness about him. Landis did not doubt that once riled he would be a fury of bony fists and lightning reactions.

Moody's eyes, green as moss, fixed Landis with a cool detachment. Here he was the captain of all things.

'Some reason you ain't tellin' me you're police?' Moody asked.

'Simple reason is I ain't here on police business. Not officially.'

'Where you from?'

'Blairsville. I'm Union County Sheriff.'

'So not only you in the wrong county, you's in the wrong state, as well.'

'That I am.'

Moody reached for the rye. 'You gonna drink with me?'

'If you'll have me.'

Moody called out for the woman. 'Dovie, fetch us in a couple of glasses would you there, sweetheart?'

Dovie brought glasses, opened the bottle, poured for them both.

'You go on and take that box o' meat there, darlin'. We can have some o' that later on.'

Once Dovie had left, Moody sipped his whiskey until it was gone. He poured another, did the same for Landis.

'So what is it you think I can do for you there, Union?'

'I had a brother,' Landis explained. 'Name of Frank Landis. Sheriff of Dade County. Couple o' weeks back he was headed out this way. Got himself run down by someone. No one seems to know anything about it.'

'I heard about it,' Moody said. 'Heard he got flattened good.'

'I spoke to a colleague o' mine. He has an uncle up this way. He said if anyone knew what my brother might've been involved in, it would be you.'

Moody smiled. 'I appreciate your directness, Sheriff Landis, but that kind of word don't paint such a good portrait o' me now, does it?'

'Man don't have to be bad to be wise.'

Moody hesitated, and then he burst into laughter.

Landis laughed with him. He couldn't help himself.

'Christ almighty, they teach you that in sheriff school, do they?'

Landis shook his head. 'No, sir. I got that dumb all by myself.'

Moody poured again. Landis thought about the drive back, what would happen if he got pulled over out-of-state. It was not a matter for consideration. Now he was here he had to find out what he could, even if he had to sleep off a drunk in the car.

'Have to say, from my limited experience of course, that most of the police I've known ain't been raised up right. That's for sure. Say one thing, do somethin' else. Shake with their right, steal with their left. Most of them so twisted they could hide behind a corkscrew. I know how people see us. Ignorant, illiterate, dirt-poor. I tell you now, folks out here had no notion they were poor 'til the likes o' Billy Graham come down here and tell 'em they was poverty-stricken. We had what we had, and it weren't no different from what other folks had. Difference with us is that you get what you see. Sure, we got ourselves a mess o' crooks and killers, but it ain't the same thing now. No one here is swearin' on the law and then breakin' it like it's nothin'.'

'Are you sayin' that you know something about my brother?'

'Not him direct, no. I don't know who got it in for him or why. What I do know is that he probably drove out and met his trouble halfway.'

'Trenton, specifically?'

'The whole o' Dade is riddled with lice, Sheriff. Place is like a rotted carcass. I'd as soon be here wi' my back broke than be around that stench.'

'You got details?'

Moody didn't respond. He smiled knowingly. Even if he had, he wouldn't be offering them up to a lawman.

'Let's just say that your brother, like so many o' them, more 'n likely got high friends in low places and low friends in high places.'

'Well, I guess there ain't nothin' left to do but keep on diggin',' Landis said.

'So long as it's not your own grave. 'Cept if you got a hankerin' for it. No good deed goes unpunished. That's what they say, right?'

'They do, yes.'

'Truth is a strange thing. Most often the more you walk towards it, the further away it seems. Sometimes it's better not to start that journey.'

'I got my brother's kid on my conscience. Even if I don't want to know what happened, I think she deserves it.'

'Family is a knot you'll never untie, Sheriff. I know that better than most.'

'I appreciate your time, Mr Moody.'

'I appreciate your whiskey, Sheriff.'

Landis got up. He extended his hand and Moody took it.

'You walk steady now,' Moody said. 'That's a narrow ridge under your feet, and a long drop on either side.'

13

On the morning of Sunday August 30, Landis received a call at home.

Marshall's words were strained, as if coming from a throat starved for air or choked up with some unfamiliar emotion.

'We got us a mess out here off of 11 up near the edge of Nottely Lake, Sheriff.'

'What kind of mess we talkin' about, Marshall?'

'Got ourselves a dead girl. Can't be more than fifteen or sixteen. Looks like she's been out here a while.'

'You called anyone?'

'Just you.'

'Okay. I'll get the coroner. Keep it together, Marshall. Don't let anyone get around there. I'll be with you as soon as I can.'

Landis called the County Coroner.

'Jeff, it's Victor. Marshall says we got ourselves a dead girl up on 11.'

'You there now?'

'Headin' out directly.'

'Okay, on my way. Guess I'll see where she's at when I get there.'

Landis put on his uniform and set off. Highway 11 went north-west out of Blairsville, on through Ivy Log, became US 19 when it crossed into North Carolina. Technically, the lake was a reservoir. Constructed back in the 1940s with the damming of the Nottely River, it was a good twenty miles long, with more than two-thirds of its shoreline still undeveloped. The reservoir came under the auspices of the Tennessee Valley Authority, whereas the shoreline was under the jurisdiction of the US Forest Service. There were homes out there, all manner of recreational spots, but it was as good a place as any to dump a corpse if you wanted it to remain undiscovered.

In Landis's seven years as sheriff, there had been two murders in Blairsville, two in Bunker Hill, one down in Suches. A dead girl in the lake might very well be accident or manslaughter, but he had a sour feeling about it before he even arrived. Marshall was a smart boy, had his wits about him. He didn't say she was drowned or fallen. He said they had themselves a mess.

Marshall had taken the fold-up barrier out of the trunk of his car and set it beside the road. Landis went on past it and pulled up behind Marshall's vehicle. The Nottely Dam was a good five miles on ahead.

An incline cut through the trees and went down to a bank of stones and sand at the water's edge. Landis could see Marshall down there. He was with another man, older, heavy-set, and the two of them seemed to be talking at each other simultaneously. Over to the left a department-issue blanket covered the body.

'This here's Enley Randolph,' Marshall said when Landis reached them. 'He come across the body a little while back.'

Randolph looked green to the gills.

'I was just down here walkin',' Randolph explained. 'I live just back there a ways, maybe half a mile or so. I come down here most Sundays afore church, just takin' the air, you know? Just mindin' my own business. And then I see that.'

He glanced toward the shrouded form on the ground.

'Poor darned thing all naked and swolled up like a balloon. Makes me sick to even think about it.'

Landis nodded understandingly.

'Deputy, you go on up the road with Mr Randolph here. Coroner's on his way. You look out for him, alright?'

Marshall put his hand on Randolph's shoulder. 'Let's go, sir,' he said. 'Get you away from this business.'

Landis waited until they had reached the top of the incline and then attended the body.

Despite all the indications of being in the water for some time – vascular marbling, skin and tissue discoloration, the grave wax and blistering – there were clear ligature marks on the throat, ankles and wrists. The coroner would confirm, but with present temperatures Landis estimated she'd been in the water for a week, maybe ten days. As Marshall had said, she was mid- to late-teens. It was hard to tell with the disfiguration. She was naked, and on her right thigh was the tattoo of a dragonfly, beneath it a series of Roman numerals. It may well have been something special before she bloated. In that moment it appeared crude and disproportioned.

The girl's eyes stared upward, vacant and lifeless. They were like black watery pearls – seeing nothing, reflecting everything.

Landis replaced the blanket once more. It was a grievous sight to see, but he covered her more out of some need to preserve whatever dignity she might still be afforded in her death.

Stepping back a good distance, he surveyed the ground around her for tracks, marks, tell-tale signs of human passage. There was nothing save the place where Marshall and Enley Randolph had been standing. Marshall had been conscientious enough to keep a good distance.

The sound of an approaching car alerted Landis to the coroner's arrival. Jeff Nelson had been coroner for five years or more. Before that the post had been held by his father.

Landis stayed where he was. He saw Nelson exchange a few words with Marshall, and then he came down the slope.

'What we got?' Nelson asked.

'Dead girl. Teenager. Ligature marks. Reckon she's been in the water maybe a week or ten days.'

'Well, let's take a look see, shall we?'

Landis left the coroner to do his work. Heading back up to the road, he was aware of the sudden flashes behind him as Nelson took pictures.

Randolph was still a bundle of nerves. From the numerous butts around his feet, he looked to have been chaining cigarettes one after the other.

'You go on and drive Mr Randolph home,' Landis said to Marshall. 'Take a full statement, make sure he's settled, and then come on back here.'

Marshall and Randolph headed off. Landis stopped to retrieve the butts from the ground.

Waiting until the coroner came back up the incline, Landis noted down his own crime-scene observations – the absence of any physical evidence beyond the body itself, the lack of disturbance in the surrounding area. The body had come down here from someplace else. This had not been the drop-point. Nelson would do an autopsy, determine time and cause of death, check for indications of sexual assault, type her blood, analyse it for drugs. All that would cross his desk in due course. His primary objective was identification, and that would begin with missing person reports and runaways.

Nelson called from below.

'Victor, drag that stretcher out the back of the wagon and get it on down here, would you?'

Landis did as he was asked, and then the two of them lifted her gently, taking care not to apply stress sufficient to get her bursting open. Her flesh was taut and slippery, but they managed it between them.

The hike back up to the road was treacherous. Nelson lost his footing for a moment, and it took all of Landis's coordination and strength to keep the stretcher steady.

'You good there?' he asked.

Nelson took his time, stabilising himself before they continued.

With the stretcher in the wagon, Landis thanked Nelson for getting out there so fast.

'I'll take her in now,' he said. 'Get a start on this.'

They shook hands and went their separate ways.

Back at the office, Landis called up every bit of information on the system regarding lost and missing teenage girls for the previous two weeks. There were six in all, three of them recovered within forty-eight hours, one reported safe and sound with her grandma in Choestoe, the last two still unverified as to whereabouts. Neither one was even close to the physical proportions or appearance of the Nottely girl.

It was highly unlikely that Nelson would get prints, not with the degree of putrefaction and tissue decay, and there was no guarantee that prints would be on file anyhow.

The other identifying feature was the tattoo. Had it remained undistorted, there might have been a hope of narrowing it down to one particular tattoo shop. As it was, that was also a long shot. The Roman numerals meant something – perhaps a date, a birthday, an event of significance.

Landis left the office and headed home. Until Nelson came back with more details, or until someone up and reported the girl missing, there was little more he could do.

Experience had taught him that worrying at something never made the something better or easier.

It was just what it was – he had someone's dead daughter on his hands, and he couldn't follow anything until there was something to follow.

14

The autopsy report came in mid-morning on Tuesday the 1st.

Nelson had not been able to get prints, but had sent over facial shots and a close-up of the tattoo.

Estimated time of death was somewhere between August 20 and 23. The girl had been dead before she went into the water. How long, he couldn't say, but the absence of water in her lungs was conclusive.

The ligature marks on her ankles and wrists were consistent with a half-inch diameter cord. They had been sufficiently tight to inhibit circulation. There were bruises and abrasions on numerous areas of the body, but nothing to suggest that blunt force trauma had been the cause of death. There was no indication of rape or sexual assault. From the visceral congestion and petechiae, Nelson had concluded that the girl had been asphyxiated. The final thing, and the thing that troubled Landis greatly, was the mention of drugs. According to the report, the blood showed clear evidence of sedatives.

Nelson had also deciphered the Roman numerals. It was a date: November 11, 1976.

Landis sat and stared at the bloated features of what had once been a pretty teenager. There were kin out there who did not know where she was nor what had happened to her.

It was the reverse of what had happened with his niece – a girl wondering why her father was dead.

Landis closed up the file. Aside from sending that image out to every sheriff's department in the state, he was at an impasse. The distortion and decay of the features was such that it would bear little resemblance to anything they might have on file. He called Barbara and gave the girl's height, weight, approximate age, hair and eye color, also the tattoo on her right thigh.

'Call up Fannin, Gilmer, Lumpkin, Towns, White and Habersham,' he said. 'Tell 'em what I just gave you. See if any of them have missings that fit that description.'

Barbara got to it while Landis went to an early lunch.

Upon his return, Mercer Gill from the *Blairsville Herald* was seated in the waiting area. He was an awkward-looking man, nose as steep as a mule's face, his knees and elbows like the corners of something.

'Mercer Gill,' Landis said. 'And what brings you down here this afternoon?'

Gill followed Landis into the office.

'Heard word you got a dead girl out near the lake,' he said.

'And where would you have heard this from?'

'Grapevine, you know?'

Landis sat down. 'I keep hearin' 'bout this grapevine, Mercer, and I sure as hell would like to get myself tapped into that.'

'True or not?'

'You set on workin' this spark into a flame, are you?'

'You got a dead girl, then it's the right of folks to know,' Gill replied.

'We're gonna play that game again, are we?'

'You gonna answer the question, Sheriff?'

'I ain't answerin' nothin',' Landis replied.

'Gonna write it nevertheless.'

'You gonna make somethin' up?'

'Gonna say it as it is. Dead girl, murdered, body found out

near Nottely Lake. Seems to me you give me something then the details'd be more accurate.'

'Now when did accurate details ever stop you from writing your pieces, Mercer?'

Gill paused. He leaned back in the chair. 'Look,' he said. 'We got jobs to do, right? We all gotta put food on the table. This here's what I do. I don't know how to do nothin' else, and to be honest I don't much want to. Got myself a bellyful o' traffic accidents and runaway cows and school pageants. We ain't had a murder here since the last one, and—'

'And I'm gonna cut you off right there, my friend,' Landis interjected, 'and I'm gonna ask you to put yourself in someone else's shoes for just a moment. Say you're right, and say I do got a dead girl, eh? Say I know nothin' about her 'cept she's dead. Well, if that's the case then her family don't know neither. You got kids, Mercer. Best as I recall you got three o' them. How would it be if one o' them got killed and the first you heard about it was a column in the *Herald*. How would that be?'

Gill didn't reply.

'That's what I was thinking,' Landis said. 'So how about you let me do my job for a while longer, and as soon as I got a handle on this, soon as I had a chance to track down her folks and break it to 'em, then you an' I can have a different discussion and you can write your story, okay?'

'You give me your word I'll get an exclusive?'

'Hell, Mercer, there ain't but one paper anyone reads in Blairsville anyhow.'

Gill paused in thought, and then said, 'Forty-eight hours.'

'Come again?'

'Forty-eight hours and then I write it anyway.'

'Now on what planet is it that a yellow sheet hack gives a county sheriff a deadline?'

'There is such a thing as journalistic responsibility.'

Landis laughed. 'You go on up there until the road runs out, Mercer. I'll let you know when there's something worth the printing ink.'

Disgruntled, Mercer Gill left the office and then the building. Landis thought to tell Barbara not to let the man inside again, but knowing Gill, he'd have shown up at Landis's home around suppertime and refused to go away.

An hour later Barbara called through from the desk.

'Looks like we got your girl,' she said. 'McCaysville. Reported more 'an two weeks back. Ella May Rayford, sixteen years old. Height, weight, tattoo all the same. Date of birth is November 11, 1976.'

Landis knew Fannin's sheriff, George Milstead. He was old school, tough as teak, came from half a dozen generations of lawmen. He was a baseball fanatic too, proud to remind all and sundry that Joe Tipton was a Fannin boy, six years in the major leagues, a .236 batting average and the survivor of a kamikaze attack in the Pacific.

Landis asked Barbara to get Milstead on the phone.

Milstead came through within a moment.

'Victor,' he said. 'You been a stranger a while now.'

'Good to hear you, George. Callin' you as I may have one o' yours here.'

'I heard word of this,' Milstead said. 'The Rayford girl, right?'

'Seems it's her, yes. She has a tattoo, date on it is November 11, 1976. I'm guessin' it's her date of birth.'

'Hang on there, Victor.'

Milstead was back on the line in a few seconds.

'That's the one,' he said. 'I know that family. Hell of a shame if it is, but then I guess it's a hell of a shame no matter whose daughter she was.'

'I'm thinkin' I should come over, maybe you and I visit with the family together.'

'You go on and do that,' Milstead said. 'That'd be fine. Combine forces an' all that.'

'I can set out now.'

'Wish it was better circumstances, but it'll be good to see you nevertheless.'

'Likewise, George,' Landis said, and hung up.

Landis walked on through to the outer office.

'Headin' on over to see George Milstead,' he said. 'You wanna run go get me a box of them licorice-lookin' cigars. Seem to recall he was mighty fond o' them.'

'Sure thing, Sheriff.'

Landis smiled. 'You ever gonna get 'round to callin' me plain old Victor?' he said.

'I ain't plannin' on it anytime soon, no,' Barbara said. 'You find a slot in your whirlwind social calendar to come over to one o' my world-famous barbecue parties, then maybe I might. Just for the occasion, you know, seein' as how we'd be out of the office.'

'You let me know when the next one is and I'll check my diary,' Landis said.

'I tell you now, all these years we known each other an' I still can't get the swing o' you.'

'Maybe that's 'cause I ain't got none, Barbara.'

15

Fannin County Sheriff's Office was located in the county seat of Blue Ridge. As a city, it was no bigger than a minute.

Blue Ridge was laid out back when the Marietta and North Georgia Railroad line was extended. Prior to that the seat had been in Morganton.

Highway 76 ran a straight west out there, all of twenty or twenty-five miles. On the drive over, Landis was conscious of the fact that this tragic business had shifted his attention away from Frank, from the thousand dollars a month, from the fact that he was now someone's uncle. Even when he'd been married, he'd never believed he'd be a father. He'd never considered the possibility that Frank would either. The Landis line would end with the pair of them – still distant, still estranged. Now there was a descendant, and even though the name might not survive, the bloodline would. Somehow the mere thought of this changed the temper of things.

McCaysville was about ten miles north of Blue Ridge and sat right on the Georgia–Tennessee state line. He guessed he and Milstead would share a few words, verify as best they could that the dead girl was this Ella May Rayford, and then they'd go visit with the family. It was the toughest of all, telling a parent that their child was dead. It went against the nature of things. Offspring should bury their forebears, not the other way around.

Milstead was grateful for the cigars.

'I'll keep 'em here,' he said. 'Wife says they smell like a hog burnin' in a tarpit.'

'How you been keepin'?' Landis asked.

'Got my troubles,' Milstead said. 'No use complainin' though. Hell, half of people don't care. Other half is happy you got somethin' to complain about.'

'How's your boy?'

'Got himself over in Atlanta doin' somethin' or other with vehicles. Fixin' 'em or stealin' 'em, I don't recall.'

Landis followed Milstead through to the office and took a seat.

'Tell me about the girl,' Landis said.

'Ain't much to tell. Her father, Vester Rayford, reported her missing back on the sixteenth of last month. She'd already been gone three days. Said as how she'd done it before, always came home sheepish and sorry. We did the usual, you know? Asked friends, people from the school. No one had seen hide nor hair o' her.'

'And the family?'

'Vester's gonna be trouble to his grave, but his wife ain't cut from the same tree. Anxious maybe, just about the general run o' things, but a good woman. Decent, hardworkin'.'

'How sure can we be that this is their daughter?'

'Sure as it's possible to be under the circumstances. Same height, weight, eye color, and the same tattoo.'

'I was reckonin' on comin' over there with you.'

'Well, she was found in your county, so she's your investigation,' Milstead said. 'Goes without sayin' that we'll help any way we can, but we all got to color inside the lines, if you know what I mean.'

'I wasn't set on deliverin' it to you, George.'

'I know that, Victor, but given half a chance I'd be all over it like lice.'

'Any help you can give will be appreciated. Right now I just want to make sure we got the right girl, and then I can start looking at where she was, who she was with, see her personal effects and suchlike.'

Milstead got up. 'Waitin' on it ain't gonna make it any easier,' he said. 'May as well go on up there and break the news.'

On the way there Landis and Milstead shared few words. Each, it seemed, was lost in some sort of reverie.

Outside of McCaysville, they took a slip road. Climbing gently towards the horizon, it became little but a dirt track. Nothing more than a thin brown ribbon between the banks of undergrowth, it appeared that with each dip and slide it seemed that ribbon might fade into nothing and leave them stranded.

To the right and out towards a dense treeline, a random scattering of weatherworn shacks came into view, seemingly held together by nothing more than baling wire and hope. There was no pattern, no sequence, as if they'd been dropped randomly from an airplane and stayed where they fell.

Milstead pulled over after a while.

'That way,' he said, indicating a path through the trees.

Landis exited the car and followed him. After fifty yards or so they came out ahead of a shallow incline. Below and to the right was a one-story house, a substantial yard, chicken coops, a couple of cats squabbling over something. They paused at the sound of the two men, eyed them for a moment, and then went back to their squabble.

Landis paused at the top of the incline. He took a deep breath and considered what was ahead of him. Children went missing and children died. Didn't matter which town, which county, it was the same everywhere. Which was better – vanished or dead?

73

If they were dead, then perhaps some sense of closure could be attained. Perhaps. But if they vanished, there was always the hope that they would return. That, in itself, was enough to have you waiting for the rest of your life. Moving on would feel like the worst kind of betrayal, as if forgetting would consign them to history.

Milstead, without a word, started down towards the house.

Landis, feeling the weight of the world on his shoulders, followed on behind.

Reaching the porch steps, Vester Rayford appeared from out back. He was a knot of silence and worry. His left nostril was gapped with an upside-down V, a gash too severe to heal and close. The scar from the upwards arc of a shrub knife had dissected his cheek, his eyelid and his forehead with a pale line that disappeared somewhere within his hair. He was a small and furtive man, his skin the color of dirt. Without a word, he stood looking at the two visitors as if he'd been anticipating them.

'Jeanette,' Rayford called out. 'Get yourself on out here.'

No one moved. The air was heavy, difficult to breathe.

The front door opened and Jeanette Rayford took a single step over the threshold.

She gave up a faint ghost of a smile for Milstead. She then looked at Landis, and in that moment Landis believed she was trying to convince herself it was something else, something unrelated, and despite the fact that the two men ahead of her were all solemn and silent, hats in hand, there was nothing in their eyes that spoke of hope.

Jeanette reached out towards the wall to steady herself.

Milstead came forward. Jeanette raised her eyebrows with a question, and the question was right there on her lips without her ever having to utter a word. It was then that Milstead slowly shook his head, and she knew for certain.

Then it was simply a question of how bad it could be. Had she been hurt, injured, beaten? God forbid, had she been raped?

'Let's go inside,' Milstead said.

Jeanette turned and went back into the house. Vester came after her.

Milstead showed them the pictures he'd brought.

For Jeanette, the grief came in stages, and the stages were like waves, and once the waves came, there was nothing at all that could be done to stop them. There was disbelief, shock, a sense of paralysis. Following on close behind there was guilt, more disbelief, a vague and disorienting attempt to locate the last thing she'd said, the last thing she'd done, the last word that had passed between herself and her daughter.

It would be a while before she got a grip on what this all meant, and only then would the pain arrive, a pain so deep it felt as if the world had closed its fist around her, all set to crush every ounce of breath from her body.

Vester Rayford looked like his mind had slipped its moorings. A vast abyss lay ahead of him, and into it he would go, nothing to slow the fall, nothing to give him any certainty that the drop would cease.

'How bad?' Jeanette asked. Her voice cracked with anticipation, and there was a hard edge of resignation in her eyes even before the sentence was finished.

Milstead looked down at the ground.

She then turned to Landis once more, believing that there might be some mistake, that Milstead was wrong, that he was there to tell her that it was something else, someone else even.

Jeanette seemed to fold in the middle as if a crease was already there, well marked from previous losses and disappointments. The heartbreak came, and it came with every kind of nightmare in tow, and she lowered her head and sank to her knees right there beside the stairwell.

They tried to help her – Milstead and Landis – but she resisted them.

Finally, she dragged herself off the floor and walked back towards the kitchen.

Vester stayed in the front hallway, his shoulders heaving, his breath coming short and fast.

Milstead and Landis followed Jeanette into the kitchen. The room was no more than eight by twelve. A single window – three panes of dirty glass, a roughly sawn plank of wood covering the hole where a fourth had once been – gave up a vague and greasy light. Beneath the window sat a beaten-up chair, cotton stuffing growing through the holes in the cover, to the right a plain deal table, on the left a heavy ceramic sink balanced on bricks, above that a two-shelf cupboard covered with netting to keep the flies out. The floor was mismatched pieces of oilcloth and linoleum that were laid straight on the dirt.

Jeanette sat down heavily.

She looked directly at Landis as if she was now seeing him for the first time.

'This is Sheriff Landis from Union,' Milstead explained. 'He was the one who found Ella May.'

Jeanette stared into the distance. Landis imagined she was looking at the last time she'd seen her daughter, perhaps trying to convince herself that she was sleeping, that this was a nightmare, that any second now she would stir and wake, that she would feel the presence of Ella May right there in the house, and her sense of relief would be greater than the grief she was experiencing.

But she did not wake, and there was no relief.

Landis took a step forward. He went down on his haunches to meet her gaze.

His heart slowed and he had to think to breathe. The world around him stepped back and faded, same as a hunter in a hollow who's fixed on a whitetail. In that moment most everything meant nothing. He figured that emotions such as these had always been there, but he'd never made them his own. Now they seemed to be a part of him, so much so that he believed he'd never be rid of them.

It was then that Jeanette Rayford felt the true force of that news. She fell towards Landis. He was there to stop her, and he put his arms around her as she closed up inside. The look in her eyes was fierce and hateful, as if the world had conspired at last to take from her the only thing that mattered.

He stayed like that for a good fifteen minutes. Eventually she cried, her body tight like a knot, fists clenched, breathing shallow.

Her child was dead. This much she knew. The full details were yet to come, and Landis didn't want rumors and assumptions stepping in where facts were needed. If Jeanette was to be told the truth of her daughter's death, then it was only right that such a truth came from him. He was the law, and the law performed a function that could not be delegated or assigned elsewhere.

'Jeanette,' he said. She neither flinched nor acknowledged his presence. Landis waited a few more moments before he said her name again.

'Jeanette, I got to ask something of you now.'

Landis could feel the cool knot of anticipation in the base of his gut. His hands were sweating, his face also, and he could not move to retrieve his handkerchief from the pocket of his pants.

'Jeanette, can you hear me?'

A twitch of response in her shoulder that might well have been involuntary.

'I have something I'm gonna need you to do now,' he said. 'I gotta take you and your husband over to the Coroner's Office in Blairsville...'

Jeanette turned slightly. For a moment her breathing hitched and stopped.

'You tell me what happened,' she said. Her voice cracked with emotion, but beneath it was a firmness that could not be denied. 'You tell me what happened to her. What happened to my girl?'

Landis started to shake his head. 'I can't—'

'You're the one who found her,' Jeanette interjected. 'So don't tell me *can't*. You the sheriff there and you can do whatever the hell you like. You tell me what happened to her.'

'Someone killed her, Jeanette. That's all we know right now.'

Jeanette was suddenly elsewhere, as if she had summoned sufficient imagination to picture her daughter.

'Sheriff,' Jeanette started, and then there was something else in her eyes, something that tore her up, because the expression on her face changed in a heartbeat from grief to fear.

'D-Did th-they... did th-they...' she started, her voice catching awkwardly at the back of her throat. 'Did th-they... you know wh-what I'm asking, She'ff...'

'No, Jeanette, they didn't do that to her.'

A momentary flash of relief, the fact that her daughter had not been assaulted and violated, and then Jeanette was shaking, pushing herself away from him.

Landis tightened his grip on her shoulder. 'Like I said already, Jeanette, I'm gonna need you and Vester to come over to the Coroner's Office with me. You're gonna have to be brave, as brave as you ever could be, and you're gonna have to take a look at Ella May and tell me that it's her.'

Jeanette's eyes were rimmed red, her face contorted with anger. 'You know who she is!' she snapped. And then she moved suddenly, twisted her body and turned to look up at Milstead. 'You can't be tellin' me that there's a mistake now. You done showed me that picture. That's my girl. That's my baby.' Her eyes widened, almost as if some small spark of hope had resided there all along, and Landis had just fanned it with his words.

Milstead shook his head solemnly. 'No, Jeanette. You know there ain't gonna be no mistake on this, but the law says that next of kin has to come down and identify the body. You know that, right?'

Jeanette's eyes flared. 'The law?' she asked. 'You're down here telling me about the law? Where was the law when she was being murdered? Tell me that much now! *Where* was the law when my little baby was being murdered?'

'Until the truth is discovered there is no truth,' Milstead said. 'We have no indication of who might have done this or why. It could have been someone here, could have been someone from out of town. The investigation has barely begun—'

'So what are you doing here with me? What the hell are you doing down here with me when you should be out looking for whoever done this thing?'

'Jeanette, I'm serious now. Me an' Sheriff Landis have a lot of work to do on this thing. First and foremost, I need to get some kind of co-operation here…'

Jeanette looked at Landis. She raised her clenched fists and started beating on him, thumping on his arms, his shoulders, his chest. The woman was strong, but he did not restrain her. It was nothing more than utter desperation and loss releasing itself the only way it could.

Eventually, Landis gripped Jeanette's wrists and pulled her close. She collapsed against him. He held her tight, as if to let her go was to see her vanish. He felt her tears making their way through the thin cotton of his shirt. He could smell the tang of something wild and bitter in her hair, the odor of the room around them. And what he felt was hopelessness. Hopelessness and futility, because he had seen this before. Ella May Rayford's life had been snatched away from her as if it meant nothing at all.

Landis glanced back over at Milstead. Milstead lowered his eyes and shook his head. In that moment, Landis wondered who the hell had made this world. With the death of his brother and now the killing of this girl, it sure didn't seem like God.

Seemed someone somewhere was hell-bent on putting ruin in his road.

16

Milstead stayed with Vester and Jeanette while Landis looked over Ella May's room and went through her personal possessions. He found nothing of any significance. What he had hoped to find, he did not know. A diary, perhaps? Something that would indicate the identity of someone involved? Such things happened in books and movies. They rarely happened in real life.

Once he was done, he left for Blairsville and the Coroner's Office. Milstead followed him, Vester and Jeanette in his car, for which Landis was grateful.

By the time Vester and Jeanette got to see their daughter's body, their rage and grief had settled into a shroud of numb despair.

After the official identification was complete, Milstead drove them back to McCaysville and the rest of their broken lives.

Landis thanked Jeff Nelson and headed for the office. He had reached the day's saturation point. He'd had to do such things as this before, but too few times to be familiar or unmoved. Jeanette Rayford's crying and cursing had rattled him to the core. He knew it was a futile wish, but he hoped that it was the last time he'd ever have to deliver such news to a family.

Barbara was gone for the day. Landis checked for any outstanding messages. There were none.

En route home he picked up a few groceries and a bottle

of rye. He was once a frequent drinker, but now reserved it for special occasions and times of stress. Enough liquor and he became insensate to the point where someone getting stuck with a knife didn't have any more meaning than his coffee got cold.

He fried up some hamburger and onions, heaped a good dose of hot sauce over it, sat out on the porch with his plate and his glass and wondered if human beings could ever be fathomed. The things he saw on the TV paled in comparison to the things real folks did to one another. Seemed to be no end to Man's imagination when it came to hurting.

After he was done eating, he went back into the house and fetched his guitar. He fumbled with it awhile, then set it aside in frustration. In that way, he was like his own father. He'd set his mind to something, invest more in the obstacles than the accomplishments, work on convincing himself it was never meant to be. Walter Landis used to tell both him and Frank the same thing: 'You got so much quit in you it ain't never gonna run out.' Other things too: 'What's wrong with you, boy? You blind in one eye and can't see with the other,' and 'I hear the words, but what you sayin' ain't worth more 'an two dead flies and a broke buckle.'

Maybe Walter was just repeating what had been said to him, because it sure sounded like he was speaking for himself.

Landis got up to fetch another drink when the phone rang. He wondered if today was bringing bad news in threes. He had to answer it. If it was important and he ignored it, then whoever was calling would come over and fetch him.

Before he had a chance to speak, Eleanor Boyd said, 'Victor, that you?'

'Ms Boyd,' he said.

'Yes, Victor, this is Eleanor.'

'What can I do for you, Eleanor?'

'Seems my daughter's taken a shine to you and your funny talkin'. She's asked me to tender another invite.'

'Well, Ms Boyd, you tell her that's awful kind of her, but I've had a hell of a day and I've got just about enough energy left to make it to my bed.'

Eleanor laughed. 'No, Lord's sake, I don't mean now. I mean for her birthday.'

'Her birthday?'

'Four days' time she's gonna be eleven years old. She's havin' a day with friends and whatnot, cake and ice cream an' all that. She knows you're busy with your sheriffin', but she said it would be nice for you to come over whenever's convenient.'

'Right. Well, sure. I guess I'll have to see if I can do that.'

'It's Saturday, Victor. The weekend, you know?'

'I know well enough that Saturday is on a weekend, Ms Boyd, but sheriffin' don't stop for birthdays or Christmas or none o' that stuff.'

'You know, you are sure as awkward as your brother. That man could be as slippery as deer guts on a doorknob.'

'I'm not meanin' anything by it,' Landis said. 'It's just that . . . well, you know, I really don't have a great deal to say to her. I know we're kin in a roundabout kind of fashion, but I'm a stranger to her.'

'She just lost her daddy. Do I need to remind you o' that? Lost her daddy, found an uncle she never knew about, and it seems to me that it would be nothin' more than good manners to make a darn effort. Hell, we ain't even but down the road.'

'I'll do my best,' Landis said.

'I'll say this and leave you to your business, Victor. Whatever history you got with Frank, if you don't get over it you'll die with it. Jenna didn't cause none o' that, and she don't deserve to be stuck with whatever you're holdin' onto about your brother.'

'I guess I'll be seein' you on Saturday, Ms Boyd.'

'I guess you will, Sheriff Landis.'

The line went dead. Landis hung up. He went for the bottle and poured himself a double.

Back out on the porch he smoked a cigarette. Seemed Frank had a reach beyond the grave, working his way back into his thoughts through his daughter. Some folks cast a longer shadow dead than alive.

Two drinks later and Landis turned in for the night.

He fell asleep with a question on his mind. Aside from the truth of her father's death, what the hell would an eleven-year-old girl want for her birthday?

17

An hour or so before he and Barbara were due to close up the office on Thursday, Landis received a call from George Milstead. It was the first time he would hear the name Eugene Russell. By no means would it be the last.

'Jeanette Rayford's cousin by all accounts. Her mother's side as far as I can figure. Anyways, it was news to me that they were blood. He's a whole bucket of joy all by himself, but his family's roots wind through Fannin, Gilmer, Murray, up into Tennessee and North Carolina, too. Had a run-in recent with his younger brother. Name's Stanley, everyone calls him Wasper.'

'Bad people?'

'Let's just say their milk of human kindness has spoiled something rotten.'

'And Jeanette went to him about Ella May.'

'Whether she went to him or not ain't the point. Nothin's secret around here. She'll have told him, maybe Vester did, or he found out for himself. Either which way, she was down here an hour back and bending my ear something terrible.'

'Sayin' what?'

'That if I didn't step up and take the reins of this thing, then Eugene might take the reins himself.'

'You told Jeanette I was runnin' this?'

'She knows that already, Victor. Like I said, 'round here there ain't no secret between two people 'cept when one of them's dead.'

'I'm guessin' he'll want to talk with me.'

'That'd be my guess too. Word of advice, go on and see him. He'll appreciate that.'

'And I'm to be spendin' my time caterin' to the needs and wants of—'

'Let me interrupt you right there, Victor,' Milstead said. 'Usually I'd say don't go meetin' trouble halfway. Stay where y'are and it might never reach you. This here is different. This whole thing is enough of a mess, what with the Rayford girl bein' from one county and dead in another, but there's communities out here, tighter than a preacher's wallet, and they can be a mighty help sometimes. There ain't nothin' goin' on around these folks that they don't see.'

'Where's he at?'

'Outside of Colwell, right where the road off of 68 runs alongside the Jacks River.'

'And you think he's gonna be of any help?' Landis asked.

'Hell, Eugene Russell would rather stand up and lie than sit down and tell the truth, but you never know with these things. All I'm sayin' is that it might be worth your while to have folks know you're onto this and you ain't lettin' go. That little girl was one of their own and they'll be takin' it personal.'

'I'll head over there tomorrow,' Landis said. 'Earlier is better. I got myself tied up with Frank's ex-wife and his daughter and I gotta be over in Trenton on Saturday.'

'How so?'

'It's the kid's birthday. According to her mother she's taken a shine to me. Asked me special to come over and bring my best wishes.'

'You never did get yourself a family did you, Victor?'

'Had a wife for a few years. I guess she saw where things were headed and bailed out.'

'I got three grown up, one of them with babies of her own.'

'Must be fine, George.'

'Expensive, more like,' he quipped. 'But I gotta say that it gives me a sense of my place in things to know that there's gonna be kin after I'm gone.'

'I guess it must,' Landis replied, believing that such a notion would forever be unknown.

'Well, I gotta head home,' Milstead said. 'You go see Russell and if you wanna come by and tell me the news, I'll be here.'

'You'll be the first.'

'And tread gentle, Victor. You go sup with the Devil, you take a long spoon.'

With that, Milstead hung up the phone.

'I'm headin' out to Colwell tomorrow,' Landis told Barbara. 'Guess I'll go straight from home. Marshall ain't takin' himself a day off or nothin' is he?'

Barbara smiled. 'Marshall'd no more take a day off than smack his granny. He's chasin' your job. The sooner he gets it the happier he'll be.'

'Well, you tell him where I'm at when you see him.'

'Will do, Sheriff.'

'You got much to do before you head out?'

'Traffic tickets. Half a dozen or so. Won't be much longer.'

Landis put on his jacket and hat. 'Okay, well I'll see you sometime tomorrow.'

He went to the door and then paused. Turning back, he said, 'Gotta go to my brother's girl's birthday party on Saturday. You got any idea what kind of gift would suit an eleven-year-old?'

'That age? Where I come from, it'd be a good skinnin' knife or her own pistol.'

'That's a hell of an idea, Barbara. Maybe I could requisition a semi-automatic from the armory.'

'Girl'd be thrilled, I'm sure.'

''Night, Barbara.'

''Night, Sheriff.'

18

Landis guessed Eugene Russell was a good five or ten years ahead of him, but he looked older than that.

In the same way as Jim Tom Moody, the outdoor life had weathered and toughened his skin. His eyes were as clear as a freshwater brook, but back of them were shadows that spoke of darker things.

Landis had brought up a haunch of deer meat strung up in wax paper. Russell's wife, Ledda – who couldn't have been more than thirty years old – took it from him graciously. She showed him back to where her husband held court.

The room in which they were seated was wide and long. There was more furniture in it than a thrift store. Hand-woven rugs were stapled to the walls. On the floor were skins of various animals.

Before Ledda left, Russell told her, 'You keep them kids out o' here a while. They don't want me comin' out and puttin' a quietus on 'em now.'

'They know well enough, Eugene,' Ledda replied.

'Well, tell 'em they got a poke o' candy comin' if they mind themselves.'

Ledda left the room with the deer meat and the message.

Turning back to Landis, he said, 'You know I didn't send you no invite.'

'I know you didn't. Jeanette Rayford was up at Milstead's. Said as how you'd be gettin' involved if Milstead didn't pull his freight on this.'

'Milstead was the one told you to come over here?'

'He advised it.'

'He's a good enough feller,' Russell said. 'For a lawman.'

'I known him a long time,' Landis said.

'And your brother got hisself kilt back a while. Run down, I hear.'

'That's right,' Landis said.

'Hell, nothin' never stops, does it?'

'Meanin'?'

'Meanin' if a feller hangs around with skunks, he's sure gonna smell like one.'

It was the second time someone had made an indirect reference to Frank being involved in something awry. Landis didn't chase it. If Russell planned on explaining further then he would do so without being prompted.

'Jeanette Rayford is your cousin, I understand.'

'Somewheres, yes. My mother's side. How much of a cousin is lost in the weave of things, but we's kin enough.'

'Did you know Ella May?'

'Not to pick out of a line-up, no. Maybe seen her at a gatherin', but that woulda been some years back. Past while I been keepin' my business close to home.'

'I'm sorry nevertheless,' Landis said. 'Ain't nothin' much like the death of a young 'un.'

'So you diggin' up the truth or diggin' a hole for yourself?'

'Right now I ain't dug up nothin',' Landis said. 'Seems the police in Trenton—'

Russell's smile cut him short.

'Trenton ain't a place I'd go lookin' for anythin' but bullshit,' he said. 'That's a dog that ain't gonna hunt right there.'

'You think…'

Russell leaned forward. 'Look,' he said. 'I don't owe you nothin', and you don't owe me nothin' in return. All I know is from George Milstead, and he says you ain't got stink on you. That's the only reason you're here talkin' with me. If I thought for a second that you were tied up in all that bad business then you wouldn't have made it as far as the porch.'

Landis raised his eyebrows in question.

Russell frowned. 'Are you actually this naïve or you pretendin'?'

'I guess I'm actually this naïve,' Landis replied.

Russell leaned back and exhaled slowly. 'Set some honey down in Trenton, you'd catch more flies than you could swat in a month. They's about one thing and one thing only out there. They got a Police Department, a Sheriff's Office, they got a City Council, a mayor, they even got themselves a courthouse and a judge, and no matter how many times you shook it up there'd always be another snake crawlin' out of that barrel.'

'Do you know somethin' specific about my brother?'

'Nope. Nothin' specific. He was the sheriff, however. He got his finger on the pulse of that thing, for sure. If he didn't know, then he was dumb as a box o' rocks.'

'You're talkin' of corruption in the administration itself.'

'Fancy way of saying they's all got their hands in each other's pockets, but yes, that's what I'm sayin'.'

'And why are you tellin' me this?'

'I mean, maybe your brother didn't do nothin' but warm himself around a fire he didn't build, but he still got warm, didn't he? Figured that I should tell you somethin' that might help you get to the root of what happened to him because you're gonna find out who killed my cousin's little girl, ain'tcha?'

'I'm sure as hell gonna do everythin' I can to find out who killed her, yes.'

There was silence between the two men for a while.

'You and your brother weren't close,' Russell finally said.

'What makes you say that?'

'You don't seem so eager to be askin' questions.'

'I ain't askin' you for anythin' you don't want to give up,' Landis said, 'but you're right about me and my brother.'

'How long since you seen him?'

'Saw him dead two weeks back. Before that it was nigh on twelve years ago.'

'I got myself a brother, name of Wasper. That's what they call him. Yo'uns might o' seen him thereabouts. Got himself one o' them Howlin' Davis motorsickles. Braggity little runt. He can talk fifteen to the dozen and still say nothin'. Half the time I wanna smack his brains out, other half I wonder if he's got any brains at all. But he's still my brother. Neither God nor anyone beneath him can change that fact. Guessin' it musta been some wrench to tear that much of a hole between you and your'n.'

'Maybe not such a wrench, and maybe the hole didn't start so big. Time unravels things fast, and all of a sudden you're looking across a valley at something you can't even see.'

'Well, your family is your business. I got my own to take care of, and that girl happened to be part of it.'

'Like I said, I'll find out what happened soon enough.'

'As for your kin, his killin' weren't no accident, no matter what anyone says. You scratch a lie, you'll find a thief.'

En route home, Landis thought about his conversation with George Milstead. He decided to keep things to himself for the meantime. What could he say? That Eugene Russell had implied that the whole of Dade County was riddled with corruption? The last thing he wanted was rumors all spread out like a week's washing.

He drove in silence for a while, and then it commenced to raining. The sound was strangely soothing to his troubled mind.

19

Landis couldn't recall the last time he'd celebrated his own birthday, let alone been invited to someone else's.

He stood on the porch of Eleanor Boyd's house with a stuffed toy monkey in a paper bag. He felt as out-of-place as a preacher in a whorehouse.

Through the door he could hear the squeals and laughter of a horde of children. He thought to leave the monkey on the porch, maybe drop a twenty-dollar bill in there for good measure, but the door opened and Eleanor looked at him with an expression of approval.

'Ms Boyd,' he said, and took off his hat.

'Victor,' she replied, and stepped aside to allow him entry.

'What you got there?' she said.

Landis opened the bag and showed her.

'You don't know much about eleven-year-old girls, do you?'

'Can't say I know much about girls of any age,' Landis replied.

A moment later Jenna came barrelling out of the kitchen. The enthusiasm of her greeting surprised him. She threw her arms around his waist.

Landis waited for her to let him go and then he handed her the bag.

'I don't know anythin' 'bout birthday gifts, Jenna,' he said.

Jenna took out the monkey. Her eyes lit up. It was a genuine reaction.

'I love him!' she said. 'I'm gonna call him Victor.'

Landis got another hug, and then she charged off again towards the clamour in the kitchen.

'Maybe I was wrong,' Eleanor said. 'Guess a monkey is exactly what she needed.'

'She seems okay. You know, considering what has happened.'

'She is. She has her moments, but she's young enough to bounce back. Kids are made of tougher stuff than we are. Takes a great deal to pull the seams apart.'

'I ain't had a chance to chase up that money thing yet. I haven't forgotten, but—'

'I got a call from one of the detectives. He said it was all taken care of. I already got some money sent over yesterday.'

Landis was puzzled. 'A detective. A police detective? Not someone from the Sheriff's Department?'

'He said he was a detective. I'm guessin' he was police.'

'He give a name?'

Eleanor paused in thought for a moment. 'Fredericks, maybe?'

'Fredericksen? Mike Fredericksen?'

'Sounds right, sure. Somethin' like that.'

'Okay, well at least it's been fixed,' Landis said.

'Well, now you're here you get to choose between playin' with a bunch of shriekin' girls or having a drink with me.'

'That's a tough call,' Landis said, 'but I think I'll go for the drink.'

There was no subtle or indirect way to ask Eleanor Boyd what needed to be asked, so he asked it straight.

They were seated in the living room, the door closed to subdue the noise, each of them acting like the strangers they were.

'You were married four years, right?' Landis asked.

'Just over,' Eleanor replied. 'February of '81 until July of '85.'

'You were pregnant when you got married.'

'I was, but that wasn't the reason for doin' it.' She smiled in recollection. 'Your brother was a character. I don't know you none, but you seem so very different.'

'How so?'

'He was a whirlwind. More fire in him than three other men. Can't lie. He swept me off my feet. Sometimes he was wound tighter'n strings on a two-dollar fiddle, other times he was the gentlest person ever. Oftentimes I didn't know whether to kiss him or tie him up, but wherever we was, he made me feel like I was home.'

'Did he talk about his job?'

'Hell no, that was like gettin' blood out of a turnip. Having said that, when he was liquored up he would get on a bus about this and that, sayin' as how they didn't treat him right, that he had to do things he didn't want to do, you know?'

'Do you think he was an honest man?'

Eleanor looked at Landis like he'd slapped her.

'I don't mean nothin' by that,' Landis said. 'I got to hearin' things, and it's raised some questions that I don't have any answers for.'

'What did you hear, and who from?'

'Couple o' times now, but more about the office, the police department. Nothin' specific, and nothin' about Frank direct, but the things said were given up without being asked for.'

'Is this about the money he was givin' me?' Eleanor asked.

'No one has mentioned that. All I know is that it didn't seem to come from his wages, and I can't fathom how he got himself a thousand dollars a month from someplace else. Even so, if it was dirty money, then why would he be putting it through a bank?'

'That's easy enough to answer. He had no choice.'

'How so?'

'It was a condition of the court when we did the custody agreement. There had to be a record of him makin' the payments.'

'I guessed that might be the case,' Landis said, 'but then why didn't he give you a cut of his wages money, have it all on record, and keep the money he was giving you for himself?'

Eleanor leaned back in the chair. She sighed resignedly. 'Look, I don't know where you're drivin' right now, but I ain't a willin' passenger. Frank was good to his word with that money, and he was devoted to Jenna. When she was around, he was about as tough as that stuffed monkey you brought over. Maybe he wasn't such a good husband, but a girl couldn't have wished for a better father. If you're diggin' up some dirt on him, then all I can ask is that you keep it away from her. Now he's gone she don't see nothin' but sunshine when she thinks of him. That's not somethin' I'll have you take away from her.'

'I have no intention of takin' anythin' away from her.'

'I'm glad to hear it.'

'I'm sorry to have brought it up, and I didn't mean no offense by it, but I had to ask.'

'You done your askin'. You got my answer. I never heard him say anythin' about any trouble he was involved in, and he didn't do nothin' to make me suspect he was.'

'Okay,' Landis said. 'Understood.'

'So I got a question for you in return. All these years, not a word between you, and this is now your life's purpose?'

'Not at all,' Landis said, 'but there's no gettin' around the fact that he was murdered. There's also no gettin' around the fact that it's a bone in my craw.'

'Well, while you're busy coughin' it loose, you be sure not to choke, eh?'

Landis nodded. He didn't have anything else to say.

'You havin' another drink?'

'Don't see a reason not to,' Landis replied, and held out his glass.

20

To Landis, it seemed he'd spent his life forgetting things better remembered and remembering things best forgot.

Some memories came up fierce and sudden. They'd hang in the air, swollen and heavy. He'd spend a day, sometimes more, fighting through them, trying to make the world seem ordinary. But it wasn't, and never would be.

Monday morning he was out on the porch. It was early, and there was rain in the breeze. He smoked his cigarette and drank his coffee. It was his routine, and had been for as long as he could recall. During those minutes he would try to find some semblance of reason for who he was and what he was doing. He guessed he was trying to rationalize his own existence. He guessed everyone did the same at some point during their lives.

Recent events had highlighted how much of an island he was. No parents, no wife, no kids, and now no brother.

Eleanor Boyd wasn't blood, but her daughter was. This fact had colored things different in his mind. That there was someone made him think of all the years there'd been no one. You don't see what ain't there until someone shows you what could've been.

He didn't long for some different life. It wasn't that at all.

It was more a case of recognizing how much he'd been the architect of his own reality. He'd built walls, endlessly it seemed, only to finally understand that he'd built nothing more nor less than a prison. He was the sole inmate. Loneliness was a face he wore for the world – pretending independence or resolute self-sufficiency – all the while convincing himself that this was what the world had done to him. That was all so much horseshit. He'd fashioned it all on his own, had even taken pleasure in his handiwork.

Landis considered the few words that Eleanor had shared about his brother. That they seemed to be polar opposites did not surprise him. They had always been different. But, from what he recalled, they had also been a good deal alike. Their mother used to comment on it. 'What one starts the other'll finish,' she'd say. Or, 'See one comin', the second'll be his shadow.'

But things were different after she killed herself. The world tipped on its axis and nothing came right again.

Without their mother, the brothers were untethered boats. They drifted with whatever currents found them, at first the same, and then in different directions. After a while, each found no sign of the other, not even on the far horizon. A while after that, both of them stopped looking.

Landis set the thoughts aside. He needed to get into the office. He had a dead girl, a sense that Eugene Russell wouldn't be anything but trouble until her killer was found, and the over-arching question regarding the motive for his brother's murder. It had been a long time since his mind had been so occupied. It served to unsettle him in a way he couldn't control, and he could see no good end to either story.

'That there Moody feller's been on the phone,' were Barbara's opening words when Landis came through the door. 'Told him he could talk to Marshall but he weren't havin' none of it. Said the things he had to say were for you and you alone.'

'He leave a number?' Landis asked.

'Nope. Said you knew where he was and it was important enough for you to go on out there.'

'Seems these people think I'm some sort of public servant.'

Barbara frowned. 'Well, if you ain't that, what are you?'

Landis went through to his office. He sat heavily, a feeling of weight all around him that he couldn't shake off. Another drive out to Murphy, more than likely another circuitous conversation, once again the feeling that he'd tied his horse to a fence that wasn't there.

Nevertheless, he had to go. There was no getting around it. Maybe this time it would be something of substance, something that would point him down a road that had a destination.

Landis went on through to speak to Barbara.

'Hey, Barb, you know who's sheriff over in Cherokee County?'

'That'd be Bill Garner,' she said, 'but he's an old 'un. Maybe he retired. Let me check.'

Barbara did so, came back to Landis in a moment.

'Yep, he's still up there in Murphy. You callin' on him?'

'Not plannin' to. Gonna go out and see Jim Tom Moody. Just wanted to know whose toes I might be treadin' on.'

'Bill Garner's so ancient he probably wouldn't notice.'

'Hell, Barb, when d'you get so creased around the edges?'

Barbara laughed drily. 'I always been this way. You just been so busy broilin' your own bacon you never noticed.'

'Meanin' what?'

'As it sounds,' Barbara said.

'You think I'm self-absorbed?'

Barbara's expression was one of bemusement. 'That's a five-dollar word out of a two-dollar vocabulary, I'll say. You ain't been readin' books now, have you?'

Landis smiled at her. 'You're a bitter old nag, Barbara Wedlock.'

'And a public servant. Just like you.'

21

Leaving the office, Landis spotted Mercer Gill across the street from the back lot.

'Sheriff Landis,' Gill called out, quickening his pace to ensure he reached Landis before Landis could get into the car.

'You ain't in the business of harassing me, now are you, Mercer?'

'Coincidence, Sheriff,' Gill replied.

'There ain't no place you could be goin' to that'd take you through the back lot of the sheriff's office, and you know that just as well as me.'

'It's been a week, Sheriff.'

'It's been six days, Mercer. You come see me last Tuesday.'

'Six days, a week. It's all the same. I got a story to write. I've waited long enough.'

'The wait don't get no shorter just 'cause you run out of patience.'

'You got a lead on who killed the girl?'

'You an' I known each other a good while now. You tell me the last time you remember me sayin' one thing an' doin' something else.'

Gill didn't respond.

'I didn't figure so. What I said on Tuesday ain't changed none. When I got somethin' worth writin' about, you'll be the first to know.'

'But, Sheriff—'

'But sheriff nothin', Gill. I got business to attend to, and you need to step out of the way.'

Gill didn't move.

Landis took a deep breath. He pinned Gill with a cold stare. 'Gill, you need to step out of the way right about now or I'm gonna cuff you and put you in the drunk tank 'til I get back.'

Gill did as he was asked. Landis pulled the car out of the back lot and headed for the highway.

Jim Tom Moody was down in the woods behind the house. Dovie – who turned out to be one of three daughters – told Landis where he could be found.

'You eatin' with us?' she asked.

'If there's an invite,' Landis replied.

'Well, he sure seemed keen enough to talk to you so I guess you's best buddies now.'

'I wouldn't go that far, Dovie.'

'He's after pumpkin blooms and whatnot. You could give him a hand.'

'What you cookin' up?'

Dovie smiled. 'Oh, whatever's there. Some bit of a pig, no doubt. 'Round here we eat everythin' but the squeal.'

Jim Tom Moody had a barrow full of greens and blooms.

'Dovie invited me to eat with you,' Landis said.

'Did she now?' Moody replied.

'If that's—'

'You ain't gonna be here long enough to eat, Sheriff.'

Landis took a cigarette and lit it.

'Heard you went over to see Eugene Russell.'

'I did, yes.'

Moody paused in his picking and sat back against the bole of a tree.

'Differences aside, that's a sorry matter if ever there was one,' he said.

'You and Russell don't see eye to eye?' Landis asked.

'Feller's one helluva piece o' crazy, if you ask me. I'd say if you know how to count, don't count on him. Regardless, his cousin's girl got killed and that ain't right.'

'Do you know something about what happened?' Landis asked.

'No, but I heard of a thing like that happenin' afore.'

'What exactly, Mr Moody?'

'Girl like that. No older than that Ella May. This one was hogtied and raped and what have you. Body dumped in the woods.'

'When was this? And where?'

'Back about six months, I reckon. Found her body in the Nantahala. Up in them woods off of 74, maybe halfway between here and Andrews.'

'And why are you tellin' me this?' Landis asked.

'Because I am,' Moody replied.

'You want somethin' in return?'

Moody shook his head. 'Not right now, I don't.'

'I'll look into it,' Landis said.

'You gettin' anyplace on what happened to your brother?'

'No. But Russell said the same as you. That maybe there was something going on in Trenton.'

'So maybe Russell is a mite smarter than I give him credit for.'

'He cross you?'

'Man's a halfback,' Moody said. 'Folks who leave and then return ain't never gonna be straight the same way. I knowed his papa. If there wasn't bad weather, he'd bring it with him. Other family seem like good people. But that Eugene has a twist in him I don't like.'

'Do you know Vester Rayford and his wife?'

'Nope. Never heard o' them afore.'

'And the girl six months back. She got a name?'

'Linda,' Moody said. 'Linda Bishop.'

Back up near the house, Dovie asked if he was leaving.

'I am,' Landis replied.

'He tell you that you wasn't welcome for dinner?'

'Not directly.'

'Sometimes I wish he was kinder,' Dovie said. 'But if wishes were horses, beggars'd ride.'

'I'm not takin' it personal, Dovie,' Landis replied. 'I'm law, and I'm used to eatin' by myself.'

'You got no wife?'

'Did have. She died more 'an ten years back.'

'And you ain't found yourself a new one?'

'Can't say I been lookin'.'

Dovie smiled. 'You're a handsome feller. You should get yourself out there to a dance or two. Sure there'd be someone keen.'

'I'll get to it,' Landis said. 'Fixin' a few things first, you know?'

'Like what went on with your brother, right?'

'Your pa told you.'

'Just that he got himself kilt.'

'Yeah, well that's a question that ain't bein' answered so I gotta keep askin'.'

'Life's a road, Sheriff,' Dovie said. 'Awful long one sometimes. Good company shortens it.'

'I'll keep it in mind,' Landis said.

'Wait up there a moment,' Dovie said.

Before Landis could reply, she'd turned and gone back into the house.

Within a minute she was back, in her hand a parcel of tin foil. She came on down the porch steps and handed it over.

'What's this, then?' he asked.

'You ever eat a boomer?'

'Can't say I have.'

'Cross between a chipmunk and grey squirrel. Fry it up with some taters. It's good.'

'That's real kind of you, Dovie.'

'Ain't nothin' at all.'

Landis started towards his car and then paused. He turned back to look at her.

'Are you this kind to everyone?' he asked.

'No,' Dovie said. 'Just the lost and lonely ones.'

22

Cherokee County Sheriff Bill Garner had taken a day off, would be found at his home. Landis took the address from the girl at the desk and drove over there.

Garner opened the door, looked Landis up and down slowly and said, 'You here arrestin' me or you after someone else?'

'Someone else,' Landis said.

Garner assumed an expression of dark inevitability. He'd spent too long digging up other people's dirt, finding too much or too little of what was anticipated. Either which way it wore a man down.

'I'm havin' myself a day off,' Garner said. 'First one since Christmas. Was set to get a right smart done around this place.'

'Well nothin' never stops.'

'Where you from?'

'Union County down in Georgia.'

'I know it,' Garner said. 'My youngest married a feller from Ivy Log. Never much took a shine to him, but what can't be cured must be endured. What's your name?'

'Landis, Victor Landis.'

'Well, you better come on in and share your woes.'

Out of uniform, Garner wore ill-fitting clothes, the color unsuited to his complexion. His house was much like Landis's own – functional and unadorned. Either he was a widow or his wife had left him for greener pastures.

They headed for the kitchen. There was coffee on the stove and Landis took some.

Seated, Garner asked the reason for the visit.

'Girl by the name of Linda Bishop,' Landis said. 'Got word she was found off of 74.'

'She was,' Garner replied. 'Remember it well. Back in February.'

'Seems I have a similar one, and was after details o' yours.'

'Seventeen years old. Choked with a rope. Looked like she'd been tied up a while before she died. Whoever did it didn't bother to dig a hole or nothin'. Left her out in the woods naked as the day she was born. We figured she was driven there. Carried past the treeline no more than twenty yards or so and dumped like so much garbage.'

'Got me something the same,' Landis said. 'Tied like that, washed up at Nottely Lake. She was from McCaysville over in Fannin County.'

'George Milstead's stompin' ground if I'm not mistaken.'

'That's right, but she was found in Union so she's my business.'

'The Bishop girl was from Rock Springs, Walker County.'

'You ever get anyplace on it?'

Garner shook his head. 'Chased ghosts for a month or two. Good family, no reason for her to go runaway. Seems she was off with friends for the weekend, never made it home. Folks reported her gone on the Monday. We found her more 'an two weeks later.'

'Who found her?'

'Folks walkin'. Out-of-towners lookin' to camp and whatnot.'

'Can I go on back to the office and look through the file?'

'Sure you can. Tell my deputy that I said it was fine. Reeve Millson's his name.'

'Appreciated.'

'You want some more coffee 'fore you head out?'

'No, but I'll stay a while if you're after company.'

'Oh, I stopped hankerin' for company a long time back,' Garner said. 'You go on and get busy. And if you figure out what happened to that little girl, I'd sure like to know.'

The file contained a stack of photos, some from the scene, others from the autopsy.

The ligature marks on her ankles and wrists were much more defined. She hadn't floated in a lake for days and swelled up like Ella May Rayford. She was a pretty girl, blonde and slim, and it was evident from the autopsy that she'd not only taken quite a beating, but also been repeatedly sexually assaulted. She'd also been drugged with a non-specific barbiturate.

The crime-scene report was sparse in detail. Just as was the case by the lake, there were no identifiable footprints or disturbances in the undergrowth. The Cherokee County Coroner estimated that she'd been out there no more than twenty-four hours. Longer than that and all manner of wildlife would have gotten her scent and come down to eat.

Landis asked Deputy Millson for photocopies of all the material in the file. Millson said he'd have to call Garner and get clearance. He did and it was given.

'You got one the same?' Millson asked Landis when he brought the pages.

'Could well be.'

'Hell of a thing,' Millson said. 'Caught between hopin' it's not 'cause that means we got a special crazy one on our hands, and hopin' it is because that means more information that could help us catch the sumbitch.'

'That's the way of things,' Landis said. 'I appreciate your help. Like I told Sheriff Garner, if I get a handle on this you'll be the first to know.'

By the time Landis got back to Blairsville it was mid-afternoon.

He asked Barbara if she'd ever eaten boomer.

'Sure I have. If it don't move, you can pretty much guarantee I'll have eaten it.'

'Woman I got it from said to fry it up with some potatoes.'

'That and some onions, maybe some bell pepper. It's good.'

'I'll let you know how it goes.'

'So what kind o' woman has taken up the task of feedin' you?'

'A kind one, Barbara. Don't read tracks where no one's walked.'

'Maybe they stepped lightly.'

Landis laughed. 'How the hell does your husband put up with you?'

'Why don't you go on over and ask him? He's locked in the basement, but he'll hear you just fine if you holler loud enough.'

23

In Landis's experience, the dead ordinarily rooted for natural causes, expiring quietly in narrow rooms for which they still owed rent. Either that or accidents – falling from high places, hit by trucks on the highway, dragged into machinery that wouldn't let them go.

Now he had two dead teenagers, one in his own territory, the other in someone else's, but both bearing similarities.

If the killings of these girls – six months apart and crossing two states – had been perpetrated by the same individual, then it would become a federal matter. The last thing Landis needed were suits getting involved – it had happened before, and it was a pressure he could well do without. Aside from working best alone, he couldn't abide the notion of some rusty-footed college kid in a starched shirt telling him how to conduct his affairs. He knew people here, and people knew him well enough to know what they could expect. He could use one word. Folks knew where he was headed. Federal people worked up a whole darn sentence to say the same thing, and no one would pay attention anyway. It was best he keep a lid on it, pursue the Ella May Rayford murder, and if that cast a light on what had happened to Linda Bishop then so be it.

And then there was his brother, of course – unrelated but no less unexpected. Frank had been dead more than three weeks, and the fact that Landis had heard nothing further from Trenton suggested that no progress had been made in the investigation. He made a mental note to call Fredericksen.

Landis fried up the boomer as Barbara had recommended. It satiated his hunger, but he didn't reckon on eating it a second time. It wasn't so much as tough, but there was a texture to it he didn't much appreciate.

He watched TV a while. Nothing caught his attention. He tried to think in straight lines, but his mind was having none of it. He kept coming back to the bodies of the girls, to the sight of his brother's busted body on the coroner's slab, to the fact that a Trenton detective – the very same Detective Fredericksen – seemed to have taken care of whatever money Eleanor Boyd was due. That it was no longer a problem was good news, but why would the police department get in on that? There had to be an explanation, but it evaded him.

Around eleven he drifted off right where he was sitting. He woke a little before three and dragged himself upstairs to bed. It was then another hour before he fell into a restless sleep. He hadn't closed the curtains and the light roused him before seven. He felt as if he hadn't really slept at all.

At the office Landis was greeted with a banner headline in the *Herald*.

LOCAL GIRL FOUND BRUTALLY SLAIN

Mercer Gill, once again shooting pool with a piece of rope, had taken it upon himself to keep the public misinformed. He'd even had the gall to report that Sheriff Victor Landis had refused to comment. He wished he'd put the man in the drunk tank, just as he'd threatened.

Of a mind to call up Gill and draw blood, Landis stayed his hand. It would satisfy a taste for revenge, but more than likely encourage Gill to string the thing out for another day. As was expected, Gill had dug up a picture of Ella May Rayford that was some years old. Portraying her as an angelic child was calculated to generate as much controversy as possible. Landis concurred with Sherman: Kill all the journalists and you'd be getting news reports from Hell by tomorrow breakfast.

Once his annoyance had settled, he called up the Georgia Sheriff's Department Pensions Office. He got someone by the name of Harold Davis, from the outset a good deal more helpful than Marjorie Whitmer.

'It's still being processed,' Landis was told. 'To be honest, these things take weeks to get through the system. I know that's not right, but that's the way it is.'

'So there's no chance that my brother's widow will be receiving money anytime soon?' Landis asked.

'You're dealing with a government bureau, Sheriff. I don't want to get your hopes up.'

'And can you tell me anyone from the Trenton Police Department been in touch with you about this?'

'The Police Department?' Davis echoed. 'It wouldn't have anything to do with the police. This is a Sheriff's Department. Totally different entities.'

'I figured as much.'

'Of course, someone could have called, but it's unlikely they would have been given any information. Strictly speaking, I shouldn't really say anything to you, but seein' as how it was your brother an' all...'

'Yes, I understand, and it's very much appreciated, Mr Davis. You've given me as much as I need to know.'

'I can see from his records that there is a dependent. A daughter if I'm not mistaken.'

'No, you're not mistaken.'

'I trust there's no hardship for the family, Sheriff.'

'It'll be fine, Mr Davis. The mother has people who will help, I'm sure.'

'Well, okay. Obviously we'll do everything we can to expedite it as rapidly as possible.'

'Thank you for your time,' Landis said.

'You're most welcome,' Davis replied. 'You have a good day now.'

Landis was troubled. Eleanor Boyd had already received money. How much, she didn't say, but that was not the point. Mike Fredericksen had taken it upon himself to contact her, to tell her it was resolved, and a payment had been made. It wasn't pension money, so where had it come from, and – more importantly – why? Money of that nature served only two purposes: To make someone speak, or to keep them quiet. What could Frank's ex-wife possibly know that Fredericksen or the Trenton Police Department wanted under wraps? Did she even know something, or did they merely need to keep her sweet? Based on the little he knew of her, she appeared forthright and unafraid to speak her mind. Was this more a matter of keeping attention off of Frank? An irate ex-wife with a child to support causing a ruckus about an unpaid pension was just the kind of thing that newspapers would relish. Mercer Gill would embroider a national catastrophe out of that all by himself. Landis guessed the journalists in Trenton would be no different.

For Landis, this perhaps gave weight to the rumors of corruption in Trenton. He considered calling Eleanor and asking her direct – how much, and how had it been paid. Once again he restrained himself. If he was going to dig into this, then the less she knew the better. There was always the possibility that she'd lied, that she'd known precisely what Frank had been involved in, that she was now in collusion to keep something hidden. There were few people who didn't have a price.

Fredericksen knew more than he was saying. Of that, Landis felt sure. Eager to pay off Eleanor, not so keen to find out who'd killed Frank. There was a contrariness here that didn't sit well.

However, Landis assumed nothing. These were threads and nothing more. Embellishment was Mercer Gill's territory and had no place in policing.

24

The dark mud held her and didn't care to let go. It filled the spaces between her outstretched fingers, and it grew up beneath and around her shoulders and crowded the spaces between her arms and torso. It clogged her ears and bound her hair into one indeterminate mass of soft color.

The rain fell straight like stairposts, and it hampered the work that was being done to retrieve her.

That she had been dead some time was evident from the degree of decomposition, but the depth of the burial had served to slow that process. Later, when she was identified, the question of what had happened to Sara-Louise Lacey in December of the previous year was finally answered.

That she was found at all was mere chance, if such a thing existed.

Satolah, Rabun County, sat just three or four miles south of the North Carolina state line. To the east, close enough to see, was the South Carolina state line and vast expanse of the Sumter National Forest. The states were divided by the Chattooga River, fictionalized as the Cahulawassee by a novelist called James Dickey. Back in 1970, Dickey had published a book called *Deliverance*. Hollywood people turned it into a movie, and thus established a misconception that people from thereabouts were ignorant, racist and sociopathic. In reality, nothing could have been further from the truth, but it made a ton of money so no one much cared.

The river itself was the only commercially rafted waterway east of the Mississippi. Known as the 'crown jewel of the south-east', it had a quarter-mile corridor of protected forest on either side. That corridor was maintained by the United States Forest Service, and it was here that work was being done to catalog shortleaf, pitch and table mountain pine as part of the effort to re-establish the forest after years of soil erosion and extensive logging.

The man who found Sara-Louise was a USFS employee by the name of Mitchell Rutherford. He hailed from Gainesville, but he'd stayed up in Clayton for the better part of three months since the Sumter project had begun.

Had Rutherford not seen the girl's hand emerge from the soil then she may well have remained undiscovered for ever. A swathe of walking fern was being lifted to track roots, and Rutherford called out to the excavator operator to shut down the machine at once.

At first Rutherford saw exposed tendrils of whitewood, the bark stripped by the excavator, but the tendrils were too uniform in length. It was a moment when the mind sought an explanation that was not forthcoming, at the same time resisting what was unmistakable. That he stopped the work was founded on some intuitive perception that something was awry.

Upon closer inspection, there was no question. It was a human hand, frail and white, and – once he'd hyperventilated a while and gotten over the immediate shock – Rutherford radioed his supervisor. The supervisor telephoned the Rabun County Sheriff's Department, and a little before noon on the morning of Friday, September 11, Sheriff Carl Parsons and his deputy, Jerry Marvin, drove the fifteen miles from Clayton to Satolah.

The rain started before they set out, and by the time they arrived it was a deluge.

Comprehensive crime-scene analysis was impossible. Parsons made the decision to get the coroner down there and get the girl out. Whatever evidence could be gleaned would have to be gleaned from the body itself. The surrounding area had already been greatly disturbed by the work that was being done.

It was the better part of another hour before Rabun's coroner, Randall Warner, made it out to the site from Clayton.

By the time he got there, Parsons, Marvin, Rutherford and two of the USFS crew had managed to get Sara-Louise out of the mud. She lay naked and black on the overturned bed of walking fern. Deputy Marvin had fetched a blanket to cover her, but Parsons said that nothing further should be done until the coroner had made his preliminary on-site examination. When it came to it, there was little of anything Warner could do.

'We'll get her to the office,' he told Parsons. 'Hell, I can't even take pictures in this damned rain.'

Marvin and Rutherford helped stretcher her up to the road, and after Warner had secured her in the vehicle, he came down to speak with the sheriff.

'Anything at all from the guy who found her?' he asked.

'They were excavating over here,' Parsons said. 'They been here a good few weeks. He says he saw her hand, stopped the machinery, immediately called his supervisor. Supervisor was the one who called me. The rest you know.'

Warner looked troubled. He was new to the job, had served for little more than a year.

'This your first homicide?' Parsons asked.

'As coroner, yes. A couple of others when I was deputy.'

'Here in Rabun?'

Warner shook his head. 'Down in Dawson. Was there for a while before my transfer here.'

'Inevitable, I guess,' Parsons said. 'It's what we do, right?'

'She must only be sixteen or seventeen. Left out here like that. The things people do to one another.'

'Whatever you can dream up, someone'll dream up worse.'

'I'll head back,' Warner said. 'You gonna follow me?'

'Yes,' Parsons replied. 'I need to find out who she is as soon as possible. Someone somewhere is sure gonna get their heart broken.'

Warner got into the car.

Parsons went back to speak with Deputy Marvin, told him to cordon off the area with crime-scene tape as best he could.

'What for, I don't know,' he said. 'From the state of her, she's been out here a good while. Anything we might have found has long been buried or washed away.'

'I'll take a good look 'round, nevertheless,' Marvin said. 'You never know, eh?'

'Except when you do,' Parsons replied somberly, and started back towards his car.

25

As Randall Warner was opening up the body of Sara-Louise
Lacey in the Rabun County Coroner's examination theater,
Landis was compiling as detailed a report as he could regarding
the similarities between Ella May Rayford and Linda Bishop.
He would not know of Sara-Louise for some time, how she'd
been bound and raped, brutally beaten, that there was the presence of sedative in her blood, that she had been missing for a
little more than nine months.

Landis's report was for the Georgia Bureau of Investigation
in Atlanta, but he had no intention of sending it right away. In
essence, it was a means by which he could assuage any criticism
should this business come to light. He had written the report,
most definitely, but he had been remiss in sending it. Better to
face an accusation of negligence rather than one of intentional
withholding of data. As a final line of defense, he could say that
though the manner and circumstances of the girls' deaths were
similar – if only from the viewpoint of abduction, the manner
in which they'd been tied and the presence of sedatives – there
was no conclusive evidence that the perpetrator was the same.

By the time Landis was done, his mind was frayed at the edges.

He wondered – if by some preternatural sense – people knew
when they were on their last journey. Had Ella May known

that she would never celebrate her seventeenth birthday? Was Linda Bishop somehow aware that she would not see in the New Year? Had Frank experienced a premonition out on I-24 as he approached the Tennessee state line on the night of Friday, August 14?

To Landis, it seemed that the primary question to address was why Frank had been out there in the first place. Answering that would perhaps reveal some threads, at the end of which would be a murderer and a motive. Where was he going? Was he meeting someone? If it had been official, he would have been both in uniform and in his department vehicle. Never one to assume, Landis nevertheless felt sure that Frank was dealing with a personal matter. He sure as hell hadn't driven out there for fresh air and scenery.

Landis waited until Barbara was gone and then locked up the office. He went home and changed out of his uniform. There was no parcel of unusual meat from Dovie Moody to fry up with onions and peppers, so Landis decided to head over to The Old Tavern.

Despite his lack of fingers, Wilbur Cobb cooked a fine chicken-fried steak. The thought of that with a couple of shots and a beer back eased Landis somewhat. He wanted some quiet to process all that was happening.

On the drive over, he erred towards darker thoughts. He'd always traveled to suit his own legs, dealing with his duties in as professional and conscientious a manner as possible. Law was never a vocation. He knew that, wasn't afraid to admit it to himself, but work had now maneuvered its way into his personal life and had taken up residence. He felt a pull towards Frank's girl, a sense of obligation and duty to afford her welfare some mind. As Eleanor said, kids were tougher in some ways, more flexible, more able to bend with circumstance and then balance themselves once more. Perhaps nothing more than a cumulative effect, but once you were grown, the emotions attendant to shock and trauma hit harder and left deeper wounds.

Landis knew that his own parents had been damaged below the waterline. Neither one of them had been equipped to raise a family. In truth, they were barely capable of holding a marriage together. In hindsight, Landis had perhaps judged Frank too harshly, but he'd spent so many years working on that judgement that it would be nigh impossible to relinquish. People had to be right, even when they were wrong. And to admit that a mistake had been made was to admit your own part in the breakdown of the relationship. Guilt was a heavy coat to wear, even when you'd tailored it yourself.

Both he and Frank – to one degree or another – were a result of their upbringing. That they'd once been so close made their estrangement all the more profound. In the face of their mother's disconnection from reality, their father's abuse and violence, they had marshaled forces. They had a common foe, and once the foe was gone they had to find something else to fight. And thus they fought one another. It was not complex. It was human nature. The trap was that each one was utterly convinced that the other was to blame for everything that had happened, and from that there was no escape.

But these things were viewed in a different light now that Frank was dead, and it was only in his absence that they were considered. If Frank had still been alive, Landis knew that neither one of them would ever have proffered an olive branch. To initiate anything resembling reconciliation would have been tantamount to admitting defeat. For all their differences, stubbornness was one thing they definitely had in common.

*

At the Tavern, Landis ordered his food, and then took his drinks to a booth. It was Friday night and the place was crowded. The hubbub of voices, the sound of laughter, even the music from the jukebox, served to remind him that life went on regardless. Yes, he had two dead girls, a dead brother, a niece who'd taken an inexplicable shine to him, yet out here were regular people doing regular things – playing pool, telling crude jokes, flirting with the waitress.

Life was no longer than a piece of rope. At some point it ran out. By then it was too late to look back and see what other threads should have been woven through it.

Landis ate his steak, drank his beer and his whiskey, and got himself up to leave. He was no sooner out of his seat than Derry Buck appeared.

'I got that vehicle out of the pound,' he said, 'but that's not why I come over.'

Landis sat down. Buck took the seat facing him.

'I read that thing in the paper,' Buck said. 'About the Rayford girl. Me an' some of the fellas over there were discussin' it, wanted to know if whoever did that was from hereabouts.'

'Why do you wanna know, Derry?' Landis asked. 'You gonna get yourselves all liquored up and go lynch someone?'

'You know somethin', Sheriff, for a smart man you sure say some dumb stuff.'

'I guess that's comin' from an expert, right?'

Buck laughed. 'I always liked you, you know? Still do. I voted for you, an' I'll more an' likely vote for you again. I know you give us a hard time every once in a while, but you're a fair man. You ain't up on some high horse about your own importance like some others I won't mention.'

'I ain't no different from anyone else, Derry,' Landis said. 'And just like everyone else, I got a home to go to.'

Landis moved, but Buck reached out and took Landis's arm.

'Hold on there a mite,' Buck said. 'Don't get all toucheous now. I come over here polite, an' I just wanna ask you a question or two.'

'Did you know the girl, Derry?'

'No, I didn't.'

'Do you know her folks?'

'I know of 'em, sure. Dan's cousin bought a car off of Vester Rayford some time back.'

'Well, whatever you read in the *Herald* was not an official report, and there wasn't no statement from me, just like Mercer Gill wrote. This is an ongoing investigation, and as long as it's ongoing then there ain't nothin' I can tell you. We get someone for this, I'm sure it'll be news all over town 'fore I can even get the cuffs on. Right now there are no suspects and no one's been questioned, so you can go back to your pool and your drinkin' and forget this idea of a Blairsville vigilante mob taking justice into their own hands.'

Buck leaned back and nodded. 'Kids is the lifeblood of a community like this,' he said. 'People take it personal, and it don't matter whether they know 'em or don't know 'em. There's somethin' about a child killer that—'

'You can stop right there, Derry,' Landis interjected.

Buck got up. He looked down at Landis. 'Fish or cut bait, Sheriff. That's all I'm sayin'. Folks think you're sittin' on your hands, they get upset.'

'Message received loud and clear,' Landis said.

Buck paused for just a moment more, and then he turned and walked away.

It took everything Landis possessed not to go on after Derry Buck and knock him to the ground.

26

Over the subsequent six days, Landis put in three separate calls to Mike Fredericksen in Trenton. Not one of those calls was returned.

All set to drive out there and confront the man on the afternoon of Thursday the 17th, Landis was detoured by a call from Paul Abrams, Dade's acting sheriff.

It was Abrams who informed Landis about the discovery of the body of Sara-Louise Lacey.

'I sort of found out by accident,' Abrams told Landis. 'Jerry Marvin, deputy over in Rabun, is a drinkin' buddy of my brother's. I don't know him personally, met him once or twice maybe, but he got to talkin' about it and my brother mentioned it yesterday. I know you had a girl over in Union found dead.'

Landis wasn't surprised. In this part of the state, it seemed that everyone knew someone who knew someone else, especially when it came to Sheriff's Office and Police Department personnel.

'That's Carl Parsons who's sheriff over there, right?'

'That's right, yes.'

'I'll give him a call,' Landis said. 'Thanks for lettin' me know.'

There was a pause at the end of the line. Landis knew that Abrams wanted to ask about Frank. Landis pre-empted the question so Abrams wouldn't feel awkward.

'You ain't heard nothin' further about what Frank was doin' that night, have you?' Landis asked.

'Not a word,' Abrams replied. 'I put some calls in to Detective Fredericksen over at Trenton Police but he ain't come back to me yet. To be honest with you, I don't know what to think about it.'

Seemed that Landis wasn't the only one that Fredericksen was avoiding.

'How you copin' with the job?'

'Same as always,' Abrams said. 'Far as I can see, there ain't a whole heap o' difference between sheriff and deputy, 'cept for paperwork and whatnot. I ain't got any dead girls, however, and I hope it stays that way.'

'Well, I'm keepin' my ear to the tracks as well, so if I get wind of anything I'll let you know.'

''Preciated, Sheriff. I hope that thing in Rabun ain't connected to yours in Union.'

'I hope so too, son. You take care now.'

Landis called Rabun County, was given the runaround before he tracked Parsons down.

'Carl, this is Victor Landis over in Union. Got word that you had a dead girl over there.'

'That we do,' Parsons replied. 'Name of Sara-Louise Lacey. Sixteen years old. She was out in Sumter Forest by the river.'

'Recent?'

'Nope. Folks reported her missing back in December of last year. Coroner says she's been dead no more 'an three, maybe four weeks, though. Why d'you ask?'

'Would be interested in takin' a look at the details. It might be connected to a girl we found here back at the end of last month. Same age, dumped in Nottely Lake.'

'Come on over if you wish,' Parsons said. 'Maybe tomorrow mornin' would be better if that suits you.'

'Suits me fine, Carl. I'll see you then.'

Landis was reminded of what Reeve Millson had said when he'd copied the Bishop girl's file for him. More killings meant more heartbreak, and yet more chance they had of identifying a pattern. If a probative link was made, then Landis would have no choice but to inform the Bureau. Just the thought of it put an ache in his gut.

Landis collected up all the photos and reports relating to both Ella May Rayford and Linda Bishop. He separated them in envelopes, and put them aside for when he left. He would go directly from home. Best to get bad news as quickly as possible. Postponing it only made it worse.

If these girls had been abducted and killed by the same person, then he was looking at a whole new mess of trouble. Sure, he could leave it be, deal only with Ella May, ignore Linda Bishop and stay as far away from North Carolina as was possible. But he'd made no progress in his own investigation. Even with Mercer Gill's inflammatory newspaper article, no one had come forward with any information. He knew of retired law enforcement, had spent time with a few of them. There was not a man amongst them who hadn't spoken of the one case, the one frustrated investigation, the one victim that – even years later – still haunted them.

If Landis was destined to be alone for the rest of his life, then he would wish to be truly alone. Dead teenage girls would not be his choice of company in those waning, twilight years.

27

Sheriff Carl Parsons eyed Landis through a blue haze of cigar smoke.

'You know what they say. Poverty'll make a monkey eat pepper.'

'You reckon I'm short on trouble?'

Parsons smiled crookedly. 'I'm sayin' that I wouldn't go tyin' things together that have no business bein' tied.'

'Three girls,' Landis said. 'Two aged sixteen, one aged seventeen. Abducted by all appearances, then bound, drugged and dumped. Ella May Rayford out of McCaysville. That's Fannin County as you know, George Milstead's territory. She winds up in Union, which is why I'm investigatin' it. Then we have Linda Bishop out of Rock Springs, Walker County. She winds up all the way over in Bill Garner's patch near Murphy in Cherokee County. Now we got this one o' yours. Mountain City girl, same MO, but at least she stayed in the same county she's from. The last two were raped and beaten, but I ain't rulin' out the possibility that the same was intended for Ella May but she died before they could get to it.'

'I see what we got, Victor,' Parsons said. 'I also see what we ain't got. And now you're off on some wild goose chase to the Feds?'

'I'm not goin' to the Feds, Carl, not unless I have to. And you're right, there's no corroborative and incontrovertible evidence that says they were all killed by the same person, but there's enough circumstantial evidence for us to get our heads together and see where we're headed with this.'

'So correct me if I'm wrong, but you want sheriffs from Union, Fannin, Walker and Cherokee to collaborate like some sort of task force.'

'I ain't tryin' to dress it up fancy, Carl. I'm just sayin' that we have a situation here that demands a good bit of attention, and it seems we'd do better to get ourselves coordinated, don'tcha think?'

'Don't misread me, Victor. I ain't averse to the notion. You spoken to the others?'

'You're the first.'

'So get to arrangin' it. Where do you plan on meetin'?'

'Walker's far west. That'll be the furthest to come—'

'Who's sheriff over there?' Parsons interjected.

'That'd be Willard Montgomery. You know him?'

'Can't say I do.'

'And he just had a dead girl from Rock Springs, you say?'

'Most times I'd say folks should keep their spoons in their own bowls,' Parsons said, 'but this ain't exactly most times, is it now?'

'Ain't like any times I seen before.'

'Well, okay. If that's what you're doin' then count me in. Just let me know when and where.'

'Appreciated, Carl.'

With the visit ended, Landis went back to the office. He set Barbara onto contacting all the relevant sheriffs and seeing how such a meeting could be organised.

'Sooner rather than later,' he said. 'More time that gets by us the less we'll have.'

'Tends to be the way of things,' Barbara replied.

*

Back at his desk, Landis plotted the three locations on a map that covered both Georgia and North Carolina. The central point in that triangle was Hiawassee, Towns County. Towns wasn't part of this thing, so it didn't seem appropriate to use it as a meeting place. Ideally, the rendezvous would be right there in Blairsville. Landis knew he'd feel more comfortable in his own territory. He buzzed Barbara, told her to run the idea by those she spoke to.

'Hey, here's an idea,' she said. 'You could get them all to come over to my place for that world-famous Wedlock barbecue.'

'Barbara...' Landis said, and then he paused. Meeting at a neutral location would not attract attention. It sure as hell would go unnoticed by the likes of Mercer Gill. He could see the headline plain as day:

MULTIPLE COUNTY TASK FORCE ADDRESSES TEENAGE SLAUGHTER RAMPAGE

'You know, Barbara, that isn't as crazy as it sounds. On account of the fact that deputies'll probably be taggin' along, you got room for ten?'

'Hell, Sheriff, family gatherin' alone is more 'an twenty people.'

'The office'll cover the cost of food and whatever,' Landis said.

'If it works for you, it works for me,' she said.

'Good enough. See what they say.'

Barbara was a born organizer, a natural administrator. Above and beyond any sense of duty the respective sheriffs might feel, she would sell them on hickory-smoked pulled pork and homemade slaw.

Almost immediately he heard her laughing.

'As my ma used to say,' she was telling someone, 'a woman can throw out more with a spoon than a man can bring home with a shovel.'

Landis left her to it. His thoughts had turned to Frank, and more specifically to the comments made by both Jim Tom Moody and Eugene Russell about something gone sour in Trenton.

28

Late Saturday afternoon, Landis was finalizing his review of all the material he had concerning the three killings. He'd worked up a page of details that each case held in common. Looking back over it, it was all circumstantial. There was nothing truly solid about any of it, but it would have to suffice.

The phone rang. It was Barbara calling from home.

'Tomorrow,' she said.

'Tomorrow?'

'They'll all be here tomorrow.'

'Tomorrow?'

'What the hell you got in there, an echo?'

'I'm surprised,' Landis said.

'That they're comin' at all or by my skills of persuasion?'

'Both, I guess.'

'Well, put your surprise elsewhere and get yourself organized,' Barbara said. 'They're gonna be here around five in the afternoon.'

'You need some help?'

'Hell no, I'll be fine. I'll let my husband out of the basement and he can pitch in.'

Landis hung up the phone with the sound of Barbara cackling at the other end.

*

Why, he didn't know, but he sat back in his chair and thought of Eleanor and his niece.

The last time he'd heard from Eleanor had been two weeks prior at Jenna's birthday party. He wondered if he'd put her nose out of joint by being so direct about Frank. Whatever grievance he'd had with his brother, still the fact remained that the woman had been married to him for over four years. They'd raised a child together too, and that responsibility had continued long after they'd split.

Landis looked up her number and called her. He was about to hang up when the line connected at the other end.

'Is that you, Eleanor?' he asked.

'Sure is. Hey Victor.'

Landis frowned. 'How'd you know it was me?'

'Well, you sound just like your brother,' she said. 'So it's either you or Frank is now calling me from the other side.'

'I wanted to see how you were doing,' Landis said. 'And to ask after Jenna.'

'Hold on there,' Eleanor said.

Away from the phone, Eleanor called out to her daughter.

'Eleanor,' Landis said, suddenly overcome with a wave of anxiety. 'Eleanor, no ... I didn't mean for you to get her.'

'Jenna!' Eleanor hollered. 'Phone! It's your Uncle Victor!'

Landis closed his eyes and took a deep breath.

'Hey, Uncle Victor,' Jenna said.

'Hi, Jenna.'

A moment's awkward silence.

'I ... er ... well, I was just wonderin' how you were,' Landis said. 'If you were okay, you know? If you needed anything.'

'Like what?'

'Oh hell, I don't know. Another stuffed monkey, maybe?'

Jenna laughed. 'I think I'm okay for monkeys,' she said. 'For now, anyhow.'

'Okay. Good to hear.' Landis scrabbled for something – anything – to say. 'So, how are things at school?'

'I guess they're fine. I can give you a better idea when I go back at the beginning of September.'

'Oh yes, right. Sure. You're on summer vacation.'

'I am.'

'Well, how is your vacation?' Landis asked, regretting his words even as they left his lips.

'I guess it was fine, you know? Normal and everything. And then my daddy died.'

Landis closed his eyes. He wanted the earth to swallow him whole and never spit him out.

'You still don't know what happened to him do you, Uncle Victor?'

'No, sweetheart, I don't.'

'Do you think you'll ever find out?'

'I sure ain't gonna quit until I do know, that's for sure.'

'Mom says you and my dad used to fight a lot. Is that true?'

Landis, taken by surprise, said, 'No, we didn't fight a lot. We had one big fight and then we didn't see each other for a long time.'

'What did you fight about?' Jenna asked.

'Family stuff, I guess. The kinds of things brothers fight about.'

'You don't remember or you don't want to say?'

'I don't know that it was one particular thing,' Landis said, knowing that nothing could have been further from the truth. 'I think it was just a lot of little things, and they just added up and added up.'

'Do you regret that you didn't make friends again?'

Landis was momentarily lost for words. The girl pulled no punches.

'Regret ain't neither use nor ornament,' Landis said. 'No sense in feeling all twisted up about something that can't be fixed.'

'I guess not,' Jenna said.

'Whichever way, I'm real sorry for what happened to your pa, and I'm doin' my best to straighten it out.'

'I think my mom is sad, too.'

'I guess she must be, yes.'

'She told me you had a wife, Uncle Victor.'

'I did, yes. A good few years ago.'

'What happened to her?'

'She died, Jenna. She got sick and she died.'

'Oh.'

'Her name was Mary. She would've been your Aunt Mary.'

'I never had an aunt,' Jenna said, 'but then I didn't think I had an uncle either.'

'Well, I guess I never thought I'd have a niece. Especially one that's now eleven years old.'

'Eleven ain't so much. I want to be thirteen.'

'How so?' Landis asked.

'Because I'll be a teenager.'

'Yes, of course. A teenager.'

'You can come to my thirteenth birthday,' she said. 'But you know, you don't have to wait that long to visit again.'

'You're right.'

'I'll tell my mom and she can make us some dinner. What do you like?'

Landis smiled. He recalled something Barbara had said. 'Oh, I'll eat pretty much anything as long as it ain't moving.'

Jenna laughed. 'Okay, we'll make sure it ain't moving.'

'I best go now. You take care, okay?'

'And you, Uncle Victor. See you soon, I hope.'

With that, she hung up the phone.

Landis sat there for a few moments, the disconnected line burring in his ear.

29

Landis and Barbara Wedlock had known one another for more years than Landis had been sheriff. Never once had he visited her home.

Arriving a while after four on Sunday afternoon, he was greeted by Barbara's husband, Emmett. Emmett had on an apron with a monogram that read: *Many Have Eaten Here – Few Have Died.*

'Pleased to welcome you, Sheriff,' Emmett said. They shook hands.

Landis knew the man's face, but, pressed on the matter, wouldn't have been able to pick him out in a line-up as Barbara's husband.

The aroma of barbecue filled the house.

'Got quite a crowd comin',' Emmett said. 'Bad business that's bringin' you, though.'

'Indeed,' Landis said, wondering what details Barbara had shared with her husband.

'Barb's out back in the yard. Follow me.'

Landis followed Emmett down the hallway and into the kitchen. From there they went through a narrow utility room with a washing machine, a drier and the like, and then out through a door into a large yard. Two tables with benches either side stood over to the right, and it was here that Barbara was seated.

She got up as Landis approached.

'Victor,' she said. 'Welcome.'

'Thank you, Barbara.' He smiled. 'I finally made it to your home.'

'Let's not make it the only time, eh?'

Emmett hovered for a moment, and then asked Landis if he wanted a drink.

'A beer'd be good, Emmett.'

'Any preference, Sheriff?'

'No preference, no. And please call me Victor.'

Emmett went for the beer.

Barbara took her seat again, indicated for Landis to sit too. The beer was delivered and Emmett went back to the kitchen.

'How long you been married, Barbara?' Landis asked.

'Almost as long as I been alive,' she said.

'You got family?'

'No, never did have kids,' she said. 'Tried. A good few times, in fact. Was never meant to be.'

'I'm sorry to hear that.'

'Maybe it's God's way of tellin' you that you ain't fit for parentin'.'

Barbara offered Landis a cigarette. He took one.

'So, what are you hopin' to accomplish today?' she asked.

'Sufficient to make a decision about how best to approach this thing. Primary question to answer is whether these three girls are all victims of the same perpetrator.'

'I seen what goes over your desk,' Barbara said. 'Seems to me that there's too many things in common for it to be otherwise.'

'Nevertheless, it's circumstantial. You can't go to the public, the press or the courts with circumstantial.'

'Well, we'll see what these other fellers have to say when they get here.'

'That we will.'

'So what's the deal with your brother now?'

The question came out of left field and caught Landis un-
awares.

'The deal?'

'Come on, Victor. This is a small place. Everyone knows
everyone. Didn't take so long for folks to start askin' questions.
You been here all this time and he ain't never visited. Things that
don't have a simple explanation is a bone that's still got meat on
it. People'll chew on it 'til it's clean.'

'He an' I had a fallin' out.'

'And the sky's blue and the grass is green.'

Landis looked at Barbara. 'What do you wanna know?'

'Only what you're willin' to tell me,' she replied.

'Hell, some folks been on the run so long they forgot where
they came from and where they're goin'. It got like that with
Frank. Ask each of us what it was all about, you'd get a different
story, and then a different story again the following day.'

'Family's a hard row to hoe most times. But what goes over
your back is gonna come up under your belly.'

'Meanin'?'

'You know exactly what I mean,' Barbara said. 'Hide something in the corner, you always know it's there. Run away from
it, you always think it's chasin' you, even when it ain't.'

'He's dead, Barbara. Trenton is dealin' with it.'

'Trenton ain't dealin' with nothin' and you know it.'

'So what do you want me to do? Go 'round the houses lookin'
for somethin' on this? I got a dead girl washed up on Nottely
Lake, and now it looks like there's two more done by the same
feller.'

'Yeah, that's your job, Victor, but I ain't talkin' about your job.
I'm talkin' about your family.'

'Frank wasn't family for a long time.'

'Hell, sometimes you say things and I don't think you got the
brains God gave a gopher. Either that, or you is so busy being

right about whatever you did or didn't do that you can't see straight. Tell you now, you gotta kill your own snakes. You don't, they come back and bite harder.'

'I didn't come here to talk about Frank, Barbara.'

'You didn't talk about him. I did.'

'Well, can we please talk about somethin' else?'

'Answer me this, and then I'll let go. You made a mistake? Was that it? You made some terrible mistake, or was it him who made it?'

'Both. Maybe me. More me than him. Christ, I don't know.'

Barbara fixed him with a look. 'Everyone makes mistakes,' she said, 'but why do folks forgive others so much more easily than they forgive themselves?'

'You want an answer to that, I ain't got one. I ain't even gonna try.'

Barbara smiled, but there was an edge to it. 'Such a man you are sometimes.' She nodded towards the house. 'He's the same. Mule-stubborn.'

Landis erred towards a defensive comeback, but bit his tongue. He wasn't going to argue with Barbara. He had to work with her every day of the week, and, just as he'd said, he wasn't here to talk about Frank. He picked up his beer and took a swig.

'Thanks for doing this, Barbara,' he said. 'For bein' the hostess an' all. You let me know how much you spent gettin' this all fixed up, okay?'

'Sure I will,' she said. 'Have a mind to charge you twice for the darn headache you give me.'

30

Five sheriffs and three deputies sat around the yard benches and ate Emmett Wedlock's hickory-smoked pulled pork. Along with it came potato salad, some greens and a bucket of dirty rice and beans.

Willard Montgomery from LaFayette over in Walker County was the only sheriff unknown to Landis. He was the same age or thereabouts, had a rangy, windswept look. He made a wisecrack about this being their own Apalachin Meeting. Reeve Millson didn't know what he meant.

'Town in upstate New York,' Montgomery explained. 'November of '57, Vito Genovese – you know who that is, right?'

'Yeah,' Millson said. 'The mafia guy.'

'That's the one. He calls a meeting of maybe a hundred or so mafia bosses, and they all show up. Feds were all over them. I think they arrested half of them, maybe more.'

Barbara and her husband came to clear up dishes and plates.

Montgomery's deputy, Scott Whitman, got up from his seat to lend a hand.

'You sit right down again, Deputy,' Barbara said. 'We'll take care of this. You folks got work to do.'

Landis looked at Montgomery, then at Carl Parsons. Both men had delivered the worst news that could be delivered to a family, much as he had done when he went to see the Rayfords with George Milstead.

Landis knew he would have to begin this thing. They were in his county, his city, and his was the invitation.

'First thing we need to nail down,' he started, 'is whether these three girls were killed by the same person.'

Each man in turn looked at Landis.

'Two of them found in different counties, only Sara-Louise Lacey out of Mountain City stayed there in Rabun.'

'Seems to me there ain't a great deal of doubt that it's the same,' Milstead said. 'I mean, if it ain't then it's one hell of a coincidence.'

'I agree with George,' Parsons said. 'The binding, the physical and sexual abuse, the drugs. Two sixteen-year-olds, one aged seventeen. I think we got a serial on our hands.'

'And if we have,' Landis said, 'and we're dealin' with someone who's crossing state lines, then it's a federal matter.'

There was a brief murmur of resignation followed by an awkward silence from all those present.

'Which none of us want to get involved in,' Montgomery said.

'I'm the out-of-stater here,' Bill Garner said. He looked at Montgomery. 'Your girl, Linda Bishop, was found in Cherokee. The rest of you are all Georgia.'

Landis leaned forward. 'Doesn't change the fact that if we make the connection between all three, then we are duty-bound to turn it over to the Georgia Bureau.'

'And if we did that?' Montgomery asked.

'Then we'd be knee-deep in college graduates with slick hair and superior attitudes before you could smoke a cigarette,' Parsons said.

'And the paperwork,' Montgomery added. 'Georgia'd be cleared of trees with the amount of forms you gotta fill in with all that duplicate this and triplicate that.'

'Seems simple enough to me,' Garner said. 'The Bishop girl

was found in Cherokee. Far as I could see from the autopsy, the blood laking tells us she was killed elsewhere, right?'

'Yes,' Landis said. 'That seems conclusive.'

'So more than likely the murder happened in Georgia and the body was driven up across the state line to Murphy. That means Murphy ain't the crime scene. It's just a secondary.'

'Which would be fine,' Landis said, 'except for the fact that murder is a class-one felony and tampering with a deceased body is a class three. That she was only left in North Carolina doesn't matter. Even if the person who dumped her didn't kill her, that still gets them a good five to ten on the tampering. Taking into account that the one who killed also dumped her, then he's a felon in both states.'

'I took the news to her family,' Montgomery said. 'I've done that kind of thing before. You know, traffic accidents and the like, but never that. Never had to tell a mother that her seventeen-year-old girl, three weeks disappeared, is naked and dead by the side of the road in a different state.'

'Hell of a thing,' Landis said. 'Me an' George there had to go tell the Rayford girl's folks the same thing.'

There was quiet around the table for a moment.

'You know what she told me?' Montgomery said. 'That girl's mother told me they'd had a fight. Wasn't nothin' serious. Just a regular mother and daughter thing. But she said something to her daughter, could remember it exactly, had been replaying it over and over in her mind ever since the girl went missing. She told Linda she would never get the life she wanted if she stayed in Mountain City.'

No one said a word, but the mood of the gathering dropped a further ten degrees.

'Beat herself up about it, I can tell you. Figured she'd run off because of that.'

'How about we turn the tampering felony investigation over to the LaFayette police?' Whitman suggested.

'It's not a case of which department handles it,' Landis said. 'It's simply that it crosses state lines.'

'We're actually getting ahead of ourselves,' Parsons said. 'We ain't yet certain that the perp was the same in all three cases. Until we know that for a fact, it's three separate investigations.'

'Hell, I'm not averse to lettin' someone just oversee all three until we know for sure,' Garner said. 'If it turns out to be the case, then whoever that is can make the call on bringin' in the Feds.'

Again there was silence. Every man present looked at every other man, each of them hoping that someone else would step up to the plate.

Landis knew he had to do it. Later he would ask himself if it was a means by which he could further distance himself from his brother's death. In that moment, however, he did not analyze it nor attempt to find reason behind the compelling need to take this thing on.

'The Rayford girl was the first one,' Landis said. 'It started there. Seems to make sense I take it.'

Not a man amongst them challenged Landis's volunteering.

'You got everything you need on the Bishop girl and Sara-Louise Lacey?' Montgomery asked.

'I got a bunch,' Landis said, 'but the simplest thing would be to copy everything and send it over. I want to make sure I'm missin' nothin'.'

'Goes without sayin' that anythin' you need from any of us, you just gotta holler,' Garner said.

'That goes for deputies,' Parsons added. 'More than happy to send Reeve over if you need an extra pair o' hands.'

'Appreciated, Carl. I'll keep that in mind. However, I'm

thinkin' that the less attention we draw to this, the less likely it'll get in the papers.'

'So we're agreed,' Montgomery said. 'I'll send over everything we have. Information about the family, notes from interviews, and Carl'll do the same with everything he has on the Lacey girl.'

'Good of you to take this on,' Garner added. 'And if the Bureau gets wind of it and it gets troublesome, then I assure you we'll all stand up and share the responsibility.'

Landis smiled. 'Reckon if it comes to that, I'll be the one in the firing line. Horse that pulls the hardest gets beat the most, right?'

31

There was more food, even a hummingbird cake and some sweet potato pie. Barbara and her husband were the most gracious of hosts, and it was close to eight by the time the gathering broke up. Sheriff Parsons and Deputy Marvin set off for Clayton, Garner and Reeve Millson to Murphy, Montgomery and Whitman to LaFayette.

George Milstead and Tom Sheehan hung back a while, and when Milstead sent Sheehan to wait in the car, Landis knew there was something up.

Milstead made his way to the end of the yard furthest from the house. He lit himself a cigarette. Landis joined him.

'Somethin' troublin' you, George?' Landis asked.

'There is, Victor,' Milstead replied. 'The Rayford girl, more than the Russells.'

'How so?'

Milstead looked away. The expression he wore spoke of anxiety.

'You spoke with Eugene Russell,' Milstead said. 'He say anythin' 'bout his brother, Stanley?'

'Not a great deal, no. Called him Wasper, said he had a Harley-Davidson and a big mouth.'

'Well, he's got more 'an that, I'll tell you.'

Landis waited for further and better particulars.

'As I told you, them Russells and Rayfords are cousins after a fashion. Eugene is the head of the snake, but Wasper ain't so keen to stay in his shadow. I know they've had their fallin' outs over who Wasper buddies up with, and some of them folks are pretty bad, but what I gotta tell you concerns Frank.'

Milstead dropped his butt on the ground and toed it out. He lit a second.

'Frank?' Landis asked. 'What's Wasper Russell got to do with Frank?'

'Maybe nothin', Victor, but I heard some things and I wanted to tell you personal before you went and heard it someplace else.'

'So tell me, George.'

'There's back story to this thing. I'll make it short. We're talkin' maybe two, two and a half years ago now. Wasper had just come out of Georgia State. He did a while for robbery. Threw his gun before they got him, so it wasn't a lot of time away. Nevertheless, he got it in his mind that Eugene hadn't taken care of him the way he should. No doubt Wasper got himself into a bunch of scrapes while he was inside, and no doubt he expected his big brother to say a few words here and there and get Wasper looked after. That's not how it worked out. He got put in hospital twice, once for a busted rib, another time someone threw him down a flight of stairs. So Wasper comes out all on fire, you see? It ain't been a smooth ride for him. Eugene, he don't give a rat's ass about what Wasper does or doesn't think about it. Eugene's a big boy, he's got his own business to attend to. As far as he's concerned, whatever trouble his kid brother gets into then he's only got himself to blame. It ain't Eugene's responsibility to clean up after him.'

'What's this got to do with Frank, George?' Landis asked, already sensing the unease in his lower gut.

'I'm on the way,' Milstead said. 'Bear with me.'

Landis lit another cigarette.

'So Wasper's bearin' a grudge. Rightly or wrongly, he feels

betrayed. Now Wasper ain't straight enough to face up to Eugene square. Wasper wants to make a point, but he's gonna go the long way 'round so it don't seem like he's the one makin' it. He gets word about some drug deal that Eugene's put together. Yet another thing that Wasper's been left out of. Anyways, he decides he's gonna derail the thing in some fashion. He ain't gonna snitch on his brother, but he's gonna make a mess of it. He hires a couple of fools to show up at the buy site, just appearing out of nowhere, create some confusion, you see? The deal goes bad, one of these fools gets winged, and he's up in the hospital with a hole in his shoulder.'

'His name?' Landis asked.

'That don't matter,' Milstead said. 'He ain't the point of the thing. Neither one of them was. The fact that they were there wasn't the issue. This clown who got himself winged was carryin' a bunch o' pills and whatnot. No drugs was one of his parole conditions. He was headed right back where he came from for another eighteen months. Then he says he's got information about Wasper Russell. He wants to trade this information for a get-out-of-jail-free card. I tell him I'm listenin'. He tells me that Wasper is tied up with some police. He says that Wasper is an informant for some detective in Dade County—'

'Mike Fredericksen. Is that where this is going, George?'

'That's where I thought it was headed, but there's more.'

'Hang fire a minute,' Landis said. 'First question is how the hell does a smalltime crook from Fannin County wind up a confidential informant for a police detective in Dade? Second question is why didn't you think to mention this when you sent me out to see Eugene Russell? That his younger brother was a CI for the cop who's supposed to be investigating Frank's murder?'

'As for the last thing, I gotta say that I didn't even think about it. That's the truth of it, Victor. Like I said, this is more 'an two years ago now.'

'And the connection between Wasper Russell and Mike Fredericksen? There's four or five more counties between the two of them.'

'Wasper Russell has spent his whole life gettin' in trouble. He's been arrested in a whole bunch of places. I don't know details, but it ain't hard to see how he could've wound up causin' trouble in Trenton.'

'Okay, so how does this relate to Frank?'

'I'm gettin' to that. You see, we got the other one in yesterday. The other fool that Wasper hired to mess with Eugene's drug deal. This is why it's all floated to the surface again.'

'And does he have a name?'

'Kenny Greaves. Same deal. Another lowlife junkie on parole. We go 'round the scenery talkin' 'bout this an' that. And we come back to this stunt he and his buddy pulled for Wasper Russell two years back. Then he tells me that he has somethin' on Wasper, that he'll give it up if we let the drug bust slide. He tells me that Wasper wasn't an informant for Mike Fredericksen at all. He says Wasper was close with someone in the Sheriff's Office, and that the someone got himself murdered.'

'Greaves said that Wasper was actually Frank's CI? Is that what you're tellin' me?'

'That's the way I read it. Greaves didn't know the name of whoever it was, but he said that this someone got himself run down when he went to a meeting up in Tennessee.'

'Does Eugene know about this?'

'Lord knows, Victor. He and Wasper have a history of crossing swords. Wouldn't be surprised to learn that Eugene knew nothin' about it. Eugene wouldn't have no issue with gettin' his own brother killed if he thought he was in bed with the law.'

Landis didn't speak for a time. He recalled his meeting with

Eugene Russell, the intimations of corruption in Trenton, the fact that they all had their hands in one another's pockets.

'So, I'm just figurin' you lookin' up Wasper Russell,' Milstead said, 'but I'm guessin' you're gonna have to do it without word gettin' back to Eugene. Maybe he can shed some light on what happened to your brother.'

Landis nodded. He was still lost in thought. The issue was not only a possible connection between Wasper and Frank, but whether Frank and Mike Fredericksen had been involved in something together. If that were the case, then it would explain Fredericksen's seeming lack of diligence in the investigation. If you're involved in the burying, you don't get busy digging it up again. Five weeks now, and not a single sign of progress.

'I appreciate you're comin' to me, George,' Landis said. 'What's the deal with Greaves now?'

'I got him on a short leash,' Milstead said. 'Penny-ante drug bust ain't no interest to me. Hell, we got ourselves more crooks than cells across the whole state. I took what he gave me, figured it was worth bringin' to you. I couldn't keep him without chargin' him, but he's dumber 'an a can o' sody pop. He's gonna believe whatever I tell him. I send word that I need to speak with him, he ain't gonna do anythin' but show up.'

Landis was struck by the irony of the situation. He'd called this meeting and agreed to head up the investigation into all three killings. Subconsciously, he knew that he'd taken it on to escape from Frank's death. Now he was being given information that would throw him right back into it. Milstead was right, though. He would have to talk to Wasper Russell, and he would have to do it discreetly. The last thing he wanted to do was go wading through the swamp of Russell family business. That was just volunteering to drown.

32

Leverage.

That's the word that occupied Landis's mind when he thought about Wasper Russell. In reality, there shouldn't have been a single reason in the world for Wasper to talk to a Union County sheriff, but that didn't change the fact that they needed to talk. And Kenny Greaves was looking an awful lot like the answer to Landis's predicament.

On Monday morning and into the early afternoon there was a raft of paperwork. Some council busybody with not enough sense to pound sand down a hole was proposing new zoning infringements and pedestrian access by-laws.

Landis would've delegated it to Marshall and Barbara, but the first question he'd be asked is if he'd thoroughly understood all the requirements and ramifications of the document. Looking over it, he figured the author had so very little on their plate that there was a need to invent work for work's sake.

By the time he was done, it was after two. He felt as if his intellect had been mercilessly blunted with a stone.

He called Barbara through from the outer office.

'First thing,' he said, 'is I want you to know how grateful I am for your hospitality yesterday. And your husband is quite the chef.'

'He has his uses,' Barbara said. 'And it was a pleasure. I hope somethin' good came of it.'

Landis smiled sardonically. 'Depends on your definition of good. What came of it was my agreement to head up the investigation into the deaths of these three girls. If we establish that the perp was the same, then we have to turn it over to the Bureau. Until that point, we can keep it in the Sheriff's Office. Carl Parsons and Bill Garner are going to be sending over all the paperwork they got. There may be something from Willard Montgomery up in LaFayette, too.'

'Okay, I'll keep a lookout for it.'

Landis paused, holding Barbara's gaze. 'The other matter,' he finally said, 'relates to my brother.'

The moment hung in the air.

'Okay,' Barbara said slowly.

'Heard something from George Milstead. If it's true, it doesn't bode well.'

''Bout who killed him?'

'About what he might or might not have been involved in that got him killed.'

'Oh.'

'So I am faced with the task of verifying what I've heard, but it's delicate.'

'How so?' Barbara asked.

'Went up to see a feller by the name of Eugene Russell out near Colwell a couple weeks back.'

'I know that family,' Barbara interjected.

Landis raised his eyebrows. 'Know them, or know *of* them?'

'Knew their father. The boys not so much. This is more an' twenty years back, mind. Bad news all over. Feller weren't no bigger 'an a wharf rat, but had a temper on him something vile. Put him in a room by himself, he'd still start a fight. Just thinkin' on him gives me the jim-jams.'

'Well, it's his younger son Stanley that interests me. Goes by the name of Wasper.'

'Then he more 'an likely takes after his father.'

'Problem I got is I need to get him talking. He's in George's patch, so I'm already out-of-county. Second thing is that his older brother, Eugene, is the big boss of the hot sauce, an' I don't want Eugene to get wind of the fact that I'm having this conversation.'

'Them folks knitted tighter than a sweater.'

'I see that.'

'And you're tellin' me this because?'

'In case you got any pearls of wisdom. Or maybe just sayin' it out loud might get me seein' it a different way.'

'You know anythin' about this Wasper?'

'Nope. I'd say Eugene was my age or thereabouts. Wasper's younger, but by how much I don't know.'

'They're over in Fannin County?'

'They are. Out near Colwell like I said.'

'And George can't get you all the information you need?' Barbara asked.

'I have an idea George wants as little to do with this as possible. Besides, I'm already gonna ask him to do somethin' that . . . well, let's just say the less it looks like collusion, the better.'

'But he came to you with this yesterday, right? When you pair were out at the end of the yard.'

'That's right.'

'That's what I figured,' Barbara said. 'Looked like some conspirin' was goin' on.' She smiled knowingly. 'I'll ask around, find out what I can. Criminal records ain't gonna be a problem. I can find all past addresses from the County Records Office or the DMV. That kind of thing, you know?'

'But discreet, Barbara.'

'When the hell was I ever not discreet?'

Landis gave her a wry smile. 'And give George a call. Ask him when Kenny Greaves pulled that stunt for Wasper Russell.'

'Don't I need to know what the stunt was?'

'Ain't important. George'll know what I mean.'

Barbara got up from the chair. At the door she stopped and turned back. 'Say, you get that niece o' yours a gift for her birthday?'

'I did. A monkey. A stuffed toy one. And before you say anything, she was smitten with it. Decided to call it Victor.'

'Well, if the boot fits,' Barbara said.

'You know, most folks don't say what they're thinking, Barbara.'

'Sure they don't, and then they spend the rest of their lives regrettin' it.'

33

Barbara, conscientious as always, came back to Landis with a raft of information on Wednesday afternoon. Not only had she been through County and Criminal Records, she'd also trawled through local history newspaper archives and spoken with George Milstead.

Eugene and Stanley Russell followed in the footsteps of a long line of crooks. Their father, Virgil, born in June of 1912, spent more than a third of his seventy-two years as a guest of various reform homes, jails and penitentiaries. His father before him, Travis Russell, was a moonshiner and bootlegger. Born in July of 1890, he got to work as soon as Prohibition was enacted. He was twenty-nine years old when he began his operation out of Sale Creek, Tennessee, but soon owned and ran stills in half a dozen or more locations through the Appalachian foothills of Georgia and both Carolinas. Seemed the man was an entrepreneur of some capability. With the government's edict that ethyl alcohol should be poisoned with pyridine and methanol, Travis hired himself a chemist and started denaturing the stuff so it could be used to make liquor. He also brewed with Vine-Glo, Sterno, medicinal wine and anything else he could get his hands on. Travis's luck ran out just a year before Prohibition was repealed. Shot by Revenue agents after a chase that ran all the way from Soddy-Daisy to Signal Mountain, he rolled his vehicle into a ditch, crawled out, and wounded two more agents before he was despatched to the hereafter in a snowstorm of government lead. He was forty-two years old. He left behind a wife, two mistresses, all of seven children between them.

Virgil Russell was twenty years old when his father died. His mother, Willa, moved him and his three siblings to Colwell. What happened to the mistresses and illegitimates went unrecorded. Willa had stowed enough money to buy a plot of land and build a house. That house has remained in the Russell family to this day, and was where Landis had met with Eugene.

Eugene was now forty-seven years old, just three years older than Landis. Wasper was thirty-nine, born in January of '53. Both of them had a history of run-ins with the law. As early as 1956, when Eugene was just eleven years old, he'd been caught attempting to steal a car. That he didn't actually steal it went in his favor. He got away with a caution. The caution didn't seem to work the magic that had been intended. On through his teen years he was a continual headache for both his mother and the authorities. At fifteen, Wasper then just seven, Eugene did his first term of detention at the Epworth Juvenile Reform School. Wasper, aged thirteen, did a year at the same place after threatening a truant officer with a knife.

Wasper's next stretch was the robbery of which Milstead had spoken. From October of '86 to May of '90, Wasper was incarcerated at Georgia State. He was released under parole and managed to keep himself out of the hands of the law until the parole term was done.

The stunt Wasper pulled on Eugene's drug deal happened in January of 1991. Alongside Kenny Greaves, Wasper had hired a junkie by the name of Holt Macklin. Macklin was the one who got himself shot by one of Eugene's couriers. He was already burdened with two charges of assault, one of grand theft auto, one of resisting arrest. He kept his mouth shut about the

Eugene Russell fiasco, but that didn't stop him getting a three-to-five at State for possession.

Macklin commenced his sentence in June of '91. In August he was found hanged in his cell. Though it was deemed suicide, the inquest had abstained from declaring it as such. An investigation was instructed, but there were no further details regarding the outcome.

An additional note in Eugene's summary concerned his affiliation to the Aryan Brotherhood. Though not proven, there were clear indications that he had associated with known members, and had been witnessed at Brotherhood rallies in Georgia and South Carolina.

Wasper, subsequent to his jail term, had been implicated in a number of investigations spanning everything from gun-trafficking to child pornography. He had not been arrested, had never been charged, but had been questioned on numerous occasions.

Landis considered everything he'd read, and wondered if Eugene had ever found out about Wasper's interference in his drug deal. If not, then would the threat of revelation be sufficient to get Wasper talking? There was no way to find out without actually doing it, and it was something that went far beyond standard law enforcement protocol and procedure. Landis himself could be held to account for coercion, intimidation, misrepresentation, and operating out of jurisdiction. And, if Wasper really was a confidential informant and engaged in any ongoing investigations, they could throw some form of obstruction into the mix.

It raised the perennial question: What if the worst course of action was still the best option?

Landis only had to think back to the first meeting with his niece. Her words still echoed in his thoughts.

If it was my brother, and no matter what had happened between us, I'd wanna know why someone run him down with a car and broke him all to pieces. And if I didn't wanna know, I'd be asking myself some pretty tough questions about why.

Chasing down Wasper Russell proved to be tougher than Landis anticipated.

Though the Colwell house was given as his place of residence, he appeared to live the life of an itinerant journeyman. An appeal to George Milstead proved no more productive than Landis's own efforts. All that could be established with certainty was that Wasper had a girl in Padena out near Blue Ridge Lake by the name of Alice Morrow. Alice had two kids – Stacey, aged four and Tyler, aged two. Their surnames were listed as Morrow. Whether or not they were Wasper's children was unknown.

On Friday evening, Landis called George Milstead at home.

'Gonna get a handle on Wasper at some point. I think we might track him down to his girl's place in Padena. Name's Alice Morrow. You heard o' her?'

'Can't say I have, but if she's hooked up with either Russell, she's gonna be a born victim or a special kind o' crazy.'

'Guess I'm gonna find out,' Landis said.

'You need me to haul Kenny Greaves in again?'

'For now, no. Maybe later. Just the fact that you've had him in recent should be enough.'

There was an audible silence at the other end of the line, and then Milstead said, 'How narrow is this line you're walking here, Victor?'

'Too narrow for both of us, George. Best if you keep out of it. Plausible deniability an' all that.'

'This is your brother we're talkin' about,' Milstead said. 'Seems to me if it was my kin—'

'I'd do whatever you asked of me,' Landis interjected. 'But right now I ain't askin' and I'm hopin' not to.'

'You know where I am, Victor.'

'I do, George, and I'm grateful for your help.'

On Saturday morning, Landis went over to see Marshall. With him he took a copy of the most recent picture of Wasper Russell.

Marshall's wife, Lilly, worked up a sour face when she saw Landis standing on the porch.

'You takin' him away on a weekend now?' she asked.

'Good morning, Lilly,' Landis said. 'Seems we're havin' a good deal o' weather recently.'

She folded her arms defiantly, though she couldn't withhold herself from cracking a smile.

'How are you, Victor?'

'I am good,' he said, 'and thank you for askin'.'

'If you're comin' in then I guess you'd best do it. Marshall's out back in the yard.'

Landis took off his hat and went into the house.

'You want some coffee?' Lilly asked. 'There's some fresh on the stove.'

'That'd be most welcome.'

Landis followed her through to the kitchen. He could hear the *thwack* of logs splitting in the yard.

'So how've you been?' Landis asked as he took the coffee.

'As good as can be expected. As Marshall's probably told you, we're tryin' for a baby. He's gotten himself all worked up about it. Sometimes he can be such a worrier.'

'I'm sure it'll be fine.'

Lilly paused, perhaps expecting Landis to say something else.

'Go on back and see him then,' she said. 'I ain't the one you come to visit, now am I?'

Landis left his hat on the table and headed out into the yard.

Marshall was all colored up from the exertion of cutting fire-wood. His tee-shirt was damp with sweat. He set down the axe.

'Hey, Sheriff.'

'Marshall.'

'Brings you here. Aside from the coffee?'

'Need you to do something for me. Gotta feller I'm after, name of Wasper Russell. Need you to take a drive over Padena way and keep a lookout on someone for me.'

'That's Fannin County, Sheriff.'

'I know where it is, Marshall.'

'Ain't Tom Sheehan able to do it?'

'He ain't. This is out-of-school.'

'This to do with them dead girls?'

Landis shook his head. 'This is about my brother.'

'Right. Okay. So I'm guessin' Dade don't know about it neither.'

'Only folks who know are them who need to, Marshall. You bein' one o' them. I know it's the weekend an' all, but this is important.'

From his expression, Landis knew that Marshall was wondering why the hell Landis couldn't do his own lookout. He didn't voice his wonder.

'Today?' Marshall asked.

'Today'd be good. And tell your wife what she'll understand. No details. And let her know that however long you're on this you'll get it back double.'

Marshall hesitated, and then he took a deep breath.

'I'll go speak to her,' Marshall said resignedly. 'You hear me gettin' stuck with a knife, I expect you to come runnin'.'

34

The call from Marshall came around suppertime on Sunday.

Landis was restringing his guitar in the hope that it would make a difference, knowing all the while it would not. His mind was a fury of unanswered questions and half-formed ideas. There was no clear path ahead of him for either investigation, and the sense of impotence and frustration was close to unbearable.

'He's showed up, Sheriff,' were Marshall's opening words. 'Arrived about ten minutes ago. Harley-Davidson, like you said.'

'I'll take 76 and 60,' Landis said. 'Be with you in about thirty minutes. You hang on 'til I get there.'

Landis put on boots and a coat. He took his own car and was on the road within ten minutes of Marshall's call.

As soon as he arrived, he sent Marshall home.

'Go calm your wife down,' Landis said. 'And don't come in tomorrow.'

'If you need me though—'

'Go, Marshall.'

Known as a shotgun house, Alice Morrow's place was one story and linear in design. The notion was that a bullet fired from the front door would go straight through and out into the back yard.

It was close to eight. Even though lights were on, Landis figured the children would be in bed.

Landis headed over, pausing for just a moment before he knocked the door.

He heard voices and footsteps inside. There was silence, then more voices.

'Who is it?'

'Open the door and find out,' Landis said.

'Tell me who you are or fuck off.'

'Open the door or I'm gonna bust it in, Wasper.'

A woman's voice. The sound of a door slamming inside.

The latch released, the door inched open. It was secured with a chain.

Wasper Russell double-took when he saw Landis.

'I know who you are,' he said. 'You ain't got no business here.'

'If you know who I am, then you know exactly what business we got.'

'My brother said you'd more 'an likely come sniffin' around. He said not to give you the time o' day.'

'You ain't gotta tell him nothin', Wasper,' Landis said. 'Wouldn't be the first time you kept a secret from Eugene, now would it?'

Wasper closed the door to with a stream of expletives. The chain was unhooked and he opened up.

He stood looking at Landis like he'd been smacked hard. Resentment permeated the air around him.

Wasper stepped aside so Landis could enter, and then he took a moment to survey the street left and right.

Closing the door, he led Landis through to the living room. Alice was evident in her absence.

Wasper sat down in a grubby lazyboy. Landis took a no-less grubby and battered sofa.

The TV was on with volume down. The place smelled of cooking oil and sweat.

In the bare light of an unshaded bulb, Wasper did not look well. How he'd wound up with his name Landis didn't know, but it suited him better than any he could imagine. His skin was yellowed and anemic. His arms were scattered with crude jailhouse tattoos. His hair, thin, black and greasy, was combed flat to his scalp. He seemed unable to sit still, his very presence a fury of agitation and nervousness.

'So what the hell d'you want?'

'I want to ask you some questions, Wasper.'

'I got nothin' to say to you.'

'My brother got himself killed. Your cousin, Ella May Rayford, too. I got Kenny Greaves in a cell in Blue Ridge. He's got a lot to say about that stunt you pulled back in '91 with Holt Macklin. I'm guessin' Eugene is still none the wiser about why that deal o' his went sour, right?'

Wasper stared at Landis. What little color was in his face drained away.

'I went up and visited with Eugene,' Landis went on. 'He didn't have a lot of good things to say about Trenton. Said the place was a swamp. I'm askin' what you know about my brother, and I don't want some parcel o' bullshit—'

'I don't know anythin' 'bout your brother,' Wasper snapped.

Landis paused for effect. He took out a cigarette and lit it.

'Me an' Sheriff Milstead go a long way back,' Landis said. 'Kenny Greaves is on a short leash right now. He's got a whole whirlwind of trouble comin' his way. I give Milstead a call and tell him to make a deal with Kenny, then Eugene's gonna know what happened with you and Macklin. Macklin went to State and got hanged. Seems to me he got the easy way out. I don't know your brother so well, but I sure as shit wouldn't want to get on his bad side.'

'What the fuck, man?' Wasper said. 'What the fuck is this? I don't know who done your brother, okay? I don't know who done it and I don't know why.'

'But you knew my brother, didn't you?' Landis asked.

'Hell, everyone knew your brother. Your brother was a bad cop, okay? He was a bad fuckin' cop and he pissed off a lot of people.'

'Which people, Wasper?'

Wasper sneered. 'Oh man, that ain't the hill I'm dyin' on. You wanna go chase them ghosts, then that's your business. That shit goes deeper than you can even imagine. Your brother was just the blunt end of a very long fuckin' stick, man. Them folks used him to keep pokin' at shit and pokin' at shit, and he did it. He did what they asked. He took their money and he looked the other way. You do that for only so long and then the shit gets too deep and you drown.'

'Meanin' what? You're gonna have to give me some specifics, Wasper. One call and Kenny Greaves'll bury you. Your brother ain't gonna mess around, right? He gets word that you and Kenny screwed up that deal, he's gonna come find you. And if he's the man I think he is, then he's gonna get to Kenny too, just the way he got to Macklin.'

Wasper frowned. He seemed genuinely surprised. 'You think Eugene got Holt Macklin killed? Is that what you think? You have no idea, do you? You don't have any idea what you're dealin' with here, do you?'

'Enlighten me, Wasper.'

Wasper got up suddenly. He walked to the window, flicked the curtain aside and looked out into the street. Whatever anxiety he'd manifested with Landis's arrival had now escalated into a state of continual agitation.

He went back to the lazyboy, sat down, stood up again, crossed the room and made sure the door was closed.

By the time he started talking again, even Landis was on edge.

'Your brother been sheriff more 'an ten years out there in Dade,' he said. 'Don't matter 'bout no election or nothin', he was gonna be sheriff for however long he played that game.'

'What game?'

'All that shit comin' down from Tennessee.'

'Drugs?' Landis asked.

'Drugs, guns, fake IDs, vehicles. Whatever, man. That's a pipeline. That's a horn o' fuckin' plenty, man. That shit keeps comin', and all them places are like a network.'

'Which places?'

Again, Wasper manifested surprise. 'You tellin' me you ain't plugged into this shit, man? Chattanooga, Huntsville, Atlanta, Memphis, even down in Alabama, right? Montgomery, Birmingham. Dade is important because it's up against the state line, but there's all sorts o' places and all sorts o' people involved in this game. The peach state is rotten to the fuckin' core, man, and your damned brother was right in the middle of it.'

'I've got no reason to believe you,' Landis said, hearing the defensiveness in his own voice even as he said it.

'And you got no reason to think I'm lyin' neither,' Wasper replied. 'You tellin' me you got Kenny Greaves down there and he's gonna rat me out, eh? He don't cooperate and he's gonna tell you all about some stunt you think I pulled with him and Holt Macklin against my own brother. Is that what you think? Sure, I know that boy. Know him well enough that he's gonna look after hisself 'fore he looks after anyone else. I don't want whatever trouble you got, and I sure as hell ain't of a mind to get run over by no damn car like your brother did.'

'Is your brother involved in this?'

Wasper laughed dismissively. 'You know yo'uns ain't growed up hard like us. This is a bad life we got. This is a mess 'fore we even get started. But you ain't no better 'an us, and that's a fact. You say one thing, do somethin' else. You all got your pockets open for whatever you can get. Police ain't no damn good just because they's police. You maybe got the law on your side, but you use it as a means o' doin' what you want outside o' the law. Your brother was a crook, whichever way you look at it, but he was way, way down on that totem pole. He fetched and carried, he delivered things, he looked the other way. If there was folks in the road, he got them out of it so other people could get where they needed to. He got paid for sure. What people did the payin' and how much I don't know, an' I don't want to know. You go dig some holes around his house and you're gonna find plenty bad shit buried.'

Wasper paused and shook his head. 'I'm all done talkin' now. You do whatever you want with what I told you, but you call up George Milstead and tell him to leave Kenny Greaves out of this. And, truth is, I don't give a rat's ass what you tell my brother. My family is my business an' it sure as hell ain't none o' your'n.'

Landis didn't speak. Wasper had said a great deal, and liars always talked too much. However, he guessed there were threads of truth woven through it. He also knew that silence was the best way to encourage Wasper to say more.

Wasper looked back at Landis. There was a sense of resignation in his eyes.

'If I was you, an' if I really wanted to know what happened to your brother, then I wouldn't be lookin' at me or Eugene or Kenny Greaves or no one else I know. You want clear water, you go find the mouth of the river. Seems to me that'd be Dade County and whoever else is on the payroll down in Trenton.'

166

'You're not the first person to tell me this,' Landis said.

'Well, you best keep your wits about you, or I'm gonna be the last.'

35

Follow the money.

It was always about the money.

Monday morning, after a fitful night of restlessness, Landis arrived at the office to find a stack of paperwork on his desk. Here were all the case notes, interviews and photographs relating to Linda Bishop and Sara-Louise Lacey. Barbara had also collected together everything concerning Ella May Rayford.

Though the triple killing should have been his foremost priority, Landis found his attention consumed by what had been said about Frank. Though he would no more trust Wasper Russell than he would a politician, the simple fact was that both Eugene Russell and Jim Tom Moody had also voiced their opinions about Frank's moral compass. Once was happenstance, twice coincidence, three times and you had a conspiracy. He could not now let it go. More importantly, he did not want to.

The thousand dollars a month. That seemed the starting point. It had gone from Frank to Eleanor, and with Frank's death that source of income had been maintained. From what Eleanor had said, Mike Fredericksen was responsible for that, or at the very least knew something about it.

Treading on the toes of the Trenton Police Department was ill-advised. He had no choice but to once again tackle Eleanor on the subject. What she knew – more to the point, whether she knew anything at all – would only be discovered by asking. The possibility that she was aware and complicit in whatever had resulted in Frank's death was also prevalent in Landis's thoughts. Pushing for details would set off alarm bells. Who would come running was unknown.

Landis thought hard on an angle, but it was not there. There was no one but himself to do this. He wondered if it would best be approached in-person, but decided against it. The more formal it seemed, the more attention it would garner. He'd seen neither Eleanor nor Jenna since the birthday party three weeks prior. Strategically, it would've been smart to have stayed in more frequent communication with them, but maintaining distance had been his habit for so long that he hadn't even thought of it. Frank's life – though no more than a hundred miles west – might as well have been on the other side of the world. He had not wanted a family of his own, and he most certainly had not wished to adopt his brother's.

The phone didn't ring more than twice before Eleanor picked up the receiver.

'Eleanor Boyd.'

'Eleanor, it's Victor.'

'Hey, Victor. I guessed you had your heart set on bein' a stranger.'

'I woulda called you before,' Landis said, 'but I got a whole mess of things goin' on and I can't seem to get out from under it.'

'Believe me, I understand,' Eleanor said. 'Days'd go by I wouldn'a see hide nor hair o' Frank.'

'So how are you? And how's Jenna?'

'As fine as can be. She's in an' out of it, you know? Been havin' some nightmares. Seems to be settlin' down now, but still a day don't go by when she don't mention him in one fashion or another. And how are you?'

169

'Me?'

'Yeah you, Victor. Don't act so surprised that someone's askin' after you.'

'Oh, I'm the same as ever, Eleanor. You can set your watch by how I am.'

'Sure seems you fixed up a lonely life for yourself, I have to say.'

'Well, it ain't so bad as all that, Eleanor. Lonely and alone ain't the same thing.'

'So did you call for a reason or just to shoot the breeze with me?'

'For a reason,' Landis said. 'I got myself a bunch o' papers relatin' to Frank's estate and whatnot. Most of it don't have much to do with me seein' as how you and Jenna are next of kin, legally speaking. One thing it's askin' is whether you're gettin' his pension, which I know you are. It's askin' for details, and I know it's tiresome but I gotta get it done and back to the lawyer people.'

'What do you wanna know?'

'You said you were gettin' a thousand dollars a month from Frank, and that has now continued, right? That got itself sorted out.'

'Sure it did, like I told you. There was some delay and whatever, but it got fixed. That feller from the police in Trenton called me about it, said he'd straighten everythin' out and he did. Ain't heard nothin' since.'

'And where's it comin' from?'

'I guess his pension, Victor. Where else would it come from?'

'Yes, I know it's comin' from his pension,' Landis said, 'but does it come as a check or what?'

'Goes right in the bank, just the same as when Frank was doin' it.'

'And do you happen to know the name of the bank it's comin' from?'

Eleanor paused. 'What the hell is this, Victor? What kinda paperwork you got?'

Landis shuffled some random papers on his desk. 'I got it right here,' he lied. 'It's headed up Beneficiary and Dependant Maintenance Provision. Part one, section five. In the instance of the aforementioned deceased or invalided party having been afforded a service pension or stipendiary—'

'I think that's about enough of that,' Eleanor said. 'Hang fire.'

Eleanor set the phone down. A drawer opened.

She was back on the line. 'Comes from Dade County First Municipal, same as always.'

'In Trenton?'

'Yeah, in Trenton.'

'Is there a reference name or number?' Landis asked.

'Just says F. Landis. No number.'

'That'll do it,' Landis said. 'Anything else they need they can go fetch it themselves.'

'So, you gonna visit again anytime soon?'

'Sure I will.'

'Well, maybe come over for dinner on a Saturday evening. Jenna would like that.'

'I'll call you,' Landis said. 'This next weekend might be tough, but maybe the one after.'

'You ain't gonna fix a date are you?'

'I gotta book time off, Eleanor. Even when I'm not officially on duty, I'm still on call.'

'You know, you might be very different from your brother in a lot of ways, but you can't lie worth a damn either. You ain't obliged to do nothin' you don't wanna do. The invite is there. Take it or leave it.'

'I'll take it,' Landis said, 'and I'm sorry for the runaround. I don't want to put you to any trouble.'

'If you think makin' some dinner for you is trouble then you ain't had much of a life, Victor Landis. And if you get all extra busy with your sheriffin' and whatnot, you just gimme a call and we'll fix it for the one after. How does that suit you?'

'Suits me fine, Eleanor. Thank you. And tell Jenna I said hi, okay?'

'I surely will, Victor,' Eleanor replied, and hung up the phone.

36

The decision to visit with Frank's deputy, Paul Abrams, was based on two things: Abrams' seeming genuine concern for the investigation, and the fact that Mike Fredericksen had not returned Abrams' calls.

Landis didn't really know the man worth a damn, but the impression he'd given when they met in Frank's office, and then again at the murder scene, had been one of directness and professionalism.

If Frank had been up to his waist in this purported Trenton swamp, there was a strong possibility that Abrams would have known about it, perhaps even have been involved. Abrams had never given Landis any reason to suspect he was complicit in anything, which meant that he was either a decent man or a very convincing liar. Landis, instinctively, erred toward the former.

Barbara found Abrams' home address without any difficulty. Landis closed up the office at five and drove to Trenton. Out near Blue Ridge – where I-76 headed southwest towards Lucius – the traffic got snarled. Whatever reservations or second thoughts he had about what he was doing, he set them aside and stayed on the road. He was in the suburbs of Trenton by seven-thirty, and had located the Abrams home.

The Abrams house sat on a good-sized plot. The yard was neat and well-tended; flowerboxes sat beneath the windows at the front and the side. The path was bordered by beds of small yellow blooms. The overall effect was that of folks taking care to present as homely and welcoming an appearance as possible.

Once again, Landis asked himself if he was doing the right thing to drag Abrams into this mess. Once again, he reconciled himself to the fact that there seemed to be no other realistic option.

For some strange reason, Landis had the impression that Deputy Paul Abrams was not surprised to see him standing there on the porch.

Opening the inner door and then hesitating for just a second before he opened the screen, Landis sensed that here was a man reconciled to inevitability.

Acknowledging Landis with a kind of forced surprise, Abrams didn't at first invite Landis in, but rather stepped out onto the porch.

'The hell're you doing here?' Abrams asked.

'Just tryin' to fix things in my mind, Deputy,' Landis said. 'Got a lot of loose ideas floating around and need some help tyin' a couple o' them down.'

'We're not doin' this here,' Abrams said. 'Not in my home—'

Before Abrams could say another word, the inner door opened once again and Carole appeared.

Frowning at her husband, she said, 'What are you pair doin' out there? Paul, what's gotten into you? Invite our guest in, for Pete's sake.'

Abrams looked back at his wife. 'I have to go out for a little while,' he said.

Carole frowned. 'What on earth are you talking about, Paul?'

'This is my doing,' Landis interjected. 'It's to do with my brother. There's something of his in the office and I need it.'

Carole nodded understandingly. 'Yes, yes, of course. My condolences again.'

'Thank you, Mrs Abrams.'

'Oh, you go on and call me Carole,' she said. 'Now can I get you some coffee before you head out, perhaps? Did you have some supper already?'

'I'm fine, thank you very much, Carole,' Landis said. 'I had myself some supper on the way over.'

'Well, good enough. I'll leave you boys to your business. It's real nice to see you again.'

Carole bade her farewell, and headed back to the kitchen.

'You know the Mountainview Grill?' Landis asked Abrams.

Abrams nodded. 'Sure, yes.'

'Meet me there.'

Landis didn't wait for a response. He turned and walked back to the car. At the end of the street, he glanced up at the rearview. Abrams was still standing in the yard.

Landis got through a hamburger and two cups of coffee before Abrams showed.

Landis stood up to greet him. Abrams waved him down, almost as if he didn't want to attract any attention to their meeting.

'I need you to keep this official,' Abrams said. 'You can't bring this to my home, you understand?'

'Well, I'm out on a limb here, Deputy,' Landis said. 'I got a bunch of questions and a bunch of answers that ain't for those questions. I'm somewhere in the middle o' that mess and I need some help findin' a way out.'

'I get that, but you can come to the office. You can call me. You shouldn't be comin' to my home.'

'Understood. Won't happen again. Got these questions, and am gettin' tired of waitin' for answers.'

'And you think I might know somethin'?'

'More like I think you might be able to help me find out something.'

'To do with your brother.'

Landis turned as the waitress approached.

'You want anythin'?' Landis asked.

Abrams shook his head.

'I'll take a refill,' Landis told the waitress. 'Nothing for my friend.'

Abrams leaned forward, his voice subdued. 'Like I said before, if your brother was in some kind of trouble, then I can assure you I didn't know anything about it.'

'I got no reason to doubt you, Deputy, but sometimes you just gotta keep diggin' and askin' questions and then diggin' some more before somethin' turns up. Right now you're pretty much the only person I can think of that might be able to solve one bit of this mystery.'

Abrams looked at Landis and waited for the question.

'My brother's pension still ain't sorted. That don't surprise me none. He's only been dead six weeks. What doesn't make sense is that he was givin' his ex-wife a thousand bucks a month, and she's still gettin' a thousand bucks a month.'

Abrams frowned.

'Eleanor Boyd told me that Frank put this money into her account every month. He'd done that ever since they split. It didn't come from his salary as far as I can tell. Where it came from I don't know, but the fact that it went directly into his ex-wife's account as a cash payment means there's no actual paper trail. If the money was good, why would he do that? Then he dies. He'll get a pension, for sure, and his kid would be entitled to financial support from that pension. The thing I don't understand is that the thousand bucks a month has continued, and it seems to be going from the same account into Eleanor's account just as if Frank was still around.'

'And you're absolutely sure the pension ain't started?'

'Not according to the pension folk I spoke to.'

'So someone's doin' that for her.'

''S how it looks.'

'To keep her quiet?' Abrams said.

'Lord knows. I spoke to her about Frank. She got defensive about him, said he was a good father, always supported her and the daughter. She said she wasn't aware of anything he might have been involved in. My gut tells me that if he was into something bad, then she didn't know about it.'

'And aside from this money, is there anything else that suggests he was involved in something he shouldn'a been?'

Landis took a deep breath. If he was going to get Abrams on side, then he was going to have to give him a much fuller picture of what had transpired.

'You hear of a family called Russell out of Fannin County?'

Abrams frowned in thought. 'Russell ... Russell.' He shook his head. 'Can't say I have, no.'

'Two brothers, Eugene and Stanley. Stanley goes by the name of Wasper.'

'I know Wasper,' Abrams said. 'Well, I heard that name before. Hard to forget.'

'Where'd you hear it?'

'Frank. On the phone, maybe two or three times. He was talking to someone by the name o' Wasper. Sure o' that.'

'And the older brother, Eugene?'

'Nope, that don't ring no bells.'

'Jim Tom Moody. Kenny Greaves. Holt Macklin. You heard them names before?'

'Not that I recall, Sheriff,' Abrams said.

'Okay. So Wasper and his brother, Eugene, also this Moody feller out of Cherokee up in North Carolina, they all said that Trenton is a swamp.'

'A swamp? What the hell is that s'posed to mean?'

'As it sounds,' Landis said. 'Lot of dirt, lot of stuff buried, lot of people doin' things they shouldn't be doin'.'

'And when you say Trenton, I'm assumin' you mean the Sheriff's Office.'

'Sheriff's, Police Department, Mayor's Office, I don't know. Some or all o' them. I ain't got details, but now I heard it three times from three different people and it won't let go.'

'But these people are—'

'I know what kind of people they are,' Landis interjected. 'And I sure as hell wouldn't trust them any further than I could spit 'em, but now I got this thousand bucks comin' from somewhere and it don't add up.'

'Is that why you're here? You want me to find out where it's comin' from?'

'I want to ask if you'd be willin' to look into it, yes.'

Abrams was quiet for some seconds, and then he asked, 'You know which bank?'

'Dade County First Municipal.'

'And it's a cash payment?'

'Eleanor says there's no reference number or anythin' like that, so I can only assume someone walked in there and paid the money over in cash.'

'And what? You think they might know who was goin' in there every month and depositin' a thousand bucks into her account? Even if they did know, they ain't obliged to give up information on any financial transaction without a warrant. You know that, right?'

'I do, yes.'

'So, what are you askin' me to do? You want me to falsify a warrant?'

'I'm not gonna ask you to do nothin' you ain't willin' to do, Deputy,' Landis said. 'You can say no right here and now and I'll be on my way.'

Abrams assumed a knowing expression. 'Of course, if I say I

ain't willin' to help you, then you're going to assume I'm hidin' somethin'.'

'I'm not goin' to assume any such thing,' Landis said. 'You got a wife, a baby, a whole career ahead of you. Hell, you might even wind up the youngest sheriff in the state. You seem like a decent, honest man to me. I bet Frank was proud to have you as his deputy. Aside from that, he's dead, and how he died and where he died doesn't make sense. I got folks as crooked as a twister tellin' me that my brother weren't no good. I got a thousand bucks I can't account for. I got his ex-wife and his kid—'

'Okay.'

Landis looked at Abrams.

'Okay,' Abrams repeated. 'I'll do what I can. That's all I can do. I'll try to find out who was sendin' that money over to Eleanor.'

'I appreciate it,' Landis said. 'However, I'll say this. If you change your mind, it's okay. If you sleep on this and figure that it's a risk you ain't prepared to take, then I'll understand.'

Abrams smiled. 'Don't really work that way, you know? Man makes an agreement, he's bound to keep it. I already thought about it while you were talkin'. Frank was a good man. At least I thought he was. He was my boss, and he treated me just fine. If it turns out that he was in on somethin' wrong, then I guess my viewpoint'll change. Until I do, he's the same as he always was. That's why I'm gonna help you. Because he helped me.'

37

Reviewing all the case notes and restudying the crime-scene photographs on Tuesday morning, Landis did not doubt that the three killings had been committed by the same person.

Without probative evidence, it was still entirely circumstantial, but the similarities were too similar – the age of the victims, the binding of the hands and feet, the drugging, the manner of disposal. The missing factor was a physical link between the girls or the sites themselves.

In the case of Sara-Louise Lacey, the fact that she'd been missing from December 27 of the previous year but only dead for three or four weeks meant that she'd been somewhere – and alive – in the interim. Both Ella May Rayford and Linda Bishop had been found within two weeks or so of their respective missing persons' reports.

Why had Sara-Louise not been murdered within the same timeframe? What had taken place in the intervening months? Where had she been? And with whom? What had they been doing with her?

The most important question was if there was a link – any link at all – between the three girls. They were from different towns in different counties. Two of them had been dumped in a different county altogether. Why these girls, and why from such diverse locations? Did they have something in common – a contact, a location, a circumstance perhaps – that would provide an explanation as to why they had been abducted? There was always the possibility that it was entirely random. The killer was a traveller, on the move all the time – a salesman, a truck driver, a farmhand, even a federal employee whose duties took him back and forth across state lines. Pick a girl up somewhere, keep her hidden someplace, kill her and then bury her in a location far away from where she'd been taken. Again, the Lacey girl didn't fit the pattern, not only because she came from Rabun and that's where she'd been dumped, but because she'd been somewhere for all those months between abduction and murder and no one had known. And only two of them had been sexually assaulted. Ella May had escaped that fate, but – as he'd considered before – that might have been solely because she'd died before such a thing could happen.

Landis couldn't even begin to imagine the abject terror that such a scenario would bring to bear upon a teenage girl. Kept in some basement, perhaps an outbuilding, a root cellar beneath a barn, someplace off the beaten track and away from neighbors. Or maybe it had been more brazen than that. Maybe it was a suburban home, the girl gagged and tied up in a sound-proofed room, mattresses up against the walls, a boarded window.

However it happened, it was a nightmarish proposition. To spend days, weeks, then into months unsure of what was going to happen to you, all the while your innocence, your dignity, your humanity being ripped away from you.

Landis selected pictures of each of the three girls – as they were, not as they'd been found – and laid them out across his desk. He walked to the window. He turned and looked back at them. Once they'd all been Jenna's age. They'd all been spoiled, pampered, adored. And now they were gone. Lives ended before they'd even had a chance to begin.

Calling it a tragedy did not even come close to expressing

the disdain and indifference that had been afforded the basic sanctity of human life.

The reality of the agreement he'd made with Milstead, Parsons, Garner and Montgomery was real enough. He'd have to go visit with the Rayfords, the Bishops, the Laceys. He would have to speak to friends, associates, the people who'd last seen each girl. He'd have to go to their schools, their places of work, their last known location. Marshall would have to help him, and he'd have to call on the respective sheriffs and deputies from each county as needed. It was a hell of an undertaking, but he could not now decline to do it. As Abrams had said only the previous evening – if a man made an agreement, he was bound to keep it.

Landis buzzed Barbara.

'You know where Marshall's at?'

'Not this moment. Can find him easy enough, though.'

'Track him down would you, Barbara? Tell him to come on back here soon as he can.'

'He gettin' a carrot or a stick?'

'Neither,' Landis said. 'Got work that needs to be done, and a good deal of it.'

'Well, that's one thing you can say about Marshall,' Barbara said. 'That boy ain't shy o' labor.'

38

Hope for the future was forever overshadowed by the sorrow of the past.

This was the underlying and intuitive sense that Landis had as he sat in the kitchen of the Lacey house in Mountain City. With the death of their daughter, their lives had come apart. There was no reason or rationale that could give them comfort. There were no guidelines or instructions on how to rebuild, how to move forward, how to reconcile the fact that the worst fear of a parent was now a reality.

That the Laceys were a good deal more affluent than the Rayfords made no difference. Though they attended church, donated to charity, bought boxes of Girl Guide cookies and provided endless candies for trick or treaters, all of it meant nothing in the face of what had happened. Evil was indiscriminate.

They had created a world. That world was there every single day. They'd taken it for granted that it would always be there, and then it wasn't.

The fact that Ed and Marion Lacey didn't question Landis's request to see them told him that they really didn't care who discovered the truth of what had happened to their daughter. They just wanted to know, as if in knowing, some of the burden of grief and pain might be dispelled.

*

On Tuesday evening and a good ways into Wednesday, both of them repeatedly distracted by the everyday demands of the office, Landis had briefed Marshall as best he could on all three murder cases.

That late morning – Thursday, October 1 – he'd dispatched Marshall to speak with Linda Bishop's folks in Rock Springs. He'd instructed him to allow the Bishops to contact Sheriff Willard Montgomery if there was any question as to why a Union County deputy sheriff was knocking on their door.

It was now mid-afternoon. He guessed Marshall was still out in Walker County, or maybe headed back to Blairsville with as much information as he'd managed to glean.

Meanwhile, here he was, asking the Laceys to go through everything they knew, everything they remembered, everything that they'd thought of since they'd learned of their daughter's death.

Landis had wanted to come here. This was the case that unsettled him the most. He wanted to know – *needed* to know – where Sara-Louise had been in those months between her disappearance and her death.

'Sheriff Parsons was over here,' Ed told Landis. 'Jerry Marvin, too. They asked everything you're askin'. We told 'em everythin' we could. Don't know how it'll help to go through all of it again and again.'

'It's just too upsettin',' Marion said. 'We ain't but got her buried this past week.' She took a deep breath and closed her eyes.

'I understand, Mrs Lacey. I really do. I'm sorry to have to bring this to you all over again, but I'm workin' with Carl Parsons over there at the Sheriff's Office, an' even though he's got all the information you gave him, and even though I read all o' that, still it sometimes happens that something is remembered after the fact, you know? Somethin' like this is ... well, there's just no way to put a tragedy like this into words. Expectin' folks to remember everythin' they can while they're dealin' with the immediate shock o' somethin' like this is just too much, you understand. That's why we come back some time later and see if there's anythin' else that's come to light.'

Ed looked at his wife. Marion looked at her husband. They both turned and looked at Landis. The atmosphere in the room was one of awkward disbelief.

'We had Christmas,' Ed started. 'Like always. She's our only child. Christmas was always just the three of us now that our folks have passed. One time – two, three years ago – she had a friend over. I think the poor girl's folks were divorcin'. Fightin', you know? Kid was right in the middle of it, and that's not what you want at Christmas time. Sara-Louise asked if we'd mind her bring the friend, and we said sure, of course. That was the only time in the last while that Christmas wasn't just the three of us. You'd o' thought she'd like to be out with her friends partyin' and whatnot, but she just wasn't that kinda girl. Kind, gentle, considerate. Conscientious with her studies. I mean, she kinda knew that we wouldn't be able to send her away to college, but that didn't seem to trouble her none. She did some volunteer work, stayed after church on a Sunday and helped put chairs and books away and the like.'

Ed looked at the ceiling. He was mustering every ounce of reserve he could manage so as not to break down.

When he spoke again, his voice cracked with emotion. 'Sh-she was a-a good girl. She was a real good girl, Sheriff Landis. She wasn't never in any trouble. Sh-she didn't go out dancin' and she wasn't smokin' cig'rettes nor drinkin' like some o' them other teenagers. She was just a sweet, sweet girl. She was our daughter...'

Ed lowered his head. Marion reached out and put her hand on his shoulder.

'Ain't right,' she said. 'Ain't fair. I mean, what kinda person takes a sixteen-year-old girl right off o' the street and just vanishes her into thin air. They told us back then, back when she went missin', that if they didn't find her within seventy-two hours then the likelihood that she'd still be alive was down to a handful o' nothin'. Well, she was alive, wasn't she? Months after she was gone, she was still alive. Where? Where was she? How come they couldn't find her? All them people lookin' for her, God bless 'em, and there was nothin'. Not a word, not a sign. How can that be?'

Landis had nothing to say that would assuage the anger, the despair, the sense of futility that these people were feeling.

'You have children?' Ed asked.

Landis shook his head. 'No, sir. Never had children.'

'Because o' your job, I guess.'

'No reason, Mr Lacey. Plenty o' folks who do my job have families.'

'Well, if you had kids then maybe you could get some kind of idea about how it is to lose one. I can't expect you to understand what's happened here.'

'No, Mr Lacey, and I am not professin' to understand what you're goin' through. The notion fills me with dread, to be honest. All I can say is that I'm workin' on this as if it's the last thing I'll ever do.'

'You mean that?' Marion said, a flash of bitterness in her eyes. 'Or is that just more words and more sympathy and more meaningless promises like all them other police fellers that said they were gonna find her?'

Landis leaned forward. He looked at Marion Lacey directly.

'You don't know me, Mrs Lacey,' he said. 'I just showed up here outta nowhere to ask you all these questions. I know it's heartbreakin' to go through all of it again, but I'm doin' this because no one's quittin' on you. I got Carl Parsons and Jerry

Marvin, I got my own deputy, too. I even got sheriffs from three other counties lendin' a hand on this.'

'I heard there was another girl,' Ed said. 'Some girl out of Fannin County.'

'Where'd you hear that, Mr Lacey?'

'It's true, ain't it? There's another girl got herself abducted and killed the same way.'

'It's true that I am investigatin' the disappearance of another girl, yes, but we have no evidence to suggest that the same person was responsible.'

'And she's dead?' Marion asked. 'This other girl from Fannin. She's dead?'

'Yes, ma'am,' Landis said.

'Some other family torn apart the way this one is,' she went on. 'I mean, you hear about it, you see these kinds o' things on the TV news, but never in a million years do you think that somethin' like that is gonna happen to you.'

Landis didn't speak. Silence settled in the room for a while. Ed and Marion Lacey sat there stunned and disbelieving and all out of things to say.

'Would it be possible for me to look at her room?' Landis eventually asked.

Without a word, Ed Lacey got up. He nodded at Landis. Landis got up and followed him out of the kitchen, down the hall, and up the stairs.

Sara-Louise's room was on the right at the top. Ed opened the door, left it open, and then walked past Landis and went back downstairs to his wife.

Once the sound of his footsteps had ceased, Landis could hear Marion Lacey sobbing all the way from the kitchen.

39

Landis did not think any additional purpose would be served by visiting with the Rayfords again. It was that case that had connected him to the Russells. The Russells were the ones who'd said Frank was bad. He couldn't help but wonder if Jeanette Rayford had riled Eugene by talking to Milstead, implying that Eugene would take matters into his own hands if progress wasn't made in the investigation of Ella May's murder. Most everything behind him was a mess of supposition and hearsay. In that moment he prayed that everything ahead of him wouldn't be the same.

That Thursday evening he sat with Marshall in the office. The lights were out in the foyer and reception. Barbara had left for the evening.

'I've delivered news before,' Marshall said. 'You know, some old feller had a heart attack, a coupla times there was a car smash. That one time a kid drowned in the Toccoa. This is all kinds of different. This there ain't no sense in. And they want you to make sense of it. The girl's folks. They look at you like you know somethin' they don't. I gotta say I never felt so useless in all my life, Sheriff.'

'I know, son,' Landis said. 'Same for all of us.'

'Went through everythin' again. Asked the same questions that's been asked a dozen times before. I mean, I was careful not to upset them, but I checked two, three times to make sure there was nothin' that they'd thought of that maybe they hadn't told Sheriff Montgomery or Deputy Whitman back in February.'

Marshall leaned back. He shook his head resignedly. His body language spoke of a man defeated.

'Just a regular girl. A regular teenager doin' teenager things. They said she was a good student, hard-working, considerate, kind. I mean, I know folks have a tendency to paint a good portrait of their own kids, but I got that this was genuine. Churchgoin' people, doin' the charity bake, a whole talent show thing to raise money for sick kids and whatnot. Just a respectable, decent, everyday American family, and then this. Their daughter gets snatched out of thin air, like she was never even there in the first place ...'

'No siblings, right?' Landis said.

'No, just her.'

'It's the same with the Rayford girl and Sara-Louise Lacey. No brothers and sisters.'

'That mean somethin', you think?' Marshall asked.

'Maybe, maybe not. What could it mean? Why would someone want to abduct girls that were only children? Or did they have something in common aside from being only children?'

'I spent a good two hours there, Sheriff, and there was nothin' out of the ordinary, not in what her folks told me, not in the girl's room. I don't think you could find a more normal family.'

'Damned if I know what kinda family this is s'posed to happen to,' Landis said. 'Is there any kinda people who deserve this?'

'So where do we go from here?' Marshall asked.

'There's either a connection or there ain't,' Landis said. 'If there is, we gotta find it. If there ain't, we're pissin' in the wind.'

'Well, whatever connection might exist, I don't think the girls' folks're gonna help us any. Far as I can see, we got ourselves a blank slate, Sheriff.'

'Seems that way, Marshall. Anyways, we're not gonna get anythin' else accomplished this evenin'. Go on home to your wife, eh?'

Marshall got up. He paused for a moment, and then said, 'What's happenin' with your brother?'

'Hell if I know,' Landis replied. 'That's another bone in my gullet. Word is he wasn't such a straight shooter, that he may've been involved in some bad stuff.'

'What kinda bad stuff?'

'You know the Russells?'

'Heard o' them, yes. You know George's deputy, Tom Sheehan? He said he had a run-in with them a while back.'

'A run-in?'

'The younger one, Wasper. Said he beat on some girl, kids too, and she was too frightened to press charges. Said he was told to back off, that it wasn't his business.'

'Who told him that?'

'Didn't come from George Milstead, I know that much. Said the police out there in Blue Ridge said he was an informant for them, that they didn't want him gettin' riled about some domestic thing that meant nothin'. This was a while back, though. Maybe six months.'

'Wasper Russell was a CI for Blue Ridge PD?'

''S what Tom told me, yes.'

'I got word he was the same for Trenton.'

'And they're out in Colwell, right? That's where the Russell place is?'

'Colwell, yes.'

'Maybe it's a state thing,' Marshall said. 'Maybe ol' Wasper's a snitch for anyone who asks him.'

'And maybe his older brother's in on the deal,' Landis said.

'Can't see how Wasper could be doin' that without Eugene knowin' about it. I met with them both. Eugene's definitely the head of that snake.'

'You want me to speak to Tom again?'

Landis shook his head. 'I'll get Barbara to see if there's somethin' on record with Atlanta. If he's a state informant, they'll know about it.'

'Okay, well if there's anythin' else you need me to do on this, just holler.'

'I will, Marshall. I'll see you tomorrow.'

Landis took his time closing up. It was past eight before he left, and though he was hungry and there was next to nothing at home, he decided not to go to The Old Tavern. He would make do with a can of soup and some saltines.

Driving away from the office, he thought about what he'd said to Eleanor, that there was a difference between loneliness and being alone. Now he wasn't so sure. Pretty much the whole of his adult life he'd kept folks at arm's-length. Was it any wonder he didn't have any friends to speak of, no one to call on, no one who would call on him? He didn't do Thanksgiving or Christmas, there were no beers and burgers in the yard after a football game. It was something about which his wife had expressed her discontent countless times in the years they'd been together. Now, twelve years on, he couldn't even say that he missed her. It was hard enough to even recollect her face. In a way, it was as if that marriage had never happened. Until recently, he would've put his relationship with Frank in the same category. That was another life altogether, and a life with which he had no connection.

However, things had changed, and though he resented those changes, there was no way to now undo them.

He felt a pull towards Eleanor, towards Jenna; the grief and loss that he'd witnessed in the Rayford house, then again with Sara-Louise's folks, had affected him in a way he could never have predicted.

Recent events had forced him to look at who and what he'd become, and, in so doing, face the fact that he didn't much care for this person.

It was a difficult admission, for it meant taking responsibility for the things he'd said and done. Blame was as redundant as guilt. He'd worn them both like a mantle. There would come a time when he'd have to unburden himself of the falsehoods. A man can lie to himself for only so long. The truth was always there, and it could not be hidden for ever.

40

First thing Friday morning, Landis again called Trenton PD.

As had happened before, he was told that Mike Fredericksen was away from his desk. He was asked if he would care to leave a message.

'I'll tell you what I want to do,' Landis said. 'I want to sit right here on this line until someone tracks him down and gets him on the phone.'

'I'm not sure that's gonna do you any good, Sheriff Landis,' the desk sergeant told him.

'Well, to hell with what's good for me or not, Sergeant. You need to get Mike Fredericksen on the line or I'm gonna drive over there and bring a whirlwind of trouble—'

'Sheriff, I understand—'

'You don't understand a goddamned thing, you hear me? I'm not hangin' up this phone. You go find Fredericksen right now. Go find him and get him on the phone.'

For a moment, Landis believed the line had been disconnected. He then understood that he'd been placed on hold.

'Sheriff Landis?'

'Fredericksen?'

'It is, yes. And before you read me the Riot Act, I gotta apologize for not gettin' back to you. I seen your calls, and I keep meanin' to get to it, but you know how things are, right?'

'I can't say I do,' Landis replied. 'Last time we spoke was the back end of August. We're now into October an' I ain't heard a word from you about what's happenin'.'

'If there'd been words to share, I woulda shared 'em, I assure you,' Fredericksen replied.

'You have nothing?'

'Bits an' pieces. I been chasin' my tail on this.'

Landis took a deep breath. 'You're tellin' me that you've made no progress in your investigation in all of these weeks?'

Fredericksen paused before speaking. When he spoke, whatever vestige of friendliness or professional courtesy had been replaced with a diffident matter-of-factness.

'I ain't one for callin' anyone up and tellin' 'em nothin',' Fredericksen said. 'And, let's be straight here, the Union County Sheriff's Department does not have any authority in this matter. Back when we first met, I asked you if you were gonna get up in this and you told me you weren't. I took you on your word, Sheriff Landis.'

'And I took you on your word that you were gonna do everythin' you could to find out who killed my brother.'

'And I have done everythin' I can, and I'm gonna keep doin' everythin' I can until I find out. You just have to let me do my job.'

'I got word that you sorted out Frank's pension.'

Silence.

'Seems Eleanor has been receivin' what she's due. I understand that you were instrumental in straightening that out, Detective.'

Not a word from Fredericksen.

'I have to say there's somethin' about this bird that don't fly right,' Landis said.

'You need to back off,' Fredericksen said. His voice was firm, direct, businesslike.

'I ain't plannin' on doin' any such thing.'

'I'm tellin' you now, Sheriff, and I need you to hear me on

this. You gettin' into this is not gonna do anyone any good, least of all Eleanor and her daughter.'

'You know, the more you say, the worse things sound, Detective.'

'Your brother—'

'Only time I wanna hear you talk about my brother is to tell me you figured out what happened to him.'

'Well, you'll be the first to know, Sheriff, and you have my word on that. I just hope you're around long enough to take my call.'

'Meaning what exactly?'

'Meaning that there's lines you seem set on crossing, people you seem determined to talk to who really don't want to talk to you, and I really don't recommend you keep on going the way you're going.'

'You're threatening me, Detective Fredericksen?'

'Me? No, Sheriff. I'm not threatening you. Let's just call it a little friendly advice.'

'I got some advice for you in return,' Landis said. 'You keep lookin' for who killed my brother. You do otherwise, an' the only place you're gonna need to look is over your shoulder.'

With that, Landis hung up the phone.

He got out of the chair and walked to the window. He breathed deeply. He focused. If nothing else, he now knew that Fredericksen was most definitely not on his side.

41

Despite Barbara's best efforts, she went round in circles trying to find anyone forthcoming about Wasper Russell.

The Atlanta PD stonewalled her, not through any direct means, but more due to the fact that she was dealing with a faceless bureaucracy of individuals. Dwarfing any county PD, Atlanta's ranks numbered in their hundreds, and she was shunted from one desk to the next, one unit to another, and came away with nothing of any substance.

'I'm guessin' either you or Marshall need to pitch up on someone's doorstep,' Barbara told Landis. 'I think it should be you. They're more likely to listen to a sheriff. Besides, it'd probably do you good to get out of here and see the bright lights.'

'Seein' the bright lights of Atlanta ain't exactly on my bucket list,' Landis said.

'Got some mighty fine eatin' establishments. Best hanger steaks I ever had was in Atlanta, and I've eaten a lot of steaks.'

'Sounds like you're sellin' me on the idea.'

'I ain't tryin' to sell you on nothin', Sheriff. I just come to a standstill on this, and I don't know who else to call.'

'An' if you can't find anyone to help, how the hell am I gonna do any better?'

'That's just plain negativity, Sheriff,' Barbara said. 'You decidin' you failed 'fore you even tried?'

Landis smiled. The woman was his conscience and confidante in so many ways.

'Give me a list of the people you spoke to,' Landis said.

'More to the point, I'll give you the name of the person I didn't get to speak to. State Attorney General's Office has a Criminal Justice Division. Inside o' that is something called the Justice Collaboration Unit. Them's the ones who deal with confidential informants, witness protection, all that kinda thing.'

'Well, I guess that's whose door I should go sit outside then,' Landis said.

'You goin' today?'

'Don't see it makes sense to leave it. Tomorrow's Saturday. Folks more 'an likely be gone until Monday. Besides, I got myself invited over for dinner with my brother's ex-wife to-morrow evening.'

'Well, how about that? We're gonna get you socializin' before you know it.'

'Duty, Barbara, not choice.'

'Oh, listen to yourself, will you? You gotta be one of the crankiest people I ever met. You ain't but forty-somethin' years old. Anyone'd think you were an oldster with the whole of their life behind them. I got at least fifteen years on you, and I put you to shame.'

Landis laughed.

'I'll get you the details you need. You want me to get Emmett to fix you up some sandwiches and whatnot for the trip, or you gonna stop someplace on the way?'

'I'll eat on the way,' Landis said, 'or maybe I'll wait until Atlanta and get one o' them hanger steaks.'

'Least I can do is get you a flask of coffee,' Barbara said.

'That'd be welcome.'

'No trouble at all, Sheriff.'

Barbara got up and walked to the door. Pausing before she

left, she turned back. For just a moment she looked genuinely concerned.

'What now?' Landis asked.

'You keep the doors locked and the lights out, no one will ever feel welcome. You do know that, right?'

'Meanin'?'

'You got time, Victor, but not for ever. I know you lost your wife an' all, and I'm sorry for that, but whatever it was that impelled you to marry in the first place must still be there. Ain't right that a man should spend his whole life on his lonesome.'

'Maybe some folk are meant to be alone.'

'Bein' alone ain't human nature. And there ain't nothin' you can do about human nature. And policin' is a job, you know. It's not your whole life.'

'I'll think on it, Barbara.'

Out beyond his door, Barbara's phone rang.

'Thinkin' ain't worth spit,' she said as she went out to her desk. 'Doin' is all that matters.'

42

Late afternoon downtown Atlanta traffic was as bad as anything Landis had ever seen.

Unused to such a jam of vehicles, he made slow progress and didn't arrive at the Atlanta Attorney General's Office until four. Without an appointment, he had to wait a further forty-five minutes. By the time he sat in front of Lieutenant Abigail Webster of the Justice Collaboration Unit, he could sense that his presence was unwelcome.

'It would have been far better if you'd made an appointment,' Webster told Landis.

'I appreciate that, Lieutenant, and I can only apologize. I'm dealin' with a case up in Union, and we're hittin' up against a few obstacles.'

'That relate to confidential human resources?'

'You mean informants, right?'

'Not a term we now employ,' Webster said, 'but yes.'

'There's a coupla fellers by the name of Russell. Eugene and Stanley. They're out of Colwell in Fannin County—'

'But you are in Union?'

'I am, ma'am, but I'm sort o' actin' as a coordination point between Union and Fannin. Sheriff down there by the name of George Milstead is workin' on this with me.'

'So what is it that you're trying to find out exactly?'

'I'm tryin' to determine if the younger brother, Stanley, goes by the name o' Wasper, is one o' these confidential human resources. If so, who's he workin' for?'

Webster hesitated for a moment, and then leaned forward across the desk. Her expression was one of bemusement.

'The entire point of a confidential resource is that it remains confidential, Sheriff Landis.'

'Save when the party involved is connected to an ongoing investigation, surely?'

'And what is the nature of this investigation?'

'That's what we can't seem to get a handle on. Could be drugs, guns, even heard word o' child pornography. I do know he was involved in some serious domestic abuse and the people down in Fannin were told to drop it.'

'And all you're tryin' to do is ascertain that this individual is working with the police down there?'

'That's right, ma'am.'

'And if he is?'

'Then I'll know not to tread on anyone's toes.'

'You can assure me of that?' Webster asked.

'I can assure you of anythin' you want,' Landis said. 'I ain't here lookin' to cause trouble, Lieutenant. I'm just tryin' to get a fix on somethin' that has me confounded.'

'Just as long as we're clear on this point. The nature of what we do here in the Criminal Justice Division is based on complete identity security, but at the same time we have a duty to work with law enforcement. After all, everyone in the Attorney General's Office is on the same side.'

'It would be a great help, I assure you.'

Webster turned to the computer on her desk. She typed for a while, scanned pages, typed some more, and then looked up.

'No,' she said. 'Stanley Russell of Colwell, Fannin County, is not registered as a confidential human resource.'

Landis's surprise was evident.

'You say there's a brother?'

'Yes, that'd be Eugene.'

Webster scanned another page. She turned back to Landis.

'I have to make something completely clear now, Sheriff Landis. The information I am divulging is to be maintained under the strictest confidentiality. This is something I am sharing with you because I have no wish to prevent you from doing your job. However, violation of the trust I am placing in you, as would be the case with any such information, could serve to place individuals in danger, or compromise ongoing investigations elsewhere.'

'I understand you perfectly,' Landis said. 'I am bound by the same law enforcement regulations as you, Lieutenant Webster.'

'Even though this is no longer an active file, what I am telling you does not leave this office, and is not to be shared with anyone, you understand?'

'Absolutely.'

'According to our records, Eugene Russell was an active confidential human resource. The file is no longer active, hence my willingness to divulge this information. Previously, and this is some years ago, he was engaged in reporting the activities of the Aryan Brotherhood in Georgia, North Carolina and Tennessee.'

'And can you tell me who he worked with in the respective Police or Sheriffs' Departments?'

'That I cannot do. One of the primary officers is still on active duty, and thus his name cannot be given.'

'Can you tell me which state the officer worked in?'

'I'm sorry, no.'

'I'm guessin' what you've told me is as much as I'm gonna get.'

Webster smiled; she seemed genuine. 'There's a fine line here, Sheriff Landis. Sometimes some very tough decisions have to be made, as you know. We balance the responsibility of public protection and safety against employing known criminals to expose greater violations of the law. It's the same with under-cover officers. They risk their own lives and the lives of others to obtain information that would otherwise remain unknown to us. Concessions are made, deals are negotiated, but all for the greater good. To an outsider, it seems thoroughly irresponsible to let a dangerous and violent individual walk the streets, but if that individual facilitates the arrest and detention of someone far more dangerous, then the end has to justify the means.'

'I understand completely,' Landis said, 'and I appreciate your confidence. I can assure you that what you've told me will go no further.'

Webster stood up and extended her hand. 'I wish you success in your investigation, Sheriff.'

'Thank you, ma'am.'

43

The night brings counsel.

Perhaps true for some, but for Landis it was not the case.

He wrestled with sleep until two or three, and then he sat in the kitchen with his cigarettes and a glass of milk. He tried to make sense of things that made no sense.

Wasper Russell lived with the possibility that Eugene would discover that he was the one who'd hired Holt Macklin and Kenny Greaves to capsize a drug deal. Macklin then dies in jail, an apparent suicide. All the while, Eugene himself has a history as an informant to someone still on active duty in the Police Department or Sheriff's Office. Landis did not know which city, nor which county. There was always the possibility that it was another state entirely. The Russells had connections not only throughout Georgia, but also Tennessee and both Carolinas. The law had jurisdictions and boundaries – law-breakers did not.

Against this was the fact that Wasper Russell was not regis-tered on that system, and yet Tom Sheehan had told Marshall that Wasper was an informant for Blue Ridge PD.

The system was Police, not Sheriff's Office. It made sense, therefore, that Eugene's contact was in the PD. Eugene's records would be in Blue Ridge, and if George Milstead did not have access to them in the Sheriff's Office, then Landis would have to deal with the police down there. Maybe George knew someone. Maybe George would be able to get what Landis needed without Landis being directly involved.

Leaving home a little after eight on Saturday morning, Landis drove the twenty-five miles west along 76 into Blue Ridge.

George was not in the office, so Landis drove over to his house. George was out in the front yard with some little kids.

'Got my grandkids here,' Milstead said. 'This here's Milly and that one there is Luke. Say howdy, kids.'

The children chimed a welcome in unison. Landis acknowledged them, and then asked Milstead if they could talk in confidence for a moment.

Milstead sent the two little ones off to find their mother.

'I need to get a look at whatever you got on Eugene Russell,' Landis explained.

'I ain't doin' that today, Victor. I see these kids rarely enough as it is. I can get Tom to help you, but you're gonna have to wait on him a while.'

'I can wait,' Landis said.

'Well, come on in the kitchen. You can get a cup of coffee. I'll find out where Tom's at and see how long before he can get back to the office.'

'That's much appreciated, George,' Landis said. He followed Milstead up the porch steps and into the house.

Landis waited an hour.

That hour had been spent not only in the company of George Milstead, but also his daughter and her husband, their two children, and a couple of the neighbor's kids. The neighbor herself – a cheery woman in her early forties called Queenie – came over and sat with Landis for a while. She seemed fascinated by all things law enforcement, said she was just addicted to true-crime documentaries and TV shows about forensics and the like. Landis humored her, answering her many and varied questions in a vague and roundabout way. When she left, she told Landis that it had been a real pleasure to meet him.

Deputy Tom Sheehan was waiting for Landis in the entrance foyer of the building.

'George said you're lookin' up the Russells,' he said.

'Whatever you have, yes.'

'I know Marshall. I spoke to him 'bout Wasper a while back. Wasper knocked some girl about pretty bad. Kids too. We were told to back off on him.'

'By Blue Ridge PD, right?'

'Yeah. They said he was working with them, that he was a valuable resource. Hell, if that lowlife's a valuable resource for anything then I'm the King of Siam.'

'You remember who contacted you from the Police Department?'

'Right now I don't recall. Maybe I made a note of it some-place.'

Landis followed Deputy Sheehan through to his office.

Sheehan left and then returned some minutes later with an armful of files. He set them down on the desk. Separating them in two, he said, 'These here are Eugene's, these are Wasper's.'

'This is everything you have?' Landis asked.

'Sure is. If there's anything else, it'll be with the PD.'

'Okay, good. This is really appreciated.'

'Well, I gotta head out and finish what I started. You take your time. I'll be back in an hour or so. You want some coffee or anything, you go on and ask Marcie out front and she'll take care of it for you.'

*

In studying the files, the thing that struck Landis immediately was that Eugene had never served a single day of confinement in his adult life. There were numerous arrests, indictments, arraignments and the like, but for even the more serious matters he received little more than cautions, fines and good-behavior bonds. The man was blessed, it seemed.

Wasper, as he already knew, wasn't so fortunate. The State three-to-five for robbery was his second strike. One more and he was out for good. Having said that, since his release in May of 1990, there were a total of eleven complaints, four police visits, three from the Sheriff's Office, even two arrests for possession with intent to supply and carrying a concealed weapon. Either one of those should have had him on a fast track back to State, but he seemed to be invisible to the judicial fraternity.

After reading through everything that Tom Sheehan had provided, the only conclusion that Landis could draw was that both Eugene and his kid brother had a guardian angel. Someone was not only keeping an eye on them, but that someone was stepping in and making problems disappear.

Landis went back through each history and made notes of arresting officers. The bulk were from Fannin. There were exchanges between Fannin and Gilmer County, also Murray and as far west as Whitfield and Walker. Eugene had been pulled over for speeding by Willard Montgomery's deputy, Scott Whitman, back in December of 1990. According to the citation, the other occupant of the vehicle was Holt Macklin. He had on him more than an ounce of coke. That was just a month before Wasper got Macklin and Kenny Greaves to mess up Eugene's drug deal. Macklin got shot during that fiasco, survived, but took a fall on the possession. That got him the three to five that commenced in June of '91. Two months later he was found hanged in his cell.

Landis made a note to get hold of Whitman. Had he arrested

Macklin on the drugs charge? If not, who had told him to back off and leave these people alone?

Landis went on reading, cross-referencing dates and locations, checking everything on the yellow sheet, and it was on the third time through that he found a phone memo that he'd previously missed. It was dated February 8, 1982. The note had been taken by the previous deputy in Fannin, Ray Floyd. It said, very simply: *Spoke to FL in Dade. Let this one go.*

Landis stared at the small scrap of paper. Just nine words, and they shifted his entire perspective in a split second. It could only be his brother. That it was a coincidence seemed impossible.

February of '82, Frank in the job little more than a year, and three years before Landis himself took up the same position in Union County.

There was a connection between Frank and the Russells, and though it might have had some credible explanation, Landis could not help but feel that it was a precursor of bad things to come.

Assumptions were not facts, however, and he knew he could not make any accurate judgement of the situation nor what might have happened a decade earlier until he spoke to this Ray Floyd.

44

'Ray is dead,' Tom Sheehan said. 'Killed himself back in early '89.'

'He killed himself?' Landis echoed.

'He sure did. March it was. March 1989. Put his service weapon under his chin and blew his own head off.'

'You knew him?'

'Sure I did,' Sheehan said. 'Knew him well.'

'Why did he kill himself?' Landis asked.

'I think that's a question that's gonna haunt me for the rest of my days, Sheriff Landis.'

Landis leaned back in the chair. 'Jesus,' he said. 'I did not expect that.'

'No one did. Did his job, seemed his usual self, nothing out of the ordinary, and then I wake up to find out that not only is he dead but I'm gonna take his place.'

'He was married? Family?'

'Nope. Never got married, never had kids. Had a regular girl, but she moved back to where she came from.'

'Which was?'

'Trenton, Dade County.'

Again, Landis's surprise was evident in his reaction.

'That's where Ray was from. That's where he grew up. He was deputy in the Sheriff's Office over there a good while before he came here.'

'When did he move here?'

'In '86.'

'And how long was he deputy in Dade?'

'Five years I reckon. I think he did the full five-year term.'

'From '81 to '86.'

'I guess so,' Sheehan said.

'So he was my brother's deputy before Paul Abrams.'

Tom Sheehan looked at Landis. Now it was his turn to be surprised.

'I guess he must've been.'

'Frank became sheriff in January of '81,' Landis said. 'Abrams told me he'd been deputy a little more than five years. From '81 to '86 it must have been Ray Floyd. Then he transferred here, was deputy under George, lasted three years and then he killed himself.'

'That would fit, for sure.'

Landis held out the phone memo. Sheehan read it.

'Spoke to FL in Dade,' Sheehan said. 'That's your brother.'

'Exactly.'

'And who's this about?'

'This is Ray Floyd gettin' word from my brother to leave Eugene Russell alone.'

Sheehan frowned. 'I thought Wasper was the informant.'

'Seems not,' Landis said. 'Or maybe they both were.'

Landis took the memo back. He wondered why George Milstead hadn't mentioned the fact Ray Floyd had been his deputy before Tom Sheehan. Maybe he didn't think it was relevant or important. Maybe, in the drift of things, he'd forgotten. Or maybe he just needed reminding.

It was lunchtime when Landis arrived back at the Milstead house.

Landis guessed that professional courtesy alone prevented Milstead from kicking him off the porch.

'Tom get you what you needed?' Milstead asked.

'He did, yes, but there's a coupla questions I got.'

Milstead couldn't conceal his irritation. 'This can't wait until Monday, Victor?'

'It can, but I don't want it to.'

Milstead sighed resignedly. 'Okay,' he said. 'We're just settin' out our lunch. I'd invite you in but this is a family thing and long overdue. You go on into town and get yourself a cup of coffee and a sandwich or whatever, and you come back here in an hour, okay?'

'Appreciated, George.'

Landis headed back to the car.

'In fact, make it an hour and a half,' Milstead called after him.

Landis raised his hand in acknowledgement without looking back.

45

Landis sat with Milstead on the back veranda.

The grandkids were whooping and hollering indoors. Milstead's daughter, Beth, brought out coffee for both of them.

'You want your cigar, Daddy?' she asked.

'I wouldn't mind one, yes,' Milstead said. 'And bring one out for my friend here.'

Beth returned with cigars and Milstead's lighter.

They sat in silence for a few minutes, and then Milstead asked Landis what was so important that it couldn't wait until after the weekend.

'Back a while,' Landis said, 'you recall I went up to see Eugene Russell?'

'I do indeed. What was that, a month now?'

'A month, yes.'

'Well, less than a week before that I met with a man called Jim Tom Moody up in Murphy, Cherokee County.'

'And what did he have to say for himself?'

'Pretty much the same as Eugene. That Trenton is all tied up in knots, that folks is in each other's pockets, that there's bad business goin' on.'

Milstead didn't respond. He just went on looking to some place beyond the end of the yard.

'Now, I know the sort o' fellers I'm talkin' to, George, but what they said they didn't have no reason to say. I go on diggin' around, and it seems that Wasper Russell is workin' as an informant for the Trenton Police Department. I go on down to Atlanta and he ain't on their system. Things don't add up, which is why I come to you. I went to the office and Tom got all them files together and I went through them. I come to the conclusion that these Russell boys are protected by some miraculous force of nature. They seem to be able to do whatever the heck they please, and they never get so much as a caution. Even found a memo from way back when Ray Floyd was your deputy—'

Milstead turned and looked at Landis. His expression was unreadable.

'Just a few words, it was. Ray Floyd had some business with Eugene Russell, calls up my brother, and my brother says that Ray should leave Eugene well alone.'

Again, a brief silence – Milstead looking, smoking, giving nothing away.

'Makes me curious why you never mentioned the fact that your deputy, the one who killed himself, used to deputy for my brother out in Dade.'

'Because it didn't have nothin' to do with nothin',' Milstead said. 'Back in '86 when Ray come over to me, I thought it was because his girl wanted to be closer to her family. Previous deputy retired, I needed a new one, wanted someone with experience. Ray put his name forward. I met him, he seemed a good man to me, and that was that. First impressions counted for shit in that instance. I got to thinkin' that your brother wanted rid of him and gave him no choice but to find a placement elsewhere. The man was a whole world of trouble. He was a drunk. He gambled, too. Owed money here and there. Got himself in a few scrapes, threw his fists around. By the end, he was just bad news for the office. Fact of the matter is that if he hadn't killed himself, then I would've had to get him canned anyway.'

'This ain't so much about Floyd himself, George. This is about why a Fannin County deputy would be contactin' a Dade County sheriff about someone like Eugene Russell, and what the hell my brother's connection with the Russells was.'

Milstead shook his head. 'The last one I can't help you with. Seems there's three people who could answer that question for you and two o' them are dead. As for Ray Floyd coordinatin' somethin' with your brother, even without their prior connection and professional relationship, it ain't no different from that meetin' we all had up at Barbara Wedlock's house now, is it? People work with people. People talk to people. I don't know what the deal was with Eugene Russell and your brother. I can only assume that your brother needed to keep Eugene sweet for some reason. It wouldn't have been the first time such a thing happened and it sure as hell won't be the last.'

'And the Russells?'

'What about 'em?'

'The Russells are Fannin County. If anyone would know what was goin' on with them, I figured it would be you.'

'You're askin' one question but I'm hearin' another,' Milstead said. 'You wanna ask me if I know somethin' about the Russells that I ain't tellin' you.'

Milstead leaned forward and rolled the ash from his cigar off against the sole of his boot.

'With me, what you see is what you get, Victor. Remember now that it was a month ago that I called you about Eugene Russell. That Rayford girl, the Russells' cousin. Jeanette Rayford came on bendin' my ear about it, sayin' all sorts of whatever that Eugene was gonna do, an' I told you to go make that visit, didn't I? I told you that that girl was one o' their own and they weren't gonna let it lie. Tell me now, if I knew somethin' about the Russells that I wanted to keep from you, why in God's name would I even send you out there?'

'I ain't implyin' nothin', George,' Landis said.

'I ain't sayin' you are. Just because I didn't mention about Ray Floyd bein' your brother's deputy, and just because I don't have the faintest notion what he was doin' lookin' after Eugene, well that don't mean squat. I've been sheriff here for sixteen years. Unless somethin' changes, I intend to go on bein' sheriff until they throw me out on my ear. You seem like a decent man, a good sheriff yourself, and I'm assumin' you're comin' at this down the right road with the intention of findin' the truth. I'd be grateful if you'd afford me the same professional courtesy, Victor. Just because I didn't say somethin' doesn't mean it was kept from you.'

'I apologize if I gave you that impression, George.'

Milstead smiled. He hadn't taken offense.

'Ray Floyd is dead. Your brother, too. I don't know what the hell motivated Ray to kill himself. I also have no idea who killed your brother. The Russells, meantime, are out there in Colwell doin' whatever the hell they do an' I guess they'll keep on doin' it until someone stops 'em.'

Landis was quiet for a time. Everything was vague. He had threads but no pattern. He had nothing to which anything else could be anchored.

'If your lure ain't catchin', go upstream,' Milstead said.

'Trenton PD,' Landis said.

'Them's the folks who're s'posed to be investigatin' your brother's murder, ain't they? You heard from them?'

Landis shook his head. 'Nothin' worth a red cent, no.'

'Gotta say I've no idea why you volunteered the way you did, what with this goin' on. Seems to me you got enough on your plate without three dead teenagers.'

'Maybe I don't want to find out the truth about Frank. Gut tells me it's no good, and I don't want to be proved right.'

'Intuition ain't facts, Victor.'

'I know that, George.'

'Seems to me the burden o' not knowing would be heavier.'

'Yes,' Landis said. 'I guess so.'

46

It was only as he crossed the Blairsville city limits that Landis remembered the dinner invitation.

It was already six, and to turn around and head back the way he'd come, to then have to sit and make small talk with his brother's ex-wife and an eleven-year-old girl, seemed altogether too much.

Once at the office, he called Eleanor to apologize.

'She ain't gonna be happy 'bout this,' Eleanor said.

'I'm real sorry,' Landis said. 'I've been out of county on some business and I just got back. I'll come another time, I promise.'

'Now you really do sound like your brother. Best in the world at makin' promises. Best in the world at breakin' them too.'

There was something about the woman's tone that irritated Landis.

'Look,' he said. 'I didn't make no promise. I said I'd do the best I could. I don't know what you expect of me, Eleanor. I'm doin' my darnedest to keep everyone happy, and sometimes it just don't work out the way I intended. I got a mountain o' work ahead o' me, and I'm tryin' to deal with everythin' all at once.'

'You get any word from Trenton 'bout what happened to Frank?'

'Nothin' yet,' Landis said. 'Did anyone come over and speak with you? Did you get a call from Mike Fredericksen?'

'I ain't heard word from no one,' Eleanor said. 'It's like it didn't ever happen.'

'No one's been in touch with you?'

'Like I said already, I ain't heard nothin' from anyone in Trenton or anyplace else.'

'Okay,' Landis said. 'I'm sorry, but I gotta go, Eleanor. You give my apology to Jenna—'

'Think it best you tell her yourself.'

'Eleanor—'

''Fore you say another word, I ain't obligin' you to be her uncle, but she's a person just like anyone else. I'm not the one you're disappointin' here. Seems to me she deserves to hear your apology direct.'

Eleanor Boyd did not wait for a response.

Landis heard voices, footsteps, and then Jenna was at the other end of the line.

'Mom says you can't come for dinner.'

'That's right, Jenna, and I'm sorry about that. I got a whole mess o' business to take care of.'

'So come tomorrow?'

'Tomorrow?'

'There's a fair.'

'A fair?'

'Sure. You know what a fair is, right?'

'Like a county fair?'

'Yes, 'cept this ain't a county one. This is just a little one, but they got rides and animals and cotton candy an' all that stuff.'

'Jenna, I would love to take you to the fair, but—'

'That's settled then. I'll see you in the morning, Uncle Victor.'

'Jenna, listen to me now—' Landis started, but the girl was already gone.

Eleanor picked up the phone.

'I think I got railroaded,' Landis said. 'Seems I'll be takin' her to the fair tomorrow.'

'Well, that's mighty good of you.'

'I don't think there was a great deal o' choice in the matter, Eleanor.'

'It's only a little thing. She'll get bored after an hour or so.'

'Okay. I'll come over early then. Say ten. I can take her for a couple of hours, an' then I need to get back to work.'

'You ain't gotta feel some sense o' duty here. I get that she's your brother's girl an' all, and whatever happened between you an' him is gonna color everythin'. I just know one thing, however. You keep on lookin' at things the same way, then you ain't never gonna feel different about them, are you?'

Landis had no response for that. She'd hit a nerve, no doubt about it.

'I'll see you both in the morning,' Landis said, and hung up the phone.

Sitting there at his desk, Landis understood that Eleanor's final words didn't only relate to his brother, they also related to his father, his mother, and pretty much everything else in his life.

He still didn't have a hold on the possible connection between Frank and the Russells. He had their word, word from Jim Tom Moody as well, that things were crooked in Trenton. He had Frank's one-time deputy, Ray Floyd, killing himself. He had threads that tied Wasper to Holt Macklin and Kenny Greaves and some kind of stunt with a Eugene Russell drug deal. He had three dead teenagers and nothing of any substance to explain what had happened to them. And there was the matter of a thousand bucks a month finding its way into Eleanor's bank account with no explanation as to where it had come from, nor why it was still being paid. Just for good measure, there was

Mike Fredericksen's veiled threat that he should back the hell off and leave things be.

Rumors, inferences, one person saying one thing, someone else saying something different, it all added up to a weight of nothing, and yet he felt that weight on his shoulders. Someone knew the truth about his brother. Someone knew what had happened to those three girls. People had answers to all of these questions, and he had to find them.

As Milstead had said, there were three people who might have some notion of what had taken place – Eugene Russell, Ray Floyd and his own brother – and two of them were dead.

Landis locked up and went home. He would sleep on it, see if tomorrow brought some other option to the fore. He doubted it. Instinct told him that Fredericksen would keep on singing the same hollow tune.

He would have to visit with Eugene Russell again, and this time he needed to come away with more than empty words.

47

Jenna, dressed up in a party frock, her hair clipped back with barettes, had chattered incessantly throughout the half-hour drive from home to the Trenton Fall Fair. Eleanor had given her a ten-dollar bill, and even though Landis suggested he hold onto it for her, Jenna was having none of it.

'They have snakes,' Jenna told him. 'They did last time anyway.'

'You like snakes?'

'What's not to like?'

'Being bitten, I guess.'

'They keep 'em in a thing,' Jenna said. 'You can see 'em through the glass. No one's gonna get bit.'

'Well, that's a load off right there.'

Jenna laughed. 'Thank you for bringin' me, Uncle Victor.'

'You're welcome, sweetheart.'

'Mom says you should come back and have lunch with us after.'

'That's real kind of her, but I gotta be someplace this afternoon.'

'Sheriffin'?'

'Sheriffin', yes.'

'Did you ever shoot someone, Uncle Victor?'

'Now, what do you wanna talk about that for?'

'I'm interested.'

'I'm gonna plead the Fifth on that.'

'Which means you did. How many?'

Landis laughed. 'Maybe not enough.'

Jenna leaned up and looked out of the window. 'Over there, you see it? Turn right and go down there.'

Landis followed Jenna's directions, and they pulled up ahead of a makeshift barrier. An elderly man in a hi-vis jacket and a Stetson waved them down. Landis lowered the window.

'Two bucks per vehicle,' the old man said. 'And you can park right over there back of those tents.'

Landis paid the money.

Once out of the car, Jenna took Landis's hand and started walking. The crescent of tents had obscured the view of the crowds that had gathered. It was just after ten, but already there were hundreds of people present. Food stands heaved with pickles, dried meats and preserves; a hot-dog franchise had attracted a queue a good thirty feet long; there was face-painting, a troupe of jugglers, a fellow on stilts dressed like Abraham Lincoln, a young woman dressed like a clown with such a host of balloons that it seemed to take all her concentration not to leave the ground. Jenna knew where she was headed. She dragged Landis by his hand at such speed that he had to jog to keep up.

Far to the right was a marquee, over the entrance of which a banner read *WILD AND WONDERFUL*.

Reaching it, Jenna made a beeline for the entrance booth. She held out her ten-dollar bill, and just as the young man in the booth was about to take it, Landis stayed her hand.

'I'm paying,' Landis said. 'You go on and keep that for yourself.'

The young man smiled. 'Seven bucks-fifty,' he said.

'So what we got here?' Landis asked.

'Snakes!' Jenna chimed. 'Like I told you.'

Landis paid up. Jenna led the way.

Landis had to admit that the presentation within was impressive. Sawdust covered the ground, and every which way he looked there was one glass case after another. There must have been two dozen or more displays in there, and snakes were not the only things on offer. Aside from the Western diamondbacks, corals, copperheads, coachwhips, massasaugas and Mojave rattlers, there were tarantulas, brown recluses, red, brown, and grey widows, Arizona bark scorpions, wheel bugs, velvet ants, and buck moth and saddleback caterpillars.

Jenna was transfixed by the deadly collection. She stood and stared as a cottonmouth unraveled itself and brought its face so very close to the glass, its tongue flickering for scent. Seemingly unfazed, she pressed the tip of her finger against the glass. Landis, instinctively, reached out to discourage her, but Jenna merely turned and smiled at him.

'He can't get out,' she said.

'You do realize how dangerous these things are, right?'

'Don't worry, I'm not plannin' on takin' one home, Uncle Victor. Besides, if he got out you could just shoot him.'

'Yeah, I guess so. Oh, aside from not havin' a gun, and the fact that tryin' to nail a fleeing snake with a handgun in a crowded tent might not be the best of ideas.'

Jenna reached out and took Landis's hand.

'Come on,' she said. 'Don't be scared. Put your hand on the glass.'

Landis kneeled down beside her. He looked at the snake. The snake looked right back at him. Raising his hand slowly, he touched the cool surface of the tank. The snake, inquisitive, moved slowly. There was an unearthly grace to the thing. Its head was no more than two inches from Landis's fingers.

'He's smiling,' Jenna said. 'You got yourself a new friend.'

Landis stood up. 'Okay, let's check out some of these other creatures, and then we can get hot dogs.'

*

Jenna did the full tour, asked questions of one of the presentation staff, and Landis watched her silently. She wanted to know everything, and every answer she got prompted yet another question. It was a good hour before they were done, and Landis headed out to join the hot-dog queue.

'I want to get my face painted like a butterfly,' Jenna said. 'Over there.'

'Run go find out how much it costs.'

Jenna was back within a minute. 'Three dollars.'

Landis gave her a five. 'You go on and do that. I'll stay here in the queue. What do you want?'

'Whatever you have is fine,' she said, and ran off.

Keeping an eye on her as she waited for her turn to get painted, Landis wondered if his brother had brought her here. More than likely, he guessed. He wasn't going to ask her. Eleanor had made a point of telling him how good a father Frank had been. And now that duty had fallen to him, though it did not feel a duty at all. He had resisted it yesterday, but now he was here he understood that for this brief moment he could forget about Frank, about Fredericksen, about the Russells and the three dead girls that had so consumed his thoughts.

Reaching the head of the queue, Landis ordered two dogs with everything, also fries and sodas. There was a seating area back of the stand. He carried the food over and set it down.

Glancing at a woman on an adjacent table, he said, 'I'm just gonna go get my kid. Keep an eye for me, would you?'

The woman smiled. 'Make it quick,' she said, 'or I'm gonna eat all of that myself.'

Landis went back around the front of the stand to call Jenna over.

Failing to see her, he walked over there. There was still a queue of children, but Jenna was not amongst them.

Catching the attention of the artist, he asked after her.

'Yay high,' he said. 'Blue party frock, barettes, wanted her face done like a butterfly.'

The artist, a middle-aged man with a goatee and a baseball cap, shook his head.

Landis turned back towards the hot-dog queue. Heading back to the hot-dog stand to see if she'd changed her mind and come to eat first, he scoured the crowds as he went. There were more people than ever. The tension that filled his chest was not unknown to him, but now it possessed an unfamiliar edge, something sharp and intense. He felt the panic rising in his throat.

'Jenna?' he called out. 'Jenna, where are you?'

People looked at him.

'Jenna! Jenna!'

Back where he'd set down the food, he gave Jenna's description to the woman, asked if she'd seen her.

'She ain't been here,' the woman said. 'I'd have seen her if she did.'

Back to the stand, back to the face-painting queue, and then Landis was elbowing his way through the throng to reach the snake tent once more.

There was no sign of her.

'Jenna! Jenna, where are you?'

His heart swelled in his chest. The sense of panic rose like a wave. His mind was crowded with unwanted thoughts, each one more fearful than the last.

'Jenna! Jenna!'

The emotion Landis felt as she ran towards him was unlike anything he'd experienced before. She was smiling, something held tight in her hand, but he was so relieved he just swept her up and pulled her tight.

'Oh, for Christ's sake, Jenna, you gave me a fright.' Setting her down, he held her firmly by the shoulders. 'What on earth were you thinkin'?'

For a moment she seemed surprised, and then there were tears in her eyes. Landis realised how hard he was gripping her. He let go, pulled her tight and hugged her once more.

'I'm sorry,' he said, 'but I didn't see you. I couldn't find you anywhere. Where did you go to?'

Jenna looked up at Landis. She blinked. A single tear rolled down her cheek.

She held out her hand. In it was a leather key fob, the center of which was a small medallion with the letter V.

'I wanted to get you this,' she said. 'So you'd remember bringing me here.'

Landis went down on his knee. He took the fob from her.

'For your keys,' she said.

'I know, sweetheart. And that is so very kind of you.'

'I'm sorry for going,' she said. 'But I wanted it to be a surprise.'

'The best one,' Landis said.

With that Jenna reached up and put her arms around Landis's shoulders.

Holding her tight against him, he felt his heart slow down. The relief was extraordinary.

'Did you get hot dogs?' Jenna asked.

'I did, but I guess they're cold now.'

'That don't matter.'

'Okay, let's go see if the woman who's lookin' after them already ate them.'

On the drive back into Trenton, Jenna – her face painted in swirls of blue and yellow – talked about little else but wolf spiders and Eastern racer snakes. Everything was interesting and everything was important. Her curiosity and excitement was near contagious. By the time he was walking her through the front door and back into the care of her mother, Landis was already looking forward to the next time he would see her.

'Thank you for taking me,' Jenna told him.

'It was fun,' he said. 'We should go other places.'

She put her arms out and he hugged her.

'You're not stayin' for lunch?' Eleanor asked.

'He's got sheriffin' stuff,' Jenna said. 'Probably gotta go shoot some folks.'

'I'm sure he ain't doin' nothin' of the sort, young lady,' Eleanor said.

Landis bade his farewells and headed out. Colwell was east a half-hour or so, and in the same direction as home.

48

What Landis was doing went against the grain, no question about it. He was heading out to speak with a man who more than likely should have been the subject of an investigation, but now seemed to be the only person who could help him find the truth of what had happened to Frank. There was a knot here, but he could not find the strand that would start to unravel it.

Landis pulled over to the side of the road a little way down from the Russell house. He went the rest of the way on foot.

Russell's wife, Ledda, was out on the porch when Landis turned down the path.

Landis recalled the trip he'd made to see Paul Abrams in Trenton. In much the same way, Landis had the impression that Ledda was also not surprised to see him.

Landis took off his hat.

'You come with news on the Rayford girl?' Ledda asked.

'No, ma'am. I come lookin' to speak with your husband.'

'He said you'd be back.'

'He here?'

'Eugene's always here, or he ain't far away. More an' likely he's in the smoke shed messin' with them sauces and whatnot. You come on up and I'll hunt him out.'

Landis took a seat on the porch. He smoked a cigarette, and then a second. He tried to convince himself that he was pursuing the only realistic option, but whichever way he viewed it, his actions seemed ill-advised.

It was a good twenty minutes before Eugene Russell came out through the front door of the house.

'Ledda tells me you ain't no further on what happened to Ella May.'

Landis got up.

'Oh, you stay right where you are, Sheriff,' Russell said. 'You don't need to be polite on my account.'

'I got no further since we last spoke,' Landis said.

'That'd be a month now.'

'Yes.'

'And you ain't no clearer on what happened to your brother neither, I'm guessin'.'

'Same story,' Landis said.

Russell sat down on the opposite side of the front door.

Before he could speak, Ledda appeared.

'Gettin' airish now,' she said. 'You boys comin' in or stayin' out?'

'We're just fine where we are, sweetheart.'

'You want somethin' to drink?'

'Not right now,' Russell said.

Ledda went back inside. She closed the door behind her.

'You come on out here 'cause you think I can help you. Is that it?'

'I think you know more than you told me,' Landis said.

'And what is it that you think I know, Sheriff?'

'Maybe you got an idea what happened to my brother. Maybe you know why Trenton don't seem to be doin' nothin' about it.'

Russell looked out towards the road. Landis had the impression of a man weighing up his words before he spoke them.

'And what's gonna come of me tryin' to help you?' Russell finally asked.

'I guess that depends on what you want, Eugene. Second, if I'm willin' to give it.'

Again there was a long pause before Russell spoke.

'Man has a right to what's his. Don't matter a damn who he is. Man works for somethin', he has a right to it. It's a fundamental thing we're talkin' about here. I ain't no thief. Never have been, never will be. Goes against my nature. Now, takin' into account the fact that I been engaged in some ventures that ain't strictly legal, I've had to associate with some folks who don't see things the way I do.'

Russell looked at Landis.

'Someone took somethin' from you,' Landis said.

'Someone took somethin' from me.'

'And you want it back.'

Russell smiled. 'Hell, it ain't so straightforward as that no more, Sheriff.'

'So what are you askin' of me?'

'I'm askin' that you leave me out of this. Wasper too. Them Rayfords as well. Anyone that's family, I want them left out of this.'

Landis didn't understand. Rather than say he didn't, he waited for Russell to say more.

'This all goes back years, Sheriff. More years 'an you been sheriff over in Union. This thing is in the weave of everythin'. Anyplace you dig, you're gonna find the same people doin' the same things, and if it ain't them it's their kin.'

'Tell me what you know, Eugene.'

'Tellin' you what I know would take the rest of today and all o' tomorrow. Even if I did, what's it worth, eh? Just one crazy feller spouting his mouth off about nothin' he can prove. You want to find the truth, you gotta do the lookin'. You gotta find your own way through this thing. But I tell you now, this ain't gonna be a joyride for you or your kin.'

'My kin?'

'You got family now, Sheriff. You got that little girl out in Trenton, ain'tcha?'

'You're sayin' that if I start diggin' into what really happened to my brother, then his daughter could be in danger?'

Russell didn't answer. He took a pipe from the pocket of his jacket. He spent a while fussing with it and getting it going.

'You think you're lookin' at two different things here,' Russell said. 'You got what happened to your brother and you got little Ella May, too. I heard word that y'all had a meetin' out in Blairsville. All the sheriffs from five different counties.'

'How did you hear that?'

'Me? I got ears like a bat.' Russell smiled. 'How I heard ain't important. What is important is that you missed out a county. Someone from Dade shoulda been there.'

'Maybe I'm gettin' the drift of this all wrong, but seems you're tellin' me that Frank's death is tied in with what happened to Ella May.'

'I didn't say that.'

'And if Ella May is connected to this, then them other two girls is as well.'

Russell turned to Landis, and through a haze of pipe smoke he said, 'You're being short-sighted, Sheriff Landis. You're seein' what's right in front of you. You ain't lookin' no further.'

'There's more?'

Again, Russell said nothing.

'How many?' Landis asked.

'You're missin' the point, Sheriff. Sometimes you get so busy lookin' at one thing that you don't see somethin' else.'

'But there's been more girls killed than just these three?'

'That ain't the question to be askin'.'

'So what question should I be askin'?'

'I guess I'd be less interested in what happened, more in how come you seem to be all on your lonesome in tryin' to figure it out.'

'Was my brother killed because he was investigatin' what happened to these girls?'

Eugene paused. His silence – though brief – seemed purposeful. 'You know, I figured you'd come on back,' Russell finally said. 'And so I thought about what I wanted to tell you and what I didn't. That's done now. I said my piece. What you go on and do with that is up to you, but you leave me and my family out of it. That's the deal here. I hear otherwise then you and I gonna have a problem, you understand?'

'I understand.'

'An' if I hear you're lookin' for me, then I'll be gone. Same goes for Wasper.'

Landis nodded, but said nothing.

'Well, I got things to do now. I don't expect to see you up here again unless you got news on Ella May.'

Russell got up. Landis followed suit.

'Blood binds folk that maybe shouldn't be bound,' Russell said. 'Me an' Wasper. You and your brother. You don't get to choose your kin. Sometimes they do the dumbest, craziest things, but that don't change nothin'. They're still yours, and you got a responsibility for them. And it don't matter how far you run, you're gonna stay tethered 'til you're both dead.'

'This is somethin' I'm beginnin' to understand,' Landis said.

Russell looked at Landis directly, his gaze unerring and implacable. Without another word, he turned and went inside.

49

Plagued by the feeling that Eugene Russell had not only implied a threat to Jenna, at the same time giving him nothing of any actual substance, Landis went back to Trenton.

Abrams hadn't come back to him with anything on Eleanor Boyd's money. That now seemed a minor detail in comparison to the possibility that the dead teenagers and Frank's murder might have some connection. This was something that he'd never even considered, for there had been nothing to suggest any relationship between them.

The reaction on Abrams' face when he saw Landis on the porch was one of immediate and significant concern.

Opening the door, he said, 'What are you doing here?'

He glanced left and right as if looking for something or someone out in the street.

'If this is a bad time …' Landis started.

Abrams opened the door. 'Come in,' he said, and gestured for Landis to be quick about it.

Landis did as he was asked. Abrams closed the front door behind him, and then, equally hurriedly, indicated that Landis should follow him.

Abrams took him to the den, told him to wait for a moment.

Returning within a few minutes, Abrams once again asked what Landis was doing there.

Landis could see the man was anxious, so much more pronounced than the last time they'd spoken.

'You seem troubled, Deputy,' Landis said.

'They took everything,' Abrams said. 'Every damned thing he was workin' on. Every file, every document, even the computer off of his desk.'

'What are you talkin' about?'

'Frank's office. I was out on a call. They came on in, flashed some IDs, took everything.'

'Who did they speak to?'

'My dispatcher. Hell, she didn't know what to do. She called me but I didn't get back to her until after they'd left.'

'They tell her where they were from?'

'Trenton PD. They said they had authority to take everythin', that it was standard procedure when it came to the murder of someone in law enforcement.'

'When did this happen?'

'Wednesday. Just a coupla days after I saw you.'

'Did she get their names, see any paperwork?'

Abrams shook his head. 'They just ran roughshod over her. She said there were three or four of them. Showed up out of nowhere. Came in, packed everythin' in boxes, loaded it up and off they went.'

'Under whose authority?'

'Damned if I know, Sheriff. They just told her to stay out of it. They said they'd be takin' care of everythin' from that point forward.'

'And so you haven't pursued the money that's still goin' to Frank's ex-wife?'

'I ain't pursued nothin'. I'm sorry, but they sure as hell seemed very clear about leavin' anythin' to do with Frank well alone.'

'And they took everything?' Landis asked.

'Every damned thing.'

Landis sat back and thought for a moment. Abrams was clearly shaken. Maybe that had been the intended effect.

'So, I need to ask you some things and I understand that you've been told not to discuss this, but it's real important.'

'I don't want to get involved,' Abrams said.

'You already are,' Landis said. 'Far as anyone knows, I ain't here. I never came here, and I will deny that I spoke with you.'

Abrams didn't respond.

'Can you tell me anythin' about what Frank was workin' on, Paul? Anythin' at all?'

'Look, Sheriff Landis, I'd like to help you, but—'

'You said he was a good man, that he took care of you,' Landis said. 'He got himself killed, and it seems to me that there's been no forward progress on that in more than a month. You owe it to him and so do I. Someone has to get this thing figured out. If we don't, then we gotta ask ourselves why the hell we're even doin' this job?'

Abrams' body language spoke volumes. He really had been rattled.

'There were disappearances,' Abrams said cautiously. 'A coupla girls vanished without a trace. I think one o' them came from Tennessee, though I can't be sure.'

'Tennessee? Is that why he was headed up there?'

'I'm tellin' you everythin' I know, Sheriff, and I feel like I shouldn't even be sayin' this much. He didn't talk to me about it, but I figured he was pretty obsessed with it. Who they were, when they vanished, what happened to them, I don't know. I really don't know.'

'Can you remember any names?'

Abrams thought for a while, and then shook his head.

'Is there anythin' else at all that he might have said, anythin' you overheard, any indication he gave you about what this was about?'

'Only thing I can remember was somethin' real strange. I didn't know what he meant, and I can't make any sense of it now, but it was about how they was volunteers.'

'Volunteers?'

'I don't know what that means, and maybe I didn't hear him right, but that's what I thought he said.'

'The girls that disappeared were volunteers.'

'That's what I made of it.'

'Volunteers for what?'

'I don't know, Sheriff. Like I said, it was just a comment, and I didn't pay much mind to it. Like I said, I could've misheard him.'

'Anythin' else you can think of?'

Abrams didn't wait to respond. His negative response was almost reflexive.

'Now, really, I would prefer it if you would go,' he added. 'I really don't want to get dragged into whatever this is. I gotta take care of my family, you understand.'

'I do, of course,' Landis said. He got up to leave.

'And you didn't hear any o' this from me, okay?'

'You have my word,' Landis replied.

It was halfway back to Blairsville that Landis remembered Ed Lacey's comment about Sara-Louise. He'd mentioned it in passing, and at the time Landis had thought nothing of it, but in light of his conversation with Abrams it now came back to him.

Lacey had described his daughter as kind, gentle and considerate, that she was conscientious in her studies. He'd also said that she did volunteer work.

50

It was mid-afternoon on Monday before Landis managed to reach Ed Lacey by telephone.

'I've been at work,' Lacey explained, 'and my wife has gone up to see her sister for a few days. Just to change the scenery, you know? All those months hopin' and waitin', and now this. We made a start on goin' through her things and Marion ... well, she was troubled so bad ...'

Lacey left the statement hanging in the air.

'I can only imagine, Mr Lacey,' Landis said.

'And the worst thing by far is knowin' she was alive for so long after she went missin'.'

Landis had no idea how to respond, so he said nothing.

'So, what can I help you with, Sheriff?' Lacey asked.

'You made a comment about Sara-Louise doin' some volunteer work. Is that right?'

'Oh sure, she did a whole bunch.'

'What was she involved in?'

'Hell, I don't know. She did things at the church with the little kids on a Sunday afternoon. She did food drives for down-an'-outs at Christmas. She baked with her mother for the town gala. An' she was a YRV girl, of course.'

Landis frowned. 'A YRV girl? I'm sorry, I—'

'Georgia Young Republican Volunteers. It's a thing she was interested in. I mean, we ain't a political family, if you know what I mean. We have our views, but we ain't standard bearers. Sara-Louise was a good deal more interested than us. Lord knows where she got it from. Anyways, it's a volunteer group for kids. Didn't cost nothin', and it was a way for her to meet and make friends of the same age and interests.'

'And this is somethin' that's all over the state?'

'Far as I know, yes. To be honest, I didn't pay much mind to it. They had get-togethers every once in a while. I'd drive her over to Clayton, one time down to Tallulah Falls for a campin' weekend.'

'And is there anything else you can think of that she did?'

Lacey was quiet for a moment, and then said, 'That's pretty much it, Sheriff. I mean, she was sixteen—'

Landis heard the hitch in Lacey's voice.

'Sixteen when she went missin'. She'd be seventeen now. Th-that's just...'

Landis waited silently as Lacey stifled his tears and caught his breath.

'I'm sorry, Sheriff...'

'Mr Lacey, you have no need to apologize to me. I'm sorry I have to make these calls, but the more we know about what she did and the people she knew, the better we'll get to grips with what happened.'

'Of course, Sheriff, and it's reassurin' to know that someone is doin' somethin' about it. Person who does this kind of thing ain't gonna stop, are they?'

'Not until someone stops 'em, no.'

'Well, I best let you get on with your work. I'm sorry I couldn't be more help.'

'You've been a good deal o' help, Mr Lacey. You take care now, and give my regards to your wife when she gets home again.'

'I surely will,' Lacey said, and hung up the phone.

*

Landis radioed Marshall and told him to come into the office as soon as he could.

Marshall was not far, and arrived within fifteen minutes.

'Marshall, take a seat,' Landis said. 'I wanted to ask you about Linda Bishop.'

'It's all in the report, Sheriff.'

'Yes, I know. I read it. There's one thing I want to find out, and seein' as how you went out there, I want you to call 'em and ask.'

'What do you need to know?'

'If she was involved in any volunteer activities. Church, community, this kind of thing.'

'I can do that. You want me to call 'em now?'

'I do, yes.'

Landis fetched Linda Bishop's file for the number and gave up his chair for Marshall.

Ten minutes later, Landis had the answer he was after. Just as was the case with Sara-Louise Lacey, Linda had been involved with this YRV group. Not for some time, but she'd been to meetings, a couple of camping weekends and the like.

Landis took his seat again.

'This is a link we haven't previously had,' he told Marshall.

'I ain't never heard o' this thing.'

'Well, you gotta get me all the info you can on it, Marshall,' Landis said. 'What's its purpose, how long has it been goin' on for, what they do. Whatever you can find.'

'Sure thing, Sheriff.'

Marshall got up to leave.

'And be discreet, Marshall,' Landis said. 'You go on up to the library or wherever, go out of uniform. Anyone asks, this is a personal interest, not somethin' official.'

'Can I ask why we're keepin' quiet on it?'

'Just in case we're diggin' holes where somethin' is buried,' Landis said.

Marshall left a little after three.

Landis wanted to speak to Vester or Jeanette Rayford. If Ella May was also part of this Young Republican group, then he had an avenue of investigation to pursue. If not, then he would pursue it anyway, but with a view to looking for something else that might have connected the three girls. He assumed nothing. It was a thin thread, and pulling at it might serve no purpose but to break it.

51

The death of Kenny Greaves was a warning. At least, that's the way Landis took it. He also figured it could only have come from Eugene or Wasper Russell.

George Milstead had told Landis that Greaves was on a short leash. *I send word that I need to speak with him, he ain't gonna do anythin' but show up.* Those had been Milstead's exact words.

Greaves had gotten himself out of Milstead's holding cell by giving up Wasper as Frank's informant. That alone should have been reason enough for Landis to go talk to the man. He'd had every intention of doing so, but had gone to see Eugene first. Now it was too late. That leash of Milstead's was too long, and someone snatched him right off the end.

Much the same as Wasper, Kenny Greaves had been a traveller. Though officially resident in Epworth, he seemed to have spent very little of his time there. Draw a straight line southwest between McCaysville and Colwell, you'd find Epworth right in the middle. However, this was neither where he was killed, nor where his body was found in the early hours of Tuesday, October 6.

Landis was still trying to track down the Rayfords to ask them about Ella May's potential connection to the Georgia Young Republicans. They were incommunicado for some unknown reason. He was all set to call Milstead, perhaps ask him to send Tom Sheehan up to McCaysville to hammer on their door. Milstead called him first, and the news could not have been more unexpected.

'Someone got to Kenny Greaves,' Milstead said.

'Got to him?'

'He's dead, Victor. Got his throat cut someplace. They put him in the trunk of his own car and drove it out along the Jacks River. I got Blue Ridge PD Forensics up there as we speak. First indication is that the thing was wiped clean as clean, but we're hopin' it'll give up somethin'.'

Landis sat down heavily.

'The Russells,' Landis said. 'It has to be.'

'Lord only knows, Victor. These people are on the edge of so many things. They get themselves connected to a whole host o' messes. The people they associate with ain't the fellers in the white hats. Coulda been the Russells, but just as likely coulda been people from out of state, people we ain't never even heard of.'

'So we wait, I guess. See if your people find anythin' that can point us in some kinda direction.'

'As it stands, there ain't a great deal else we can do. I'll keep you posted, Victor.'

Landis hung up the phone.

He asked Barbara to come through.

'Need you to keep tryin' the Rayfords for me,' he told her. 'Need to know if their daughter was engaged in any voluntary activities. Church groups, clubs, school things. Anything she was a member of, any weekends away, any camps she went to and the like.'

'Sure thing, Sheriff. You in or out this afternoon?'

'Out for a while. Gonna go take a drive, get my head straight. Too many things happenin' too fast and none of them make any sense to me.'

'Well, if I get anywheres on this I'll radio you,' Barbara said.

'An' I got Marshall out lookin' up a whole bunch o' things for me. Let me know if he comes back to the office.'

Landis took his car and headed out of Blairsville.

He went northwest to Nottely Lake, parked on the road right where Ella May Rayford's body had come ashore. He opened the door, and sat sideways, his boots on the ground, his line of sight down to the water's edge. He remembered the struggle he and Jeff Nelson had in getting that stretcher up the incline. He remembered the swollen body of that poor girl. He remembered having to tell her parents that their child was dead.

It was true, of course. Didn't matter who you were, we all got buried in the same dirt. But how you wound up dead mattered a great deal. His own brother run down time and again, his body broken, his desperate efforts to move even when the pain must have been beyond understanding. Three dead girls – abducted, drugged, bound, then suffocated or beaten to death. Kenny Greaves, his throat cut, his life abruptly at an end.

The last highway. That was something you would never know. Where it would start and how it would end.

Landis lit a cigarette. He leaned forward, his elbows on his knees, and he closed his eyes.

Reconciling himself to the possibility that Frank had been involved in something bad seemed to be right at the heart of this spider's web of seemingly unrelated occurrences. Right from the get-go, the implications and inferences had been there – from Jim Tom Moody, from Eugene Russell, and then the fact that Ray Floyd, Frank's deputy, had committed suicide was yet another red flag to Landis.

And then there was Fredericksen. Not only had he made no progress, he was sorely averse to Landis taking any kind of interest in what had happened to Frank. The man was all-too-quick to tell everyone that he was doing his job, that he had it in hand, but as far as this was concerned, he wasn't even showing up to work. A man never does nothing. A man is always doing something. Just because you can't see it doesn't mean it's not happening.

And now Landis had this Young Republicans thing. That had only come to light as a result of Paul Abrams' recollection about something Frank had said. The fact that he'd said it at all was due to an investigation he was involved in, all the files and records of which had been removed from his office by Trenton PD.

It all came back to Trenton. That was where Frank was based, and Dade was where he was killed. He'd been going on into Tennessee, or maybe meeting someone coming down. Who, and why? How his actions – whatever their intent – had then warranted his murder was yet another mystery.

The radio went off in the car. Landis turned and unhooked the handset.

'Sheriff, I got George Milstead after you. Says best you go on over there.'

'Okay, Barbara,' Landis said. 'Call him back. Tell him I'm on the way.'

Landis ground out the cigarette butt in the ashtray and started the engine. He swung around and headed for Blue Ridge.

He was ill at ease. He sensed the answers he was seeking were those he was most unwilling to hear.

52

The photographs of Kenny Greaves' body in the trunk of his own car were laid out on George Milstead's desk at the Fannin County Sheriff's Office. They were brutal and unforgiving.

Landis believed he had a strong stomach, but the gaping wound in Greaves' throat went almost bone-deep. He had been dead for some time before he went in the trunk. The blood that caked his clothes was dried hard and black, and there were no traces on the interior of the trunk.

'The car's clean,' Milstead said. 'Whoever did that knew what they were doin'.'

Landis sat down. He breathed deeply.

'You know, the thing that still nags at me is this whole drug deal thing with Eugene Russell,' Landis said. 'I get that Macklin and Greaves were sent to make a mess of it, but it don't seem possible that Eugene wouldn't then find out that Wasper was behind it. Macklin hangs in his cell in ... when was it?'

'August of last year,' Milstead said.

'And now we got Kenny Greaves with his head damned near cut off.'

'You think Eugene had 'em both killed?'

'That's my gut,' Landis said. 'But the thing that don't make sense is how Eugene doesn't know Wasper was behind it. You said that Eugene'd have no issue with killin' Wasper if he thought he was workin' with us. Maybe Wasper wasn't involved at all. Maybe it was just Macklin and Greaves, and that's why they're both dead.'

'Okay, so let's look at it from a different angle,' Milstead said. 'Maybe Eugene wanted the drug deal messed up and he told Wasper to hire Macklin and Greaves to do it.'

'Why would someone want their own drug deal blown?'

Milstead shrugged his shoulders. 'These people don't do things the way we do 'em, and they sure as hell don't think the same way. Maybe it was someone else's shipment. Get it stolen by these guys, and then you get to sell it without ever payin' for it in the first place.'

'Which opens up the possibility that either Wasper or Eugene gave these guys up as the ones who stole it, and they were never directly involved in the killings.'

'Who the heck knows, Victor. Like I said, these people think different from regular folks.'

'Is there anything else from the car?'

'They're goin' through it now. Told me they'd have everythin' done by close o' business today.'

'You mind if I wait?' Landis asked.

'Be glad of the company,' Milstead said. 'I'll get some coffee. You make yourself at home.'

In Milstead's absence, Landis struggled to string a line between the many different aspects of what he was dealing with. He kept coming back to Frank's connection to Eugene Russell, the nature of their relationship, whether they'd been complicit in something. To Landis, it seemed almost certain that this was the case. It also seemed certain that Fredericksen was involved. If not, why was no effort being made to find the truth of Frank's death, and why had every case that Frank was working on now been confiscated by Trenton PD? Sure, both PD and Sheriff's

Office worked in tandem, but – at least in theory – the Sheriff's Office was the senior law enforcement unit.

Answers had to exist in those files and documents. If they were damning, then perhaps they had already been destroyed. Then again, there was another possibility altogether. If Frank's involvement was potentially compromising for others, then maybe the seizure of existing case files from the Dade County Sheriff's Office had been nothing more than a smokescreen, a means by which any evidence could be removed.

Again, based on little more than his sense for people, Landis didn't doubt that Mike Fredericksen knew a great deal more than he was telling. Mike Fredericksen, whether he admitted it or not, was right in the middle of this thing.

Milstead returned with coffee.

'You know Mike Fredericksen over in Trenton PD?' Landis asked.

Milstead shook his head. 'Can't say I do. Why?'

'My line keeps snaggin' on him. Somethin' about the man ain't right. He's the one s'posed to be figurin' out who killed Frank. Not a word from him since it happened. Last thing was Trenton PD had every ongoing case picked up from my brother's office, and I'd put money on Fredericksen bein' the one who done it.'

'When the hell does PD have authority over us?' Milstead asked.

'Exactly.'

'This is a whole mess you're dealin' with, Victor.'

Landis didn't reply. He was already looking at how to get under Mike Fredericksen's skin.

The phone rang on Milstead's desk. Milstead picked it up.

A handful of words were exchanged, and then Milstead nodded at Landis.

'Something in Greaves' car we need to see. They got it over at the pound.'

It made no sense to travel separately, so Landis rode in Milstead's car.

They stopped at lights. Landis looked out at the people on the sidewalk. A thousand different stories walked by, and those stories changed every time they were told. Life was anything but straight lines. Sometimes things got so twisted up there was no way to untwist them. Bad memories had a way of shifting over time, as if the mind found a means by which they could be accommodated. No one ever really recovered from the past; they just found a way out of it with as little damage as possible. And things were never really forgotten either. People just chose not to remember.

Out of nowhere, Milstead asked about Frank. Landis was caught off-guard.

'Ain't nothin' I can say that's gonna make a great deal o' sense,' Landis said.

'There must've been somethin' specific to put such a divide between you. I mean, hell, it ain't none o' my business, but ... well, I got a curious nature.'

'Sometimes you find things out,' Landis said, 'and there ain't no way to forget them. Ain't no way to forgive neither.'

'I guess that's family,' Milstead replied. 'Me, I'm fortunate in that way. We have our differences, sure, but they work themselves out in the run o' things.'

'Maybe me and Frank would've figured a way through, you know? Can't see how, and now it's too late.'

'I got a brother. Two sisters as well. Don't know how I'd feel if one o' them got murdered.'

'Let's hope you never find out.'

'Amen to that, Victor. Amen to that.'

A crime-scene analyst from Blue Ridge PD met Landis and Milstead in the front office.

'This is Bob Natchwey,' Milstead said.

Landis and Natchwey shook hands.

'Come on through,' Natchwey said. 'I got a bunch o' things here that you need to take a look at.'

They followed Natchwey out through a door at the rear of the office and down a corridor. Left and right were car bays, various vehicles jacked up above inspection pits. Men in overalls shone lights, other men took notes. There was the intermittent glare of flashguns that lent the scene a surreal quality.

At the far end of the bay, a series of tables were positioned in a parallel sequence. Each one held a collection of objects – clothing, shoes, tools, torches, gas canisters, the various and assorted things people stowed in their cars.

On the table that Natchwey indicated, the assortment was of a very different nature. Here Landis and Milstead were shown coils of rope, a hessian bag, cable ties, a pair of heavy-duty bolt cutters, a shovel. To the right in a clear Perspex tray was a small labeled bottle and a packet of hypodermic syringes.

Milstead looked over the items and turned to Landis.

'What is that?' Landis asked, indicating the bottle.

'Thiopental,' Natchwey said. 'A sedative. Powerful enough. Fast, but short-acting. Gets used for minor surgeries, sometimes alongside other anaesthetics.'

'Difficult to obtain?' Milstead asked.

Natchwey shrugged. 'Guess that depends on how you obtain it.'

'Everything you'd need to abduct someone,' Landis said.

'That was my take,' Natchwey said. 'Hence my callin' you over to take a look.'

'Anything else we need to see?' Milstead asked.

'I got an address,' Natchwey said. 'Most o' one, anyways.'

Taking a baggie from the end of the table, Natchwey passed it to Milstead. Inside the bag was a corner of torn newsprint; on it was scrawled *1225 Oakwood*.

'Oh hell,' Milstead said.

'That's the Rayford place, right?' Landis asked.

'Yep.'

'I was tryin' to track 'em down,' Landis said. 'Somethin' I come across yesterday I wanted to ask them about.'

'In relation to the girl?'

'Yes. Something that might link all three of them together.'

'No time like the present,' Milstead said. 'Let's head over there now.'

Milstead turned to Natchwey. 'Want you to make this a priority. This may be connected to the abduction and murder of a McCaysville teenager. Call over to the office, tell Tom Sheehan to get you everything we have on file about Ella May Rayford. I need you to go through this and find anything – hair, blood, semen, anything at all – that might put that girl in this car.'

Natchwey said he would get onto it immediately, and then showed the two sheriffs out of the building.

Once in the car, Milstead voiced the question that was at the forefront of Landis's mind.

'You think Kenny Greaves did all three?'

'I'm assumin' nothin',' Landis said. 'Still circumstantial. I'm hopin' that forensics comes back with somethin' probative. If that girl was in that vehicle, then Greaves becomes the prime murder suspect, sure. Beyond that, we need to speak to Rayford.'

'What was the question you had for him?'

Landis relayed what Paul Abrams had told him over in Trenton. He explained the possible connection to the Georgia Young Republicans group.

'Can't say I ever heard o' them,' Milstead said.

'I got my deputy diggin' up whatever he can,' Landis replied.

Once outside of the Blue Ridge city limits, it was little more than ten miles north to McCaysville.

Though the journey took no more than a quarter hour, neither man said another word for the duration.

53

Little more than a month had passed since Landis and Milstead had been in this very place.

Jeanette Rayford opened the door to them. She was barely recognizable. Already of diminutive stature, she now appeared twice as drawn and twice as fragile. Landis guessed she couldn't weigh more than eighty or ninety pounds.

'You comin' with bad news or no news?' she asked Milstead. 'Because neither ain't good.'

Milstead, hat in hand, answered her question with a look.

Jeanette lowered her head. 'You best come on through.'

The kitchen was unchanged. The memory of Jeanette breaking down and sobbing in his arms came back to Landis with some force. He took a seat, Milstead too. Jeanette stood at the sink, her hands gripping the edge behind her.

'It takes the two o' you to tell me you don't know who killed my baby?'

'Jeanette, believe me, we have been workin' on this and nothin' else all this time. We've made some progress, but there's some questions we need an answer to.'

Jeanette didn't reply.

'Where's Vester at now?' Milstead asked.

'Oh, he's up with his brother,' Jeanette said. 'Been gone a week. Asked him not to go, but he weren't havin' any of it.'

'An' he left you here by yourself?'

Jeanette shook her head resignedly. 'I been married to the man a good while,' she said. 'I don't know what he's thinkin' half the time, and I'm guessin' he knows less. He told me if I didn't want to be alone then I should go stay with my sister.'

'Where does his brother live?' Landis asked.

'Over there in Tennessee. Spring City.'

'You any notion of when he's comin' back?' Milstead asked.

Jeanette sneered. 'Yesterday. He said. If that man ever kept a promise in his life, it would die o' loneliness. Lord only knows when he'll show.'

'You have an address for your brother-in-law?' Landis asked.

'You gonna go on up there and drag him back for me?'

'If I find him, I'll surely tell him to get himself back here.'

Landis passed over his notebook and a pen. Jeanette wrote down the Spring City address.

'Another question I have for you relates to your daughter,' Landis said. 'I'm after knowin' whether she was involved in some kinda volunteer work.'

'Volunteerin' for what?'

'Oh, anythin' at all, Jeanette. Church, school, clubs, charities and the like.'

Jeanette thought for a while and then shook her head. 'She weren't that kinda girl, you know? I mean, I ain't sayin' that she was only interested in herself, but she wasn't much one for get-togethers and whatnot. Hard enough to get her a birthday party fixed up. She liked bein' home and she liked her own company. Fond o' animals too, but Vester wouldn't let her have no dog or nothin'.'

'Did you ever hear of something called the Georgia Young Republican group?'

Jeanette frowned. 'What, is that like a politics type o' thing?'

'Exactly,' Landis said. 'A group for teenagers who are interested in politics.'

'Because you think she was interested in somethin' like that?'

'It's somethin' we're lookin' into, that's all,' Landis said.

'My Ella May wouldn't know the difference 'tween George Bush and a walnut tree. Lord no, she weren't interested in any such thing.'

'Okay,' Landis said, an edge of disappointment in his tone.

'We really appreciate your seein' us, Jeanette,' Milstead said.

'That's all you wanted?'

'For now,' Landis said. 'And we'll see if we can't track down your husband for you.'

Jeanette pushed herself away from the edge of the sink. There was a flash of bitterness in her eyes.

'Well, you find him you tell him he better get his sorry self back here pronto, or his head's gonna get a pump knot with one o' them darn fryin' pans.'

Ten minutes later Landis and Milstead were back on the road south to Blue Ridge.

Landis asked if there was a map in the car.

'Bunch o' them in the glove,' Milstead said.

Landis went through them, dug out one that covered the northwestern corner of Georgia and the southernmost edge of Tennessee.

He found Trenton, then traced a line northeast along 24 to Wildwood and the place where Frank's body was found.

Looking further and following the line of the Tennessee River, Landis came to the intersection with 127.

As he'd thought, if you took that road and kept going for sixty miles, you'd wind up in Spring City.

He closed up the map and put it back in the glove.

'You wanna go out there?' Milstead asked.

'Need to find the man,' Landis replied.

'You gonna head up there today?'

'I figure so.'

'I ain't goin' with you,' Milstead said. 'I wanna stay here and keep on Bob Natchwey for any more forensics evidence in that car.'

'Makes any sense to you that Kenny Greaves did these things?'

'If you're askin' me was he capable, then I'd say yes. If you're askin' me whether he acted alone, then I'd say no. That boy sure wasn't no bright light in the harbor. If he did them things, then I reckon someone told him to, and that's all there is to it.'

54

Landis called Barbara before he left Milstead's office. He told her he wouldn't be returning to the office that afternoon.

'Has Marshall come back with anythin'?' he asked.

'I ain't seen him all day,' Barbara said.

'Okay, I'll catch up with him tomorrow.'

Landis headed out immediately.

Spring City, Rhea County, Tennessee was a hundred miles northwest of Blue Ridge.

Back in the 1870s, it had been known as Sulphur Springs, then Rheaville, then Rhea Springs. Much of the original town was lost to flood and fire. What little remained was now submerged beneath the Watts Bar Lake. Relocation brought with it yet another name.

Covering little more than two and a half square miles with a coal-fired plant dominating the skyline, it seemed to Landis that the one-time stop on the Cincinnati Southern Railroad line wasn't somewhere you'd visit for the wildlife or the scenery. For some reason, founded in nothing but intuition, he sensed that Vesper Rayford was either hiding or running away. He recalled Rayford's reaction when the news of his daughter's death was delivered, that stunned silence, the way in which he'd seemingly disappeared while Landis spoke with Jeanette. Rayford had asked neither of them a single question about Ella May's murder. Throughout their visit to the house, even on the drive to Blairsville to identify his daughter's body, the man had barely uttered a word.

By the time Landis arrived it was after seven. He was roadkill hungry, so he stopped at a bar and took a steak. Once again, he felt it would have been better to be out of uniform, but the urgency with which he wanted to find Vester Rayford had been paramount in his mind.

Before leaving, he asked the barman for directions to the address Jeanette had given.

'It'll seem like you're drivin' right on out of town,' the barman said, 'but just keep on goin' 'til you see a fork in the road. Take the left, and it's a ways down there on the right. There's an old gas station on the corner so you won't miss it.'

Landis followed the route he'd been given. After ten minutes of driving he felt sure he'd fouled up someplace, but then the gas station came into view. Dilapidated and broken-down, the canopy collapsed on one side, the station had long been abandoned. As if to give some idea of time, a rusted '70s Chrysler New Yorker sat in the forecourt, its windows punched out, a mess of weeds growing out of the trunk.

Landis turned. He looked out for house numbers, but they were unclear. Wide expanses of scrub and scald ran between the plots. Swathes of buckthorn had invaded in a sea of orange.

Again, he had the sense of being lost, of having missed something. He started to turn around, and then noticed a further slip road that ran away from the main route and to the left. At the end was a mailbox, on it the name *RAYFORD*.

Heading down there, the rutted track jolted the suspension something awful. The overhang of trees created the effect of a tunnel, and it was a good quarter-mile before he came out ahead of a wide, low-slung house. A veranda ran the full length of the front, the banister and steps rotted in places. The paintwork had dried and cracked; leaves of faded white had peeled away from the façade. The yard ahead of the house was nothing but patches of dried-out grass, here and there a low shrub, a couple of tree boles, the hammered dirt of an irregular pathway from the house to a small barn on the right.

Landis parked up and waited for any indication that his arrival had been noticed. He left it a good five minutes. Neither in the house itself nor anywhere in the yard was there movement. He got out of the car and made his way to the porch.

Before he'd even raised his hand to knock on the screen frame, he sensed someone to his left.

Turning slowly, he was confronted by the barrel of a small caliber rifle – little more than a rat gun – but at the range of no more than six feet it would have punched a clean hole through his skull.

Landis raised his hands. He didn't look anywhere but ahead.

'And who in Christ's name are you?' the man behind the rifle asked.

'You gonna put that down and act polite, or we gonna have ourselves a stand-off here?'

'Answer the question.'

'Landis, sheriff out o' Union County. Out here lookin' for Vester Rayford. I'm guessin' you'd be the brother.'

'You guess right, sheriff out o' Union County. And what the hell makes you think I'd know where Vester's at?'

'Spoke with Jeanette back in McCaysville. She said there was a good chance he might be holed up here with you.'

'Did she now?'

'She did,' Landis said.

'And what business you got with my brother?'

'I'm the one who found his girl,' Landis said. 'I'm out here with news.'

'You ain't here to take him in?'

Landis shook his head. 'I got no reason to take him in. He ain't done nothin' I know of.'

There was a moment's hesitation.

'What you got on your belt there?'

'I got a .44,' Landis said.

'Be mighty courteous o' you to take it off and set it down. Left hand. Slow as it gets.'

Landis did as he was asked, unbuckling the belt and letting it slide to the ground. He moved it aside with his foot, his hands still raised.

'Good 'nough. Can stand easy now.'

Landis lowered his arms and turned to look at Rayford's brother.

The likeness was such that he and Vester could have been twins.

'What's your name?' Landis asked.

'Gil,' Rayford said.

'You expectin' trouble?'

Gil cracked a wry smile. 'I always expect trouble,' he said. 'Then when it comes there ain't no surprise.'

Landis looked the man over. He was worn-out, that was certain. His eyes were those of someone who was used to being kicked by life – enough to wonder if next time he shouldn't just stay down.

'You gonna put that pea-shooter down now?' Landis asked.

Rayford lowered the rifle.

'So, he here or not?'

'Depends if you with him or against him.'

'Meaning?'

'You don't look like the dumb type, Sheriff,' Rayford said. 'They got his girl, didn't they?'

'Who did?'

Rayford frowned. 'Hell, maybe you are that dumb.'

'Ain't no shame in admittin' it,' Landis said. 'Means I come here aimin' to make sense o' things.'

'You stay right where you are. I'm takin' you on your word that you ain't here to cause trouble.'

'My word is good, Gil.'

'Maybe you go on back toward your car a while. Smoke a cigarette. Leave your pistol right where it is.'

Landis backed down the steps, turned and walked to the car. By the time he reached it and looked back, Gil Rayford had gone.

Giving up his weapon was bad form. Landis knew that. In that moment, however, form was the least of his concerns. Gil Rayford knew something, and if Gil knew, then so did Vester. Of this there was no doubt. The simple fact that he'd spoken of the girl, that someone had got her, was enough for Landis. There were answers here, and Landis was determined to get them.

Two cigarettes went by before Gil reappeared. He came through the front door and stood behind the screen. He no longer carried the rifle.

'You can come on up now,' he said. He opened the screen, picked up Landis's belt and holster, and waited.

Landis nodded in acknowledgement and started walking.

55

Vester Rayford was three sheets to the wind.

He sat awkwardly in a worn-out armchair, the cushion beneath him spilling twisted tongues of horsehair. In his hand he held a jar of liquor, and he looked at Landis through the red-eyed haze of drunkenness.

The room in which he sat was open-plan, long and poorly lit. At the far end a breakfast bar separated living room from kitchen. The sink was high with unwashed dishes. An old birddog lay on the linoleum, barely raising its head at the interruption to its day.

'Sheriff Landis,' Vester slurred. He shifted so as to better focus his attention.

'Vester.'

Gil Rayford walked on past and stood behind the breakfast bar.

'Get yourself sat,' Vester said.

Landis pulled a chair out ahead of a circular table beneath the window. A legion of dead flies littered the sill. A long-vacated spider's web triangulated the lower left corner of the frame.

'Maid's on vacation,' Vester said.

Landis nodded. 'Mine takes a lot o' them too.'

Vester took another drink, and then held the jar out towards Landis.

'You want some?'

'Thanks, but no. I'm good, Vester.'

'So what you got for me? What you doin' trackin' me all the way out here?' He grinned foolishly. 'You do realize you're in Tennessee now, don'tcha?'

'I know where I am, Vester. An' I just come from your place. You come on out here and left your wife alone, you know.'

'Told her to go to her sister's. Hell, she spends more time with that woman than she does with me anyhow.'

'I came to tell you that maybe we got the feller who killed your Ella May.'

Vester closed his eyes in slow motion. He opened them the same way. He looked like a sunning lizard.

'Maybe?'

'We're waitin' on some forensics and whatnot, but it looks pretty tight.'

'This feller got a name?'

'Kenny Greaves,' Landis said.

Vester's eyes widened, and then he let out a raucous snort of laughter.

'Kenny Greaves? You gotta be foolin' yourselves somethin' bad if you think Kenny Greaves did that to my girl. Lord, that boy couldn't pour piss out of a shoe if the instructions was on the heel.'

'You know him?'

Vester shook his head. He took another sip. 'Hell, I know all o' them. All them wrong 'uns. I know 'em to a man.'

'How many wrong 'uns we talkin', Vester?'

'Anyone tied up with them Russells is a wrong 'un far as I'm concerned. And that goes for police, sheriff's people, whoever. They got mixed up in this business, then they're just bad through to the bone.'

'What business, Vester?'

Vester frowned. His head swayed. He looked at his brother, then back at Landis.

'Why in hell's name you think your brother got killed, eh? You musta asked yourself that question a thousand times since it happened. You blind, or you just don't wanna see?'

'Maybe a bit o' both,' Landis said, 'but I want to understand what's happenin' here. I wanna know who killed him, sure I do, but I also wanna know how come your Ella May got killed.'

Vester lowered his head. There was the defeated man, the broken spirit. Despite the blunt mask of liquor, just the thought of his dead daughter tore a hole right through him.

'Worst kind o' thing to happen to a father,' Vester said, his voice cracking with emotion. He looked up at Landis. 'You don't got no kids, do you?'

Landis shook his head.

'They's your life, your blood, your everythin'. They come along and the whole world is a different place. You get to see everythin' around with new eyes. It's like bein' given a chance to live your life twice over, fix things, make things right, find some peace. The worst things happen, you come home to that and it ain't so bad anymore. Man needs to feel that, you know? Man doesn't have kids there's always gonna be a hollow part in his soul.'

Vester took a hefty swig from the jar.

'An' they took that away from me. They ripped her right out of my arms. That's what they did.' He shook his head. Tears filled his eyes. 'They killed her and then threw her aside like a bone that been chewed to the last.'

'Who, Vester? Who did these things? If it wasn't Kenny Greaves, then who was it?'

'Hell, maybe that poor dumb shit of a boy done it, but he didn't do it alone. He would never have done it hadn't there been someone tellin' him so.'

'And you know there were other girls,' Landis said. 'Two

others. One out in Walker County, another they found up near Sumter.'

'Two?' Vester said. 'Two ain't even close to what they done.'

'So who is they, Vester? Who's doin' this?'

Vester smiled. It was a cruel expression. 'Seems your brother woulda been the best person to answer that question, eh? Him and that cop buddy o' his.'

'Which cop, Vester?'

'That piece o' shit lyin' two-faced asshole, Fredericksen.'

'Mike Fredericksen from Trenton PD?'

'That's the one. He told me it'd be alright. He told me that I'd be safe, that he had it all covered. He told me not to worry about a darn thing, and yet here I am. I gotta come hide out in my brother's place to keep away from that business.'

Landis leaned back. He looked over at Gil. His expression was implacable. He'd remained silent throughout, seemed set to stay that way.

'I don't know what the hell went on between you and Fredericksen,' Landis said, 'but I need to get this straight. What you're tellin' me is that Fredericksen and my brother had some-thing to do with these girls gettin' killed, that there's more than three o' them, and that you and Fredericksen had some kind o' deal that relates to this.'

Vester leaned forward. He was unsteady for a moment but gained his balance.

'One thing I know, an' I tell you this for free, Sheriff Landis. Your brother was a good man. Sure, he had his circumstances. He weren't no different from anyone in that respect, but when it came down to it, he was a good man. Maybe he done some wrong things, but he did them for the right reasons. Hell, if he hadn't o' been law, I figure he would've burned the lot o' them to the ground. Fredericksen I ain't so sure about. I didn't meet him more than three or four times an' he never said much of anythin'. Your brother was always the one who done the talkin'. But Fredericksen was there, for sure, and it sure seemed to me that he and your brother were all tied up together in this thing. Frank was the one who gave his word, and I trusted him. Didn't seem to me I had much choice. I told 'em what they wanted to know, and Fredericksen told me just as plain as day that it would be fine, that no trouble'd come to my door. But it came, didn't it? It came anyway, no matter what he said, and it was the worst kind.'

'What did you tell my brother, Vester?' Landis asked. 'What was he tryin' to find out?'

'How to stop 'em. How to get all o' them stopped from doin' what they was doin'.'

'Who, Vester? Stop who?'

'Them Russells, goddamnit. Ain't you been listenin' to nothin' I been sayin'? To stop the Russells from takin' them girls.'

Landis knew he'd heard right. He didn't need Vester to repeat himself.

'Did the Russells find out that you'd spoken with my brother?' Landis asked.

'Sure they did. Hell, them people can find out anythin' they want.'

'Is that why Ella May was killed? Did they get Kenny Greaves to kill Ella May because they thought you were workin' with the police?'

'I don't know who killed her,' Vester said. 'Maybe Kenny, maybe Wasper, maybe someone else. Hell, they know enough people who'd do that sort o' thing, and do it for free. All I know is she's dead, and it's my fault. It's my goddamned fault for tryin' to do the right thing. Jeanette told me to keep the hell away from all o' that. Did I listen? Did I hell. Just went ahead and opened my goddamned mouth, didn't I? Just like I'm doin' now.

'Cept it's different this time, 'cause they already taken from me the only thing that matters.'

'So Frank was tryin' to take down the Russells, an' he was workin' with Mike Fredericksen out of Trenton PD. You gave up some information about Eugene.'

Vester didn't reply.

'Tell me this, Vester. Do you think that Fredericksen betrayed my brother? That he was the one who got him killed?'

'I don't know no more than what I already told you. Best you go ask him yourself, eh? Go find out if you get a welcome from that man. He's the one who knows what the Russells is doin', and he knows how far it goes.'

Out on the porch, Landis put on his gun.

Gil Rayford eyed him directly, and there was a question in that look.

'We ain't gonna find ourselves surrounded by fellers with guns in the middle of the night, now are we?'

'If you do, then it ain't gonna be my doin', Gil.'

'Gonna tell you straight. All o' this ain't my business. All I got is my brother, and he come up here askin' if he can lay low a while. Maybe he ain't no tiger of a man, but I ain't never seen him in such a state. Like he said, folks all got their own circumstances, but he ain't a liar and he ain't got no part in whatever them Russells been doin'. Them lot's my kin too, but I knowed from the first time I met 'em that I didn't want nothin' to do with 'em. You get a sense for these things, and sometimes you just gotta trust it. I knowed their daddy when I was a kid. He was a bitter man, poisoned through and through. That's the root of it right there. Them kids o' his done got the same poison in their veins.'

'I know 'em,' Landis said. 'I been up there to Colwell, out to

Padena to see where Wasper stays with his girl. Didn't much care for them, I gotta tell you.'

'Seems your brother didn't care much for them either, an' look where it got him. I guess I should tell you to mind yourself, but I think you're the sort of feller who does what he wants no matter what anyone says.'

'This has put a twist on things,' Landis said. 'If what Vester says is true, then maybe Ella May got killed to hurt him for what he done. Friend o' mine told me that Eugene Russell wouldn't blink to kill his own brother if he thought he was in with the law.'

'Sounds 'bout right to me,' Gil said. 'They don't think regular ways.'

'Tells me I gotta stop thinkin' regular if I wanna understand 'em.'

'Hell, you don't need to understand 'em. You just need to corner 'em an' kill 'em. Fox come stealin' your chickens, you don't figure out his take on life. You just blow his fuckin' head off.'

'I'm law, Gil. It don't work that way.'

'Your brother was law, wasn't he? Whatever the hell needed doin', he tried doin' it right, and look where the hell that got him.'

Landis extended his hand. Rayford took it.

'Appreciate your hospitality, Gil. I gotta friend over in Fannin County. I'll tell him to keep an eye on Jeanette.'

'And you keep an eye on your own kin,' Gil said. 'Seems to me you're walkin' into a war that's already started, an' there's casualties enough already.'

56

Throughout the drive back to Blairsville, Landis's thoughts were a storm.

If he'd strung things together correctly, then the killing of Ella May Rayford was not connected to the deaths of Linda Bishop and Sara-Louise Lacey. At least not directly. Ella May's death had been a revenge killing for something, and that something looked an awful lot like Vester Rayford's collaboration with the Dade County Sheriff's Department.

Frank being on the right side of this had not occurred to Landis. That Mike Fredericksen might very well have been the one to betray not only Frank, but also Vester Rayford, was yet another turn in the road that he hadn't seen coming. There was also the money that was still going to Eleanor Boyd. Why, and from whom? And was she being paid to keep her mouth shut?

Landis was hunting blind. He knew that, and had known it from the start. Now there was an about-face to take into account, that the Russells were behind this, that Frank had been in their line-of-sight, that they had been responsible for his murder. Had Kenny Greaves been the one to kill him, driving back and forth over his busted body until he was sure the job was done? Or maybe Wasper was behind the wheel for that little joyride.

Either which way, Landis knew he had to get to Fredericksen. Fredericksen had worked with Frank. Fredericksen was demonstrably derelict in his investigation of Frank's death. If Fredericksen was working with the Russells, watching their back, taking money, getting them into the system as confidential human resources to keep the law off of them, then this was a whole other pit of snakes.

By the time Landis reached home he was beat. He kicked off his boots, got himself into jeans and a shirt, and dug around in the freezer. He found a couple of pork chops that still looked the right color and put them on a plate over a pan of simmering water to defrost.

Fetching down a bottle of rye, he poured out a good three inches and went to the porch to smoke.

Come January, discounting the identification of his body, it would be twelve years since he and Frank had been in the same room.

Landis remembered the last words he'd said to his brother.

For you, there ain't never gonna be a light in these windows. You ain't never gonna get a welcome here. You may be kin, but from here until the end of time you don't exist to me.

Without a word, Frank had turned and walked away. He'd gotten in his car and was gone before Landis had closed the screen and locked the front door.

The house had then been emptier than he'd ever remembered it. He could hear his own breathing, maybe even the blood in his veins, the beating of his heart. He'd taken a drink, and then another. He'd kept on drinking until everything inside was dark and silent. Then he'd slept, and woken to the first day of the rest of his life.

That could have been yesterday, and it could have been a thousand years ago. There was no frame of reference within which to place what had happened between them. Nothing like that had happened since, simply because Landis had never allowed anyone to get that close. If you didn't have it, no one could take it from you.

In its place had come routine, predictability, one day following the next with no discernible difference. He did not engage or connect or invite. He did not take the time to make friends. He had acquaintances, colleagues, superiors, juniors. In the midst of this he was a small island, about which the ocean of life went through its tides and storms.

That was the way he'd wanted it to be, and that was what it had become.

He knew he could no longer maintain it. If what Rayford had told him was true, then both Eugene and Wasper Russell were fully aware of what was happening here and had lied to his face. He'd been drawn into a web that connected not only them, but the sheriffs and deputies of four other counties, the police departments of two other cities, a corrupt detective, confidential informants, and the parents of at least three dead girls. Last but not least, there was Frank, and Frank was at the center of all things.

Perhaps he'd brought it all on himself. Perhaps it had been his own weakness that was to blame. And maybe if he could conquer that weakness, he could live without regret.

That he might one day forgive Frank for what he'd done had seemed impossible to Landis.

Now it looked like the world was set to change his mind.

57

'It's been around for years,' Marshall said. 'Started back in the fifties when Eisenhower was president. Ain't been a Republican governor in Georgia since the 1870s so they were looking to get a whole raft of grassroots things going to sway the vote. The Young Republican Volunteers was a sort of community drive activity thing, you know? They had dances and swap meets, bake sales, events with celebrities and the like. Don't seem to me like there's a great deal goin' on with it, but they got the best part of ten thousand names in their database.'

'Where are they based?' Landis asked.

'Well, they got five administrative offices. Macon is central, then you got Valdosta for the south, Columbus is west, Trenton is north and Savannah is east.'

'Trenton has an office?'

Marshall nodded in the affirmative.

'And this is state-funded or what?'

'GOP backs it, and then there's member donations as far as I can tell.'

'What age you gotta be to join this thing?'

'Thirteen to eighteen-year-olds.'

'So somewhere on record you got a list of ten thousand teenagers. Names, ages, addresses, parents' names too, I guess.'

'Exactly.'

'And it's public?'

'No, not public. To access the register you gotta go through the Republican Party headquarters in Atlanta.'

'Which means a warrant or a subpoena.'

'You're lookin' to cross-check all the girls in that register against ongoing missing persons, right?'

'That's what I was thinkin', yes.'

'Well, me an' Barb can get onto that. Ain't gonna be overnight, but the sooner we get started the better.'

'You're gonna need to get simultaneous requests from George Milstead, Carl Parsons, Bill Garner and Willard Montgomery. I want as much pressure on this as we can muster. Get it to Judge Brennan if you can. He's a good man. He ain't gonna make this any more complicated than it needs to be.'

Marshall got up.

'And tell Barbara to get the names of all the officers of that chapter in Trenton.'

After Marshall left, Landis sat quiet for a while and considered his next course of action. He knew he was going to stir up trouble, but he didn't much care. If it had all been in-county it would have been different. Not necessarily easier, but the information he needed would have been more accessible without attracting too much attention. Not only was he dealing with Dade, he was looking for the background and connections of someone within Trenton PD. Fredericksen was in his crosshairs, and he had to be absolutely certain before he pulled the trigger. He figured he'd only get one shot at this, and if he missed then he would become the target.

The only personal contact he had within Dade was Paul Abrams. The man was already spooked, and Landis doubted whether he'd be willing to go digging around. He'd expressed concerns not just for himself, but for his family. That alone suggested the possibility of inferred threat, but from whom? Was

Fredericksen so entrenched with the Russells that he could use them to intimidate a deputy sheriff?

Landis knew he was making assumptions. Even as he considered such a possibility, he knew it was based on nothing but fragments of information from unreliable sources. He alone would have to find out how Fredericksen was involved in this mess. He had no leverage. He had no card up his sleeve. There was nothing that directly implicated Fredericksen in any aspect of this. The only means of approach was Frank's still-unexplained death. That seemed to be the only premise upon which he could approach the man.

Landis had last spoken with Fredericksen two weeks prior. In that time, he'd heard nothing from him or anyone else in the police department. Fredericksen had said there were officers out canvassing, that a reward had been posted, that he was using every resource at his disposal. Another week and it would be two months since Frank got himself run down and left for dead. Landis still had no clue why he'd been out there on his own, nor why he was heading for Tennessee.

If he could connect Fredericksen to the Russells, and the Russells were behind these abductions and killings, then whatever Frank had been doing would not have been in vain.

As it stood, that was the only thread Landis could hold onto, and even as he grasped it, it felt tenuous and fragile.

58

Landis was met with a dismissive reception at the duty desk of Trenton's police department.

'Detective Fredericksen is away this week,' he was told. 'Annual leave. If you want to see him, make an appointment for some time after next Monday.'

'Next Monday ain't gonna work for me,' Landis said.

The duty sergeant frowned. 'I don't know else I can tell you, Sheriff. He ain't here, and that's all there is to it.'

'Can you give me his home address?'

'Now, you know I can't do that.'

'Give me his telephone number then.'

'I can direct you to a detective who's actually workin' this week if you like.'

Landis held his ground. 'No, it's Detective Fredericksen that I need to see.'

'Okay, well as I said, he ain't gonna be here until next Monday, and more 'an likely he's gonna have a backlog of business to take care of.'

'You ain't gonna help me, are you?' Landis asked.

'Well, I'm bein' as helpful as I can. You asked to speak to someone who ain't here, and then you asked for information you know I can't give you. You ain't exactly makin' this simple, now are you?'

'What in hell d'you think I'm gonna do if you tell me where

he's at, Sergeant? You think I'm here for any other reason than official business? I drove all the way over here from Union to speak to the detective an' I'd appreciate some cooperation. Ain't we all in the same business here?'

'I have no idea what business you got with Mike, but you know as well as I do that a man's time away from his work is sacred. How would you feel if someone showed up on your doorstep when you were takin' some vacation with your family?'

'I guess that'd depend on how important it was.'

The sergeant shook his head exasperatedly. 'Hell, you're set on makin' this as tough as can be, ain'tcha?'

'All I'm askin' is you point me in the right direction. Let me worry about whether Mike Fredericksen has an issue with it.'

The sergeant hesitated, and then there was a moment of recognition.

'Landis,' he said. 'You ain't related to that feller from the Sheriff's Office who got himself killed, is ya?'

'That was my brother, yes. And Detective Fredericksen is the one who's investigating what the hell happened.'

'Okay, well that shines a different light on things. I'm gonna give you his address now, but I have no idea whether he's gonna be there or not. Maybe he's away someplace with his wife and kids. You're just gonna have to take a drive out there and see for yourself.'

The sergeant located the address on the computer. He wrote it down on a piece of paper and passed it over the desk to Landis. He told him to turn left away from the building, go three blocks, then take a right towards the highway. 'You'll find it on down there. You get lost, you ask someone.'

'I appreciate it,' Landis said.

'Let's hope Detective Fredericksen does too, eh?'

*

A little before six, Landis stood on the porch of the Fredericksen house and knocked on the door for the third time.

There was no response. Instinct told him the place was empty.

Walking back to the road, he surveyed the front of the building, then looked at the adjacent properties on each side. The one on the right was lit up, so he tried it first.

The elderly woman who answered seemed altogether unsettled by the sight of a sheriff on her doorstep. It was one of the few scenarios where the uniform lent an authority that was useful.

Landis took off his hat.

'Ma'am,' he said. 'My name is Sheriff Landis out of Union County. I've come over here on a business matter to speak with your neighbor, Mike Fredericksen. There don't seem to be anyone home, and I was wonderin' if you know where they might be at.'

'They's away on vacation,' the woman said. 'Been away since the weekend. Don't expect 'em back 'til next.'

'And did they say where they were goin', perhaps?'

'Not specific, no. Near about every time they're off to the state park, though. Them kids love it over there.'

'The state park? You mean Cloudland?'

'That'd be the one. Cloudland Canyon. I think they take themselves a cabin up there, do all the fishin' and walkin' and whatnot. I ain't never been there, but I heard it's real pretty.'

'That's really good of you, ma'am. Thank you for your time.'

'You gonna go over there and see him?'

'That's the plan. If he's there, of course.'

'Well, you tell him you spoke with Edie. Tell him Edie says he needs to deal with his outside trash before he takes off again. Had all sorts of mess to clear up with raccoons and the like.'

'I surely will, ma'am. And thank you again.'

From the glove compartment, Landis took a state map and folded it out over his knees. Cloudland Canyon State Park was less than fifteen minutes' drive down Lafayette Street.

Once again, the authority of a uniform gave Landis an advantage he otherwise wouldn't have had.

The receptionist at Cloudland Canyon State Park was immediately forthcoming when he enquired after the Fredericksen family. Assuming that she couldn't refuse a sheriff, she gave Landis the number of the cabin where the Fredericksens were staying and directions to find it.

It was a longer drive from the entrance to the residential facility than it had been from Fredericksen's house to the park itself. The route was clearly signposted, and Landis pulled over beneath a high overhang of trees just a short walk from his destination.

He waited a while, smoked a cigarette, took a little time to focus his thoughts on what he was doing. Whichever way he came at it, he didn't see another way of digging up any further information. Fredericksen was connected to Frank, to the Russells, to whatever was happening in Trenton. Fredericksen was a part of whatever the hell this was, and if nothing else, he could confirm or deny the assumptions Landis had made.

Leaving the car, Landis walked a couple of hundred yards further and came out at the edge of a wide clearing. Eight identical cabins were situated in an imprecise circle around a central children's play area. Set back at differing distances and angles, each cabin was separated by a border of low trees, a good degree of privacy afforded each one.

Counting from left to right, Landis identified the Fredericksen cabin. Lights were on, but there was no one visible inside or out. Assuming there would be a yard behind the cabin, Landis started around the perimeter, keeping well inside the treeline.

Behind him and to his right was the road where his car was parked. The sun would set within the hour. The air was alive with insects. Clambering over low fallen branches, all the while keeping the cabin in view, he stumbled a couple of times, scuffing the knees of his pants, once or twice pausing to catch his breath. Beneath his hat his scalp itched something furious; sweat darkened his shirt beneath the arms and across his chest.

When he reached a point that brought the rear of the cabin into view, he could see an inflatable pool. Here and there toys were scattered across an expanse of grass. A swing set, a gas-fired barbecue, a long table, benches either side, a second smaller table with a canvas sunshade over the top.

A woman, presumably Fredericksen's wife, sat on the back steps of the cabin. A little boy, no more than three or four years old, sat in her lap. Though Landis could not hear them, the child seemed to be fussing about something or other.

Landis crouched low with his back against the trunk of a tree. He loosened his tie and unbuttoned his shirt collar. He waited and watched.

Within a few minutes, Fredericksen appeared. In tow were two young girls. Fredericksen shared a few words with his wife, and then went back into the cabin. The girls headed for the swing set.

Landis, already feeling tension in his knees and his back, got to his feet. He backed up and stood behind the tree. He considered how best to deal with this scenario, whether to return the way he'd come and approach the cabin from the road, or wait a while longer, perhaps until everyone was back inside the cabin. Then he could head down the incline to the yard and see if he could get Fredericksen alone.

After another fifteen minutes, he decided that nothing would be accomplished by staying where he was. He had established that the Fredericksens were here, the presence of children sufficient to avoid any unnecessary confrontation, and that making himself known in the most direct way possible was the sole option remaining.

Landis took a step backwards and started to turn.

The all-too-familiar sound of a hammer being cocked was followed by the sensation of a cold muzzle against the back of his neck.

'Seems you didn't get the message, Sheriff,' Fredericksen said.

Landis didn't speak. He didn't turn.

'Left hand. Ease out that pistol and hand it back here. I don't give a goddamn why you're here. You're trespassing, intimidating my family. Try anything and I'll knock you senseless.'

Landis did as he was told. He unclipped his holster, withdrew his .44 and passed it backwards.

Fredericksen took it, and then jabbed Landis in the neck once more.

'Walk,' he said. 'Back to your car. And slowly.'

59

Landis sat in the passenger seat. Fredericksen sat directly behind him.

Though Landis could count on one hand the number of times he'd had to draw his weapon in all his years of service, the mere fact of having it taken from him gave him a sense of vulnerability and impotence.

'You must take me for one dumb son-of-a-bitch,' Fredericksen said. 'You don't think I told them to call me if anyone showed up here looking for me?'

'Why would anyone be looking for you, Detective?'

'You can cut that shit out right now,' Fredericksen replied, in his voice an edge of real aggression. 'What in hell's name do you take me for?'

'I don't take you for anything,' Landis said. 'I came to talk to you. You weren't home. Your neighbor told me you were out here so I drove over.'

'So what the fuck are you doin' hidin' up in the trees?'

'I guess I wanted to get the lay of the land. I didn't know what to expect.'

'Well, I guess that makes two of us. Only thing that surprises me is that they sent you.'

Landis started to turn. Once again, the gun was at the nape of his neck.

'They sent me?' Landis asked. 'No one sent me. I came out here on my own.'

'I ain't buyin' that for a second.'

'I ain't sellin' anythin',' Landis said. 'I came to see you about my brother. Went to Trenton PD. They said you were on leave. Went to your house. A woman called Edie told me where you were. She also said you gotta deal with your outside trash before you take off.'

'What the hell are you talkin' about?'

'Just relayin' a message, Detective. She said you had raccoons all up in your trash and she wasn't happy about it.'

Fredericksen didn't speak for a few moments, and then he said, 'What makes you think I'm gonna believe a word you're sayin'?'

'Why would you assume I was lyin'?'

'Because you ain't no good. I know that for a fact.'

'You don't even know me. We've spoken twice. You don't have any reason to—'

'I know what your brother told me about you.'

Landis didn't know what to say, and so he said nothing.

'I'm takin' your silence as confirmation that you know exactly what I'm talkin' about.'

'What happened between me and my brother is long-gone, and now it don't matter a damn. He's dead. I don't know why. I don't know what he was into that would make someone want him dead. I don't have the faintest notion what he was doin' headin' up into Tennessee that night. Enough to know that someone run him down and killed him and you're the one who's s'posed to have answers on that.'

'The Russells sent you, didn't they?'

'The Russells? What the hell're you talkin' about?'

'Heard you been out there. More than once.'

'Sure I did,' Landis said. 'They got cousins, name of Rayford, and their daughter got herself killed. I'm trying to figure out what happened to her. And how the hell d'you know I went out there anyways?'

'Ain't so difficult to keep tabs on you. You been stickin' your hand in a hornets' nest all over the place. You got Milstead and Garner involved, I hear. Montgomery from out in Walker. You treadin' on some very thin ice, just like your brother, and I don't need to remind you what happened to him.'

'Any which way you read it, that's a threat.'

'Read it how you like, Sheriff.'

'So what the hell you gonna do now?'

'Same as I did before. Tell you to leave this thing alone. I got my own family. I got three little 'uns down there. I got the same message I'm givin' you. Only difference is I understood what it meant. You ain't got a wife an' kids to concern yourself with, but I do. You keep pushin' on this thing, who do you think they're gonna come talk to next, eh? You think just 'cause they killed a sheriff, they wouldn't kill me, too? And you? You wanna wind up dead in a drive-by that never gets solved? I sure as hell don't, and I ain't havin' you drag me back into somethin' that I got well out of, you understand?'

'The Russells threatened you? Are they the ones who killed Frank?'

Fredericksen laughed dismissively. 'Oh, you really have no clue, do you? Or maybe you're just pretendin'. You're tellin' me you have no idea where this goes? The Russells are doin' whatever the hell they're doin', and they're gettin' away with it. You ask yourself why? Has it even crossed your mind that these people are protected?'

'By the confidential informant thing, right?'

'Oh, so you do have some notion about this?'

'I went up to Atlanta. I spoke to them. I was told that Wasper wasn't on their system, but Eugene was. I got word that he was an informant for Frank, and then—'

'Eugene Russell ain't no damned informant, for Chrissake. Jeez, you just seem to believe everythin' you're told, don'tcha? Frank said a few things about you, but he didn't say you were stupid.'

'So tell me, Mike. Tell me what the hell is going on here?'

Landis heard Fredericksen lean back in the seat behind him. He went quiet, and stayed that way.

'Tell me what you know,' Landis said. 'Tell me what the hell I'm dealin' with here. I got three dead girls. I got a dead brother. I got rumors about him bein' crooked, about you and him bein' involved in somethin' together that got him killed. I got word from two or three different people, none of them I'd trust as far as I could kick 'em, sayin' that Trenton is a swamp. I got some kids' volunteer thing goin' on which two o' them girls belonged to, and they got offices all over the state. Oh, an' before I forget, I got you tellin' Frank's ex-wife that his pension is sorted when it ain't darn well sorted at all. She's still gettin' a thousand bucks a month, and it sure as hell ain't comin' from the department.'

'Christ almighty, Landis, I can't believe you're still alive. You sure been busy, ain'tcha?'

'I been doin' my job, which is more than can be said about you.'

'Forget about death threats. Seems to me you got a death wish. You need to take a long, hard look at what you're doin' an' ask yourself if this is a road you wanna keep headin' down. Tell you now, there's a very strong likelihood, I'd say it's guaranteed, that you're gonna wind up the same damn place as your brother.'

'Tell me one thing,' Landis said.

'You can ask. You might not get an answer.'

'Was Frank bad? Was he on the take? Was he involved in somethin' with the Russells?'

Glancing up at the rearview, Landis saw Fredericksen shake his head resignedly.

'You really didn't know him worth a damn, did you?'

'Tell me, Mike. Tell me where that money came from. It wasn't comin' out of his own pocket. It was goin' to Eleanor from someplace else, but he wasn't smart about it, was he? He put that money through a bank, for Christ's sake.'

'He didn't have any choice. That was money for his kid. He had to do that. The court told him he had to do that.'

'So where the hell did it come from?'

'It came from me, goddamnit! I paid it to her. I put it in a bank and paid it to her. An' I'm still payin' it now, aren't I?'

'What?' Landis asked. 'Why the hell would you do that?'

'Because... because he needed me to, okay? Because I owed him more than you can ever imagine. Because he was in trouble payin' back debts that were set to bury him. Because them Russells sent someone to hurt my family and he took care of it. Hell, that man was more a brother to me than he ever was to—'

Fredericksen fell short of speaking his mind.

Landis knew what Fredericksen was going to say. He didn't need to hear it.

'An' now he's dead, isn't he?' Fredericksen said. 'An' I ain't gonna let his kid go without, not after what he did for us.'

'What did he do, Mike? What did Frank do?'

'He got that son-of-a-bitch killed. That's what he did. The one the Russells sent. He got him strung up.'

'Macklin? Are you talkin' about Holt Macklin?'

Fredericksen leaned forward suddenly. Landis turned. The man's expression was one of genuine surprise.

'What the hell're you askin' me about this for if you already know?'

'I didn't,' Landis said. 'I had no idea that your family was threatened. I knew Macklin was supposed to have committed suicide, but I didn't know Frank had anything to do with it.'

'Well, now you do. Now you know, okay? An' I'm out of this, you hear? You stay the fuck away from me, away from my family, an' if you have any sense at all in that head o' yours, you just back the fuck off and stop turnin' over stones. Likely you'll find somethin' underneath one of them that's gonna bite.'

'What about Ella May, Mike? Why'd she wind up dead?'

'Why'd you think?'

'I'm thinkin' that Vester Rayford was your informant? Was he givin' up information on the Russells?'

'You know, up there it's all about family. They talk about how family is everythin', how they all gotta stick together, how blood is all that matters. Well, it don't seem to matter worth shit when it comes to money. An' it matters even less when it comes to self-preservation. You go on askin' your questions, Sheriff, an' let's see what happens. You're on your own now.'

Fredericksen opened the rear door. He paused before he got out.

'Don't come lookin' for me again. Don't call, don't come to my house, don't go to the office.'

'But—'

Fredericksen jabbed the gun into Landis's shoulder.

'I'm puttin' your gun in the trunk.'

Landis sat motionless as Fredericksen exited the car. He walked back, opened the trunk, put Landis's gun inside.

Fredericksen came back to the open window.

'Turn around and go back to Union,' he said. 'And if you want my advice, fuckin' well stay there.'

Landis watched in the rearview as Fredericksen walked away. He went on watching him until he disappeared into the trees.

60

Landis didn't sleep.

He lay awake until the sun broke over the horizon. His mind raced headlong into all kinds of turmoil.

If he believed Jim Tom Moody and the Russells, then Frank and Mike Fredericksen were on the wrong side of everything. If he believed what Fredericksen had told him, then the Russells were being protected by someone at state level. Vester Rayford had given up information on the Russells, and the killing of Ella May had been the penalty for his betrayal. Maybe Kenny Greaves had killed Ella May. Maybe someone else had done it and Greaves was the patsy. However it had happened, it was cruelty of the worst kind. Don't kill the man, but kill something he loves. Let him carry that burden for the rest of his life.

Maybe Frank had been on his way out to Spring City that night of August 14. Had he been meeting with Rayford? The Russells – or someone in their employ – had been out there waiting for him, and he'd been murdered as a warning to anyone who might have had an interest in what was going on. If we can get to a sheriff, we can get to anyone.

The State AG's Office Collaboration Unit had Eugene on their system as a resource. That would keep both the police and the Sheriff's Office off his back. Protection like that – warranted or not – would give him free rein to do whatever the hell he wanted. If that was true, then what was he doing? Girls abducted, beaten, raped and strangled. Rayford had said that there were more besides Linda Bishop and Sara-Louise Lacey. What did the volunteer organization have to do with it? Was that database being used to select girls? Who was doing the selecting? Was this some kind of sex-trafficking operation?

Intuitively, Landis erred towards the picture painted by Fredericksen and Rayford. Rayford was terrified and in hiding, to the point that he'd abandoned his wife back in McCaysville. Fredericksen was a police detective, yet he'd been sufficiently backed off by Frank's killing that he'd ceased any further efforts to investigate. That would also explain the removal of all the files from Frank's office. Someone had told him to get them, perhaps to destroy them. Now he was determined to do anything to protect his own family. Understandably, Fredericksen knew that anyone could be gotten to, and he was not prepared to put his wife or children in jeopardy.

A little before five, Landis stood silently in the kitchen. He'd brewed coffee, tried to eat but had no appetite. He was chaining smokes to the point of nausea. He knew he was walking around the edge of a swamp, but the swamp was entirely different from the one he'd believed was there. How deep it went, and how far he'd now waded into it, he did not know. If it was as bad as he suspected, then Fredericksen's warning carried a great deal of weight. The Russells – on their own initiative, or at the behest of someone else – had murdered one sheriff already. To have also killed Fredericksen would have attracted too much attention. Frank's death was enough to have Fredericksen close everything down and walk away. And Frank had died for two reasons, it seemed. Not only had he threatened whatever operation the Russells were involved in, he'd also had Holt Macklin killed in prison. Macklin was part of the Russell crew, as had been Kenny Greaves. This raised yet another question regarding Wasper. Had he really capsized his brother's drug deal? Had he really been so determined to exact some revenge against Eugene for this imagined abandonment in prison? Or had that been orchestrated by Eugene for some ulterior motive? Or was the whole thing yet another lie, a means by which a further misdirection could obscure the truth of what was going on?

Questions led to further questions, and yet – at the heart of all of them – was the need to know why Eugene Russell was being protected at state level. Who was pulling the strings in Atlanta, and why?

An hour later, Landis got ready for work. He was physically exhausted, but his mind ran at speed. There were many decisions to make, the foremost of which had already been made. He could not let it lie. He would not back off and leave it be. If not for his brother, then for the lives of the girls that had been so mercilessly brought to such a horrific end.

No, he did not have children. No, he did not have his own family to consider. Nevertheless, he had his brother's. Beyond that, there was also a sense of obligation to the truth, and it weighed heavy on his mind and in his heart.

61

Marshall and Barbara had spent much of Wednesday preparing the warrant for the Georgia Republican Young Volunteers records.

Landis read through it. His impulse was to drive it up to Judge Brennan at the Union County Courthouse and file it right away, but he decided against it. Within days it would be in the hands of the State Attorney General's Office, thence to whoever was coordinating the GRYV down there. It would alert them to the fact that Landis was now continuing an investigation that had been pursued by his brother. If Landis was right, Russell would then be swiftly informed, and Landis could very well find himself the victim of a hit-and-run or an inexplicable shooting.

The Attorney General's Office supported numerous departments – Corrections, Public Safety, Juvenile Justice, Pardons and Paroles. It also oversaw the actions of the Prosecution Division, a unit devoted solely to investigating and prosecuting fraud and corruption within the state's own departments and agencies. If there was someone within the AG Office hell-bent on covering Eugene Russell's tracks, an approach to Prosecutions would be a futile avenue. Beyond that, there was the Georgia Bureau of Investigation. Despite the fact that the Bureau was also under the same umbrella, they would ultimately be answerable to Washington. Past experience told him that getting the Bureau involved would entail innumerable reports, endless interviews, not to mention a convoy of SUVs and sedans gridlocking the streets of Blairsville. A dozen or more federal agents trawling through the countryside looking to talk with the Russells and their cohorts was unthinkable.

Landis then thought of Abigail Webster of the Justice Collaboration Unit.

Calling Barbara through from the outer office, he asked her to find out what he could about the woman.

'What do you need to know exactly?' Barbara asked.

'How long she's been police, where she came from before she worked for the Attorney General, anything notable on her record, and also her personal life. Is she married, does she have kids.'

'Can I ask why?'

'I'm lookin' to find out if she's reliable. If I can trust her to get me the information I'm after without going through channels.'

Barbara frowned. 'Why am I thinkin' this ain't such a good notion?'

'Because there ain't any other way to think about it,' Landis said.

'What the hell have you gotten yourself into? More importantly, are you gonna be able to get yourself out?'

Landis paused for a moment. 'Sit down, Barbara.'

Barbara did so.

'I'm tellin' you these things because it's weighin' heavy on me, an' I know you can be trusted to keep your mouth shut.'

Barbara didn't speak.

'This thing with my brother and the killings of these girls seem to be connected, yet I ain't quite got the full measure of it yet.'

'Your brother was bad?'

'I thought so, but I'm thinkin' the other way.'

'And you're followin' his tracks?'

'I am, yes. At least that's what I think I'm doin'.'

'Is this to do with the Russells?'

'Seems so.'

'Then it's a wicked business you're headin' into. Near about every time I hear that name it's followed by somethin' real unpleasant. They's all gaumed up with the worst kind o' filth imaginable. Guns, drugs, murders, the lot.'

'How come you know 'bout them?'

'Hell, you hear it once, you pass it over. You hear it a hundred times you start reckonin' there's some truth behind it.'

'Well, it looks like they're the ones that got Frank.'

'That's just heartbreakin' to hear, Sheriff.'

'I also learned that Frank may have arranged to get someone killed in Georgia State Pen.'

'If whoever got killed was connected to the Russells, then he more 'an likely got what was comin' to him.'

'Name was Holt Macklin. I don't doubt he was a bad 'un, but murder is murder, whichever way you look at it.'

'This Macklin a killer?'

'Does that make a difference?' Landis asked.

'Genesis 9:6 If anyone takes a human life, that person's life will also be taken by human hands.'

'Well, by that reasonin', looks like Frank got what was comin' to him, too.'

'There's a balance in all things, Sheriff.'

'You still believe that? After all we've seen?'

'Day I stop believin' that I may as well call it quits,' Barbara said. 'You gotta believe in somethin', right? Even if it's just "an eye for an eye".'

'Yeah, and then the whole world is blind.'

Barbara smiled. 'Gettin' all philosophical don't suit you none. You's a lawman, always have been, always will be. You're decent and honest, and that counts for a lot in this world. Sure, you ain't exactly the life and soul o' the party, but that's okay. Someone's gotta steer the boat or we all end up drownin'.'

'So, I'm after gettin' these records,' Landis said. 'I wanna know if there's more kids that belong to that Republican thing that's gone missin' or been killed. I send that warrant, and all hell's gonna break loose. If there's someone up there that has a mind to keep that information to themselves, I don't want them forewarned.'

'You think that's what's goin' on?'

'I don't know, but I want to find out.'

'Hence you're after this Webster woman to see if she's gonna break the law for you?'

Landis nodded.

'There ain't no goin' back now. She could just as likely turn you in.'

'So what would you do if you were in my shoes?'

Barbara smiled. 'I'd probably do just exactly what you're plannin' on doin'.'

'So let's do it,' Landis said. 'Let's find out what we can about her, and then I'm more an' likely headin' right back to Atlanta.'

62

Abigail Webster was Atlanta-born and raised.

She was third-generation police, her father and paternal grandfather both career cops. Now forty-six, she'd graduated with honors out of the academy. She'd risen to Lieutenant through what appeared to be good, solid endeavor and industry. Her arrest record as a beat cop was substantial, but both in Vice and Homicide she'd shown herself to be a detective of initiative and strong resolve. She'd been invited to move to Internal Affairs on two occasions, but each time she'd declined. An offer to work in the Attorney General's Justice Collaboration Unit had been accepted in 1981, and she'd assumed the senior position in that unit three years later.

Married for fourteen years, she was the mother of two kids. Marcus was eleven, Greta was nine. Her husband, Anthony, was a Battalion Chief for Atlanta Fire Rescue. He managed stations in Hills Park, Adamsville, Washington Park, Grove Park, Riverside and Brookview Heights. The Webster home was in Johns Creek, Fulton County.

Landis looked up Fulton County's sheriff. He didn't know the name or the man.

The deciding factor that affirmed Landis's decision to visit with her was the children. If rightness was not on his side, then perhaps an emotional appeal to her as a mother would compel her to assist him. If she refused, then at least he could ask her to keep this matter to herself until he'd obtained the information he wanted through standard channels.

'So you're headin' down there?' Barbara asked.

'I am.'

'You need me to get onto anythin' else while you're gone?'

'Put together a list of every sheriff in the state,' Landis said. 'I know that's a lot—'

'A hundred and fifty-two,' Barbara said, 'but you know that you have the authority to cross county lines in the pursuit of a felon. You can go anyplace you want to find 'em and bring 'em back.'

'I know that, Barbara,' Landis said, 'but I ain't gonna go to every county to check on missing persons, now am I?'

'An' it's me who's gonna be makin' a hundred and fifty-two phone calls, right?'

'You an' me an' Marshall,' Landis said. 'Why, you got somethin' better to be doin'?'

'Oh, I'm sure I could think o' a whole heap o' things.'

'Well, you think o' them while you're makin' that list, an' then you can get right to 'em when we're done with this.'

'You know, you better not get yourself killed doin' this,' Barbara said. 'I ain't got a mind to be workin' for no one else.'

'Hell, Barb, there ain't no one else who'd put up with you.'

Assuming Webster would be working until the end of the day, Landis didn't set out right away. He corralled his thoughts, made notes on all the things he wanted to discuss with her, and then headed home to change out of uniform.

He ate before he left, and made up a flask of coffee for the journey. He thought about Frank, about their respective lives, their broken history, and he knew his viewpoint about his brother had changed. The better part of twelve years in retrospect, he knew he'd refused to face his own responsibility for what had happened between them. It was true, of course, that the more significant the relationship, the harder the impact of its failing. Little thought was given to those who meant nothing.

Ever since the first conversation with Jim Tom Moody just two weeks after Frank's death, Landis had assumed the worst of his brother. Moody had said that Trenton was corrupt. Painting with colors from his own memory, Landis had been all too willing to accept that Frank was part of that corruption. After all, it suited him to have Frank be the bad guy, not only then but now. It made him right for viewing things the way he did – that everything that had happened had happened because of Frank, and he'd been nothing more nor less than the unwitting victim of circumstance.

But it was not true. Nothing but the truth resolved unanswered questions. It was the same for all of life. At the bottom of every irreconcilable difference was a lie. It was the lie that kept it going, twisting things in such a way as to obscure reality. No matter how you took it apart, if the facts were concealed or altered then the conflict would remain.

Admission of his own responsibility for the division between himself and Frank would perhaps be the beginning of letting go. That Frank had to die to bring this about was the real tragedy, for now there would never be a chance to repair what had been broken.

Frank was gone, and with him the impossible hope that they could once again be brothers.

Landis knew he would have to live with that for the rest of his life. He also knew that if things went south, that might not be very long at all.

63

Landis waited until Abigail Webster had been home more than an hour before he headed on up to the porch and knocked the door.

There was already a truck in the drive, presumably the husband's, and he guessed that she'd want to get out of her uniform, see to the children, attend to the everyday for a little while.

When Webster saw Landis standing on her porch, the expression of surprise was quickly followed by concern.

She opened the door.

Landis expected an immediate barrage of questions – what was he doing at her home, why had he come, what on earth was he thinking?

There was none of that.

'You should have forewarned me,' Webster said.

'I didn't want to be refused.'

She stepped back, held the door wide.

'I guess you'd better come in then,' she said.

Landis went through into a wide hallway that opened out into a kitchen on the right.

'Is this a bad time?' he asked.

'Let's just say that there ain't gonna be a good one.'

Webster closed the front door.

'Wait there,' she said.

She headed into the kitchen. Words were exchanged.

Returning, she said, 'Follow me.'

Landis did so, passing the kitchen doorway as he went. Webster's husband and kids were seated at a breakfast bar. Without a word, all three of them watched him pass by. They did not acknowledge him, and he made no effort to apologize for his unexpected arrival.

At the end of the hallway, Webster went left and out through a door into the garage. An impressive range of tools was secured on the wall. On the far side was another door. Unlocking this, she held it open for Landis. He went through and found himself in the back yard. To the right and along the length of the house was a veranda. An arrangement of chairs surrounded a low table. The floor was scattered with toys. After collecting them up and putting them in a trunk behind the chairs, Webster took a seat. Landis followed suit.

'I think I know why you're here,' she said. 'But you tell me what the hell is goin' on.'

'I came to ask for some help,' Landis said.

'With?'

'Same people I spoke of when I came to see you at your office.'

Webster leaned her head back and closed her eyes.

'You seem set to drag me somewhere I really don't want to go,' she eventually said.

'I ain't gonna drag you anyplace,' Landis replied. 'Besides, you don't seem the draggin' type.'

Webster cracked a smile. 'So, what are you gonna do if I don't agree to help you? Render an emotional appeal or threaten to shoot my dog?'

'The first then the second, I guess.'

'Tell me your troubles, Sheriff.'

'Seems to me you have a notion of your own,' Landis said.

'Based on our previous discussion, I'm thinkin' that you got your teeth into the Russells. You want information that's gonna be denied you because one o' them is protected.'

'I don't want to follow channels for that reason. I don't want to be stopped from doin' this.'

'So give me the backstory.'

Landis told her all that she needed to know.

'But you got three dead girls, an' only two of them might be connected by this volunteer thing, right?'

'I think that the Rayford girl was killed for a different reason, but by the same people.'

Again, Webster paused. She looked down the yard. Landis could hear the machinery of her mind.

'I don't want to help you,' she said, 'but you're gonna make me feel obliged, aren't you?'

'It ain't a matter of obligation to anythin' but the truth, Lieutenant.'

Webster smiled. 'If we're going to be thick as thieves, you can at least call me Abigail.'

'Abigail it is. My name is Victor.'

'Well, Victor, you're crossin' a line that's very clear here. If you can't get this volunteer register thing on your own and you're comin' to me for it, then both of us are breakin' a whole host of confidentiality protocols. It isn't a minor matter, and it could mean the end of both our careers in law enforcement.'

'The end has to justify the means. That's my only defense.'

'And if you're wrong? What then? What happens if these people have absolutely nothin' to do with it?'

'Then I guess no one'll hear about it.'

Webster shook her head resignedly. 'In some other world, maybe. The world I'm from, there ain't gonna be no gettin' around it.'

'You can deny it.'

'I thought you just said somethin' about an obligation to the truth.'

'Truth is relative, Abigail. I'm just not gonna let it lie. If you can't help me, then I understand. You got a family. You got kids. You got all manner of obligations and people who rely on you. You also got one hell of an impressive service record. Those things I don't have. I just got a bone in my craw on this thing, and I also got the possibility that there's more girls who've been abducted and killed.'

'You really believe that?'

'I do, yes. But I also believe that three is already enough.'

Webster looked at Landis for some seconds and then said, 'You got a smoke?'

Landis lit it for her. She smoked a while. Halfway down, she put it out beneath the sole of her shoe.

'Quit more 'an five years,' she said. 'Look what you're doin' to me.'

'Maybe all you gotta do is point me in the direction of someone else,' Landis said. 'I'm comin' to you because you're the only person I know. If you can think of someone else . . .'

'I ain't gonna send you to someone else, Victor,' Webster said. 'I just gotta reconcile this in my own mind.'

'If you need time . . .'

Webster leaned forward. 'We take an oath. We pledge allegiance to uphold the Constitution and the laws of the state. We defend citizens against all enemies, foreign and domestic. That's what we promise to do. What happens when the enemies are within? What happens then? What about breaking one law to uphold or enforce another? Whose side are you on? More to the point, how will it be viewed?'

'I already made my decision,' Landis said, 'but you and I have completely different circumstances.'

'You have no wife, no kids?'

'I had a wife. She's dead now. We never had kids.'

'And your brother got murdered.'

'Yes, he did.'

'And the Russells did that, too.'

'That's how it appears.'

'Christ almighty, Victor, you really worked up a sad story, didn't you?'

'I guess I did. That wasn't the plan, but when do you ever plan to screw up your life?'

'You ain't gonna get me feelin' sorry for you,' Webster said. 'That is somethin' I ain't gonna do. Sympathy never did anyone any good anyhow.'

Landis nodded. 'Okay,' he said. 'I'll head out. You think it over. Let me know as soon as you can.'

'I thought it,' Webster said. 'I am somewhere between feelin' like I don't have a choice and thinkin' to hell with it. I mean, what's the worst that could happen, eh? Headin' towards fifty, unemployed, maybe even facin' a jail sentence. Never work in law enforcement again, can't pay my mortgage, can't feed my kids. And my husband works for the city so they'd probably tar him with the same brush. I'd have to go back to East Point and live with my folks.'

'I got a couple of empty rooms in Blairsville,' Landis said.

Webster gave Landis a wry smile.

'Sometimes you gotta do what you know to be right, irrespective of the consequences.'

'I keep tellin' myself that.'

'Does it help?' Webster asked.

Landis shrugged. 'I'll let you know.'

64

On Friday morning, Landis called both Barbara and Marshall into his office.

'I'm hopin' by Monday we'll have this register,' he explained.

'You submitted the warrant?' Marshall said as he took a seat.

'I went a different way.'

'She's gonna help you,' Barbara said matter-of-factly.

'Who's helpin'?' Marshall asked.

'Best you don't know who, Marshall,' Barbara said.

'Are we breakin' the law?'

'Bendin' it some,' Landis said. 'But don't you worry yourself about it, Deputy. This blows up then I'm the one in the firin' line.'

'Hell, you might be the captain, but we're all on the same boat, ain't we?' Barbara said.

'Bail out, then,' Landis replied. 'I won't hold it against you.'

'Didn't mean it that way. Meant that if you go down, then I'm goin' with you.'

'Well, let's hope it never gets to that, eh?'

Marshall was still baffled. 'So someone is givin' you this register of names. All these volunteer kids, right?'

'That's right,' Landis replied. 'Ten thousand or thereabouts. We're gonna have to go through the entire thing, take out all the boys, then cross-check every girl by county against deceased or missing persons.'

'Hell, I'm plumb wore out just thinkin' about it,' Marshall said.

'It's called policin', Marshall,' Barbara said. 'If you didn't already know, this is what you signed up for.'

Landis leaned forward. 'All you're gonna be doin' is what I tell you to do, Marshall. If this gets to be a mess, you just say you were followin' orders. That ain't a lie. The less you know about how I got this information, the better. All you gotta think about is the fact that there's three dead girls, maybe a good few more, and the better job we do here, the less likely it is that there'll be any more.'

'I ain't sayin' I won't do it, Sheriff,' Marshall said. 'I just ain't got a habit for bein' halfway on things.'

'Do the job I need you to do, but be content with gettin' halfway in trouble, okay?'

'Meantime?' Barbara asked.

'Meantime, as best you can, clear your desks of anythin' outstandin'. Once we get this information we're gonna be flat out.'

Marshall got up. He opened his mouth to say something and then seemed to change his mind.

'If you're gonna say it then just say it, Marshall,' Landis said.

'I guess you're gettin' into whatever happened to your brother. I ain't never said how sorry I was to hear of it.'

'I appreciate that, Marshall.'

'I also guess I don't want you to wind up dead. You're a good man, fair and decent, and there don't seem to be too many o' them around these days.'

'Well, Marshall, if that's what happens I'll be expectin' you to run for sheriff come the next election.'

'I would, you know? The hell with it. I know I'm young, but I could do a good job I reckon.'

Barbara stood up. 'Don't go gettin' your hat measured,

Marshall. We'll come out the other side o' this with no more dead sheriffs if I have anythin' to do with it.'

Landis smiled. 'You pair are somethin', you really are. Lord only knows what I'd do without you.'

Barbara smiled. 'More 'an likely be in a great deal more trouble than you already are.'

65

True to his word, Landis fulfilled his promise to go to dinner at Eleanor's place on Saturday evening.

He called early afternoon to make sure it was still on.

'Hell yeah,' Eleanor said. 'Jenna's been askin' after you.'

'How's she gettin' on?'

'You can come find out for yourself.'

'Shall I bring anythin'?'

'Just yourself, Victor. That'll suffice.'

'Okay, then. I'll see you around seven.'

Landis ironed a shirt and dug out a sport coat he hadn't worn for years. Unused to socializing, the last time he'd dressed up was for his brother's funeral.

On the drive over to Trenton, he listened to music on the radio. He forced himself not to work up an anxiety about what he was doing. It would serve no purpose.

He arrived on time. Eleanor opened the door, but Jenna was right behind her within a moment. She edged past her mother and threw her arms around Landis.

'We're havin' tuna casserole,' she said. 'I helped make it.'

Eleanor looked him up and down.

'You scrub up pretty good,' she said.

Landis smiled awkwardly.

'Come on an' get yourself inside.'

In the kitchen, the table was laid up for four. One of the seats was occupied by the stuffed monkey.

'You takin' a beer?' Eleanor asked.

'I will, thank you,' Landis said. He sat down beside the monkey.

'So, how're you gettin' on?' Landis asked Jenna. 'I guess you're back in school.'

'I am. It's okay, I guess. I suck at math, but everythin' else is pretty good.'

'What's your favorite thing?'

'History.'

'What you been learnin'?'

'Just about the civil war an' stuff.'

Eleanor put a bottle of beer in front of Landis, and then sat down herself.

'Also about stuff in England,' Jenna said. 'The pilgrims comin' over an' all that. What happened to the Native American Indians. How we killed so many o' them and took the land and whatever.'

'A bad business,' Landis said.

'People are crazy,' Jenna said. 'I mean really crazy, right?'

'Some, some not. I think most folks are decent. That's my experience anyway.'

'I guess,' Jenna said, and then added, 'Two Victors at the table. Uncle Victor and Monkey Victor.'

Landis raised his bottle. 'Here's to Monkey Victor. I guess he must be partial to a bit of tuna casserole, right?'

'No, he just gets bananas.'

'Well, he seems pleased enough anyways.'

Eleanor tended to the food.

'I ain't much of a cook,' she explained. 'At least that's what Frank used to say.' She caught herself, glanced at Jenna. Jenna seemed to pay no mind to the comment.

'Anyway, it is what it is. If it sucks, you don't gotta eat it.'

'I'm sure it'll be just fine, Eleanor.'

A tray of casserole was centered on the table. There was a bowl of green beans and some corn too.

Landis hesitated. He was unsure of dinner protocol.

'So let's eat,' Eleanor said. 'It don't taste no better cold.'

Jenna made up a plate for Landis. It was as good as any he'd had before. He said as much.

'I like it too,' Jenna said. 'But mostly because I made it.'

Landis took a second helping. He was hungrier than he thought.

'I'll take it as a compliment as opposed to the fact that you probably haven't eaten all day,' Eleanor said.

'It was really good,' Landis said, 'so thank you to both of you.'

Eleanor cleared away the plates.

'We got red velvet cake,' Jenna said.

'Which we're gonna have a little later, young lady,' Eleanor said. 'You go on and watch TV for a little while. I wanna have a talk with your uncle.'

Jenna looked at Landis with a dismissive expression. 'Grown-up stuff, right?'

Landis looked at Eleanor for support.

'Boring stuff,' Eleanor said. 'Money an' bills an' whatnot. We won't be long then you come on back and serve up the cake, okay?'

'Okay,' Jenna said. She slid off the chair, grabbed the monkey, and took off into the living room. Moments later the sound of the TV filtered through into the kitchen.

'Money an' bills?' Landis asked.

'No. That's all fine. I just wanted to ask about what's happenin' with this investigation into Frank's death.'

'Right,' Landis said. 'Well, as it stands not a great deal. I'm workin' on it, Eleanor, an' I got a whole bunch more questions that need answers.'

'Isn't this guy from Trenton PD s'posed to be dealin' with it?'

'He was. I guess he still is. However, this is personal for me so I ain't got reasons to get busy with other stuff.'

Eleanor leaned back in the chair. In that moment she seemed so very tired.

'I just wanna know, I guess,' she said. 'I mean, we were divorced for more years than we were together, but that don't change the fact that he was Jenna's dad. Sometimes she looks at me, says things, you know, and I can see him.'

'I guess so. I know it's tough, but whatever happened with him is a good deal more complex than some random hit an' run. I mean, sure, as a sheriff, I got the authority to go into any county I want chasin' a felon, but right now I ain't got a felon to chase. You're just gonna have to be patient with me, Eleanor. I'm doin' the best I can, believe me, and I ain't quittin' 'til we know what really happened.'

'I need to know for her too,' Eleanor said, nodding towards the living room. 'She asks about him, about you, about why he got killed. She ain't stupid. I told her it was an accident but she don't believe a word o' that.'

'She said the same to me.'

Eleanor frowned. 'When?'

'First time I came here. After the funeral.'

'What did she say?'

'She said that you told her Frank had been killed in a car accident, but she knew it was a lie.'

'Really?'

Landis nodded. 'She also asked me to find out what happened. She said that it had been her brother then she'd wanna know why someone had run him down and broken him all to pieces. Those were her exact words.'

'Oh my God,' Eleanor said, visibly shocked. 'I had no idea.'

'She also said that if I didn't want to know too, then I should ask myself some tough questions about why.'

'And what did you say?'

'I didn't say nothin'. She was right.'

Eleanor stayed silent for a while. Her expression said enough.

'So, to be honest, until she said that to me, I was kinda prepared to let it go. I mean, maybe I wouldn't have. Maybe it would have worked its way under my skin an' I'd be doin' this anyway, but that was the clincher.'

'You sayin' that you would have let it be, that you wouldn't have investigated this?'

Landis sighed resignedly. 'Hell, I don't know, Eleanor. Me an' Frank... see, you gotta understand that I bore a grudge toward him that was something fierce. I held onto that for a long time, kept it goin' in my mind pretty much every day. I figured that what happened between us was his doin', not mine. Time changes that. That he got killed changes it even more. Now I see it different.'

'I'm the same,' Eleanor said.

'The same? How?'

Eleanor took a deep sigh. 'Jesus,' she said. 'I'm not even capable of thinkin' about this.'

'Look,' Landis said, 'I know it ain't none o' my business...'

'We were married for five years. Hell, not even five years,' Eleanor said. 'I mean, I knew what I was gettin' into. At least I had some inklin'. Your brother... well, you know all about your brother, I guess. He was a personality. Let's put it that way. He was a big personality. He had an opinion sometimes, and it might've been the dumbest opinion to ever leave someone's lips, but he just got on a horse about it and rode the darn thing to death. First of all, that was one o' the things that made him special, you know? He didn't give a good God darn what other folks said or thought, and you could respect that. After a year, two, it just got wearisome. It was like bein' in a fight with somethin' you couldn't even see, an' it just wore me down. I mean, he wasn't only to blame. I ain't the easiest person to live with. Always two sides, right?'

Landis nodded in agreement. He knew what had happened between Eleanor and his brother but he wanted to hear it from her directly.

'I guess I started to see the seams comin' apart at the start of '84. It all went to hell, but it was kinda slow motion, little by little. He was here less and less. He was away with work stuff more an' more. I got it in my head that there was another woman, an' I still don't know to this day whether that was the case. You ain't got an answer for somethin', you just invent anythin' that will explain what you think is goin' on, don't you?'

'Yes,' Landis said. 'I know that well enough.'

'Anyways, it got kinda crazy. I was drinkin', he was drinkin', and after a year o' that we had to get away from each other before one of us wound up dead.'

'And Jenna was just a little kid while all this was goin' on.'

'She was indeed, so she ain't had the easiest time of it, that's for sure. Never ceases to amaze me that she ain't a great deal more trouble than she is. All things considered, she's kinda bulletproof.'

Landis was not upset by what Eleanor was telling him, but it served to remind him of all that he'd both loved and despised about his brother. It also reminded him of the death of his own wife and what he'd learned about her after she'd gone. The walls of his own world had collapsed around him and left him buried beneath a tonnage of emotional rubble. Even now, these many years later, he was still clambering out of it with eyes full of dust.

Eleanor reached out and touched Landis's hand. 'You know, I know we never met before Frank and I got married. I knew about you, of course, and I would've come to your wife's funeral. Frank said that things were so bad between you that I knew he'd never have let me anyway. I think things would've gotten real ugly.'

'Things were ugly enough without you,' Landis said. 'We were already enemies before you got married. I wasn't even aware of it. I saw him after my wife died. Just once. That was the last time I seen him … I mean, before I had to go on out to Trenton and identify his body.' Landis took a deep breath. 'I busted his nose, Eleanor. I got so mad at him I busted his nose.'

'What the hell? You did that? He told me some feller in a bar did it.'

'That was me. No one else.'

'Why in God's name? What the hell did you fight about?'

'It don't matter now, Eleanor. It really don't. Brothers, right?'

Eleanor leaned back. She closed her eyes for a moment.

'The man was a hurricane o' trouble, I'll give him that much. Never a dull day, right?'

'Like you, I got to the point where enough was enough. Didn't matter we were blood, I just didn't want him around anymore.'

'Do you regret that?' Eleanor asked.

'Regret is pointless.'

'I know that. Don't mean you don't still feel it.'

'Like I said, time changes things. What I thought I was mad at wasn't what I was mad at. I look back and I understand his way o' seein' things. At least some of it. He did what he thought was right. I did, too. They just weren't the same things.'

Eleanor spent some time in her own thoughts, and then she smiled and said, 'I'm gonna have a shot of whiskey and a smoke in the yard. You wanna join me?'

'Sure thing,' Landis said. 'And then we get cake, right?'

'As much as you can eat.'

*

Landis left at nine. He'd watched TV with Jenna, talked about this and that, eaten the cake, and then had one more smoke out in the yard with Eleanor.

He wanted to tell her what he knew, but couldn't find the words to fit. He figured he would tell her at some point, but later, after he'd learned the truth of Frank's death.

Driving back to Blairsville, he felt as if he was driving away from half of his life. That was how it now seemed, that he was inextricably connected to Eleanor, to his niece, to that house in Trenton where his brother had once lived.

Back then, all those years ago, he had refused to listen to Frank, and then refused to listen to himself. The world he'd built for himself was soundless. Now it was filled with voices, and though many of them he did not want to hear, it was still strangely preferable to the interminable silence of the past.

66

The information that arrived from Abigail Webster late on Monday morning was better than Landis had hoped.

The stack of pages she'd sent over had been printed from a single perforated run. Understanding what Landis was trying to do, Webster had limited her search to the names of girls. Counting the names down one sheet, Landis estimated there were just over two thousand in total. Alongside the names were ages, addresses, the relevant county, also the regional office that covered those counties. Dividing the pages into three, he, Barbara and Marshall would each have about seven hundred names to go through. The amount of work that had been saved by Webster's conscientiousness was significant.

It was clear from the start that teenage members of the Georgia Young Republicans came from right across the state. It spanned one hundred and fifty-two counties, each with its own sheriff, and each would need contacting with a separate list of names to cross-check. Whichever way it broke down, it was an unenviable task, but Landis saw no other means by which they could gauge the scope of this thing.

Landis, even before he began the laborious task, had an intuitive certainty that the result of their endeavor would be a substantial list of missing teenagers from right across Georgia.

Landis determined that Macon – as the central hub – covered counties for roughly fifty miles in each direction. Valdosta encompassed everything from Dooly and Pulaski down to Lowndes, Echols and the Florida state line. Savannah covered the east – Jefferson to Screven and right on to South Carolina. Savannah was responsible for everything west to Alabama.

Intent on establishing whether his initiative was founded on anything but guesswork, Landis instructed Barbara and Marshall to focus on the counties that were managed by the GRYV office in Trenton. This territory ran all the way from Dade to Rabun, on down around Atlanta, Athens and a little way north of Augusta. They worked quickly, identifying by county name, Barbara typing as they went. Though it took the better part of four hours, they finally had a list detailing close to four hundred names from twenty-nine different counties.

Satisfied that this was a realistic starting point, Landis first noted the counties that bordered Tennessee and both Carolinas, then their southern neighbors. Thirteen counties in all, Dade to the west, Rabun the most easterly. From those alone Landis counted thirty-one girls. None of them came from Union or Fannin.

Aside from Linda Bishop, there was only one other girl from Walker County. Sara-Louise Lacey was one of four from Rabun. Landis had Marshall call both Willard Montgomery and Carl Parsons. Both came back negative on the additional names. Landis crossed them off the list.

With ten counties remaining, Landis had Barbara type up fax despatches to the relevant sheriffs of each. Marked urgent, the list of girls for each was given along with dates of birth and places of residence. To ensure swift responses, he divided the counties between Marshall and Barbara and had them follow up the faxes with a direct call to the relevant offices.

They waited patiently. Barbara made coffee. Landis went out behind the building and smoked.

By six that evening, all ten offices had responded.

The three of them sat at Landis's desk and looked at the information they'd been sent.

Going back six years, there were a total of seven outstanding and unresolved missing persons reports. There was one girl each from Catoosa, Whitfield and Gilmer. White had two, Habersham the same. Aged between fifteen and eighteen, seven girls had vanished into thin air, never to be seen again.

'And this is just from thirteen counties,' Barbara said. 'We got another hundred and thirty-nine to go.'

'Unless this is localized to the north,' Landis said.

'How d'you figure that?'

'The Russells are up near Colwell. If they're behind this, then maybe they keep their business as close to home as possible. You abduct somebody, you wanna get them off the road and out of sight as quickly as possible. I could be wrong, sure, but that would make sense to me.'

'Even so, we're only talking forty or fifty miles down to Gainesville,' Barbara said. 'You run a line west from there to Rome or Cedartown you've got dozens more counties to consider.'

'I understand that, Barbara,' Landis said, 'but already we've got seven more girls that could be part of this thing. I'm thinkin' that we make a start with these and see where it takes us.'

'So what's next?' Marshall asked.

'Get onto the respective offices and ask for copies of whatever they have on each of these girls.'

'They're gone for the night now,' Barbara said.

'So send the requests. Hopefully they'll come back to us first thing tomorrow.'

Marshall picked up the list of names. 'So – what? You figure we got some sort of ... I don't know, like a sex-trafficking thing going on here? And whoever's behind it is using this database of teenagers from the volunteer thing?'

'I don't know what we got, Marshall,' Landis said. ''Cept two dead girls an' a further seven missin' whose names are on this list. That's enough for me to get awful busy awful quick.'

'I'll take care o' this,' Barbara said. 'It ain't gonna take long. You go on home to your wife, Marshall.'

'You sure?'

'I'm sure she cooked you a fine dinner. Wouldn't want it goin' to waste now, would we?' She glanced at Landis. 'As for you, you ain't got no one cookin' anythin', so you can stay and do this with me.'

67

Again Landis did not sleep well.

The night was interminable, his mind preoccupied by a single thought. They had requested and received outstanding missing persons reports for the counties in question. They had not asked for unsolved murders.

His recollection of the images of both Linda Bishop and Sara-Louise Lacey crowded around him like the vestiges of a nightmare. It was a sickening thing to consider. What kind of people did this? Seemingly devoid of all humanity, who would abduct, rape, torture and kill a teenage girl? Could they even be considered human?

Landis could not conceive of this being the work of one individual. As Marshall had said, perhaps it was some kind of trafficking operation. Someone at State was aware of this, had helped to cover it up, had provided protection for Eugene Russell and whoever else was involved. If not directly implicated, they had condoned and sanctioned it by the mere fact that they knew it was happening and had turned a blind eye. For what? Money? Surely nothing so base and self-serving?

But greed was at the heart of so much evil, whether it be individual or global. History – if nothing else – demonstrated that no matter how degraded and destructive an act could be imagined, the reality of what people were capable of was infinitely worse.

These were people without conscience, without morals, without guilt. And perhaps Frank had walked this road before, and it had taken him all the way to his death.

Landis went early to the office. He took a pin board and set it on the top of a filing cabinet beside his desk. To the left he put a picture of Ella May, in the center the images of Linda Bishop and Sara-Louise Lacey. Over to the right he would put photographs of the other seven girls who had disappeared. If nothing else, it would keep him focused on what he was doing, and – more importantly – why. He did not doubt his own resolve to see this through to the end – whatever that might be – but he wanted a constant reminder that this was a personal crusade. Families had been shattered with violence. Heartbroken parents waited patiently, knowing all the while that when the news came it would be worse than they'd imagined. Closure would never be achieved until the precise details of what had happened were revealed. Even if there was no body, even if the mortal remains of their child could not be laid to rest, at least the interminable question would be answered and they could – perhaps – move on.

The fear that Fredericksen had manifested was as real as any other part of this. Landis wanted to believe the man. He did not know why Frank had been burdened by such debts that he couldn't meet the payments for Jenna's support, but the fact that Fredericksen had stepped up and made good said a lot about the man. It also said a great deal about the loyalty he still had to Frank. Facing this together, Frank and Mike Fredericksen had pursued this as far as they could until the intimidation and threats had become real. Fredericksen could not risk the well-being of his wife and children. Every man had a point at which he had to stop. Landis, having no one reliant upon him, was still very far from that line. The mere fact of continuing this investigation, the involvement of Abigail Webster, the other sheriffs who'd met at Barbara's, even the simple fact of requesting information from a further five county sheriffs, would put him in the crosshairs.

Landis knew that his brother's life had been sacrificed to hide the truth. Perhaps the only way to now attain closure was to put his own life on the line to reveal it.

68

It wasn't until late afternoon on Wednesday – two months to the day since Frank's murder – that all the requested files on the missing girls came in.

Landis and Barbara went through them together. They pinned pictures on the board.

Ten girls looked back at them. The youngest – Nicole Crawford out of Graysville, Catoosa, reported missing back in November of 1989 – was nothing more than a child in Landis's eyes. Smiling at him from a picture that had been taken on some long-ago summer day, her eyes bright with life, it seemed the worst kind of horror. He remembered how he'd considered that someone might possess an intuitive inkling that this would be their last day, but looking at this teenager, he believed that this would have been the furthest thought from her mind.

The others – Dorothy Blake from Dalton, Whitfield; Nancy Morgan from Ellijay in Gilmer; Allison McCormick and Sarah Buchanan from Robertstown and Leaf in White County; Melissa Franklin from Clarksville and Erin Howard from Cornelia in Habersham – spanned all of six years. The earliest – the McCormick girl – had disappeared on her way home from school on Wednesday October 1, 1986. According to the file, she'd walked the same three-quarter mile route every day, most often alone, and somewhere between a sighting at a convenience store where she bought a pack of watermelon-flavored Big

League Chew and the road that led away from the highway and down to her home, she'd just vanished into thin air.

In all cases, the investigations undertaken had been thorough and comprehensive. Parents, relatives, friends, teachers, even handymen and gardeners who tended to the relevant properties, had been questioned. Fliers were posted, volunteer search parties were established, and extensive canvassing of the locality of each disappearance had been carried out.

In every case the efforts of the sheriffs, deputies and citizens had come to nothing.

Barbara stood by the window. For a while she said nothing. She just stared at the faces, the expression on her face one of disbelief.

'We could have done more,' Landis said. 'I could have done more for Ella May. I feel that I could have … Christ, Barbara, I feel like I should've been all over this right from the start.'

'That ain't gonna serve any purpose,' Barbara said. 'It was one girl. She wasn't even from here. She was George Milstead's responsibility more than yours. I know she was found here, but she was from McCaysville. Besides, your own damn brother got killed just two weeks beforehand. I'm impressed that you even showed up for work.'

'Even so …'

'Even so nothin',' Barbara interjected. 'What good is it gonna do, eh? What possible good is it gonna do for any of us to think about what we might've done. We didn't know, did we? We thought it was an isolated case. We're now weeks down the line, and here we got somethin' that we could never have predicted. Not in a million years. I mean, hell, the Bishop girl was found dead back in February, and the Lacey girl had been missing for how long by the time they found her?'

'Disappeared in December of last year. But she'd been dead

only a month or so. She was alive and somewhere for all that time intervenin'.'

'Okay, so there we are. Just recognize the fact that you're on it now, okay? You're doin' somethin' about it. Anythin' you do now is gonna make a difference, ain't it? We get to the bottom o' this, and we'll have saved how many girls that would've otherwise wound up the same darn way?'

'We'll never know, will we?'

'We won't. You're right. But no matter how much you're gettin' rained on, you gotta keep your powder dry, ain't cha? Mentally speakin'.'

Landis gave a wry smile. 'You're just an endless source of some off-kilter homespun wisdom.'

'Make light of it, why don'tcha? Women know these things. Men don't, so they gotta be told. Sometimes they gotta be told a hundred times afore they get it.'

'I got it, Barb.'

'You sure now, or you want me to say it again?'

'No, I got it,' Landis replied.

He took a seat at his desk. Barbara sat facing him.

'So, where you goin' now?' she asked.

'General or specific?'

'Both.'

Landis looked over at the photographs once more. 'Common denominator is the volunteer organization. All of them were registered save Ella May, but it looks like she was killed as some kind o' warning to Vester Rayford. Because of the drugs in her system and the way she was tied, we're attributing her death to the same person that killed Linda and Sara-Louise. It pains me, but I'm now assumin' that these other seven are also dead. They're buried somewhere and ain't never been found.'

''Cept for the fact that the Lacey girl was alive for eight months or so before she was murdered.'

'So maybe some of them are still alive. If so, where are they?' Landis nodded towards the pin board. 'I mean, the McCormick girl has been missing for six years. If she's alive then she's twenty-two years old. If this is some kind o' teenage sex-traffickin' thing, then what happens when the abducted girls ain't no longer teenagers?'

'I think we got our answer to that question already,' Barbara said. 'Maybe they just get worn out and thrown away.'

Landis nodded resignedly. 'Hell, I can't stop thinkin' 'bout the parents, you know? And what about brothers and sisters. Can you imagine havin' to grow up—'

Landis stopped mid-sentence.

'What?' Barbara asked.

'Did you see any brothers and sisters? In the files? Did you see mention of any brothers and sisters in any of these investigations?'

Barbara got up. She brought the files from the table on the other side of the office. Handing half of them to Landis, they started to go through them again.

'They're all only children, aren't they?' Landis asked. It was a rhetorical question.

'Certainly appears that way,' Barbara said. 'So what the hell ...'

'More likely to be alone. Siblings attend the same schools, hang out together, have friends in common. Maybe these girls were more likely to go out alone to see folks, to walk back from school on their own. It mayn't be somethin', but it would be a helluva coincidence if they were random and yet every one o' them turned out to be the only child in the family.'

'And how does this help us?' Barbara asked.

'I don't know, Barb, but it sure as hell lends itself to the notion that they were bein' selected, don't it? Someone was goin' through that register and pickin' teenage girls. They were bein' chosen, weren't they? Because of their age, how they looked, where they came from, how easy it would be to follow them, abduct them...'

'Hell, Sheriff, you make it sound like some sort of factory process.'

'So maybe that's what it is,' Landis replied.

Barbara shook her head in dismay. 'I'm strugglin' with this, I have to say. I find it hard to believe that anyone could be that wicked. I mean. Lord almighty, what kind of person are we dealin' with here? And what kind o' preparation d'you get for investigatin' somethin' like this? All the years I been here, and that's a good few years more than you, and I ain't never seen anythin' that comes even close to what we're lookin' at here. I mean, it ain't like they done lessons for this in sheriff school, is it?'

'Sheriff school,' Landis said dryly. 'The old alma mater. I remember it well.'

'Just thinkin' on it makes my head hurt,' Barbara said. 'I don't think I'm gonna sleep until this thing's set to rights.'

'Well, no one's dealin' with it but us, and we gotta figure out where we go from here.'

'Don't see we got any choice but to find out who has access to these records in Atlanta. Seems to me there's gotta be a link between that and the Attorney General's Office. Someone in there is coverin' tracks for Eugene Russell, ain't they? Someone's got the authority to make everyone look the other way when they start snoopin' into that man's business.'

'I seen him twice,' Landis said, 'an' both times he pointed me in the direction of Trenton. He got me thinkin' it was Frank that was involved in this, that Frank was as crooked as the day is long. He was just misdirectin' me, that's what he was doin'.'

'Man's got more twist in him than a rattler.'

'So, now we need to know when he got registered as a

confidential informant. Someone did that, for sure, and it wasn't Abigail Webster. If it had, she woulda said so.'

Barbara got up and went back to her desk. She returned with the notes she'd made when looking up Webster's history.

'Been there for eleven years,' she said. 'Headed it up since sometime in '84.'

'Let's follow that up, Barb. See if you can't find out who else works there, who was runnin' it before Webster, eh? That should be easy enough to find out.'

'I'll get onto it,' Barbara said.

'And where the hell is Marshall?'

'Oh, he's taken his wife to the doctor's office.'

'She sick?'

'I think she's pregnant, Sheriff. I'm guessin' our Marshall's gonna be a daddy soon enough.'

Landis didn't reply. A question hit him broadside. What would have happened if he'd done the same, if things had worked out with his wife, if he'd been an attentive husband and raised a family?

Perhaps, after all, it was better that he was alone. If something happened, there would be no one left behind to grieve.

69

With the information that Barbara brought to Landis when he arrived on Thursday morning, the feeling was one of disbelief.

He had no trust in coincidence, and thus the effect of the news was all the more disconcerting. It seemed there was a pattern to all things, that he was somehow caught in the middle of some grand deception, a trick of the universe, and that with each step forward he was walking behind someone who had had orchestrated everything to unnerve and unsettle him.

Ray Floyd, prior to deputising for both Frank and George Milstead, had served in the Police Department. Why he moved from the PD to the Sheriff's Office, Landis did not know. It did not matter. What mattered was that he'd worked in the Attorney General's Justice Collaboration Unit for the four years between 1977 and 1981.

Landis called Webster, found her absent from the office. He called her twice more, leaving messages each time. He could imagine he was the last person from whom she wished to hear, but he impressed upon her assistant the urgency required.

It was after noon when she returned the call.

'I just have a question,' he said. 'I'm hopin' you can answer it for me.'

'Okay.'

'You took your current position back in 1981 if I understand correctly.'

'Yes, that's right.'

'Who was your predecessor?'

'My predecessor here?' Webster asked.

'Yes. Who headed up the unit before you?'

'Why are you askin' this, Victor?'

'I got a name here and I'm just tryin' to verify somethin', that's all.'

'His name was Jim Whelan.'

'He was Police Department?'

'Yes, of course. This position is always held by someone in the PD.'

'And did you know someone called Ray Floyd?' Landis asked.

Again, a moment's pause. 'Floyd? No, I can't say I know anyone by that name.'

'Can you find out if a Ray Floyd worked in that unit before you started? As far as I see he must've been there from some-time in '77.'

'Sure I can, but I'd really like to know why.'

'I need to know who registered Eugene Russell as a confidential human resource, Abigail. I'm thinkin' it may have been this Ray Floyd.'

'Okay, I'll check it out.'

'And what happened to Jim Whelan?'

'Jim retired early,' Webster said. 'Health, I think. He wasn't retirement age.'

'And do you know where he went?'

'I have no idea. If you want, I can try and find out.'

'Be really appreciated if you could.'

Once more there was silence for a few moments, and then Webster said, 'I'm guessin' you got what I sent over.'

'I did, yes.'

'You gettin' somewhere with it?'

'Somewhere I didn't wanna be goin', but yes, I am.'

'I gotta tell you, I'm on eggshells, Victor. I feel like I'm waitin' for a bomb to go off someplace.'

'Same here,' Landis said. 'I plan to have that happen as far away from you as possible.'

'Well, I did what I did. I have to take responsibility for that. I'll get this information and come back to you.'

'If I ain't here, give whatever you find to Barbara Wedlock. She's my dispatch up here.'

'Will do,' Webster said. 'You take care now.'

The line went dead. Landis hung up. He sat back and closed his eyes. A deep sense of fatigue invaded him, both physically and mentally. He wanted this thing to end. He wanted to come through and out the other side with all his questions answered. He needed to, if not for the memory of those missing and murdered, then for his own sanity. The world had shifted and changed. It was a darker place than he'd ever known it to be. Though he had no regrets about what he was doing, still it had served to highlight so many things in his own history that could have been different.

Building a case that could be successfully prosecuted was entirely dependent upon probative evidence. Hearsay, rumor, circumstantial material, statements from unreliable witnesses, unsubstantiated facts – no matter how compelling they might appear – were as much use as shovelling smoke when it came to the law.

The law – in and of itself – was designed to protect the innocent and damn the guilty. Good intentions didn't count for anything. Good intentions so very often paved the way to hell.

No matter Landis's belief that Eugene Russell – protected by someone in the Justice Collaboration Unit and thus given free rein to break whatever laws he chose – was ultimately responsible for the abduction, rape and murder of teenage girls, it counted for nothing unless Landis could prove it. He did not have a motive. He had no witnesses, reliable or otherwise. He had a spider's web of seeming coincidences that had led him toward a conclusion that could be entirely wrong.

There was always a danger in assumption. Based on an initial premise, all later information was interpreted to agree with that original premise. Objectivity was sacrificed in the name of justice, revenge, even a vendetta. Even later facts that contradicted initial perceived certainties were discounted, not because they were untrue, but because they didn't fit the predetermined pattern.

Landis was aware of this, even as he gave instructions to both Barbara and Marshall. He had to be willing to have his reality broken apart and scattered to the four corners.

He had to be willing to admit he was wrong, and – from past experience – he knew this would not come easy.

70

Landis overslept on Friday. He did not care. Once awake, he did not hurry to the office.

He took coffee, even made eggs, and then stood on the veranda at the back of the house for a good fifteen minutes before leaving the house.

Webster had called and given Barbara the answers to Landis's questions. Yes, there had been a Ray Floyd in the Justice Collaboration Unit between '77 and '81. He had worked for Jim Whelan directly. Maintaining a position of considerable authority, Floyd had supervised aspects of witness protection, registration of confidential resources, even coordinating with the State Board of Pardons and Paroles.

In 1981, Floyd had transferred from PD to the Sheriff's Office. Between '81 and '86, he was deputy under Sheriff Frank Landis of Dade County. Subsequently he moved to Fannin County to deputise for Milstead. After three years of service he'd committed suicide. It was also Ray Floyd's signature that was to be found on a number of documents relating to the acknowledged status of Eugene Russell as a valued source of information. With Floyd's authority, Russell had been protected by the very law that he'd then proceeded to routinely violate.

As for Jim Whelan, his was a different story altogether, and here Landis saw an opportunity to pursue a line of investigation that had remained unknown to him.

Whelan, also a PD Lieutenant, had taken early retirement on the grounds of ill health in 1981. Abigail Webster had been his replacement as head of the JCU.

According to the information from Webster, Whelan – at the time, forty-five years old and a department veteran of some twenty-two years – had moved back home to Dalton in Whitfield County. Beyond that, there was no additional information. Landis assumed he was still out there, though anything could have transpired in the intervening eleven years. The man would be in his mid-fifties, and though the medical grounds that prompted his retirement could have been anything from high blood pressure to terminal cancer. Landis needed to find out if he was still alive, if he was still in Dalton, and if he could shed any light at all on why Ray Floyd had used his position to hide Eugene Russell's activities from the eyes of the world.

Landis set Barbara onto tracking down Whelan.

While she made calls, Landis had Marshall assist him with a full documented brief detailing all the events that had brought them to the current point in their investigation.

Covering everything from the news of Frank's death, his meetings with Jim Tom Moody, both Russells, the council of the relevant sheriffs at Barbara's house, and both Atlanta trips, he wanted to clearly detail the path he'd taken. It was easy to see why he had followed this road, but equally clear that the road was – in essence – founded on a chain of suspicions and assumptions.

However, nothing changed the fact that three girls were dead, perhaps many more. At least seven girls were still missing, and all but Ella May Rayford were members of the Georgia Young Republican Volunteers.

The conclusions Landis had arrived at were strung together

with tenuous threads, but they were still threads. He had to trust that anything further would serve to add strength and substance to those threads.

A little after three Barbara appeared in the doorway.

From her expression, Landis knew she'd turned up something important.

'This Whelan feller,' she said. 'He's alive an' kickin' alright. He ain't in Dalton no more. He lives outside o' Trenton. Very respectable by all accounts. Family man. Has a son in the Gainesville PD. Other son's an architect in Athens. Our Mr Whelan is a member of the Lions Club, a Rotarian, a regular contributor to various charities…' Barbara paused.

Landis raised his eyebrows.

'And treasurer of the Trenton chapter of your volunteer lot.'

Once again, Landis had the sense that something beyond his understanding was tying things together behind his back.

'All roads lead to Trenton,' he said quietly.

Getting up, Landis walked to the window. He parted the horizontal slats of the blind and looked out toward the street. Everything was the same, nothing out there had changed, and yet he felt that the entire world had shifted on its axis.

'I'm guessin' you'll be headin' out there to see him,' Marshall said.

Landis nodded.

'Now?' Barbara asked.

'In a while,' Landis said. 'I need copies of everything. The files from the different offices, pictures of the girls, everything. I need Whelan's address, whatever else you can find out about his service record, his personal life, the son in Gainesville. Just get me whatever you can find out about the man.'

Landis glanced at the clock.

'I'm goin' home to change,' he said. 'I'll be back in an hour or so. Whatever you've got by then will have to do.'

Landis turned and looked at Barbara and Marshall. He nodded his head resignedly, looked down at the floor, then back up at them.

'Okay,' he said. 'Enough now. This comes to an end, one way or the other.'

71

Trenton sat in a valley. High on the south side were a number of substantial properties that afforded a view that went far beyond the city below.

Landis followed a winding road bordered by lush shrubbery and high banks of trees. Up there, the feeling of space and light was considerable. The landscape was some of the most beautiful that Georgia had to offer.

Parking at the road's edge a couple of hundred yards from the Whelan house, Landis went on foot the remainder of the way. He was out of uniform. He carried the documents, files and photographs that had been prepared at the office in a leather despatch case. The less official this seemed, the better. Landis went with no preconceptions. In the brief time it had taken him to head home and change, Barbara had found out little else about the man.

Looking up at the impressive façade of the house, Landis estimated it was a good three or four hundred thousand dollars' worth of real estate. The lawns were manicured, the beds orderly. A sprinkler silently misted the grass. Maybe the Whelans came from a moneyed family. Maybe the guy was whip-smart when it came to managing his police pension. Whatever the reason, the Whelans didn't seem to be going without.

Though the property was gated, they were open. Landis

walked on up. Before he'd gotten within fifteen yards of the front porch, a curtain moved in a lower window.

Arriving at the screen door, Landis raised his hand to press the bell. The door opened before he reached it.

A middle-aged woman looked him up and down disapprovingly.

Landis took off his hat.

'If you're here sellin' things, I can assure you, you ain't got nothin' we want,' the woman said.

Landis smiled. 'No, ma'am, I ain't sellin' nothin'. My name is Landis. I'm the sheriff over in Union County. I was hopin' that Mr Whelan might be home.'

The woman frowned. 'I know your name from someplace. Landis, you say?'

'Yes, ma'am. My brother was the sheriff here in Dade.'

'Oh lord, of course. That's where I know it from. I was mighty sorry to hear about that. I didn't know him personal, of course, but I knew his name. My condolences.'

'Thank you, ma'am. That's real kind o' you.'

The woman relaxed. She smiled. 'I'm Florence Whelan,' she said. 'Jim's my husband, and yes, he's home. He's always home. Please do come in, Sheriff.'

Florence stepped back and opened the door wide. Landis went on into the house.

If the exterior had been impressive, the interior was in another league altogether.

Landis knew nothing of antiques and the like, but the place was as elegantly furnished as any place he'd ever seen. It was more high class than the best hotels in Atlanta.

'You have a beautiful home, Mrs Whelan,' Landis said.

Florence waved her hand dismissively. 'Oh, we do try, you know? We're fortunate, of course. My husband's family were in the furnishings business for many years. Collectors, they were.

Hoarders, more accurately. Lord, the things they had you would not have believed!' She laughed. 'After my father-in-law passed on, it was our responsibility to organize and catalogue, to arrange the auctions, to get the bulk of it sent all over the country. Some of it even went to Europe, if you can believe that. It took years to sort it all out. Anyways, my husband held onto a few things that were either really special or particularly sentimental.'

Florence checked herself. 'Listen to me rattlin' on about somethin' that's just as dull as paint dryin'. Let me take your hat. Please come on through and we'll see where Jim's at.'

Landis followed Florence Whelan through one extravagant room after another. The kitchen alone was pretty much the footprint of Landis's entire house.

Out back of the kitchen and along a wide corridor, Landis followed Florence into a large glass-roofed sunroom. Luxuriant foliage and blooms climbed the walls. The floor was tiled in a mosaic pattern of deep turquoise. The room was of sufficient size to feature a number of different bamboo chairs and sofas, even a wide canopied swing seat.

'Jim?' Florence called out. 'You have a guest, my dear!'

Landis stood and waited. It was not long before there was movement at the far end of the sunroom.

'Here he comes,' Florence said, and started down the room.

Whelan – wheelchair-bound – appeared from behind a tall ranging plant, in one hand a small trowel.

Evidence of a stroke was clear. The right side of Whelan's face had sagged. He seemed to resist his wife's proffered assistance. He handed her the trowel without a word, and with some difficulty, got up from the chair.

'This is Sheriff Landis from Union County,' Florence said.

Whelan's expression did not change. He peered at Landis as if his eyesight was not so good, and then he slowly nodded.

'Sheriff Landis,' he said. He raised his hand and waved him over. 'Come, please.'

Landis crossed the room.

'Florence, I think we'll have some coffee. You'll take some coffee, Sheriff Landis?'

'Thank you, yes,' Landis replied.

Florence left her husband to deal with their visitor.

With a little difficulty, Whelan shuffled toward a wicker chair and sat down heavily.

Having witnessed his seeming resistance to any help, Landis offered none.

'Sit, sit,' Whelan said.

Landis did as he was asked.

'I know who you are,' Whelan said. 'I was awful sorry to hear about your brother.'

'You knew him?'

'By name, and due to the fact that he was sheriff, but we weren't nothin' more than acquaintances. I have to say I ain't heard nothin' 'bout what happened to him save that he was killed. They got to the bottom of that yet?'

'Not yet no, Mr Whelan, but we're workin' on it.'

'Well, I wish you all the luck in the world, Sheriff. That's a mighty bad business when a lawman loses his life in the line o' duty.'

'You were in the PD for a lot o' years, weren't you?'

Whelan nodded. 'Sure I was. Over twenty years. And then ...' He looked down at himself. 'And then something like this happens and you cannot imagine how many things you took for granted just ain't so simple no more.'

Landis turned at the sound of Florence returning with coffee for both of them. She set a tray down on a low table.

'I'll not fuss while you're talkin',' she said. 'You go on and serve yourselves.'

Landis thanked her. He waited until she'd left before he continued talking.

'I was interested in your time at the Justice Collaboration Unit,' Landis said.

Whelan frowned. 'What about it?'

'You had a colleague out there who wound up deputising for my brother here in Dade.'

'You mean Ray Floyd, don'tcha?'

'I do, yes.'

'Tragic what happened to that man.'

'His suicide.'

'Yes,' Whelan said. 'Helluva thing. Makes you wonder just how much you don't know about what's really goin' on with folks.'

'How many years were you there?' Landis asked.

'From '76 to '81. Ray came in around '77, as far as I recall. Yes, that'd be right. I'd been there a little more than a year. He was a good cop. Diligent, hard-working. He an' I got along just fine.'

'You must have both left 'round about the same time.'

'That's right, yes. He said he wanted to get out of the police. He was lookin' to start a family. He figured he would be happier in the Sheriff's Office, you know? He wasn't never happy in Atlanta. He was raised on a farm, if I remember rightly, wanted to get away from the city.'

'So he came here.'

'He did, yes. I mean, we didn't stay in touch. I got sick pretty soon after he'd gone. I took early retirement, went back to Dalton, then decided I'd come out here.'

Whelan looked around the room. 'My father died. He was a wealthy man. He left me a bunch o' money, and I figured I may as well set myself up someplace where I'd be happy dyin'.' He smiled. 'And Florence, well she has this notion o' bein' some sort of Georgia society hostess or somethin'. We got this place because o' her. Hell, she don't come from nothin' at all, but there ain't a great deal wrong with havin' aspirations, now is there?'

'Nothin' wrong with that at all,' Landis said. He went ahead and poured a cup of coffee for Whelan, then one for himself.

'So why're you here?' Whelan asked.

'A whole mess o' reasons, to be honest. I'm lookin' into what happened with my brother, an' I got a hold o' some folks out in Fannin County who may be involved. But then there's this other thread I'm tuggin' on that has to do with the death of a teenage girl out of McCaysville. Went missin' back in the middle of August, an' we found her dead a coupla weeks later. Then we got another one, found dead up in Cherokee County, but she was out of Rock Springs over in Walker County.'

Whelan frowned. 'I must've missed somethin' here, Sheriff,' he said, 'but I'm not gettin' the connection between what happened to your brother and this thing you're sayin' 'bout these dead girls.'

'They may not be directly connected, Mr Whelan. Like I said, this is a whole mess I'm tryin' to unravel. The thing that ties 'em together is that whatever happened to these girls may've been somethin' my brother was diggin' into.'

'And you're sayin' that whoever killed these girls might've killed your brother too?'

'Maybe,' Landis said. 'That's where this thing looks to be goin', but I really ain't sure.'

'And where do I figure into this, Sheriff?'

'Well, you see, the thing is that the person who may be behind all o' this was one o' the confidential human resources that Ray Floyd signed off on when he was workin' in that unit over at the Attorney General's Office. That classification, that this character was a valuable informant, kept him safe and sound. Anyone started lookin' in his direction, well it was simple enough to back them off.'

337

'And you think this person – all these years later – is the one responsible for this trouble?'

'I have a notion that this goes way back, Mr Whelan. I'm comin' to the conclusion that there may've been a great many more missin' and murdered girls, and that this feller up in Fannin ain't the only one involved.'

'Yes, yes, I see,' Whelan said. 'An' this feller? He got a name?'

'Russell,' Landis said. 'Eugene Russell.'

Whelan, pensive for a moment, then shook his head. 'Can't say I heard o' him.'

'And there's another connection which, in all likelihood, ain't gonna come to nothin', but it does warrant lookin' into.'

'And what's that?'

'Two o' the girls we found belonged to something called the Young Republican Volunteers. And then we dug a little more and found out that there were some outstandin' missing persons reports across other counties, and a number of those girls also belonged to this volunteer group.'

Whelan's eyes widened in genuine surprise. 'I know it,' he said. 'I'm the treasurer for the Trenton branch. I mean, not that that entails a great deal. I don't even attend the meetings. I just keep an eye on their donations and books and whatnot for the annual revenue inspections.'

'Do you remember if Ray Floyd had anythin' to do with it?'

Whelan seemed genuinely perplexed. 'With the Young Republicans? Not to my knowledge, no. I mean, you're talkin' more 'an ten years ago now since I worked with him. Then, like you say, he transferred out of the PD to the Sheriff's Office and came here to Dade to work for your brother.'

'So you had no contact with him after you returned?'

'None at all, no.'

'You see, Mr Whelan, I got my hooks into an idea, and I appreciate I could be wrong by a mile or more. I got Ray Floyd gettin' everyone to look the other way by registerin' someone as a confidential informant, and then that someone gets access to names, addresses and personal details of all them girls in the volunteers group, you see? I think this has been goin' on for some years now, and I think maybe there's a good many more than three or four girls been killed.'

'But why, Sheriff? Why are they bein' killed?'

'I'm thinkin' it's some kind of traffickin' thing, you know? That's where this is headin'.'

Again, Whelan's dismay was evident. 'I know these kinds of things go on,' he said. 'I wasn't born yesterday. But here? I mean, you just never really consider that such a thing could be happenin' in your own back yard, do you?'

'Not until it does, no.'

'So what was it that you thought I could help with?' Whelan asked.

'I'm not so sure, to be honest,' Landis said. 'Ray Floyd worked for you, then he worked for my brother, and then he went to Fannin to work for George Milstead. He then kills himself in '89, and three years later my brother gets murdered. Like I said, I think Frank was investigatin' those missin' girls, and he stepped all over someone's toes.'

'And lost his life because of it.'

'Seems so, Mr Whelan.'

'Such a waste.' He shook his head. 'Sometimes you just can't help but wonder at the state of the world, can you? You imagine the worst, and then someone goes and does something far worse. Is there no end to how bad a person can be?'

'I guess not.'

'I don't know that I can be of any more help to you than I've already been, and I ain't sure I've been any help at all, Sheriff. All I can do is wish you the best o' luck trackin' these Russell fellers down. I sure as hell hope you find 'em before they get wind o' your scent.'

Landis looked at Whelan. He smiled and nodded.

'I sure appreciate that, Mr Whelan.'

'Not at all, Sheriff.'

Landis finished his coffee. He told Whelan to thank his wife for her hospitality. He said he'd see himself out.

Whelan let him go with a handshake.

Out in the maze between the sunroom and the front door, Landis met Florence.

'Pleasure to meet you,' she said. 'I hope you had a good visit with Jim, and I really am so very sorry about your brother an' all.'

'That's most kind o' you, ma'am,' Landis replied. He retrieved his hat. 'And thank you for your hospitality.'

At the end of the driveway and before he passed through the open gates, Landis glanced back.

Florence Whelan raised her hand in farewell. He echoed the gesture.

Reaching his car, he was wrestling with those final words of Whelan's.

All I can do is wish you the best o' luck trackin' these Russell fellers down.

Landis had only mentioned Eugene. Whelan had said he'd never heard of him. So why the hell would Whelan think there were more?

72

By the time Landis reached Blairsville, he was not only convinced that Jim Whelan knew precisely who he was looking for and why, but he also doubted the veracity of Ray Floyd's suicide.

Perhaps Floyd's death was as much a murder as Frank's. Perhaps Floyd had signed those documents under Whelan's instruction. After all, Whelan was head of the unit, and was now in a position where he could easily access the register of every member of the Young Republicans.

The man had money, no shortage of it, and though both he and his wife had spoken of a considerable inheritance from Whelan's father, Landis still possessed an intuitive sense that he was on track to the heart of this thing. In the absence of anything else to trust, he had to trust his instinct. One way or another, if he pursued what he believed to be the truth, then he would confirm it or rule it out.

It was past eight by the time he got home. He was frayed at the edges, desirous of respite from the relentless stress of the investigation.

The fridge and cupboards were empty – as was so often the case – so he headed out to The Old Tavern to eat. He knew he'd drink a good deal, so he walked. It was no more than half a mile and he could use some air.

Even Wilbur Cobb, a man seemingly unused to social banter, commented on Landis's appearance.

'You look like a man who's had his fill o' whatever's goin' on,' he said as he poured Landis's whiskey.

'Runnin' on fumes,' Landis said.

'Work or personal?'

'Good helpin' o' both right now, Wilbur.'

'What you need is a wife.'

'I had one o' them already.'

'I know you did, but she's dead. Been dead more 'an ten years if I remember rightly.'

'You do,' Landis said. 'I guess my mind still ain't straight on it.'

'That's why you should get yourself a new 'un. Sittin' 'round maunderin' ain't never did do nothin' good and never will.'

'I ain't maunderin', Wilbur.'

'Sure looks like it from where I'm standin'.'

Landis downed his whiskey, edged the glass forward for a refill.

'Regret is a road we all been down afore,' Cobb said.

'I get about enough of that talk from Barbara Wedlock,' Landis replied.

Cobb laughed. 'Well, maybe she's as smart as me then.'

'I appreciate your concern, Wilbur, but 'round about now'd be a good time to stop talkin' and fetch that steak.'

Cobb laughed. 'I guess I'm pissin' in the wind,' he said. 'I'll keep my lifetime's worth of wisdom to myself, then.'

'Yeah, you best do that.'

Cobb set the whiskey bottle beside Landis's glass. 'Go on an' help yourself, Sheriff. On the house.'

Landis nodded his thanks. Cobb went out back to get the steak.

*

A meal and three drinks later, Landis left The Old Tavern.

The walk seemed further on the way back than it had been heading out. There was a chill in the air. It was halfway through October, and he could feel the season was aiming for winter.

Arriving home, he fetched down a bottle and poured one last drink. He went out and sat in the back yard. He smoked a couple of cigarettes. For a brief while, the world slowed down some and he was grateful for it. He knew, without a doubt, that it would all get back up to speed in the morning.

He thought about his niece, about Eleanor Boyd too. He thought about Vester Rayford, the Bishops, the Laceys, and all the other parents of girls who were no longer home. He thought about the kind of men who valued a human life no more than they did an empty bottle.

Existence was blunt and brutal and unforgiving. Sometimes it seemed you only got things to see them taken away. Other times you never got them in the first place.

He didn't know the reasons for this, and he didn't try to figure it out. Maybe the answers to all the mysteries of the universe were right before his eyes. He'd been so busy looking or so busy telling himself that it couldn't be that simple that he didn't recognize them, even when they were served up on a plate.

Mary was dead. That much he knew. He also knew he'd been derelict, uncaring, distant and quiet. She'd been dying. They'd both known it. Perhaps the greater guilt was not the abandonment during those last months of her life, but the fact that he'd never really been much of a husband at all. He had failed her, and in so many ways. He'd loved her, had always loved her, but with a heavy heart.

And at that final revelation – when he understood the signs that had been there all along – he'd found excuses for himself that were nothing but excuses.

In hindsight, he understood that he'd held open the door for everything that happened. He'd then closed it and walked away, choosing not to remember that he'd been the cause of so much unnecessary heartbreak.

He'd not taken responsibility for what transpired nor how it had turned out. He'd blamed Mary, and he'd blamed his brother. His brother most of all.

The past could not be undone, no matter how hard he tried.

The past was marked clear all the way back to the beginning of his life. He could follow in the same direction, or forge a new and different path in the hope that the destination would be better.

Landis knew this was a decision he had yet to make. He was headed towards it – of that he was sure – but first he needed the courage to forgive himself for what he'd done.

For years, he'd carried that burden. For years, he'd hidden from the truth. Now it was right there in front of him, and there was no way to avoid it.

73

A little after nine, morning of Saturday October 17, the walls of the world collapsed.

The telephone – insistent and unforgiving – roused Landis from sleep. He was aware of the cloud of liquor that still fogged his thoughts. He thought to ignore the phone, but it refused to ignore him in return. It just rang and rang. Whoever was at the other end seemed determined to reach him, no matter how long it took.

'Victor,' Eleanor said, her voice urgent, distressed.

'Eleanor. Yes. What's up?'

'Jenna's gone,' she said. 'Jenna's gone, Victor! She went to the store. I let her go. This morning. I let her go to the store, Victor, and she's not come back.'

Landis's head cleared. 'When? When did she go, Eleanor?'

'This morning, Victor. Maybe an hour ago. Not even an hour. I don't know what to do.'

'Okay, okay. First things first, have you been to the store?'

'Yes, of course I've been to the store.'

'What did they say?'

'They said she never arrived.'

'How far away is it?'

'Christ, I don't know. Maybe a quarter mile, maybe a half. I don't know, Victor. I don't know how far it is!'

Eleanor started crying. She was beside herself.

'Eleanor, listen to me now. You stay right where you are. I'm on my way, okay?'

'Maybe I should go back to the store. D'you think I should go back there, Victor?'

'No, Eleanor. Stay right there. I'll be with you as fast as I can. And call Trenton PD. Tell them what's happened.'

'Okay,' she said. 'Hurry, please. Please get here, Victor. I don't know what to do. She's gone. My baby's gone.'

'I'm hangin' up, Eleanor. I'm leavin' now.'

Landis took the department car, lights and siren all the way.

The highway was clear and he made good time. A two-hour journey took him little more than an hour and a half, but it was the longest hour and a half of his life.

Eleanor was out in the front yard. She saw Landis's car turn at the end of the street and came down the path to the sidewalk. Still in her robe, her face was red, her eyes swollen. She started talking before he'd even had a chance to get out of the car.

'Tell me where the store is, Eleanor.'

'It's down that way. It's on the right. It's a 7-11. She wanted to go by herself. She's done it before, Victor. She's been so many times before. I didn't even think about it.' She put her hands over her face. 'Oh my God, what have I done?'

Landis put his arms around her. She sobbed hysterically. Just as had happened when he gave the news to Jeanette Rayford, he felt the tears soaking through the front of his shirt.

'I need to go down there,' Landis said. 'I need a picture of her, and I need to know what she was wearin'.'

Eleanor described Jenna's clothes, and then she took a recent picture from a small frame on the windowsill in the living room.

'Is there anythin' else you can tell me, Eleanor?'

'She took her monkey, Victor. She took that monkey with her. The one you gave her.'

That small detail hit Landis like a hammer.

Eleanor got up. 'I'm comin' with you,' she said.

'No. You need to stay here in case she comes back. And did you call the police?'

'Yes, yes, I called 'em. They gave me the fuckin' runaround, Victor. They said they'd send someone out later. They told me she wasn't a missin' person until she was gone for two days! Two fuckin' days, Victor! She could be dead. She could be lyin' dead somewhere. Or hurt. She could be hurt real bad somewhere and they ain't even gonna start lookin' for her!'

'I'm here,' Landis said. 'I'm here now, Eleanor. You go on back in the house. I'm gonna go down to the store and see if anyone saw her. You wait here. I'll be back soon, okay?'

'Don't go, Victor. Don't leave me here!'

'Eleanor, you need to stay in the house, you understand? You need to stay right here in case Jenna comes home.'

Eleanor gathered herself together as best she could. 'Yes, yes, okay. I'll stay here.'

'Okay. Don't go anywhere.'

'Is she gonna come home, Victor? Is my baby gonna come home?'

'Yes,' Landis said adamantly. 'She's comin' home, Eleanor. Whatever happens, she's comin' home.'

The elderly man at the 7-11 was no help. He'd not seen the girl in the picture.

Landis gave him Eleanor's phone number.

'You see anyone fittin' that description, even if they're with someone else, you call that number,' Landis told him.

Landis headed back to Eleanor's place.

Seated in the kitchen, her head in her hands, she was an emotional wreck.

Landis felt as if his heart had been ripped out of his chest, but what Eleanor needed most of all was an anchor. He had to remain decisive, forthright, certain of what he was doing.

This was a warning – a personal one – and it was clear enough.

Landis figured that Jim Whelan had contacted the Russells. The Russells – or someone in their employ – had taken Jenna right off the street no more than a half mile from her house.

'I'm going for help,' Landis told Eleanor. 'I know you don't wanna stay here by yourself, but right now that's what I need you to do.'

Eleanor – now speechless – just stared at him in abject despair.

'I have a notion of what's happened. I need to move fast. The quicker I get onto this, the better, you understand? I can't take you with me.'

'But … but what if …'

'Eleanor, you need to hear what I'm sayin' now, and you need to trust me, okay? You need to let me deal with this.'

Eleanor didn't respond.

'I'm gonna call my deputy, Marshall Turner. I'm gonna have him come over here and stay with you, alright?'

'You gotta bring her back, Victor. You gotta bring my baby back to me.'

'I know, Eleanor, and I will. You have my word on that.'

Landis started towards the door.

'Do you know where she is?' Eleanor asked. 'Do you know where Jenna is?'

'I don't know where she is, no. But I know someone who's gonna help me find her.'

74

Mike Fredericksen's initial reaction was just as Landis had expected.

Anger; beneath that a sense of inevitability. Landis was the last person in the world that Fredericksen wanted to see.

He came down the porch steps and stopped Landis right there in the front yard.

'I told you—' he started.

'They took Frank's girl,' Landis said matter-of-factly.

'You what?'

'The Russells. I'm sure of it.'

'Oh my fuckin' Christ! What the livin' fuck almighty—'

'You gonna help me or what?' Landis asked.

Fredericksen looked at him. He closed his eyes and lowered his head resignedly. The weight of the world fell on his shoulders.

'I need an answer, Detective. I need an answer right now. You gonna help me with this?'

'Fuck, of course I'm gonna help you,' Fredericksen snapped.

'Okay, then I need you to get focused, okay? I need you to get your family somewhere. Doesn't matter where. They need to go now. Tell your wife whatever you need to tell her. Get her in a car with them kids o' yours and send 'em as far away as they can get.'

Fredericksen was nodding in the affirmative before Landis had finished talking.

'Yes, yes,' he said, 'they can go to—'

'I don't need to know,' Landis said, 'and I don't want to.'

'What are you gonna do now?' Fredericksen asked.

'I'm headin' to Colwell. To the Russell place. That's where I'm startin'. You deal with your family, and then go speak to your colleagues. Tell them this is serious. Tell them we ain't waitin' forty-eight hours to see if this kid shows up, you understand? I'm gonna get my deputy over to Eleanor Boyd's place now.'

'Yes, yes of course. And what do you want me to do?'

'Give me your home number. I'll call you as soon as I'm out of Colwell. I'll know where I'm headed from there and you can come meet me.'

'Okay, yes.' Fredericksen turned and started towards the house. He stopped, turned back. 'If they kill that little girl...'

'Don't even think it,' Landis said. 'Not even for a second.'

Another two-hour drive, all the while his mind fighting against images of Jenna drowned, Jenna strangled, Jenna dead.

Russell had lied to him, misled him, threatened him, and now he'd invaded his life and taken the only thing that really mattered.

When Landis thought of the man, his feelings were filled with nothing but brutality and violence. If anything had happened to that girl, he would not stop until every one of them was dead or in jail.

Landis drew his .44 before he got out of the car and headed down to the Russell place.

It was silent. There was no sign of anyone. A solitary dog watched him from a cage. Passing it, Landis went up the porch steps and hammered on the door.

He waited thirty seconds or so, and then he hammered again.

'You got no business here,' Ledda Russell said.

Landis turned. She had come out from behind the house and was there at the far end of the veranda. The expression on her face was one of disdain.

'Where's Eugene at, Ledda?' Landis asked.

'How the hell am I s'posed to know that? Man's a law unto himself, ain't he?'

'I'm askin you again, Ledda. Where's Eugene at?'

'Hell, Sheriff, even if I knew I wouldn't tell you.'

Landis crossed the veranda in a half dozen steps. He was less than ten feet from her. He did not raise his gun, but he made sure she saw it.

She sneered contemptuously. 'What the hell're you gonna do? Shoot me?'

'He's done somethin' real bad,' Landis said. 'You tell me where he's at, maybe he's got a hope o' comin' out o' this alive.'

'Is that so?' She laughed. 'Well, if I know Eugene, he'll give you the runaround somethin' awful. You may's well go search all creation, you'll not find him lest he wants to be found. I should know. Been married to the man for long enough.'

'You ain't gonna help, are you?'

'Never was, never will. Now you best git off my property afore I set the dog on you.'

'Set the dog on me, I'll fuckin' kill it.'

'Oh, go to hell, Sheriff.'

Ledda gave Landis one more disparaging look, and then turned and walked back down the side of the house.

Landis felt his blood boiling. The urge to follow her and knock her to the ground was almost impossible to contain. His teeth gritted, he headed back to the road. He kicked the dog's cage as he passed it. The dog leapt up, roaring at him. Landis leaned down and roared back.

En route to the Whelan place, Landis pulled over for gas.

He called Fredericksen, told him where he was headed, said he'd meet him there.

Fredericksen said he would leave immediately.

'You speak to your people at the department?' Landis asked.

'I did. They're on it,' Fredericksen said.

'Get on the road,' Landis said. 'See you in Padena.'

75

Even though he was in Fannin County, Landis did not inform George Milstead of his intentions or actions. As was his prerogative, he had the lawful right to cross any county in pursuit of a felon.

Landis's initial unwillingness to report what he believed to be an inter-state investigation to the federal authorities had been based on lack of evidence. He also believed that the more people who were involved, the less progress would be made. Now his unwillingness was based on mistrust. Who was involved, and how deep this thing went stayed his hand.

This was now his responsibility, and with the assistance of Mike Fredericksen, he believed he could track down Eugene Russell and bring Jenna home. Now there was no law aside from what was right. If it cost him his job, even his life, then so be it. He believed, and believed with everything he possessed, that if the roles had been reversed – if it had been his daughter – then Frank would have done the same for him.

Now it was not only a sense of justice that drove him forward, but amends to the memory of his brother. He would make this right for Frank, and then perhaps there was a chance he could make it right for himself.

It was five in the evening. The lights in Alice Morrow's house were on.

Landis parked down a block and walked the rest of the way. He hoped Wasper was there. He prayed that he was there. If he wasn't, then perhaps Alice would know where to find him.

The signs of violence were written bold across Alice's face. She looked frightened even before Landis said a word.

Her right eye was swollen, her cheek bruised. A thin cut centered her forehead above the bridge of her nose.

'If you're lookin' for Wasper, he ain't here,' she said.

'Can I come in?' Landis asked.

'I don't want no trouble,' Alice said.

'Looks like you got plenty enough already,' Landis replied.

Alice looked down. When she looked up, her eyes brimmed with tears.

'Sometimes he ain't so bad,' she said.

'Those ain't the times I'm worried about.'

Alice stepped back, drew the door wide.

Landis went on into the house.

In the kitchen, Alice offered Landis a drink. He declined. He asked her to sit down.

'I'm after him 'cause he'll know where his brother's at,' Landis said.

'Knowin' Wasper, wherever Eugene's at he'll be taggin' along like a lost puppy.' She shook her head. 'Hell, if he heard me call him Wasper he'd bust a gut.'

'You need to get yourself out o' this mess, Alice.'

'Folks who ain't in a mess always say that.'

'But what about the children?'

'What about 'em?'

'They're his, right?'

'Hell no, they ain't his kids. Their daddy's long gone. An' Wasper ain't never been a daddy to them.'

'Where's your folks at?'

Alice frowned. 'Hell business is it o' yours?'

'It ain't, 'less you wanna make it so.'

'Meanin'?'

'Meanin' maybe I could be some help to get you back there. That's all.'

'I go someplace, Wasper'll chase me. He ain't gon' let me go nowhere he don't want me to be.'

'An' if he weren't around, what then?'

Alice's eyes widened. It served to accentuate the injuries to her face.

She half smiled. It was an expression of both resignation and disbelief.

'That man'd come back and haunt me from the fuckin' grave,' she said.

'Him and Eugene's done somethin' bad, Alice. Real bad. I need to find them, an' quick.'

'What they done?'

'They took a kid. Eleven-year-old girl. Took her from her momma this mornin'.'

Alice shook her head. 'No way he done that. He ain't got the nerve to do no such thing.'

'Maybe his brother's the one that done it, but Wasper'll know about it, and he'll know where to find Eugene.'

Alice leaned forward, her elbows on the table, her head in her hands.

'Oh, for chrissake almighty, could this get any worse?'

'It will if I don't find him,' Landis said.

'I don't know where he's at, okay? If I did, I'd tell you. If he ain't with his brother, then he could be any number o' places.'

'Tell me some o' them, then. Is there a bar he goes to? Some place he hangs out when he ain't here or back in Colwell?'

'You been to their place?'

'That's where I just come from.'

'An' I'm guessin' neither one o' them was there or you wouldn't have come here.'

'Just Ledda, an' she ain't sayin' nothin'.'

'Now there's a surprise, ain't there? Poisonous fuckin' witch that she is.'

'So tell me where he might be, Alice.'

'He's over here Saturday nights,' she said. 'That's his routine. He has a coupla places he goes to for drinkin' an' whatever. Place up near where 60 meets 76. Truckstop kind o' place. Bikers go there. That's where he usually goes afore he gets here. Gets himself oiled up real good.'

'What's it called?'

Alice thought for a moment. 'I can't remember the name of it. But you go north on up 60 and you'll find it. There'll be a dozen or more bikes outside. Hell, you'll hear it 'fore you see it.'

'Okay,' Landis said. 'I appreciate it.'

He got up from the table.

'You gonna hurt him or what?' Alice asked.

'Not 'less I need to,' Landis replied. 'If he's there an' I find him, he ain't much likely to be back here tonight anyways.'

'You want a word of advice? You get to killin' either one o' them, you better kill 'em both. An' kill 'em twice just to be sure.'

76

Fredericksen was already across the street in his car when Landis left the Morrow house.

'I'm after Eugene,' Landis told him. 'Ledda won't tell me where he's at, so I'm chasin' Wasper. There's a place up on 60. His girl said he might be there. If he ain't, then maybe someone can point us in the right direction.'

Fredericksen paused before speaking. He looked ahead through the windshield. His hands gripped the steering wheel. His knuckles were white with tension.

'Tell me about the money, Mike.'

'The money?'

'This money that you pay to Frank's wife.'

Fredericksen looked dismayed. 'You really don't know, do you? You really have no fuckin' clue what happened.'

'I'm askin' now, ain't I?'

'It can wait.'

'If you an' I are gonna work on this together, then I need to know whose side you're on. I need to know how come Frank was in so much debt that he couldn't take care o' his own family.'

'Your wife got sick. You were the one who was s'posed to take care o' her. That was the way it was meant to go, right?'

'My wife? What the hell d'you know about my wife?'

'I know she was dyin'. I know you bailed out on her at the earliest available opportunity. So where did she go, eh? You ever ask yourself that? More to the point, why did she even need to go someplace else?'

'You knew about Frank and Mary?'

'I ain't talkin' to you through the damned window, Victor.'

Landis walked around the back of the vehicle and got in on the passenger side.

Fredericksen looked at him. Landis felt transparent, as if every thought and feeling he'd ever possessed was visible to the man.

'You ran away,' Fredericksen said. 'There ain't no other way to see it. And your brother? Hell, your brother took it on himself to visit her, to take care of her, to pay for medicine, hospital bills, to pay for all the things you shoulda damn well paid for. That's why he was in so much debt, for Christ's sake. Everythin' he had, and more. He gave up everythin' to look after your damned wife to the very last.'

'He took her from me,' Landis said.

'Is that what you've told yourself all these years? That he took her from you? Jesus Christ, man, you are livin' some twisted version of the truth. That's about as much of a lie as you can tell, and you know it.'

'He betrayed me,' Landis said. 'She betrayed me. They were together, goddamnit. For nearly a year they—'

'They what?' Fredericksen asked. 'They were human fuckin' beings, Victor. That's what they were. What the hell did you expect? You didn't give a good goddamn about that woman's pain. You were the one that betrayed her, not the other way around. She needed you and you just fuckin' let it all go to hell.'

Landis closed his eyes.

'Fuck man, you can lie to the world for all of time, but you can't lie to yourself. An' if you wanna keep on tellin' yourself whatever version of the story minimizes your guilt, then that's your business. I know you know what happened. What really happened. Frank knew too.'

Landis breathed deeply. The dam he'd so carefully constructed was insufficient to hold back the reservoir of emotion in his chest.

'Did... did Eleanor know?'

'She didn't know a goddamned thing, Victor. Okay, so Frank cheated on Eleanor with Mary. And then Mary died. You found out after she was dead, right?'

'After the funeral, yes,' Landis replied.

'Well, a month later Frank married Eleanor. Sure, Eleanor was already pregnant with Jenna. That's not why he married her. He married her because he loved her. But he loved Mary, too. Loved her a great deal more than you did, it seems.'

Landis lunged sideways. He grabbed the lapels of Fredericksen's jacket and pushed him back against the door. He felt rage and hatred towards the man.

Fredericksen did not fight back. He slowly raised his hands to make it clear he was not going to resist. He just looked at Landis with a detached expression.

'I'm to blame now?' he said.

Landis said nothing.

'Go ahead, Victor. Now that Frank ain't around, you can make me the fuckin' bad guy. This shit is on you. I know it. You know it. Hell knows what kind of life you've been livin' all these years, but it sure as hell ain't the kind of life I'd want.'

Landis shoved Fredericksen once more, and then he let go.

Fredericksen straightened his jacket. He seemed unperturbed by Landis's outburst.

'You want me to help you find the truth of what happened, then you gotta start tellin' yourself the goddamned truth. You're a fuckin' hypocrite, Victor. Frank wasn't to blame for what happened between him an' Mary. You were.'

Landis lowered his head. He felt the seams coming apart. The diligently constructed façade was weakening. In truth, he knew it had never been founded on anything but sand. Now the tide had come in. His entire world was faltering.

'You're a tough guy,' Fredericksen said. 'I get that. But being honest about what happened takes more fuckin' courage than anythin' else.'

Landis breathed deeply. He kept on breathing. That was the only thing he seemed capable of doing in that moment.

'So, there we fuckin' have it,' Fredericksen said. 'Your wife got sick. You didn't wanna deal with it, so you took off. Your brother stepped up. You buried yourself in work or whatever the hell else you could find. An' now they're both dead an' you're the only one who's holdin' onto a version of the past that ain't true.'

'What did Frank say, Mike?'

Fredericksen shook his head. 'He said a lot o' things, Victor. At the start, it was all angry and bitter. Later, it was just fuckin' sad. Most of all, he said he wished it could all go back to how it was before Mary got sick.'

'The same,' Landis said. 'The same damn thing for me.'

'Past is past. You can't change it, no matter what you do. Only thing you can do is change the way you think about it.'

Landis hesitated, and then he opened the door.

'Follow me,' he said. 'We're gonna go see if Wasper's up at this biker's place.'

Fredericksen reached out and grabbed Landis's forearm.

'You know these people ain't gonna play fair, right? This is more 'an likely goin' real bad.'

Landis didn't speak, didn't even look at Fredericksen.

'How far you prepared to go with this, Victor? You set to kill 'em, ain't you?'

'I'm set to do whatever it takes to make it right,' Landis replied.

'That for you or for your brother?'

'For Jenna. 'Cause she's the only kin I got left.'

77

Alice Morrow had been right.

Landis could not have missed the truckstop had he tried. Music could be heard from the highway, and outside the bikes were lined up in two or three rows. He remembered Eugene's comment – that Wasper was *a braggity little runt with a Howlin' Davis motorsickle.*

Landis pulled over a good hundred yards away. Fredericksen pulled up behind him.

'That's the place,' Landis said.

'I know what he looks like,' Fredericksen said. 'How we doin' this?'

'He would recognize you?'

'I doubt it,' Fredericksen said.

'So go on in. If he's there, get him aside. Tell him you think you clipped his bike with your car. Get him out here through the back door to take a look.'

'That's the best you got?'

'You wanna go in there guns drawn and have a stand-off with a hundred bikers?'

'Okay. So get close. You see me come out o' there with him then I don't want to be standin' there like some dumb jasper wonderin' where the fuck you are.'

'I'll be here.'

Fredericksen headed off to the bar.

Landis stayed back a moment, and then followed him. He walked down the side of the building and then around the back to the rear exit.

A wide expanse of open ground ran the length of the bar. It was bordered by heavy fencing. At the other end of the building half a dozen bikers were drinking and laughing with a couple of girls. They were far enough away for Landis to be untroubled by the possibility of their interference.

The rear exit led onto a short, raised deck. A rail ran around the edge of it, and then there were four risers down to the ground.

Landis stayed in the shadow afforded by the deck. He refrained from lighting a cigarette even though he badly wanted one.

He did not think about Mary, about Frank, about everything Fredericksen had said in the car. He would at some point, and he would have to deal with the hurricane of regret and guilt that he knew was on its way. Now was not the time. Now he needed to stay focused on nothing but Jenna.

Wasper Russell stumbled out of the exit full of liquor and expletives.

Fredericksen was apologizing, explaining that it was dark, that he'd had a few too many, that he was sorry, that he would make it good.

'Fuckin' bullshit, man,' Wasper said. 'This is just fuckin' bullshit. If you fucked my bike, man, I tell you … if you fucked with my bike …'

Wasper reached the bottom of the steps and turned to his right. Landis let him pass by, and then stepped out behind him. Fredericksen hung back.

Wasper hesitated, turned back to Fredericksen. He saw Landis.

363

'What the fuckin' Jesus God almighty—'

Landis grabbed Wasper's arm with his left hand. With his right, he pressed the muzzle of his .44 into the small of Wasper's back.

'Not a fuckin' word, Wasper.'

Wasper, rage flaring in his eyes, wrestled against Landis's grip.

'Hey, get the fuck off of me!' he hollered.

Landis dug the gun in hard and sharp.

Fredericksen turned at the sound of voices behind them.

One of the men from the huddle started walking towards them.

'What the fuck is happenin'?' he called out.

Wasper turned, opened his mouth to holler back.

Landis let go of Wasper's forearm and grabbed him around the throat.

Fredericksen walked back the way they'd come to meet the biker.

Landis pushed Wasper back against the wall. He put the muzzle of the gun under Wasper's chin.

'Not a fuckin' sound out of you,' Landis said.

Wasper, his eyes wide, glanced left towards Fredericksen. Fredericksen was exchanging words with the biker. The biker asked a question. Fredericksen answered. The two of them laughed.

Landis moved Wasper away from the building and out towards the road. Wasper resisted, and it took all of Landis's strength to keep the man moving. Small and wiry he might have been, but his whole body was a knot of muscle.

Fredericksen caught up with them. He grabbed Wasper's arm, and between the two of them they manhandled him to the cars.

Landis shoved Wasper to his knees. He pressed the gun against his forehead.

'Where's Eugene at?' Landis asked.

Wasper sneered contemptuously. 'Go fuck yourself.'

Landis cocked the weapon.

Wasper didn't flinch.

'Where's Eugene at, Wasper?' Landis repeated.

'Go to hell, Landis,' Wasper replied.

'One more time, Wasper,' Landis said. 'I'm askin' you one more time...'

'An' then what? You gonna shoot me in the fuckin' head? Is that what you're gonna do? Out here with a hundred damn witnesses? You ain't got the balls, Sheriff. You're gettin' yourself involved in somethin' that really doesn't concern you. Just like your damn brother.'

Wasper laughed. It was not forced. He seemed to be genuinely amused.

Landis grabbed the collar of Wasper's shirt in his fist. He twisted it hard, twisted again. The knuckles of Landis's hand were hard up against his throat, so much so that Wasper's eyes widened and he gasped for breath.

Fredericksen grabbed the back of Wasper's hair, and pulled down hard.

Wasper, unable to scream, bared his teeth, his eyes wide, gasping for breath with difficulty.

'Eugene,' Landis said. 'Where the fuck is he?'

Wasper mustered every ounce of energy possible. He pushed back against Landis. Landis lost his balance for a moment, and then heaved back with his full weight.

Wasper hit the wing of the car with considerable force. He dropped to his knees. Undeterred, he looked up with utter hatred in his eyes.

'Let me fuckin' go,' he hissed. 'Let me fuckin' go now or you'll wind up just like your asshole of a brother.'

Landis hesitated, but just for a second. With the heel of the

.44 he swung hard and low. He caught Wasper's jawline just below his ear. The man went down like a stone.

Landis looked up at Fredericksen.

'Get his feet,' Landis said.

'And do what with him?'

'Put him in the trunk of my car.'

'What?'

'Put him in the fuckin' trunk, Mike!'

78

Landis saw signs for a motel off the highway. He took the turning. Even as he did so, he heard Wasper thumping and kicking the roof of the trunk. He pulled over and waited for Fredericksen to come to a stop behind him.

The engine off, Wasper was making a hell of a noise. Landis opened the trunk. Wasper reared up suddenly, and Landis hit him square in the bridge of the nose. Before Wasper had a chance to start screaming, Landis put an oily rag in his mouth. He cuffed him with his hands behind his back.

'Make a sound an' I will drag you into the trees and beat your head to a pulp.'

The defiance in Wasper's eyes had dimmed, but it was still there. Whatever might be said of him, he had a good deal of fight.

Before he closed the trunk, Landis hit him once again.

'What the hell are you plannin'?' Fredericksen asked. 'You gonna try and trade him?'

'Best idea I got,' Landis said. 'You think different?'

Fredericksen shook his head. 'Doin' best I can not to think at all right now.'

'We'll take a room at the motel. Wasper is gonna tell us where Eugene's at.'

'That's what you're gonna do? Put him in a motel room and torture him?'

'These people are fuckin' animals, Mike, but they're at the bottom end of the food chain. This goes all the way into the AG's Office in Atlanta. These people have been protected by a guy called Jim Whelan. That's what I figure anyway. I'm guessin' we hurt Wasper enough then we're gonna find out, right?'

Fredericksen didn't speak.

'You got any doubts about this, you go on home, Mike. Like you said, I ain't got kids or family of my own. I got that little girl and Frank's ex-wife. I ain't havin' this on my conscience.'

'I'm thinkin' maybe you ain't in the best frame o' mind to be makin' decisions right now, Victor.'

'That's where you're wrong. I reckon I'm in the best frame o' mind.'

Landis walked around the side of the car and got in. He started the engine and pulled away. He was no more than twenty yards away when Fredericksen's lights came on and followed him down the road to the motel.

Wasper's nose was busted. There was no doubt about that.

One of his nostrils was clogged with congealed blood, and when he spoke he struggled to breathe.

Landis dragged him through to the bathroom and filled the sink. He ducked Wasper's head into the water until the involuntary need to inhale and exhale cleared his airways.

Landis dragged Wasper bodily up onto the toilet. Using Fredericksen's cuffs, he linked the pairs together and looped them beneath the wide ceramic pipe behind and beneath the toilet bowl. Tearing a towel into strips, he then bound Wasper's feet together and tied them behind the base of the unit. Wasper was going nowhere.

Snarling and spitting, his face a mess of blood, his nose swollen and twisted to the right, his left eye already twice its size and barely open, Wasper was still a small tornado of resistance.

Landis tugged off Wasper's boots and socks. He then sat on the edge of the tub and waited for Wasper to wind down some.

Fredericksen stayed in the bedroom. He was seated on the edge of the bed, had a line of sight right into the bathroom. He said nothing, his face implacable.

Once it seemed that Wasper had quietened down, Landis took the rag out of the man's mouth.

Immediately, Wasper let rip.

'You have no fuckin' idea what you're doin'! Let me fuckin' go right the fuck now and I might only kill you. Go on with this bullshit, an' that little girl and her ma are gonna get—'

Landis used the back of his hand. The blow was fierce. Wasper's head lolled sideways, then backwards.

He held up the rag. 'Quit your hollerin', Wasper, or this is goin' back in your mouth.'

'Fuck you, Landis!'

Landis sat down on the edge of the tub again. He straightened out the rag and draped it over his knee.

'I need you to tell me where Eugene's at,' Landis said. 'I need you to tell me everythin' you know 'bout what's been goin' on. I need you to answer every question I got or I'm gonna kill you. You understand me?'

'I understand you're a fuckin' dead man. That's all I understand right now.'

Landis pushed the rag into Wasper's mouth. Wasper tried to spit it out, but it was futile.

Reaching behind him and to the right, Landis opened the medicine cabinet above the sink. From it he took a polythene-sealed toothbrush. He stripped off the polythene, held Wasper around the throat, and then pushed the toothbrush into Wasper's ear. Landis kept on pushing until Wasper's eyes widened and he started to scream. The sound was low and muffled, but there was no doubt that the pain Wasper was experiencing was excruciating.

Landis paused.

'You ready to talk?' he asked.

Wasper's eyes closed. He shook his head, his head then jerking back and forth as if he believed he could wrest himself free of the restraints that held him.

Landis applied pressure to the toothbrush.

Wasper's eyes bulged. His face reddened. Sweat broke out across his forehead. He fought and twisted and kicked, but he was tied so securely to the toilet that his efforts came to nothing.

Fredericksen got up and came through the doorway. He watched silently as Wasper writhed in agony.

Landis stopped. He withdrew the brush.

'You ready to talk?' Landis asked.

Wasper nodded once, twice.

Landis removed the rag.

'Kill me,' Wasper said. 'Do it. Just fuckin' do it.'

Fredericksen drew his .38. He cocked the hammer. He put the muzzle against Wasper's forehead.

'You know somethin',' he said. His voice was calm and unhurried. 'There ain't a great deal I can think of that would make me happier, Wasper. But you ain't gettin' off that easy.'

'We're gonna be here 'til we got what we need to know,' Landis said. 'We ain't playin' games no more, my friend. This is a whole mess o' trouble you're in, and it's only gonna get worse if you don't answer up.'

'I ain't tellin' you nothin', Wasper said.

Fredericksen held the muzzle of the gun against the broken bridge of Wasper's nose. He pushed. Wasper screamed. He pushed harder, harder again. There was a sound like choking. Wasper's eyes rolled back into his head and he passed out.

Landis looked up at Fredericksen.

'Let's have a smoke,' he said. He backed up out of the doorway, and dropped his .38 on the bed.

79

By the time Wasper started talking it was nearly midnight.

Three broken fingers, a fractured clavicle and multiple abrasions, cuts and bruises did not seem sufficient motivation for the man. When Fredericksen went out to his car and came back with a tire level, Wasper paid attention. The threat of shattered shin bones and the likelihood he'd never again walk unaided seemed to push him beyond whatever reprisal he feared from his brother.

Landis did not think about what they were doing. He did not think about the law, nor the personal consequences of kidnap and torture. He did not consider anything beyond the immediate moment and the information he needed from Eugene's brother.

Fredericksen, similarly, now seemed driven and vindictive. The individual cuffed and tied to a motel toilet was the target for his rage and retribution.

Wasper was frightened now; that was clear. It had taken a considerable degree of violence, all of it carried out silently, methodically, by a sheriff and a police detective, to make him realize that this would end one of two ways: Either he would tell them what they wanted to know, or he would be dead. Self-preservation kicked in, and hard.

Wasper's head hung low. He breathed with difficulty. He had long-since stopped howling, understanding perhaps that no one was coming to his rescue, least of all his brother. They had beaten him to within an inch of his life. He was now at breaking point, and the prospect of more pain and suffering was beyond his tolerance.

Landis sat on the edge of the tub. His hands were bruised and bloody.

Fredericksen had dragged a chair in from the bedroom. He sat astride it, his .38 in one hand, in the other a wet towel that he'd used to suffocate Wasper.

'You gonna tell us what we need to know?' Landis asked.

The nod of Wasper's head was almost indiscernible, but it was there.

'Where's he at, Wasper?'

Wasper looked up. His face – his eyes swollen, his mouth a bloody mess – was like some crude Hallowe'en mask.

'I want out,' he said.

'You want out?' Landis asked. 'You want out o' what?'

'Everythin',' Wasper slurred. 'You gotta get me out.'

'You want immunity?' Fredericksen asked. 'Is that what you want?'

Again, the almost-imperceptible nod.

'You don't get anythin' 'til you start talkin',' Landis said. 'The more you tell us, the better it'll be for you.'

Wasper started crying. It was pain, exhaustion, defeat. The man was overwhelmed – trapped whichever way he turned.

'He has a place, okay? Up in Tennessee.'

'Where exactly is this place?'

'Signal Mountain. He's got a cabin out there on the river.'

'The Chickamauga?' Landis asked.

Wasper nodded.

'How far from Signal Mountain?'

Wasper told him how far, the direction he should take off the road, what the place looked like.

'Tell us about the girls,' Landis said.

Wasper looked up. 'The girls,' he mumbled.

'These girls were abducted for what, Wasper? Who took 'em, and why?'

'M-money,' Wasper said. 'Took 'em for money. They make good money.'

'Money?' Fredericksen asked. 'Who's payin' for them?'

'Anyone … anyone who wants 'em.'

'For what?'

'Hookers, porn stuff, carryin' drugs, whatever. Hell, use your imagination.'

'Where do they go?' Landis asked.

'Anywhere. Up north. Everywhere. Canada. All over.'

'And you took 'em? Is that what happened? You an' your brother took 'em?'

'Lot o' people.'

'Kenny Greaves?' Landis asked. 'Holt Macklin? People like that?'

'Them, yeah. Others, too.'

Landis looked at Fredericksen. Fredericksen looked like he was ready to kill Wasper right where he sat.

'Tell us how it worked, Wasper,' Landis said.

Wasper lifted his head with difficulty. 'You gonna help me, right? You gonna get me out o' this.'

'You tell us, then we'll talk,' Landis replied.

Wasper started sobbing again. His mouth was bleeding. Blood bubbled from his nostrils.

Fredericksen leaned forward. He whipped the towel right across Wasper's face.

'Talk,' he said. 'Talk right now, or—'

'Okay, okay,' Wasper gasped.

'They're bein' trafficked,' Fredericksen said. 'To where, Wasper? Where exactly?'

'Every damn where, for fuck's sake. Loggin' camps. To the

border. Into damn Mexico. Wherever there's money. They go wherever there's money to pay for 'em.'

'An' your brother runs all o' this?' Landis asked.

Wasper looked up, genuinely perplexed. 'What?'

'Your brother. Eugene. He runs all o' this?'

Wasper tried to laugh. He grimaced in pain. 'My brother?' he said. 'You think my brother's got the fuckin' sense to organize all o' this?'

'This goes to State, doesn't it?' Landis asked. 'Ray Floyd, Jim Whelan...'

'What the fuck?' Wasper said. 'What the fuck, man? Jesus Christ, you fuckin' kidnap me and bring me here an' beat the shit outta me an' you already know what's goin' on?'

'Was Floyd in on it, or was he killed because he was investigatin' it?' Fredericksen asked.

'Floyd? Ray fuckin' Floyd? Jeez, that's a blast from the damn past, eh? Yeah, he was in on it. He got Eugene on that informant witness protection thing, whatever the fuck that was.'

'So why did he kill himself?' Fredericksen asked.

'He didn't kill himself. He bailed out, man. He got scared. He started makin' noises. Eugene had to take care o' him, didn't he? He had to make sure he didn't go talkin' to the Feds or whatever.'

'How many girls, Wasper? How many girls we talkin', and for how long?'

Wasper shook his head resignedly. 'I don't fuckin' know, do I? I lost count, man. I lost fuckin' count. Dozens o' them.'

'And they were all selected from this volunteer register?' Landis asked.

'That, yeah. An' different places. Child Services. They even got some people to set up foster places an' then they took them girls right out o' there and shipped 'em off.'

Fredericksen leaned back in the chair. He dropped the towel to the floor. He looked at Landis in disbelief.

'Did Kenny Greaves take your cousin, Wasper? Did he take Ella May because Vester Rayford was talkin' to my brother about this?'

Wasper looked up. The fear was still there, but now there was a deep resignation in every aspect of his expression and body language. 'She weren't meant to die, you know? Kenny fucked it up. Kenny was just s'posed to take her so Vester would keep his damned mouth shut.'

'What did he do, Wasper?'

'I don't know. I don't fuckin' know, okay? He tied her up, he drugged her. Whatever. She suffocated in the trunk of his car.'

Wasper closed his eyes. He slowly shook his head. He was broken. 'You gotta help me now,' he said. 'You don't help me, I'm dead.'

'We need to know about Frank's daughter,' Landis said. 'Eugene took her right? Eugene took Frank's daughter, didn't he?'

Wasper nodded.

'And where is she? Right now, where the fuck is she?'

'At the cabin, I guess,' Wasper said. 'That's where they all go.'

'And the dead ones? What happened to the dead ones we found?'

'They was the ones Eugene kept for himself. Kept 'em a while. Kept 'em there. An' when he was done with 'em he ditched them, didn't he?'

'Eugene killed them and got rid of the bodies?' Landis asked. 'That's what you're sayin', Wasper.'

'Some o' them. Kenny, too. Holt Macklin as well. Eugene'd say get rid o' this one or that one, and so they did. We took 'em away for him.'

'Did you kill any o' them yourself?' Fredericksen asked.

Wasper's head jerked upward instinctively. 'No! No, I didn't fuckin' kill any o' them!'

Landis leaned forward. He put his hand on Wasper's shoulder. 'You're gonna testify,' he said. 'That's your only ticket out o' this mess. You're gonna testify to everythin' you told us, and maybe you got a hope that you ain't goin' to prison for the rest o' your miserable, shitty life. You understand me, Wasper?'

'You gotta help me,' Wasper slurred. His breath caught in his chest. He coughed. He started sobbing again.

Landis slapped him hard. 'You understand me, Wasper? You're gonna testify against your brother an' everyone else who's involved in this, and then you might just have a prayer.'

Wasper didn't respond.

Landis got up. He and Fredericksen left the bathroom, closing the door behind them.

'We go to the cabin,' Landis said. 'We take Wasper. We trade him for Jenna.'

'You think Russell's gonna give up the only card he's got?'

Landis shook his head. 'I doubt it, but I ain't got a better notion right now.'

'Leave your cruiser here,' Fredericksen said. 'We'll take my car. We don't want to be announcin' our arrival.'

80

It was two on Sunday morning. The moon was a pale crescent. The sky was dense with clouds. What little light there was gave up nothing beyond ten or fifteen feet.

Eugene Russell's cabin was not so much a cabin as a sizeable compound with numerous outbuildings and barns. The central house was two-storied and set back beneath the overhang of a tall range of trees. Around the perimeter of the property was a fence of no more than five or six feet in height.

Down to the left was a steep incline that ran all the way to the edge of Chickamauga Lake.

Fredericksen's car, Wasper gagged and bound in the trunk, was up along the road and a good quarter-mile away. Landis had questioned whether the man would suffocate.

'Right now, I don't care,' Fredericksen had said. 'Eugene only needs to know we've got him.'

Though there was a single light burning in the lower half of the house, everything was quiet. As far as Landis could tell, there were no dogs – at least not outside – and both he and Fredericksen stayed low and silent a good twenty feet from the fence before they moved.

They would attempt entry to the house at the rear.

Both carried torches, their sidearms, and Fredericksen had a pump action. Landis had with him a tire lever.

Once they had made their way around to the rear of the house, they again laid low beyond the fence and waited.

For what seemed a small eternity, nothing but the sound of their breathing, the internal awareness of both pulse and heartbeat, they watched. After a good twenty minutes, Fredericksen moved. Landis followed him. They crossed the final span of cover afforded by the trees and approached the fence. Landis went over first, landing silently and then crouching down. Fredericksen followed suit. The two of them made their way across the yard to the building.

Fredericksen indicated right toward the slanted roof of a storm cellar.

Secured with a heavy chain and padlock through the handles, Landis could not see any way to breach it aside from the hinges. Though sizeable, they had weathered and rusted. With sufficient leverage and force, there was a hope that they might come away from the wood.

Fredericksen crouched in the lee of the cellar entrance. Landis, kneeling on the side furthest from the lighted window, worked the edge of the tire lever beneath the door. Given a half-inch of leeway, he would perhaps be able to get the lever beneath the hinge itself.

On the first attempt, the lever slipped suddenly. In the silence, the sound was a gunshot. Landis hunkered down, Fredericksen too, and they waited for any indication that they'd been heard.

Landis left it a good three or four minutes before he tried again. This time, he took it slowly, easing the lever up and down, feeling the wood straining against the hinge above it. After another five minutes or so, there was sufficient room to get the lever beneath the hinge plate itself.

The sound of the screws twisting up and out of the wood that had held them for countless years was shrill and penetrating. It seemed to echo back at them again and again from the trees.

Landis was sweating from the exertion. His heart hammered in his chest. The triangular plate of metal buckled against the force being applied. One screw remained steadfast and tore a hole through the hinge itself. Landis kept going. It took another ten minutes to get the first hinge free. The second one surrendered more readily. The heads of three screws snapped with almost no effort. With the hinges free of the frame, he and Fredericksen could lift the right door back over towards the left. It was heavy and awkward, but they succeeded.

The cellar was pitch-black. Landis went down the steps first, Fredericksen right behind him, and it was not until they reached the bottom that Landis switched on his torch.

What they saw could not have been described as anything but a prison. Spanning the footprint of the house above, the cellar had been lined along each side with dense steel cages. Within the cages, each one no more than six by eight, was a filthy mattress, odd articles of discarded clothing, lengths of rope, sections of chain, and a battered steel bedpan. The floor was stained with wide patches of excrement, urine, perhaps blood.

Landis and Fredericksen went in opposite directions. The cages were empty.

'How many?' Landis asked.

'Sixteen down that way. You?'

'Same again.'

'This is where they kept them,' Fredericksen said. 'This is beyond belief. This is just beyond anything I imagined.'

'I don't think there's anyone in the house,' Landis said.

'That's what I'm gettin',' Fredericksen replied.

'That way,' Landis said, indicating a walkway to the left with a door at the end.

The door was unlocked. Through it a flight of stone steps led upwards. The door at the top was also unlocked.

Once through it, they were in the kitchen. If the place was

empty now, it had not been empty long. A day-old newspaper was on the table. There was food and milk in the refrigerator. The cupboards, though not well stocked, had canned and dried goods, cereals, a sack of flour.

Landis and Fredericksen searched the property. Fredericksen found a room stacked ceiling-high with moving boxes. Opening one, he found articles of clothing – jeans, sweatshirts, underwear, shoes. A second revealed the same. He counted over forty boxes.

Other rooms were much the same as any regular house. People lived there, presumably Eugene, Ledda, Wasper, whoever else was involved in this. They went on living their lives, watching TV, making breakfast, while down in the cellar teenage girls – bewildered, terrified, afraid for their lives – screamed and sobbed until their throats were raw. What they must have experienced was beyond imagination. Landis could only assume that they thought they were going to die. That was true, but what was ahead of them – drugged into oblivion, prostituted out, used up and then thrown away like so much trash – was even worse.

In the room that overlooked the back of the property was a single bed. The sheets were filthy. The window was covered with a blanket. Landis scanned the room. Something in the corner caught his eye. He flicked on his torch.

Jenna's monkey looked back at him.

Landis crossed the room and picked it up. His heart was a clenched fist. He closed his eyes and made himself breathe. Had it not been a conscious action he believed he would have suffocated right where he stood.

He turned at the sound of Fredericksen entering the room.

'What you got there?' Fredericksen asked.

Landis turned and showed him.

'It's Jenna's,' Landis said. 'I gave it to her for her birthday.'

'He's left that on purpose, hasn't he?'

Landis didn't respond for some seconds, and then he nodded. 'I'm takin' it with me. I'm holdin' onto it until I can give it back.'

'Where's he taken her?' Fredericksen asked. 'Where would he go?'

'He's runnin',' Landis said. 'He'll have figured for this. He'll have another place, maybe. He'll have money hidden. I figured he'd maybe go to Whelan, but I doubt it. He'll know Whelan's compromised. Wherever he is, Wasper ain't enough. He ain't enough to be sure we get Jenna back.'

'So what do you wanna do?'

'Get hold of Milstead. Get him out to Colwell to arrest Ledda. Then we got Eugene's wife and his kid brother to barter with.'

'And what about this place?' Fredericksen asked.

'We're cross state now. We got an active felony kidnapping. Soon as I know that Ledda's in Blue Ridge, we call the Feds.'

81

Back at the cars, Fredericksen took Wasper out of the trunk and got him into the back seat. There was no fight left in him. Fredericksen would drive him to Trenton PD, and from there the necessary calls to coordinate the different agencies would be made.

Before they headed out, Landis put the monkey in a polythene evidence bag.

The search for Jenna was paramount. The more help they could muster, the better.

Landis and Fredericksen arrived a little after four.

Wasper was secured in lock-up and a doctor was brought in to tend to his injuries.

George Milstead was roused from sleep a little before five. Landis explained what was going on. Milstead called his deputy, Tom Sheehan. They were on their way to the Russell place in Colwell before six. Milstead said he would take Ledda Russell back to Blue Ridge, that he would call Trenton as soon as the woman was in custody.

'Just so we're clear,' Milstead said. 'If she gets mean, I will shoot her where she's standin'. That woman's had it a long time comin'.'

'I may still be here,' Landis said. 'If I'm not, get dispatch to radio Fredericksen.'

Milstead came back to Landis a little before seven-thirty.

'We got her,' he said. 'Like a wild fucking cat she was, but we got her.'

'Don't book her in,' Landis said. 'I need you to keep it quiet. I don't want anyone but us knowin' she's there.'

'You plannin' on comin' to get her?' Milstead asked.

'Maybe,' Landis said. 'I gotta see how this thing plays out.'

'I'll be here,' Milstead said, and hung up.

Landis then called the Tennessee and Georgia Bureaus respectively. To both offices, he faxed the full report he had previously written with Marshall. He added the up-to-date information regarding the suspected abduction of Jenna.

Tennessee said they would secure the place out near Chickamauga and get a forensics team in there. Georgia would send a unit to Trenton to get inside the Whelan house.

Finally, Landis called Abigail Webster.

'Abigail, it's Victor Landis. I got Eugene's brother here in Trenton. This is one for you. He's agreed to testify.'

'How bad is it?'

'Real bad. Hell, I don't even know how bad. A good deal worse than we thought. I got the Feds in on it. Tennessee are goin' to one of Russell's places in Chickamauga. Georgia are out to Whelan's place.'

'Jim Whelan?'

'Looks that way, yes.'

There was silence at the other end of the line.

'And Eugene Russell's took off with my brother's kid.'

'Oh my God, Victor. Is there anythin' I can do?'

'Right now, no. You'll need to come get Wasper from Trenton, but I'll tell you when. We had to get rough with him. He's gettin' fixed up by a doctor. I might need him yet, but once we're done he'll need secure transport to Atlanta.'

'I'll take care of it,' Webster said. 'Just let me know when and where.'

'Okay, I gotta get goin'.'

'Yes, yes of course. An' I hope you get her back real soon, Victor.'

'I'll get her, Abigail. Even if it kills me, she's comin' home.'

The last call Landis made was to Eleanor Boyd. It was seven, and from the sound of her voice Landis doubted she'd slept at all.

'Have you got her? Have you got Jenna?'

'No, Eleanor, but we're on it. We're pretty sure she's here in Trenton.'

'Where? Where is she? I'm comin' there now.'

'No, you need to stay right there.'

'But—'

'Eleanor, listen to me. I got two sheriffs, people from the Attorney General's Office. I got the Bureau from both here and Tennessee on this. You need to trust me on this. She's comin' home. I gave you my word, an' I'm keepin' it.'

Eleanor started to say something, but Landis interrupted her.

'Is Marshall there?'

'Yes, he is. He's been with me all night.'

'Put him on the phone, Eleanor.'

Eleanor did as Landis asked.

'Marshall, I need you to take Eleanor to Barbara's place. That'll be safer than stayin' where you are. And keep her there, okay? We're stayin' in Trenton. I got the Feds en route. You keep her there and let me get the girl, okay?'

'Sure thing.'

'Soon as I have word, I'll call.'

'Understood,' Marshall replied.

'Hang in there, son,' Landis said. 'It won't be long before there's news.'

Just before nine, a four-vehicle convoy of SUVs pulled up ahead of Trenton PD.

Senior Special Agent Allen Lowell was the first to question the physical state of Wasper Russell.

'Things got rough,' Landis told him. 'Right now I got an eleven-year-old girl kidnapped by Eugene Russell. I got Jim and Florence Whelan in a place outside of the city. We get the girl back, then you can drag me over the coals about how we all arrived at this point, okay?'

Lowell closed the office door.

'I ain't askin' any more questions about it, Sheriff. Your department and how it conducts itself ain't none o' my business. If what you're tellin' us is correct an' we got a sex-trafficking operation goin' on here an' a whole host of missing and dead girls, then how we got to this point is the least o' my concerns. As of this moment, I need to know everythin' you got about the girl.'

'I got a unit headin' out to a Russell place in Chickamauga. All I got is a toy that belonged to Jenna that tells me she was there.'

'And you think there's any possibility the Whelans have her?'

Landis shrugged. 'Unlikely, but there's always a chance he dropped her there and took off alone.'

'Okay, then I need the best you can do as far as layout, entrances, exits, anything else you can tell me about the property itself.'

'I been there once,' Landis said.

'I appreciate that, Sheriff, but I ain't got time to be requesting blueprints from the county plannin' office. You just need to tell me everythin' you remember an' some of the things you forgot, too.'

Landis sat down. Exhaustion and hunger was catching up with him.

'You ain't slept an' you ain't had no breakfast, I'm guessin',' Lowell said.

'Don't matter right now,' Landis replied.

'Sleep I can't help you with, but tryin' to think clearly with an empty belly ain't easy.'

Lowell opened the door and summoned one of his team.

'Go out and find a diner,' he said. 'Get me bacon, pancakes, coffee, eggs, whatever else they got. Bring enough for two.'

The agent went on his way. Lowell closed the door once more.

'Okay,' he said. 'Everythin' you can tell me, right from the start, and everythin' you can give me on Whelan, his wife and the property.'

Landis leaned back in the chair and started talking.

At half-past nine, Lowell got word from the Tennessee Bureau Agent-in-Charge that the Chickamauga cabin had been secured. They had a forensics team on-site already, but the task ahead of them was far beyond what they'd anticipated. A second team had been requested from Nashville. Word had already been relayed that they were on the road.

Lowell met with Fredericksen and Landis in the makeshift operations room provided by the Trenton PD.

'This is Bureau,' Lowell told them. 'This is interstate felony whichever way you look at it. You don't need to be on this, but I understand that this is your niece that we're talkin' about here.'

'It's also my jurisdiction,' Fredericksen said.

'I ain't sayin' you can't be with us, but you've both been up all night, and a man who ain't slept has slower reaction times. We're dealin' with someone here who has more than likely murdered or ordered the murders of numerous people. This is not a man who wants to be taken in. You understand precisely the kind of individual we're dealin' with here, and I need you to just take a step back. This is my responsibility now. Hell, if it weren't for you and what you've done so far, I wouldn't even be here. I wouldn't even know about it. That don't change the fact that I cannot risk any mistakes here. The people I brought with me have done this before. They have been trained for it. They know exactly what they're doin'.'

Fredericksen raised his hands. 'I ain't gettin' in your way here,' he said.

Lowell turned to Landis.

'Sheriff?'

'How would it be if it was your kin?' Landis asked.

'I'd want the best people on the job, sure, but I can't deny that I'd have to be there.'

'So let me be there,' Landis said. 'I made a promise to bring her home.'

Lowell hesitated, and then he nodded.

'You comin' along?' he asked Fredericksen.

Fredericksen glanced at Landis. 'I go where he goes,' he said.

Lowell stood up and walked to the door. He opened it, hesitated, and then closed it once more.

'Just on a personal note,' he said. 'If this thing is what it appears to be, if this has been goin' on all these years and if it really does involve officials in the Attorney General's Office, then the fallout is goin' to be considerable. Don't expect your lives to get quiet any time soon. The press are gonna be all over this. This'll be like doin' damage control on ... hell, I don't even know what to compare it to. But whatever happens, I just wanna say that you did a hell of a job.'

'We ain't done,' Landis said. 'I need that little girl back.'

'You're right,' Lowell said. 'Let's go bring her home.'

82

Lowell's first action was to coordinate surveillance of the Whelan property.

Utilizing all the resources at his disposal – Sheriff's Office, Police Department and his own people – he stationed units at each entry and exit point. Situation reports came in from the team deployed overlooking the back of the house.

In the office at Trenton PD, Lowell briefed Landis, Fredericksen and two of his own people on the approach he wanted to make.

'The fact that we have complicity in a suspected kidnapping gives us probable cause. We'll have a warrant imminently, but I'm not waiting. We can ask permission. If they refuse, then we have to provide the warrant. If Russell is there, he'll leave. The exits away from the property are covered. He can be pulled over. If he doesn't comply with a request to pull over, then it's officer evasion. The key thing we want to avoid is a flight. If he has that child, then any high-speed pursuit puts the child's life in danger.'

'Who goes to the house?' Fredericksen asked.

'Myself and Agent Young,' Lowell said. 'Sheriff Landis has been there before. That will give them forewarning. I'm hoping that the presence of federal agents on their porch will rattle them. If they do something – anything – that gives us reasonable cause to enter the property, then we have the advantage we need.'

'You actually think Russell would be dumb enough to take her there?'

'I guess we're going to find out, aren't we?' Lowell replied.

'And Jim Whelan?' Landis asked.

'If Jim Whelan has been complicit in this, and I have every reason to assume that he has, then he's looking at spending the rest of his life behind bars. If he was complicit in the murders themselves, then the State will push for the death penalty. If his wife was aware of it, then she's an accomplice. As for Russell himself, he's Tennessee. They haven't executed anyone for over thirty years. They seem to have lost their taste for it. However, there's no reason we can't have him tried in Georgia.'

'How long to get a warrant?' Fredericksen asked.

Lowell shook his head. 'Like I said, it's imminent, but we're not waiting. We also have to consider the possibility that it won't get authorized anyway. A search warrant has to be very specific. It needs to be based on direct information, something that a law enforcement official has actually seen. We don't have that. This is hearsay and circumstance. I'm not certain enough of that to take a gamble. Informant information can also be used, but we have an issue there.'

Lowell paused and looked at Landis.

'I don't disagree with what you did or how you did it, but any public defender will see right away that Wasper Russell was beaten, an' badly. That then becomes the basis for an appeal against the original warrant. Anything we see or find as a result of that warrant becomes inadmissible.'

For a few moments, there was silence in the room.

'That's where we are,' Lowell said.

'I got one question,' Landis said. 'Say Russell is there an' he runs, how quick can you get more people out here to ensure he doesn't evade capture?'

'We have enough people on-site to stop him. If, for some

reason, he gets through, then I'll have the entirety of both the Georgia and Tennessee Bureaus to call on. I can get helicopters in the air within thirty minutes. I can close every road out of the state. I assure you, whatever it takes, we will hunt this man down. He's comin' back here, either in cuffs or on a gurney.'

Out near the Whelan house, Special Agent Lowell confirmed that all units were in place and that a clear line-of-sight had been established for all exit points on the property.

Landis and Fredericksen were in separate vehicles on the road ahead. Landis was silent. If this went wrong and Jenna was killed, he would only have himself to blame. Everything that had occurred since his brother's death had brought him to this moment. This was Frank's daughter, just eleven years old. Her life on his conscience was something from which he knew he'd never recover.

Through binoculars, Landis watched as Lowell and Young went up the porch steps. The door opened before they knocked.

Florence Whelan gave no indication that she was unsettled by the appearance of two federal agents at her front door. Words were exchanged. The door was then closed, but Lowell and Young stayed right where they were.

It wasn't long before the door opened again. This time it was both Whelans, he in his wheelchair, she standing beside him and to his right.

Lowell and Young again produced ID. More words were exchanged. Whelan was shaking his head, already backing up, his wife then stepping around behind him to close the door on the visitors.

With the front door shut, Lowell and Young turned and made their way back to the car. They headed up the driveway to the road.

'We were about as welcome as a rattler,' Lowell told Landis and Fredericksen.

'She knows, doesn't she?' Landis said.

'She knows enough,' Lowell replied.

'So now we wait,' Fredericksen said.

'We do,' Lowell replied. 'I'm leavin' one car here. The rest of us go to the roads behind the property. If Russell is there and makes a run for it, he's leavin' that way.'

Alongside the upper roads, dense woodland afforded cover for the half dozen vehicles that were stationed there.

Lowell had them separated by thirty or forty yards each way. If Russell turned either left or right, there would be more than adequate time for his escape to be blocked. Foremost amongst concerns was the prevention of a high-speed chase or a gun battle.

With no knowledge of what might be occurring in the house below, Landis was on edge. For him, more than anyone else present, this was personal. He stayed close to Lowell, listened as reports came in from the various agents. One after the other, it was the same. No sign of movement, no indication that anyone was intending to leave the property.

'You get any word back on the warrant?' Landis asked.

'Nothin' as yet,' Lowell replied. 'We gotta act like it's never comin'.'

Landis walked up into the trees. He smoked one cigarette after another. After a while, Fredericksen joined him.

'Eugene Russell ain't here, Mike. Nor is Jenna.'

'You can't be sure o' that.'

'Sure as I need to be. He ain't a fool. He knows we're onto him. He's taken Jenna as insurance. He's reckonin' on her bein' his getaway ticket.'

'So, if he ain't here and he ain't out at the cabin, where's he gone?'

'Not a clue.'

'Ledda?'

'That's what I'm thinkin'.'

'You wanna go get her?'

Landis nodded. 'Wasper too.'

'What you gonna tell Lowell?'

'Exactly what he wants to hear,' Landis said. 'This is his operation, right? Let's leave him to it.'

83

Landis and Fredericksen left Trenton PD with Wasper Russell before noon.

Wasper was Fredericksen's case. No one questioned him about what he was doing or where he was going.

They took 76 east in Landis's car. It was a good two-hour drive, but being Sunday the highway was clear.

Arriving in Blue Ridge, Landis pulled over a block from Milstead's office. He looked back over his shoulder at Wasper. Wasper's spirit was as bruised as his face. Aside from the odd expletive, he'd said nothing throughout the journey.

'He's gone an' left you,' Landis said. 'So much for brotherly love, eh? I'm guessin' the only things he loves are himself and money.'

Wasper sneered. 'You're gonna give me a lecture 'bout brotherly love, are you?'

Landis didn't evidence his reaction, but the comment cut to the quick.

'I'm goin' in to get her,' Landis said to Fredericksen. 'He moves a muscle, knock him flat.'

George Milstead did not conceal his surprise when he saw Landis. Surprise was quickly replaced with concern.

'And where the hell are you gonna take her?' he asked.

'I'm figurin' it's best you don't know, George.'

'She's in my custody, Victor. My county. My jail, goddamnit.'

'But you didn't book her.'

'No, I didn't. I did what you asked, but I didn't reckon on you comin' to get her.'

Landis paused before speaking. He knew the more people he told, the more likely this would wind up on the grapevine that Mercer Gill was so fond of harvesting.

'We can take a moment in your office, George?'

Milstead hesitated, and then nodded.

Closing the door behind him, Milstead waited for an explanation.

'They took my niece,' Landis said.

Milstead closed his eyes for a moment. He shook his head and sighed deeply. 'Lord almighty,' he said quietly.

He crossed the room and sat down at his desk. Landis remained standing.

Milstead looked up at him. 'You do what I think you're gonna do and it'll more 'an likely end your career.'

'It ain't about policin' anymore, George. Say it was one o' yours? Your granddaughter, maybe.'

'Hell, you don't have to explain nothin' to me, Victor. An' I sure as hell ain't gonna try and convince you of anythin'.'

'So give her to me. In cuffs. And let's do it discreet, okay?'

'Like you asked, she ain't in any booking log. I ain't even got her in a cell. I locked her in a supply room.'

'She make a fuss?'

'She knew it was comin'. Mouthful of curses, but little else. Said she wasn't talkin' to no one, no matter what we did.'

'Well, we'll see if that holds up in practice, won't we?'

George hesitated, and then he got to his feet.

'Let's go fetch her then.'

*

'Oh, here we go again,' Ledda Russell said when she saw Landis.

Her expression was disdainful.

'You ain't in no place to look down on anyone,' Milstead told her.

Ledda ignored him. She kept staring at Landis.

'You think I'm gonna tell you a single thing, you better think again,' she said.

Landis smiled. 'Hell, Ledda, I ain't expectin' you to tell me anythin'. I'm after everythin'.'

'You all can go burn in Hell. You ain't no good. None o' you. Your brother was about as much use as a three-legged hound, and you ain't no much better.'

Milstead had handcuffed Ledda to the upright of a metal shelving unit. He uncuffed her, cuffed her again when her hands were free. He gave the key to Landis.

'Where you set on takin' me?' she asked.

'Same place I'm taking your brother-in-law,' Landis said.

'You got Wasper?'

'I got Wasper, an' I got the Feds pickin' up the Whelans. It's pretty much a done deal for all of you.'

'Oh, I don't think so,' she said. 'You ain't got Eugene, and you ain't gonna get him. If there's one thing I can guarantee, that'd be it.'

Landis turned to Milstead. 'Appreciate your help, George.'

'Least I can do, Victor. An' gimme a holler if you need help diggin' a hole to bury this one.'

Ledda laughed condescendingly. 'Only ones who's gettin' buried is you pair. An' your brother's daughter, I'm guessin'.'

Landis was about ready to beat the woman into the hereafter.

'Shame there ain't some way to cuff her mouth, eh?' Milstead said.

'Oh, she'll be polite enough by the time we're through,' Landis replied.

Milstead opened the door and followed Landis and Ledda Russell out into the corridor.

'See you on the other side o' this, Victor.'

'Sure as daybreak,' Landis replied.

Landis put Ledda in the back of the car with Wasper. He cuffed her right hand to the seat post behind the footwell. He did the same with Wasper's left, and then cuffed them together in the middle.

They didn't say a word to one another.

Fredericksen was in the driver's seat. He had the motor running.

'I gotta make a call,' Landis said.

Fredericksen waited while Landis crossed the street to a booth on the corner opposite the Sheriff's Office.

He was back within five minutes, took the passenger seat.

'Who'd you call?' Fredericksen asked.

'Someone who's very interested to see this pair,' Landis said.

'Where we headed then?'

'Straight ahead,' Landis replied. 'McCaysville.'

84

It was a little after three-thirty when Fredericksen turned off the main road and headed down to Vester Rayford's place.

Landis had last seen him over in Spring City with his brother on the 6th.

Before they were twenty yards from the front porch, the front door opened and Vester came out.

Fredericksen came to a stop. Landis got out and walked on up to the house.

'Sheriff,' Rayford said.

'Vester.'

'I'm ready for them.'

'Where's Jeanette at?'

'Had her sister come get her. She don't live but three or four miles away. Told her to stay there 'til I said otherwise.'

'This goes a great deal farther than what they did to your Ella May.'

Rayford didn't reply.

'You thought about what's gonna happen if you get into this?'

'I thought about what'll happen if I don't.'

Landis nodded. 'Okay then. Where we puttin' them?'

Rayford indicated a point towards the trees to the right. 'Root cellar back there. I don't use it much. It's big, though. Big enough to hold 'em. Deep too. Ain't no one gonna hear a thing.'

Landis looked back at Fredericksen and nodded.

Fredericksen got out of the car.

'Who's your sidekick?' Rayford asked.

'His name ain't important, Vester. Just enough to know he's here on the same terms as us.'

Fredericksen uncuffed Ledda and Wasper from the seat posts. They came out of the vehicle on the passenger side, still cuffed together.

Vester Rayford came down from the porch and walked towards them.

Ledda Russell recognized him immediately. For Wasper it took a moment longer.

'Cousin,' Rayford said.

Ledda squinted at him. 'You ain't family,' she said. 'Never was, never will be.'

Rayford smiled faintly. 'Still a lady, I see.'

'Eugene gonna skin you alive, your wife too,' Ledda said.

'I guess we'll see about that,' Rayford replied. He took a bunch of keys from his pocket.

'Let's go,' he said to Landis.

Rayford started walking, Landis following him, Fredericksen behind Ledda and Wasper.

The five of them headed on beyond the treeline towards the root cellar.

Excavated into the incline beyond the trees, the cellar was built of split trunks, the roof supported by two central braces, each of them half the girth of a man. The back wall was racked with shelves. Old preserve jars sat alongside rusted cans, spiders' webs woven thick between them, and to the right a hammer and a handful of nails sat on a workbench. Beneath it was a wooden stool. The place smelled of dirt and damp seed.

Fredericksen and Rayford barred the door. Landis took the

cuffs off Ledda and Wasper. He had Ledda put her arms behind her and around the brace. He cuffed her once more. He did the same with Wasper.

Rayford then pulled Wasper's arms up so they were bent at the elbow. He hammered nails through two or three of the links and into the wooden brace. He did the same to Ledda. The position in which they were secured was uncomfortable, stressful to both the shoulders and neck.

Landis took the stool from beneath the workbench and sat down ahead of Ledda.

Fredericksen and Rayford stood back against the wall to the right.

Wasper struggled some, but it was futile. He was going nowhere and he knew it. With his broken fingers and fractured clavicle, the painkillers he'd been given now wearing off, he was in a considerable amount of pain. More troubling to him was the fact that he'd already spoken to Landis. Ledda would know this, and that was as good as telling Eugene. Landis figured that the only thing that kept him from breaking down completely was his sister-in-law's presence.

'You an' I gonna have a heart-to-heart now, Ledda,' Landis said.

'You an' I ain't gon' have nothin' of the sort.'

'Wasper here gave up the cabin. I got Feds all over it like ants. I can only guess what went on there, but I'm figurin' the reality is a lot worse. Seems Tennessee don't much care for the chair anymore, but we ain't plannin' on havin' you tried there. We're keepin' you in Georgia. Here we have no such moral or ethical reservations. Here we do eye-for-an-eye. This is my state, and just for Ella May alone, we got you for a capital crime.'

'You got nothin',' Ledda hissed.

Landis took out a cigarette and lit it.

'You listen up too now, Wasper,' Landis said. 'I'm gonna tell you exactly how this goes.'

Wasper raised his head. Whatever defiance remained in his eyes had long since dimmed.

'They shave your head first. Then they shave the calf of one leg. They tie you in the chair with straps to your wrists, waist and ankles. They fix an electrode to your head and your calf. There's a wet sponge under the electrode. That ensures really good contact. They tighten up those electrodes and you feel the water running down your face and the back of your neck. You get to wait a while. They make sure your heart is beating. They check your pulse. You wait a while longer. They drag it out somewhat, you know? Some folks have been known to pass out there and then. They wake 'em up. They want you fully conscious for this. They want to really build up the tension. Folks piss themselves. They cry. They always cry. They plead. They beg. They say they're sorry. Don't matter how vicious, how cruel, how tough you tell yourself you're gonna be, when it comes to that moment you ain't nothin' but a terrified child.'

Landis took another draw on his cigarette.

'Oh, they tape over your eyes. I forgot that. Yeah, they tape over your eyes and sometimes they put a diaper on you.'

Wasper let out a pained gasp.

'Two thousand volts. Two and a half thousand. It goes on for minutes. The body can heat up to over two hundred degrees. Your eyeballs actually liquefy. Massive internal organ damage. I mean hell, they're cookin' you alive, aren't they?'

Wasper started to cry.

Ledda turned and looked at him. For just a split second, Landis saw a flash of vulnerability in her expression. It was gone as fast as it had appeared, and she looked back at Landis with pure contempt.

'Your head can burn,' Landis continued. 'That's happened a

good many times. Actual flames comin' out of your face. One time the chair broke down halfway through. Guy was still alive, screaming at the top of his voice. They had to haul him off the thing, scrape all the charred skin off of the chair and the electrodes, repair the chair and then do it all over again. Took more than an hour.'

'Oh, fuckin' hell,' Wasper gasped. 'I don't know, okay? I don't know anythin' else. I don't know where's he's gone.'

Landis nodded understandingly.

'I'm askin' Ledda here.'

'Fuck you,' Ledda snapped. She glanced at Wasper. 'An' you keep your damned mouth shut now, boy. I ain't tellin' you twice.'

'Where's he gone, Ledda?' Landis asked. 'Where's Eugene gone?'

'I don't know. I don't know where he's fuckin' gone! Don't matter how many times you ask, you're gonna get the same damned answer.'

Landis turned to Rayford. 'Vester, I'm set to put some nails through her hands now, but you're more 'an welcome to do it.'

Rayford didn't hesitate. He picked up the hammer once more, gathered up a couple of nails and stood behind the brace.

Ledda struggled wildly. She screamed at Landis. Landis slapped her hard across the face.

Rayford put the point of a nail against Ledda's right hand and pushed. It broke the skin. Her eyes widened suddenly. She spat at Landis and then started screaming once again.

Landis nodded at Rayford.

With a single blow, Rayford drove the nail right through the palm of Ledda's hand and into the wood beneath.

She let out a guttural roar, and then her head lolled sideways. For a moment she seemed unconscious, and then she came to. She lifted her head. She instinctively tugged forward, and this merely served to exacerbate the pain she was already experiencing.

'Do it again, Vester,' Landis said.

'Tell him!' Wasper shouted. 'Tell him where Eugene is, for fuck's sake!'

Rayford didn't hesitate. Once again, and with a single blow, he drove a second nail through Ledda's hand.

Ledda screamed. Her eyes rolled upwards to white, and for a few moments she was delirious with the pain.

Landis slapped her, slapped her again.

'Where is he, Ledda? Where's he gone? Where's he taken my niece?'

'Fuck you!' Ledda screamed. 'Fuck you! Fuck all o' you!'

Landis turned to Fredericksen.

'Gag her, would you? I'm gonna break her shins.'

Fredericksen removed his tie and gagged Ledda. She was wild with hate and fury. She wrestled back and forth, but she knew she wasn't going anywhere.

Fredericksen got up. He took the hammer from Rayford. He hefted it in his hand. Taking a step back, he raised the hammer.

A moment before he let fly, Ledda howled through the gag.

Landis paused.

Ledda started nodding furiously.

'You wanna say somethin'?' Landis asked.

Ledda kept on nodding.

Fredericksen loosened the gag. Ledda gasped for air. Her throat was raw from screaming.

'I-if I te-tell you wh-where he's gone...'

'You tell me where he's gone, Ledda, and we talk a plea deal.'

'You gotta give me your wo-word.'

Landis smiled. 'I ain't gotta give you nothin', Ledda,' he said. 'You take it for what it is. You tell me where he is or I snap your shins right here and now, an' then I'm gonna dig a hole and bury

Wasper alive right in front of you. However this turns out, I'm gonna find Eugene and I'm bringin' my niece home. You help me, then maybe you got some slight hope of makin' it out of this without the chair.'

Ledda lowered her head. No matter the bluff and bravado, when it came to real physical pain there were few who could bear it. Self-preservation overcame loyalty, promises, even family oaths.

'He's got another cabin,' she said. 'Signal Mountain. Up near there.'

'Where exactly?'

'Down to the river. A mile or so out towards Powells Crossroads.'

Ledda paused. She breathed deeply. 'Ah Jesus Christ, you fuckers.' She started to cry, less now because of the pain and more because she'd done exactly what she'd promised herself she would never do.

Landis leaned forward. 'Is that where my brother was headed? Was he goin' on out there to find Eugene?'

Ledda looked up at Landis. Her expression answered the question.

'Was it Eugene who killed him, Ledda? Was it Eugene who run him down and killed him?'

'Guess you're gonna get a chance to ask him for yourself.'

Rayford secured the cellar door with a heavy padlock.

He walked on up to the house, Landis and Fredericksen following. When they reached the car, Rayford turned and said, 'Of a mind to burn the place down with the pair o' them inside.'

'Be smarter if you didn't,' Landis said.

'I know, Sheriff, and I ain't gonna do it. Guess I just wanted to say it out loud.'

'If this goes how I want, we'll be back tonight.'

'An' if it don't?'

Landis looked at Rayford, then out towards the root cellar. 'You find a Fed called Allen Lowell out of the Georgia Bureau. You tell him I asked to use your place. You went with your wife to her sister's place. Have the pair of them corroborate. You don't know what happened while you was gone, but you came on back and found them pair in the cellar.'

Rayford nodded. 'If I get word you're dead, then I'm lightin' them up like I said.'

'Forensics'll know when they was burned, Vester. The timeline'll get you. You got a wife to look after. You give 'em to Lowell, okay? He'll make sure they fry.'

Rayford didn't reply.

'I need your word, Vester. Too many people have been killed that shouldn'a been already. I appreciate you doin' what you done to help us, but that's gonna have to be enough.'

Rayford hesitated a moment longer, and then he nodded.

Landis turned to leave.

'One other thing 'fore you head out,' Rayford said.

He went back up into the house, returned a couple of minutes later with a Winchester 70 and a box of shells.

Handing it to Landis, he said, 'You go on an' get that little girl back now, Sheriff.'

Pulling the car onto the road, Landis said, 'You got any doubt about comin' with me?'

'Too late for that,' Fredericksen replied.

'You think what I'm doin' is wrong.'

'I think what they did is worse.'

'You understand there ain't no simple way out of this for either of us.'

'I know that,' Fredericksen said.

'But you have a wife and kids to think about.'

'Only reason I still got a wife and kids is because of your brother.'

Neither spoke again until they were heading west on 64.

85

Eighty miles or so from McCaysville, Signal Mountain sat at the south end of Walden Ridge, Hamilton County. The Tennessee River followed a course a thousand feet beneath.

Northwest out of the town, Route 27 ran adjacent to the river to meet Powells Crossroads. Much the same as the landscape surrounding Nottely Lake, high banks of trees lined the water. It was down along here, a mile or so from the junction of 27 and 127, that Eugene Russell had a second cabin. From what Ledda had told them, it was an A-frame, much smaller than the one at Chickamauga, and it sat in a clearing some eighty yards or so from the river's edge.

Though it was dusk, visibility was good. Landis drove along the high road, Fredericksen looking out for a turning that would take them down towards the water. Three-quarters of a mile along, a clear track appeared. Landis pulled over. He and Fredericksen exited the vehicle and started down on foot. Landis took the rifle. Fredericksen carried his revolver and a PD-issue pump action. If the information they had was correct, they would find Eugene's place within a quarter mile.

Progress was slow. The undergrowth was dense. Darkness fell quickly, and by the time they reached the river itself, visibility was down to nothing.

It was Fredericksen who sighted a cabin. An A-frame, just as they'd been told, but no guarantee it was Eugene's. Through the scope of the rifle, Landis could read the plate on the truck parked to the side. Had he been in his department vehicle, he could have radioed in the number and confirmed ownership. Without such a resource available, they would have to gain a vantage point from where they could see into the building itself.

With the agreement to meet back at the same point, Fredericksen took a route that ran behind the property. Landis made his way towards it, and then headed left until he was closer to the river. Here he shouldered the rifle and climbed into the lower boughs of a tree. Though the view was not unobstructed, he could see through the front windows of the cabin. A single light burned at ground level. Using a branch to support the rifle, he watched for any sign of movement. For minutes there was nothing. He wondered where Fredericksen was. There was no evidence of him or anyone else in the vicinity of the cabin.

Feeling the strain in his shoulders, Landis tried to shift into a more comfortable position. It was then that he caught a fleeting shadow somewhere near the truck. Training his scope as steadily as he could, he held his breath.

The truck door was opened, and in the few seconds that the internal light was on, he saw Eugene Russell. There was no doubt in his mind. He would know Eugene Russell anywhere. Exiting the vehicle, Russell went back into the cabin.

Landis came down from the tree and headed back the way he'd come. He needed to find Fredericksen and establish some sort of strategy. He knew that if he gave himself time to consider what was happening to Jenna, the terror she must be experiencing, what Russell was capable of doing, he would lose it. He made himself focus on the simple fact that Jenna was the only card that Russell held. If Russell killed her, it was all over. She was the bargaining chip that would extricate him from the situation he was in, and thus it made sense for him to keep her alive. Russell would also know that it was only a matter of time before someone caught up with him. The Signal Mountain property had been unknown to Landis, and was more than likely unknown to anyone but Ledda, Wasper, perhaps the Whelans. Nevertheless, Russell had perpetrated so many felonies and maintained such a level of corruption, all the while maintaining ties that ran right into the heart of the justice system, that Landis could not afford to underestimate the man's intelligence and foresight. Russell would know that Jenna's kidnap would warrant federal intervention, and thus all the resources at their disposal. The advantage that Landis possessed was the speed with which they'd located him. They had left the Whelan place no more than six or seven hours earlier. Even if Lowell had arrested the Whelans, even if he'd then discovered the absence of Ledda and Wasper, there was no way for him to know where they'd been taken. Marshall knew nothing, and – if he'd done as Landis instructed – he was now with Eleanor at Barbara Wedlock's place.

Landis kept moving slowly, listening, watching, stopping periodically for any sign of movement around the cabin. Keeping the front of the cabin in his line of sight, he reached the point of departure. Fredericksen was not there. Landis resisted the urge to go looking. He stayed right where he was. He stayed silent. He barely breathed. Every once in a while he raised the rifle to his shoulder and scanned the side of the cabin, the truck parked outside, the little he could see of the trees left and right.

Ten minutes passed. It seemed a great deal longer. The sound of someone approaching raised the hairs on the back of Landis's neck. He crouched low, laid the rifle on the ground and withdrew his pistol. When he was sure it was Fredericksen, he made the slightest sound. Fredericksen crouched down beside him.

'It's Russell,' Landis said. 'He came out to the truck and I saw him clear enough.'

'So how d'you wanna play this?'

'As it comes,' Landis said. 'I ain't waitin' on Feds. He's got Jenna. She's either there or he's hidden her someplace else and is gonna use her as leverage to get himself out of this. He'll have figured this out. He'll have some place he's headed. He'll have money, maybe a new ID, people who'll protect him.'

'So what, you're gonna go on up there and knock on his damned door? What's to say he won't shoot you soon as he sees you? Seems from what Ledda said that he's the one who killed your brother. Done it once, I don't doubt he'll do it again.'

'You a hunter?'

'What?'

Landis picked up Rayford's Winchester. 'You know how to use this?'

86

Between the treeline and the cabin porch ran a twenty-foot pathway bordered by stones.

Landis stayed back in the shadows. Russell's truck was to the right and down the side of the building. Fredericksen would be out there somewhere in the darkness.

Landis's heart thundered in his chest. What he was feeling was unlike anything he'd experienced before. Movement took a conscious decision. Breathing, too. There was a sensation of motion without even taking a step, as if some deep inner part of himself was trying to run. He understood that what happened now would determine whether both he and Jenna came out of this alive. He questioned his own willingness to die. To die for Frank's daughter. To give up his own life for her. Would he do that?

He tried to silence his mind, to focus on nothing but one foot in front of the other. He started down the pathway, his gun still holstered.

Ten feet from the porch steps he looked up at the windows. There was still no sign of movement, still no more lights.

Holding his breath, he willed himself to keep it together, to stay calm, to give no impression of fear. In truth, what he felt was something so far beyond fear that he would struggle to define it. Paralysis. Terror. Hysteria. Even those things were inadequate.

'Eugene Russell!'

The sound of his own voice was that of a stranger. It reverberated out into the night and came back at him in triplicate.

Once the echoes had died away, there was nothing but the distant sound of the river, the faint susurrus of wind in the tress.

'Eugene Russell!'

Once again, the sound went out there and hung in the air.

The faint snap of a twig underfoot to his left. He turned. At first there was nothing, but then a figure emerged, the twin barrels of a shotgun leveled at his head.

'You got anythin' on you but that pistol?' Russell asked.

'No.'

'Real slow, left hand, you unbuckle that belt and drop it.'

Landis did as he was told, all the while watching the unerring steadiness of the shotgun barrels, sensing some strange cousin to relief that he was now at the point of no return.

'You take a good three or four steps back now,' Russell said.

Landis did so.

'Get on your knees, Sheriff. You pitch forward, head to the ground, and put your hands behind you where I can see 'em.'

Once again, Landis did as Russell instructed.

Russell gathered up Landis's belt and holster. He backed up once more, told Landis to get to his feet.

'Keep your hands out where I can see 'em, and you walk on up to the house.'

Landis moved slowly, Russell ten or twelve feet behind him, the shotgun directed at back of Landis's head.

'Go on an' open up the door,' Russell said. 'Walk on in the house real slow. There's a switch on the wall to your right. You put the light on there, and then you keep on goin' 'til I tell you to stop.'

Landis opened the door, turned on the lower light, walked forward.

'Okay, stop right there.'

The cabin was sparse. There was nothing but a table to the right, a gun rack, a couple of chairs, and over to the left a heavy wooden trunk, on top of which was a suitcase.

'Go get one o' them chairs,' Russell said. 'Set it ahead of the fireplace there and sit yourself down.'

Landis complied.

Russell put Landis's gun down behind the trunk. He took a second chair and set it facing Landis on the other side of the room.

The shotgun still trained at Landis's midriff, Russell just looked at him for a good minute or more before he sat down.

'I'm guessin' you got Ledda someplace.'

'You'd be right,' Landis replied. 'Your brother too.'

'Which one told you about this place?'

'Your wife.'

'She dead now?'

Landis shook his head.

'You hurt her though?'

'Less than I was ready to.'

Russell smiled. 'But enough for her to open her damned mouth, right? Hell, I knew well enough she would fold. Should never have told her 'bout this place.'

'I'd have found it,' Landis said. 'My brother did, didn't he? Came on out here to arrest you, I'm guessin', but you knew he was comin' and killed him before he arrived.'

Russell shook his head slowly. 'You know, for a lawman, I gotta say I liked your brother. Don't ask me why 'cause I can't tell you. Maybe 'cause he was so damned perseverin', you know? He was a dog with a bone, that boy. A real starvin' dog, mind. He just didn't know the meanin' o' quit.'

'Reckon you knew him better than me,' Landis said.

'Maybe I did. But it don't matter a damn now, does it? He's dead.'

'You done it once, I know you can do it again.'

'Kill you? You think that's what I want?'

'I can't say I know what you want. I come on out here to ask you.'

'Same as what anyone wants,' Russell said. 'For folks like you to leave me the hell alone, let me live my life, you know?'

'I'm gonna let you do that, Eugene.'

'If I give up the girl.'

Landis nodded.

'Well, I figured that's how it would be, so we gotta make some agreements now, you see?'

'I know we do. I'm ready to hear 'em.'

Russell took a deep breath. He leaned back in the chair. He crossed his legs, rested the gun on his knee.

'You didn't come alone, did you?' he asked. 'Who you got out there? Fredericksen?'

Landis didn't reply.

'You best tell me or we're done before we even got started, Sheriff.'

'Yes,' Landis said. 'I got Mike Fredericksen with me.'

'Okay. Well, I don't know what the hell you figured he was gonna do, but he ain't no use to you. You was gonna have him shoot me when I left? You think she's here? Is that what you think? You were gonna convince me to hand her over if you let me go, and then you were gonna have Fredericksen shoot me as I drove away? Was that your plan?'

'Somethin' like that.'

'Well, she ain't here. I got her, but she's someplace no one's gonna find her. Ledda, Wasper, the Whelans, they can all go to hell. They don't know where she is, and you ain't got a hope in hell of findin' her lest I tell you.'

'So what do you want?'

'I'm gonna leave. You're comin' with me. We're gonna drive on up to the highway. I'm gonna let you out. I'm gonna head on to wherever the hell I'm goin'.'

'And you'll tell me where to find her.'

'Sure I will. An' by the time you get there I'll be long gone. I'll be history, Sheriff, and you'll never find me.'

'No use askin' for your word 'cause I know you ain't gonna give it.'

Russell laughed. 'An' even if I gave it, you know it don't mean shit. At least not to you.'

'So what's stoppin' me from takin' a chance right now? You kill me sure, but Fredericksen's out there with a rifle. You put one foot outside an' he'll take your head off.'

'Because you still got a little hope, ain'tcha? I could surprise you and do what I say I'm gonna do. I might just tell you where that little girl's at. As long as there's a possibility o' that, then you gotta keep believin' it, right? You kill me, an' you ain't never gonna know.'

Russell was right. Landis knew it. There was no point trying to convince himself otherwise.

'How do I know she ain't already dead?' Landis said.

'You don't,' Russell replied, 'but hell, Sheriff, I ain't a monster now, am I? But that don't mean I ain't capable, an' it don't mean I won't do it if it comes to that. But right now she's got some use to me. Same as all o' them. You gotta play the cards you're dealt, right?'

'If this is how it's gonna be, then let's get on with it.'

Russell stood up. He took keys from his coat and tossed them to Landis.

'Get that suitcase there,' he said. 'Go on out to the car and put it in the trunk. Then you come on back here. We're goin' out there with me right behind you, just in case that buddy o' yours is dumb enough to take a shot at me.'

87

They drove for half a mile.

'Slow down,' Russell said. 'Pull over up here.'

Landis slowed the truck and came to a stop.

'Leave the keys in and the engine running,' Russell said. 'Get out slow and walk over to the trees.'

Landis got out and walked. He didn't turn around. He heard Russell get out. The back door of the truck slammed shut.

'On your knees, hands on your head.'

Landis complied. He felt the barrel of Russell's shotgun against the back of his skull.

'Your brother was dead 'fore he even come lookin' for me,' Russell said. 'Same goes for you. This was none o' your goddamned business. But you couldn't leave it alone, could you? You couldn't just leave it alone. You had to go on puttin' a stick on the hornets' nest. Pokin' an' pokin' like dumb kids, the pair o' you. Well, you got me riled, I tell you. An' now I'm gonna kill you and leave you here in the damned dirt, Sheriff. And the last thing you're gonna think of is what I'm gonna do with that little girl. How old is she now? Eleven, twelve years old? There's good money right there, I'll tell you. But, just for you, I'll take a cut on that price 'cause o' what I'm gonna do to her 'fore I sell her on.'

Landis felt the rage rising in his chest. His eyes closed, his fists clenched, he started to hyperventilate. His every muscle was tense. He felt sick with terror, not for himself but for his niece.

Russell jabbed Landis hard with the barrel of the gun. Landis lost his balance and fell forward. He was on his hands and knees. He tried to get back up but Russell swung the stock of the gun sideways and connected with Landis's shoulder.

Landis dropped again, rolled onto his side, then onto his back. He lay there looking up at Eugene Russell.

Russell was but a silhouette against the lights from the truck, but Landis could see his face, half in shadow, half out. The smile on the man's face was depraved, the anticipation of what he was going to do writ large in his eyes.

'I tell you now, Frank's little bitch gon' get growed up so fast...'

The ghost of lights to Landis's left. The sound of a vehicle.

Russell – just for a second – lost his focus.

Landis let fly with everything he possessed, kicking upwards and sideways into Russell's right leg. He felt it connect. The gun went off, the sound deafening. Shot tore into the trees.

Russell dropped to one knee. Landis was on his feet.

The car came to a shuddering halt across the road not twenty feet away, and suddenly the entire tableau was bathed in brilliant light.

Russell stood up and swung the discharged shotgun towards Landis. Landis moved fast, ducking sideways and to the left, but the stock caught him broadside across the side of the head. Stunned, he dropped, but then he heard Fredericksen's voice.

'Drop the fucking gun! Drop the fucking gun now!'

Landis, dazed and disoriented, saw nothing but movement somewhere to his left, and then he heard a second shot. It was deafening. It thundered out into the darkness.

Russell twisted sideways as a bullet struck his shoulder. He staggered awkwardly, dropped the shotgun, fell backwards to the road.

Fredericksen was over him, the barrel of the Winchester pointed directly at Russell's head.

'Victor! Victor, you okay?'

Landis groaned as he sat up. The pain in his jaw and along his cheekbone made it impossible to speak. He nodded and dragged himself upright. He stumbled when he moved, falling once again to his knees.

'Victor! Victor, you gotta come help me!'

Pure necessity drove Landis. He crawled towards Russell. Between them, he and Fredericksen managed to turn Russell over.

Fredericksen held out a pair of cuffs with his left hand. Landis, despite a wave of nausea and dizziness, took them from him. He cuffed Russell's hands behind his back, and then Fredericksen hauled the man to his feet.

Fredericksen and Landis manhandled Russell to Landis's car. Landis opened the trunk. Before he put Russell in there, he took the evidence bag with Jenna's monkey and put it on the back seat.

Russell was bleeding profusely, but he was conscious. They lifted him together, put him on his side, and then closed the trunk.

'Were going back to the cabin,' Landis said.

'Where is she?' Fredericksen asked.

Landis shook his head. The shock hit him then. He moved sideways and leaned against the rear wing of the car for support. He started to retch, dry at first, and then he was violently sick.

88

Victor Landis stood over Eugene Russell. Fredericksen had fired at close range, and the exit wound in Russell's shoulder was a gaping hole the size of a fist.

Despite the pain, Russell was conscious, still able to speak. Landis knew that the only hope of now finding Jenna rested on the man's inherent urge to survive.

'I need to know where Jenna is. That's the only hope you got of walkin' away from this,' Landis said.

Russell, his head down, looked up at him. 'Walk away? Only place I'm walkin' to is the chair. That's what you said, ain't it?'

'That's what I said, yes. But that ain't what I'm sayin' now.'

Russell frowned. 'You're lettin' me go?'

'You got a hole in you. You're on foot. Maybe you make it back to your truck, maybe you don't. Even if you do, where you gonna go? I got a notion you ain't even gonna be able to drive. But let's say you can. Let's say you make it out onto the highway. How far you gonna get before you get pulled over? How far before you need gas and someone calls you in, huh? I'm guessin' not too far. But that's what we got, Eugene. You tell me where she is, I let you go.'

Russell looked hard at Landis as if trying to discern the sincerity of what he was saying.

'You really think I'm gonna buy this?'

'Hell, I don't have any idea how you think,' Landis said. 'One thing I do know is that this is where we're at. Maybe you got people you can call. Folks who'll come runnin' if you ask 'em. If you're anywhere near as smart as I think you are, I reckon you got as good a chance as anyone of makin' it out of this alive.'

Russell looked over at Fredericksen. He stood silent, his back against the wall, the Winchester aimed at Russell's chest.

'No use lookin' at him, Eugene. It ain't his niece we're talkin' about. I make an agreement with you, he's gonna keep it. You don't tell me, well he shot you once, an' he'll be more than happy to shoot you again. I got an agenda here. You got somethin' I want, and I want it bad enough to let you run. That's a trade I'm willin' to make. A life for a life. Jenna Landis for Eugene Russell.'

Somewhere in Russell's eyes there was a light of hope. Landis saw it clear as day.

'You got money, an' plenty of it. You get all the way to Mexico an' you don't never come back. Slim chance, sure, an' maybe you ain't a gamblin' man, but if it was me? If it was me, Eugene, I wouldn't be askin' if I'm gonna keep my word, I'd be askin' if you really have any other road to take.'

Russell didn't speak. The wound in his shoulder was a through-and-through. There was no bullet inside of him. In Russell's eyes, Landis could see he was turning over everything he'd been told. Would Landis do what he said, or, once he knew the whereabouts of the girl, would he kill him? If he didn't, could he then make it all the way back to the truck on foot? Would he be able to drive? Without his wife or his brother to help, who would he call? How long would it take for them to reach him? Would he bleed out before he got help?

Landis took out a cigarette. He offered one to Russell. Russell took it.

Landis knew Jenna was alive. He knew it in his bones. It was the only leverage that Russell had, and there was no way he would've given it up. He had to get the man talking. He had to make Russell believe that he would keep his word. He knew from experience that if Russell told him one truth, then the likelihood of him telling another was far greater.

'Tell me what happened to Frank.'

Russell shook his head. 'Hell, even you must believe in an eye-for-an-eye.'

'Holt Macklin.'

'Holt Macklin, yeah.'

'My brother killed him?'

'As good as. Holt was up there in the State Pen. Your brother had him killed. Who did it, I don't know, but I know for sure that your brother set it up. Someone got early parole, someone got a deal they wouldn't have gotten before. Christ only knows what he gave 'em, but he had someone kill Macklin.'

'Because Macklin killed Ray Floyd. Because he threatened Fredericksen's family.'

'Why the hell you askin' me this shit if you already know?'

'You had him do that though, didn't you?'

Russell looked over at Fredericksen. 'Him and your brother gave me more grief an' heartache than anyone else I know,' he said. 'They's all over us like fuckin' ants, man. This one here got the message loud an' clear. Your brother didn't.'

'What did you do? Set up a meeting?'

Russell sneered. 'Oh, sure. I invited him over for drinks, you know? Said he should come on up to Tennessee and we could have a smoke and shoot the breeze.'

Landis gritted his teeth. He'd never felt the urge to kill someone as strongly as he did in that moment.

'Why did he come, Eugene?'

''Cause he knew about the girl from Mountain City.'

'Sara-Louise Lacey.'

'I don't remember. Whatever her name was don't matter. The one out o' Mountain City. He got word she was still alive.'

'And she was, wasn't she? We found her in September, an' she'd been dead less than a month.'

'If you say so, sure.'

'An' he got word from you, didn't he? You made sure he got word. You had someone tell him she was out this way, that maybe he could find her and bring her back. Is that what happened?'

Russell just looked at Landis. All the answer that Landis needed was right there in the man's eyes.

'How did you get him out of the car?'

'We set her down right there. Right there in the road, Sheriff. He come on out to see to her. Checkin' to make sure she was still alive. Wasper was down there hidin' someplace. He comes out and knocks him in the head. He went down like a stone, man.'

'An' then you ran him over.'

Russell looked down, and then away towards the front of the cabin.

'Dog eat dog, ain't it? You gotta do these things sometimes. It wasn't personal.'

'You run over him three, four times. That sure seems personal to me.'

'What's done is done. There ain't no goin' back. An' whatever the hell I did counts for nothin', does it? I figured that was the end of it. But I didn't figure on you lookin' to see what happened, did I? Hell, 'fore I met you I didn't even know you existed.'

Landis breathed. He quelled the rage in his chest. He knew now. He knew what had happened to his brother. Nothing could change that. Now he could only look to the thing that could be changed.

'An' now you tell me where the girl is.'

Russell looked over to Fredericksen.

'Say I do tell you, what's stoppin' either one o' you from killin' me?'

Landis ignored the question.

'Tell me an' we got a deal, Eugene. Otherwise, I'm gonna burn this place to the ground with you inside it.'

Russell gave the faintest smile.

'That's amusin' to you?'

'Ironic.'

'Ironic? You burnin' to death in this place?'

Russell looked back at Landis with a cold stare. There was nothing there – no compassion, no empathy. Whatever human-ity the man might have possessed was long since dead.

'Why ironic, Eugene?'

Russell didn't respond. He gave that same sly smile.

'She's here,' Fredericksen said.

Russell's eyes widened suddenly.

'That's why it's ironic. She's here, Victor.'

Landis stood up.

'She ain't here,' Russell said. 'For Christ's sake, how dumb d'you think I am?'

Landis leaned down, his face just inches from Russell's.

'Tell me again, Eugene.'

'She ain't fuckin' here,' he said, but his voice faltered, and when he looked away towards Fredericksen, Landis knew.

'Keep him quiet,' Landis said. 'Not a fuckin' sound from him.'

Russell opened his mouth to speak. Fredericksen moved fast. He had the muzzle of the rifle inches from Russell's heart within a second. Fredericksen shook his head. Russell said nothing.

'Jenna!' Landis called out. He started moving. 'Jenna! Jenna, are you here? Make a sound! Make a sound so I can hear you!'

Landis walked the length of the cabin. He called out, waited in silence. He moved, called again, stood stock-still and held his breath.

'Jenna, it's Victor!'

There was nothing. Dead quiet.

Landis walked back to Russell. He grabbed him around the throat.

'She's here, isn't she? Tell me where she is!'

Russell didn't respond. He just looked back at Landis with hatred.

Landis started moving again. He made his way around the cabin, knocking on the walls, calling out Jenna's name time and again. Listening, waiting, moving again. He went upstairs. There was nothing but a single room, a wooden bed, a few personal items. There was an empty cupboard. He dragged it away from the wall, kicked the wall behind it. Turning over the bed, he scoured the floor for any sign of a trap. Again, there was nothing.

Downstairs once more, panic rising in his chest, beneath that rage and fury and a sense of real despair.

'Where is she?' he shouted. 'Where the fuck is she?'

Russell, wordless, closed his eyes.

Landis wanted to kill him right where he sat. He wanted to beat him to the ground, and just keep on beating him until there was nothing recognizable remaining.

Landis headed out of the cabin. He walked the perimeter. He called Jenna's name, screaming now at the top of his voice. It echoed out into the darkness and came back at him like a taunt.

'Jenna! Jenna! Jenna!'

Running back towards the porch, he lost his footing. Barely able to keep his balance, he fell forward. The side of his face collided with the ground with some force, and for a moment he lay there stunned.

Everything went quiet. His heart stopped. His breathing, too. He rolled over on his back and looked at the vast blackness above him. He felt defeated, broken, impotent. He was running blindly, shouting into nowhere, and he knew that if he didn't find her now, he more than likely never would.

He summoned every ounce of strength remaining. He rolled onto his side, put his hand beneath him and started to get to his feet.

He stopped. He stayed right there on his knees.

Did he hear something? Or did he imagine he'd heard something?

Holding his breath, he listened.

There was nothing.

Landis stood up. He took a step forward. He closed his eyes. 'Jenna!'

Back to his left, he turned suddenly. There was something. There had to be. It couldn't have been his imagination.

'Jenna! Jenna!'

There it was again. To the left and back near the outer wall of the cabin. He took five or six steps, and then he heard it beneath him. The hollow sound. The sound of his footsteps on the ground and something empty beneath. He raised his foot and stamped down. No doubt. No question now. There was something beneath – a space, a cellar, a hole in the ground. On his knees, frantically scrabbling to dig the dirt away, handful after handful, and then the resistance of something solid, the feeling of wood, and the sound of something beneath, someone screaming for help – faint but discernible, getting louder as he focused on it.

'Jenna! Jenna! It's Victor!'

And then his name came back to him. Not an echo. The sound of his niece calling out for him. Calling out his name. Louder now, as clear as anything. And he was pulling away handfuls of dirt as fast as he could, exposing the door beneath. Faster, furious now, sweeping armfuls of earth aside until he found a recess, a handle within, dragging it up, unable to move it, moving more dirt, his heart thundering, blood pounding in his head, his eyes wide, seeing everything, feeling everything.

Finally, enough leverage, tearing at the handle and dragging that door back with every ounce of strength he possessed, and the smell of damp that rushed up at him, feeling the uppermost rung of a wooden ladder right there at the edge of the hole.

'Jenna!' he called out.

'Uncle Victor!'

89

Wrapped in a blanket, holding onto the monkey as if it was a lifeline, Jenna lay on the back seat of Landis's car.

Her face, dirty and tear-streaked, her eyes wide with shock, Landis held her for a long time. Her whole body trembled like a frightened bird.

After a good while, he picked her up and carried her into the cabin.

Russell was silent. He knew he was done.

'This is Mike,' Landis told Jenna. 'He was a real good friend of your daddy's. I just gotta do somethin', so he's gonna take you back to the car for just a minute.'

Jenna looked up at Landis. She put her arms around his shoulders and pulled him tighter.

'It's okay, sweetheart. Everything's okay now. You go with Mike here for just a minute an' I'll be right there.'

She looked up at him, her eyes wide with fear.

'You're safe now. Nothin's gonna happen. We're leavin' in just a minute. We're takin' you home to your momma.'

Landis looked at Fredericksen and nodded.

Walking towards him, he took the Winchester. Fredericksen lifted Jenna out of Landis's arms. She looked at him once and then closed her eyes.

'Go to the car. Stay in the back with her,' Landis said. 'I'll be a coupla minutes.'

Fredericksen left the cabin. Landis waited until he heard the car door slam.

Russell looked up. 'Guess we're goin' on a drive then, eh?'

Landis shook his head. 'No, Eugene, we ain't goin' on any drive.'

Russell opened his mouth to say something.

'We're all done talkin',' Landis said. 'Get up now. On your feet.'

Russell didn't move.

'Up!' Landis repeated, and with the stock of the rifle he shoved Russell in the side of the head.

The chair fell sideways, Russell too. He lay there for a moment, the pain searing through him, and then he got to his feet.

Directing Russell ahead of him, the muzzle of the gun in the small of his back, they left the cabin.

They walked around the side and then Landis told him to get down in the hole.

'I ain't gettin' in no damned hole,' Russell said.

Landis took a step forward and kicked Russell's legs out from under him. Russell fell forward, arms wide as if he could somehow stop himself, but he twisted sideways and dropped the eight or ten feet into the darkness below.

Landis stood over the hole and looked down at the man. Even in that moment, there was nothing but hate and defiance in the man's eyes.

'So do it,' Russell said. 'Fuckin' do it, man. Just fuckin' shoot me an' get it over with.'

The first shot took out Russell's left knee. The bone shattered into a mess of pieces.

The scream that erupted from the man's lungs echoed out into the night.

'Ain't so simple,' Landis said. 'Last thing you deserve is a quick killin'.'

Landis fired again, hit the right leg and destroyed the shin.

He stepped back. He wouldn't last more than a few hours down there. He would bleed out, or maybe his heart would surrender to the pain. Whatever happened, that deep hole was the last place he would see.

Landis set down the rifle. He kicked at the top of the wooden ladder until it broke free. Once he'd pulled it from the ground, he walked a good ten yards and hurled it into the trees.

Returning to the hole, he looked down at Eugene Russell. Closing the door over him, he then dragged fallen branches, rocks, a dozen or more cut logs from the side of the cabin and piled them over the door. He kicked the dirt back until there was no sign of it.

He stood for a few moments, his heart slowing, his breathing deep, and then he turned and walked back to the car. After twenty feet, he couldn't hear Eugene Russell's screaming anymore.

90

Barbara Wedlock was out on the veranda of her house before Landis had even killed the lights.

Within a heartbeat, Eleanor was past her, rushing down to meet them.

Fredericksen came out from the back seat with Jenna in his arms.

Eleanor was there to take her, tears streaming down her face.

'Oh baby, oh my poor baby. Oh my God, what did they do to you?'

Holding her then, looking at Fredericksen, at Landis, back to Fredericksen.

'Victor,' she said. 'Victor…'

'Take her on up to the house,' Landis said. 'She's okay. She ain't hurt. Get her cleaned up. Barb will help you.'

Eleanor hesitated, glanced back at the house as Barbara came down to meet them, and then she started crying again.

'Go,' Landis said.

Barbara reached them.

'Let's go, dear,' she said, and she steered Eleanor back up the path.

Landis waited until everyone was inside and then he turned to Fredericksen.

'We got ourselves a storm o' trouble to sort out,' Fredericksen said.

Landis nodded. 'Best get started, then.'

91

It was the end of October. Despite the fact that fall had well and truly arrived, the day was bright and warm.

The gathering at the Wedlock place had been arranged by Barbara and her husband. Once again, the man had cooked up a feast.

Milstead had come over from Blue Ridge. Fredericksen was there, as was Abigail Webster. Eleanor and Jenna were helping Emmett in the kitchen. Barbara had Marshall fetching drinks and ferrying things out to the yard.

'She talked, and once she got started she didn't stop,' Abigail told Landis. 'As is so often the case, Ledda Russell was more interested in saving her own skin than anything else.'

'Heard the DA gave her a deal,' Fredericksen said.

'They didn't push for the death penalty,' Abigail said. 'That was the best she could hope for, and that's what she got.'

'And Wasper?'

'Same,' Abigail explained. 'It'll be life without parole for the pair o' them.'

'You think Eugene'll ever turn up?' Milstead asked.

Abigail looked at Fredericksen, then at Landis. 'I read your statements,' she said matter-of-factly. 'Your Agent Lowell, despite his seeming conscientiousness, seems not to have noticed the fact that they were almost verbatim.'

Landis, deadpan, said nothing.

'But I'm guessin' that he was faced with the word of two law enforcement officials versus the word of two sociopaths.'

'A lot happened, and it all happened so fast,' Fredericksen said.

'Hey, I ain't askin', Mike,' Abigail replied. 'Just seems a hell of a shame that Eugene Russell will never see the inside of a cell.'

'When he took off with that girl away from the cabin, the only thing that mattered was bringing her back,' Fredericksen said. 'Once Victor got her out of the car, Russell was gone. I mean, hell, I chased him as far as I could. It was dark, and those woods out there are—'

Abigail raised her hand. 'I read the report. You ain't under any obligation to explain anything to me.'

Milstead leaned forward. 'So how big was this thing? How far did it go?'

'There's a chance we'll never know,' Landis said. 'Florence Whelan rolled over on her husband. That's when it started to unravel. Lowell's now got his own dedicated task force. This thing went through the Republican Volunteers, Child Services, adoption agencies, foster homes. These kids were being sold into slavery. There ain't no other way to look at it. Prostitution, drug couriers, everything you can imagine. Last I heard they were tracking this south to Florida, north to New York. Heard that kids were being shipped to Canada, Mexico too.'

'I saw his press briefing,' Abigail said. 'He's intent on keepin' goin' until they find out what happened to every last one.'

'I saw it too,' Fredericksen said. 'They're setting up a second task force to track where all the money went. It ran into millions.'

'Is it true they retracted Ray Floyd's suicide?' Abigail asked.

'Yes,' Landis replied. 'Wasper said Holt Macklin killed him. Holt and Greaves worked for the Russells. It was Greaves who was told to kidnap the Rayford girl. Apparently, Eugene never meant to have her killed. That was Greaves' mistake. As for who killed Macklin, I guess we'll never know for sure, but there's a strong possibility that Frank was behind that.'

'Well, he ain't here to defend himself,' Abigail said.

'And he'll get his full service pension,' Fredericksen said.

'And so he should,' Milstead said. 'Sometimes the good a man does outweighs everything else.'

Landis turned at the sound of voices.

Eleanor and Jenna were coming down from the back door bearing plates of wings and ribs.

'Who's hungry?' Jenna asked.

'Gimme enough ketchup, I'll eat roadkill right off the tarmac,' Landis said.

He waited until Jenna had set down the plate, and then he held out his hand. She came towards him, and he wrapped her in a hug.

'You good, sweetheart?'

'Sure,' she said.

'Looks like you did a mighty fine job in the kitchen.'

She shrugged. 'Emmett did all the cookin'. I just watched.'

'You gonna sit here and eat with us?'

'I'm gonna go tell Marshall first. Barbara's got him doin' somethin' with her car.'

Landis watched her take off. Eleanor came down from the house, Barbara and Emmett too. It had been little more than a month since a meeting had taken place in this very yard. In a matter of weeks, everything Landis had persuaded himself was true had turned about-face. The world wasn't different. He just saw it a different way.

'That's a smart young lady there,' Barbara said. 'Hard to believe she's your kin, Victor.'

'That one's gonna outshine the lot of us combined,' Landis replied. 'Just you wait an' see.'

92

The ceremony to replace Frank Landis's state-funded headstone lasted no more than twenty minutes.

In its place was a simple black marble upright that read:

FRANK LANDIS

09.09.47 — 08.14.92

LOVING FATHER, HUSBAND AND BROTHER

Landis, Eleanor and Jenna were the only ones in attendance.

Afterwards, Eleanor said they should head out for dinner somewhere.

Landis agreed, but said he wanted to have a few moments alone with Jenna.

Eleanor nodded understandingly. 'I'll meet you back at the car.'

'You got anythin' you wanna ask me about what happened?' Landis asked his niece.

Jenna looked up at him, artless and innocent. 'Not particularly,' she said.

'Your father,' Landis said. 'You know he was a good man, don't you?'

'Sure I do,' Jenna replied. 'It was you who thought he wasn't.'

'I was wrong. I made a mess o' things and I'm sorry for that.'
Jenna reached out and took Landis's hand.

'We all make a mess o' things sometimes,' she said.

Landis looked at his brother's marker. He felt a wave of grief.

'You wanna come go with us an' get some dinner then, Uncle Victor?'

Landis smiled. 'Sure sounds like a bunch o' fine to me, sweetheart.'

Jenna laughed. 'Still talkin' funny, ain'tcha?'

'I guess some things ain't never gonna change.'

Jenna led the way, in one hand the monkey, in the other the hand of her uncle.

Credits

R.J. Ellory and Orion Fiction would like to thank everyone at Orion who worked on the publication of *The Last Highway* in the UK.

Editorial
Emad Akhtar
Celia Killen
Sarah O'Hara

Copy-editor
Clare Wallis

Proofreader
Linda Joyce

Editorial Management
Jane Hughes
Charlie Panayiotou
Tamara Morriss

Audio
Paul Stark
Jake Alderson
Georgina Cutler

Contracts
Anne Goddard
Ellie Bowker
Humayra Ahmed

Design
Nick Shah
Tómas Almeida
Joanna Ridley
Helen Ewing
Rachael Lancaster

Finance
Nick Gibson
Jasdip Nandra
Elizabeth Beaumont
Sue Baker
Tom Costello

Production
Paul Hussey

Inventory
Jo Jacobs
Dan Stevens

Sales
Jen Wilson
Victoria Laws
Esther Waters
Frances Doyle
Ben Goddard
Jack Hallam
Anna Egelstaff

Operations
Sharon Willis
Jo Jacobs

Rights
Susan Howe
Krystyna Kujawinska
Jessica Purdue
Ayesha Kinley
Louise Henderson